JAN - 6 2016

D0282770

THE CYCLOPS INITIATIVE

ALSO BY DAVID WELLINGTON

Positive

JIM CHAPEL MISSIONS
Chimera
"Minotaur"
"Myrmidon"
The Hydra Protocol
The Cyclops Initiative

THE MONSTER ISLAND TRILOGY
Monster Island
Monster Nation
Monster Planet

THE LAURA CAXTON VAMPIRE NOVELS
13 Bullets
99 Coffins
Vampire Zero
23 Hours
32 Fangs

THE FROSTBITE WEREWOLF NOVELS
Frostbite
Overwinter

AS DAVID CHANDLER
Den of Thieves
A Thief in the Night
Honor Among Thieves

THE CYCLOPS
INITIATIVE

A JIM CHAPEL MISSION

DAVID WELLINGTON

WM
WILLIAM MORROW
An Imprint of *HarperCollins*Publishers

THE CYCLOPS INITIATIVE. Copyright © 2016 by David Wellington. All rights reserved. Printed in the United States of America. No part of this book may be used or reproduced in any manner whatsoever without written permission except in the case of brief quotations embodied in critical articles and reviews. For information address HarperCollins Publishers, 195 Broadway, New York, NY 10007.

HarperCollins books may be purchased for educational, business, or sales promotional use. For information please e-mail the Special Markets Department at SPsales@harpercollins.com.

FIRST EDITION

Library of Congress Cataloging-in-Publication Data has been applied for.

ISBN 978-0-06-224883-1

16 17 18 19 20   OV/RRD   10 9 8 7 6 5 4 3 2 1

For Mom, who taught me to love books

This book would not have existed without certain individuals I would like to thank. They include (but are not limited to) Russell Galen, my agent; Lyssa Keusch, my editor; as well as Rebecca Lucash and Jessie Edwards at Harper. Thanks for bringing Jim home.

PROLOGUE

Silence.

Ten thousand feet up there was nothing to hear, except the faint scratching hiss of the wind as it spilled across carbon fiber control surfaces. Riding high on a column of warm air, the old Predator's engine barely ticked over. It was very good at conserving its energy. It was very good at waiting patiently. Waiting and watching with its single, unblinking eye.

Chuck Mitchell was asleep at his post.

He had the best of all possible excuses. His wife had given birth to a beautiful little girl three weeks ago. Mitchell hadn't slept more than a couple of hours a night since—he'd been far too busy sitting up at night next to the crib, watching her squirm and wriggle, counting her ten perfect fingers, her ten perfect toes.

But if anyone needed to be awake at his job, it was Mitchell. He worked at the busiest port in America, scanning cargo containers as they passed through on their way to grocery stores and warehouses and schools across the country. It was his job to oversee the PVT portal monitor, a device that scanned those containers for radioactivity. All day long the containers passed through his station, one every few seconds—more than sixty million a year. They went under a giant yellow metal arch and came out the other side, and nine hundred and ninety-nine times out of a thousand, nothing happened.

That thousandth time Mitchell very much needed to be on top of his game.

So he did his best to fight the tide of sleep that kept washing over him. He mainlined coffee. When that wasn't enough, he would jab himself in the leg with a pen—anything to help him wake up.

It was a losing battle.

The cargo containers were all the same. They didn't stay in front of him long enough for him to even know what was inside them. Even before dawn it was warm at his station, warm enough to make him feel cozy and complacent. Even the noise of the giant rolling belt that carried the boxes was a droning, repetitive sound that just lulled him back to sleep. Staying awake was just about impossible.

There was only one thing that could possibly yank him back, one sound.

A steady, persistent ticking. The sound he heard in his nightmares. The sound the detector made when it picked up stray gamma radiation.

Mitchell's eyes shot open. He nearly fell off his chair. Without even thinking about it, he slammed his palm down on the big red button in front of him, stopping the belt, freezing the cargo container in place under the arch.

The ticking sound didn't stop.

The old Predator could see in color, though the first early light made everything the same three drab shades of gray. Below, in the sprawling yard, the boxes stood in ziggurats twenty high, bluish gray and reddish gray and yellowish gray. The Predator's eye swiveled back and forth in its socket as it looked for patterns it could recognize.

The drone was an old model, one of the first wave of UAVs to see real action. It was obsolete now, and it had been declawed—stripped of its weaponry and most of its fancier software. It should have been decommissioned a year ago.

But it could still fly. It could still loiter up there, so high up it looked like just another bird, a speck against the blue sky. It could still see—its camera eye had not grown nearsighted over the years.

It still had one more mission in it.

Mitchell pulled a lead-lined vest over his shoulders. The same kind dentists wore when they took x-rays of your jaw. He jumped down from his station and took a hesitant step toward the cargo container.

The PVT equipment kept ticking away.

Mitchell knew that most likely this was a false positive. There were all kinds of things that gave off gamma rays—everything from fertilizer to kitty litter to bananas. The chances that this box was full of, say, weapons-grade plutonium were vanishingly small.

Like every box in the port, this one came with a sheaf of papers listing its contents and tracing its route across the oceans. The sheet on top was just a list of bar codes. He waved a handheld scanner over the box's codes. If the bill of lading said it was full of kitty litter, he would have a little laugh and go back to his chair and fall asleep again. It had to be kitty litter, right?

The box's forms all claimed it was full of plastic water bottles. Empty bottles. That definitely wasn't right—he flipped through the sheets until he found what he was looking for, the declared weight of the container. The box was heavy. Heavy enough that it had to be filled with metal or stone, not empty plastic bottles.

He hadn't thought his day could get worse, but it just had.

Someone had shipped this box with counterfeit paperwork. Somebody had wanted to make sure nobody knew what was really inside.

Mitchell closed his eyes and tried hard not to panic. Was this the moment he'd trained for? He'd never actually seen radiological cargo come through his post before. It had just never happened. But when he took this job, he had known it might.

His duties at this point were clear. He was supposed to alert his superiors and then open the box and make a visual inspection of its contents.

Mitchell licked his lips because they were suddenly very dry.

If he did what his job required, if he popped the seals on that box, he might expose himself to the radiation inside. Most likely it wouldn't be enough to actually hurt him. Most likely it would be like getting a single chest x-ray, nothing that would have long-term effects on his health.

Most likely.

There. The drone had found the pattern it was looking for. Near the docks where the big ships came in, it made out the rectangular silhouette of a box sitting underneath a yellow arch.

The drone shifted its control surfaces a few degrees, turned about on its circling course. Then it put its nose down and opened up its throttle, launching itself into a powered dive.

"I can't," Mitchell said, aloud. "I just can't. Not with the baby . . ."

He stared at the box, knowing what he was supposed to do. Knowing he would probably get fired if he didn't do it.

Knowing he couldn't.

If he got sick now, if he couldn't work, who would take care of his perfect little girl? His wife had quit her own job to look after the baby. If he got sick—

He would go and find his supervisor, go and explain. He turned on his heel and started to walk away from the box, away from—

He didn't get very far.

The drone weighed nearly five thousand pounds. It had a top speed of three hundred miles an hour. Dropping out of the sky like a javelin, it was moving even faster than that when it struck the cargo container.

Its eye hit the steel side of the container and shattered in a million shards of glass. Its nose, made of carbon fiber and Kevlar, disintegrated on impact.

But its wings were edged with pure titanium. They smashed into the container with enough force to tear through the box's metal walls, to pulverize its contents and send them flying, a thick roiling column of powdered metal that hung glittering in the air until the wind caught it.

The noise of the impact could be heard five miles away.

"Oh God, no, please," Mitchell whimpered.

He couldn't hear his own voice. His ears weren't working. The after-image of the flash filled his eyes, made him blind. He could still feel pain, though.

He was down on the concrete, and he felt like half his face had been scraped off. There was blood on his cheek, wet and hot. He struggled to get up, but he couldn't move. He couldn't even get up on his knees.

As his eyes slowly cleared he saw pools of burning jet fuel all around him, saw chunks of dull gray metal strewn everywhere.

He still couldn't hear anything.

That wasn't the worst of it. Something had hit him in the back. Something hard and sharp. His first thought had been that he'd been struck by a bullet, but it had been much bigger than that and it had knocked him down like a giant hand pressing him against the floor.

Whatever it was, it was still back there. He was—he was impaled on it.

Blood was pouring from his stomach. From where the piece of debris had punched right through the lead vest he wore—and the flesh inside it. He'd been so worried about radiation. That didn't seem so terrifying anymore.

In the distance he heard the sirens of emergency vehicles, coming closer.

He wondered if they would make it in time.

He wondered if he would ever see his little baby girl again.

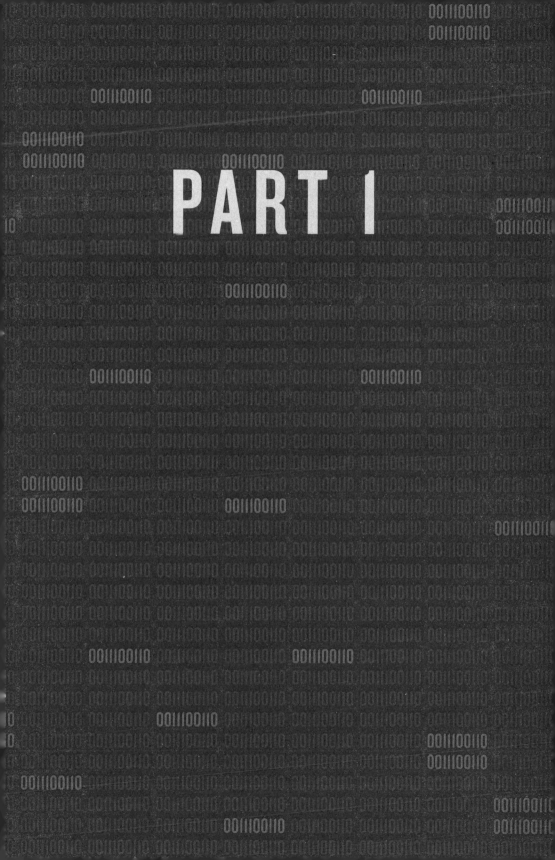

PART 1

"If I were you," the marine said, "I'd think real careful about my next move. There's a lot riding on this."

Jim Chapel stared the man right in the eye. As usual, there was nothing there. Years of clandestine missions in the Middle East had given Marine sergeant Brent Wilkes total control over his facial expressions. The man just didn't have a tell as far as Chapel could see.

And he was right—there was a lot at stake. Chapel glanced down at the table and did a mental calculation. Two sixes showing, and Chapel only had queen high. If Wilkes wasn't bluffing, the game could be over right here.

Chapel sighed and threw his cards down on the table. He found that he couldn't care less. "Fold," he said.

Wilkes's mouth bent in a fraction of a grin and he grabbed for the pot—nearly a full bag of potato chips. He stuffed them in his mouth one after another with the precision that marked everything he did.

Chapel had spent three months in the smelly motel room with Wilkes, as much as sixteen hours out of every day, and he still couldn't get a read on his partner. Wilkes didn't seem to care about anything except poker—he didn't read, he didn't watch TV, he just wanted to play cards.

After the first week, Chapel had realized how outclassed he was and had refused to play for money anymore. They didn't have anything else to wager with, so they'd played with potato chips instead. It didn't seem to matter to Wilkes. He played the game to win, not to make money.

The floor around the marine's chair was littered with a drift of empty potato chip bags. He ate each little crumb of chip that he won, scouring the table bare, but then he just dropped the empty bags on the floor, completely uninterested in keeping the room clean. At the end of each day Chapel picked up the bags and threw them out, knowing he would get to do it again the next day.

And meanwhile nothing whatsoever changed with the case.

They were holed up in the motel because a high-profile black marketeer had taken a room there, too. The motel was a place where he could meet and make deals with military personnel from the nearby Aberdeen Proving Ground. A lot of very expensive military hardware had gone missing from Aberdeen, and intelligence suggested it all came through this motel. Chapel had identified one Harris Contorni as the buyer, a former army corporal who had been dishonorably discharged. He'd gathered enough evidence to show that Contorni had connections to East Coast organized crime. Chapel had thought that once he identified the culprit his involvement with this case would be finished. After all, chasing low-level crooks like Contorni was way below his pay grade.

Instead he'd been ordered to see the case through. Which meant a semipermanent stakeout of the motel where Contorni lived. Chapel had planted listening devices all through Contorni's room and phone and car and then he'd moved into a room three doors down and then Wilkes had shown up and Chapel had gotten the worst sinking feeling of his life.

His boss had given him scutwork to do. And then he'd assigned Chapel a babysitter just in case.

It was a pretty clear vote of no confidence.

And one he'd earned, he supposed. He'd screwed up badly the year before on a mission in Siberia. Put a lot of people in danger. Even though he'd fixed things, even though he'd completed his mission, he knew his boss, Director Hollingshead, must have lost a lot of faith in him.

"Wanna play again?" Wilkes asked.

"Not now," Chapel said. He looked at the cards scattered across the table and realized he didn't even care enough to pick them up and put them away. This case was turning him into a slob—breaking his lifetime habit of cleaning up after himself.

Months had passed with no sign whatsoever that Contorni was putting together another deal. Months of doing nothing but breathing in Wilkes's air. Chapel was losing his edge. Getting rusty.

"All right," Wilkes said. "You mind if I run down to the store, get some soda? All these chips I keep winning make me so dry I don't even piss anymore. I just fart salt."

Chapel waved one hand in the air, careful not to express disgust. It would just encourage worse behavior. Wilkes left without another word.

When he was gone, Chapel checked the laptop on the nightstand, but there was nothing there. Contorni hadn't made a call in six hours, and though he'd driven approximately sixty miles in his car over the last twenty-four hours, he had gone nowhere near the Proving Ground. Nothing. As usual.

Chapel sat down hard on the bed. He considered doing some calisthenics, but the room already smelled like sweat and dirty laundry. Maybe later. Instead he reached into his pocket and took out his handsfree device. He stared at it for a while, knowing he was probably making a mistake, but then he shoved it in his ear and pressed the power button.

"Angel," he said, "are you there?"

"Always, sugar," she replied.

He closed his eyes and let himself smile a little. That voice . . . it was like having someone breathe softly on the back of his neck. It made him feel good like nothing else did anymore.

He hadn't spoken to Angel in weeks. He'd missed it.

He had never met her. He had no idea what she looked like or where she was located. He didn't even know her real name—he'd started calling her Angel and it just stuck, and now even his boss referred to her that way. He'd chosen the name because when he was in the field she worked as his guardian angel. If Chapel needed to look up the criminal record of a deadly assassin or just find the best route through traffic during a car chase, she was the one with the answers he needed. More than that, she had walked him through some very tricky missions. She'd saved his life so often he didn't even keep track anymore.

She had become more than just a colleague to him. Among other things, she was the only woman in his life, now that his girlfriend had dumped him.

While he was working the stakeout, though, he barely got to talk to Angel at all. There was no need for her special skills on this mission, no need to occupy her valuable time with the running tally of how many poker hands Chapel lost or how many days had passed without new intelligence.

"Anything to report?" she asked. "Or are you just checking in?"

"Nothing," he told her. He wondered what he sounded like to her. There'd been a time she respected him, even admired what he'd achieved in the field. Had her esteem for him dropped as she listened to him grow more and more dejected? "Any word from the director? Any new instructions, any hint of reassignment?"

"You know I would call if there was," she told him. There was something in her voice, a cautious little hesitation. She was waiting to hear why he'd called.

It was too bad he didn't have a good answer. He couldn't very well tell her that he'd called because he was lonely. Every time the two of them spoke it cost taxpayer money. Maybe something more than that, too. He knew she worked with other field agents—even Wilkes knew who she was, though he said he'd only worked with her once, and briefly. Maybe right now she'd been in the middle of saving somebody else's life and he was distracting her. Though he supposed she would have told him so, or just not answered her phone.

"What about that other thing I asked you to look into? Did you turn up anything more on Wilkes?"

"I'm still not sure what you're hoping to find," she said.

"I just want a better idea of who I'm working with here. I need to be able to trust this guy when push comes to shove."

Angel sighed. "You know I can't tell you much. He's a Raider, as I'm sure you've already figured out."

Chapel didn't need any great detective skills to turn up that piece of information. Wilkes had a Marine Corps logo tattooed on his arm and the distinctive haircut of a jarhead. If he was working for Hollingshead's directorate (the Directorate for Defense Counterintelligence and HUMINT, or DX), that meant he was special ops—specifically the United States Marine Corps Special Operations Command, MARSOC, the Raiders, the newest branch of secret warriors in SOCOM. He would be what the service called a critical skills operator, which meant he would be trained in everything from unarmed combat to language skills to psychological warfare.

All well and good. But there was something about Wilkes that bothered Chapel. The guy was just too self-contained. He never gave anything away, never spoke of himself, never so much as blinked at the wrong time or laughed at a private joke. Chapel had met plenty of vets with PTSD, people who were stuck inside their heads, reliving a bad moment over and over. They acted a little like that, but in Wilkes's case there was something more. He didn't seem like he was stuck. Instead he acted like a panther in a cage at the zoo. Watching the world through hooded eyes, giving nothing away. Waiting for something to happen. Maybe he had some dark secret he didn't want Chapel—or Hollingshead—to know about.

"And you say his record is clean. No red flags anywhere in his file."

"None," Angel replied. "He served a bunch of tours with military intelligence in Afghanistan and Iraq. When he got home, about three years ago, he was recruited by Director Hollingshead personally. He checks out—I vetted him myself."

"And you worked with him, too, on a mission," Chapel said.

There must have been a certain tone in his voice. "Are you getting jealous?"

Chapel forced a laugh. "Hardly."

"You know I'm yours, first and last," Angel said. "You were on mandatory vacation. A mission came up, and he and I were just free at the right time. Don't worry, Chapel. Nobody's replacing you in *my* heart."

It felt damned good to hear that.

He just wished he was sure Director Hollingshead felt the same way.

Chapel respected and trusted his boss implicitly. He would even admit to loving the man, the way a soldier loves a worthy commanding officer. Hollingshead was fair-minded and he took good care of his people. But he was also a pragmatist.

If he was going to replace Chapel, then Wilkes was a perfect choice. Chapel was rushing toward his midforties, way older than any field agent should be, while Wilkes still had plenty of good years in him. Chapel had been badly wounded in combat, and in Siberia he had screwed up a vital mission by misjudging a foreign asset. Wilkes was tough as nails, smart as a whip, and had no bad marks on his record at all. It would just make sense to put Wilkes on the most vital missions and have Chapel make a more or less graceful descent into, say, an analyst position or have him work as a consultant or, God forbid, run stakeouts for the rest of his career.

If Chapel had been in Hollingshead's place, he would make the same decision.

It didn't mean he had to like it.

"Chapel, are you okay?" Angel asked. "You went quiet there."

He shook himself back to attention. He realized he'd been sitting there ruminating while Angel was on the line. He was so comfortable with her, so utterly at home talking to her that he'd let his brain shut down.

"I'm . . . fine. I . . ."

Maybe it was time to lay his cards on the table.

His mouth was suddenly dry. He swallowed thickly and said, "I'm fine, Angel. I just need to know something. You and I have been through so much, I'm hoping I can count on you to tell me something even if you have orders not to."

Angel didn't respond. Maybe she was waiting to hear what he said next.

"I need to know—is my career over? Because it's pretty much all I have left." He shook his head, even though she couldn't see him. "When

Julia left, when . . . when Nadia died, I . . . I guess I started to wonder about what I'm doing. About what kind of life I can have now. I took my time and weighed things and I think, well, I think if I can keep working, if I can keep going on real missions, then it'll be okay. All the sacrifices I've made, everything I've had to do, it doesn't matter. Not if I can still be of some use. But if I'm being put out to pasture, I'm not sure I can keep—"

He stopped because there was a click on the line. A soft mechanical sound that could have meant anything. Maybe somebody else was listening in, or maybe Angel had just changed the frequency of her signal, or—

Three annoying beeps sounded in his ear. The tones that indicated a dropped call.

"Angel?" he said. "Angel, are you there?"

Angel's equipment was the best in the world. There was no way she could get cut off like that, not just because of a bad cellular link or rain fade or anything like that.

"Angel?" he said again.

There was no reply.

TOWSON, MD: MARCH 21, 07:36

When Wilkes got back, Chapel was still trying to raise Angel. He had a phone number for her, one he'd never written down, only memorized. There was no answer on that line. It didn't even go to voice mail. It just rang and rang. He tried to get in touch with Director Hollingshead next, calling a number for a pet store in Bethesda that was a front for the Defense Intelligence Agency. The woman on the other end of the line listened to his access code, then told him to hold the line while she connected him.

At least he got an answer this time—the woman came back and told him the director was not available to take his call. Chapel knew better than to ask if he could leave a message. His access code had been logged— Hollingshead would call Chapel back as soon as he could.

Wilkes had returned with a two-liter bottle of soda and with his own phone in his hand. He kept trying to get Chapel's attention, but Chapel just waved him away. If something had happened to Angel, if she was in trouble, he would move heaven and earth to help her. Nothing else mattered. Even his mission was less important. If Harris Contorni was in the middle of selling backpack nukes to Iran in his motel room three doors down, well, that would just have to wait.

Wilkes finally did get his attention by grabbing Chapel's phone out of his hand.

"What the hell do you think you're doing?" Chapel demanded.

Wilkes didn't reply. He just tapped Chapel's phone screen a couple of times with one finger while unscrewing the top of his soda bottle with his other hand. Then he handed the phone back and took a long slug of cola.

Chapel looked down at his phone. Wilkes had opened an app that decrypted incoming messages from the Pentagon. What he read there made him swear under his breath.

ABORT CURRENT MISSION.
W AND C TO REPORT NGA HQ
FOR BRIEFING 0900.
AUTHORIZED POSEIDON.

"Poseidon" was Director Hollingshead's code name for the month, which meant he'd sent for the two of them personally. The headquarters of the National Geospatial-Intelligence Agency were in Fort Belvoir in Virginia, less than an hour away. The two of them just had time to clean up and get their uniforms on before they had to leave.

All of which was fine—but the first line of the message was what made Chapel's eyes go wide. They were being told to abandon their stakeout, just for a briefing? Something truly serious must have happened.

"When did this come in?" Chapel asked.

"Five minutes ago. Looks like you were too busy to notice," Wilkes told him. He took another long pull on his soda, then capped the bottle and threw it on the bed. "What were you up to?"

Chapel tried to decide how much he trusted Wilkes. "Something's going on with Angel," he said finally. "Her signal cut out and I can't get her back on the line."

"Maybe it's something to do with this briefing."

Chapel shook his head. No way to know. "You take the first shower. I'm going to keep trying to reach her."

FORT BELVOIR, VA: MARCH 21, 08:51

Chapel had an office at Fort Belvoir—as did half the intelligence staffers in America. It was an enormous, sprawling facility packed with the headquarters of dozens of agencies and offices and directorates large and small. He'd worked there for ten years, back before his reactivation as a field agent, but that had been in the southern area. The NGA headquarters was in the northern area, a region of the fort he'd rarely visited. He'd never even seen the NGA building before.

He had no idea why he was being summoned there. Normally he would have called Angel to ask her—to get some idea of what he was walking into before the briefing began. But she still wasn't answering her phone.

Wilkes played with the radio the whole way there, trying to find some news broadcast that might give them an idea of what had happened. There was nothing. Some freak wildfires in Colorado caused by a massive lightning strike. The governor of New Jersey was in trouble again for reasons so boring Chapel just tuned them out. There was nothing to explain why Hollingshead had canceled a six-month investigation just so two operatives could attend a briefing.

When they arrived at their destination, Chapel just took a second to look at the place. What he knew about the NGA was limited. The National Geospatial-Intelligence Agency was responsible for SIGINT and imaging, he knew that much—it was a clearinghouse for all kinds of intelligence ranging from satellite data to radio broadcast intercepts to paper maps of sensitive areas. Its mission was just to collect information that might be useful to other agencies, and as far as he knew it didn't carry out operations on its own; it just provided support. He knew that it was supposed to have been vital in locating Bin Laden in Abbottabad.

Apparently the kind of support that paid off.

The NGA building was the third-largest federal building in the D.C. area. Only the Pentagon and the Ronald Reagan Building were bigger. Much of its size came from its unusual shape. From above—say, from a satellite view—the structure looked like two enormous concrete parentheses framing a central atrium like the world's biggest greenhouse. The atrium was five hundred feet long and more than a hundred feet wide. It was big enough to have its own weather system. As the two of them headed inside, Chapel couldn't help but look up at the massive span of arching trusses overhead that screened the sky.

The atrium was full of people headed from one side of the headquarters to the other, some in military uniforms, some in civilian clothes. None of them looked particularly scared or tense, but maybe they didn't know what was going on either.

Wilkes was already moving ahead toward a security station that blocked the main entrance to the complex. Chapel rushed to catch up—then slowed down when he saw there was a metal detector station. Of course there was. If he hadn't been in such a rush, he would have thought about that in advance.

"Just step through, sir," the attendant said. She was a middle-aged woman with that look security professionals get, like they've seen literally everything and none of it was particularly interesting. "There's a line behind you."

He gave the woman a smile. This was always tricky. "I'm afraid I'm about to make your day more complicated," he told her. "I—"

"No firearms are allowed inside," she told him, running a practiced eye up and down his uniform. "No weapons of any kind. If you're worried about your belt buckle, you can take your belt off."

"It's not that," Chapel said. "I have a prosthesis."

Her world-weary stare didn't change. "You'll have to remove it."

He considered arguing but knew there was no point. So while everyone in the NGA stared he unbuttoned his uniform tunic and then stripped out of his shirt until he was naked from the waist up. In a government office building.

Anyone seeing Chapel like that would take a second to realize what was different about him. His left arm, after all, looked exactly like his right one. It was the same skin tone and there was the same amount of hair on the knuckles and the forearm.

That appearance ended at his shoulder. There his arm flared out in a pair of clamps that held snug against his chest and back. He reached over with his right hand and released the catches that held the arm in place, then pulled the whole thing off and put it in a plastic bin so it could be scanned.

As it ran through the machine, the attendant didn't even look at him. She studied her screen making sure there were no bombs or weapons hidden inside the prosthetic. The fingers of the artificial hand ducked in and out of her x-ray scanner, as if reaching out of the guts of the machine for help.

At least a hundred people, most of them in civvies, had stopped to watch. Some of them pointed at him while others whispered to each other with shocked expressions on their faces.

Chapel had been through this before. He tried not to let it bother him. On the other side of the security barrier, Wilkes watched with a sly smile. He knew about the arm, of course—they'd been living together for months now. Most likely he just wanted to watch Chapel squirm. Well, Chapel did his best not to show his embarrassment.

When the scan was done and Chapel, sans arm, had passed through the metal detector, the attendant picked up the prosthetic and handed it back to Chapel. He started to take it from her, but she held on a second longer.

"Sir," she asked. She looked like she was having trouble finding the right words. Finally she just said, "Iraq?"

"Afghanistan," he told her.

She nodded. "I have a cousin. Had . . . had a cousin. He died in Iraq. Sir—do you think it was worth it?"

Chapel wanted to sigh. He wished he knew the answer to that one himself sometimes. It wasn't the first time anyone had asked him the question, though, and he knew what to say. "I'm sure he thought it was. I'm sure he went over there to serve his country, even knowing what that could mean."

The woman didn't look at him. She just nodded and gave him his arm back.

By the time he put the arm and his uniform back on, Wilkes was nearly jumping up and down in impatience. "Come on," he said. "We're going to be late."

FORT BELVOIR, VA: MARCH 21, 09:03

They were given guest badges and instructions on how to find the briefing room. It was a little strange they were allowed to proceed without an escort, but Chapel supposed their security clearance spoke for itself. The two of them hurried through a series of windowless hallways and down several flights of stairs because they had no time to wait for an elevator. When they arrived at their destination, Chapel estimated they were at least one floor underground. He knew what that meant—he'd been in enough secure facilities in his time to know you put the really important rooms in the basement, where anyone inside would be safe from an attack on the surface.

Chapel pushed open the door and found himself in the largest, most high-tech briefing room he'd ever seen. Every wall was lined with giant LCD screens, some ten feet across, some the size of computer monitors. Currently they were all showing the same thing: a murky picture of a stack of shipping containers, with a deep fog or maybe a cloud of dust swirling between them. The view didn't give him any useful information, so instead he looked at the people gathered in the room.

There were a lot of them. Maybe fifty. Half were dressed in military uniforms from every branch of service—even the Coast Guard and the National Guard were represented. Judging by the insignia they wore, Chapel, a captain in the U.S. Army, was the lowest-ranking man in the place except for Wilkes, who was a first lieutenant. He recognized some of the faces because they belonged to generals and admirals.

The other half of the crowd wore civilian clothes—conservative suits and flag pins. He recognized far fewer of them because he rarely dealt with civilian agencies, but he could tell right away they were all intelligence people by the way they kept glancing at one another as if they expected to be stabbed in the back at any minute.

Chapel definitely recognized one man in the room, a man in an immaculate navy blue suit with perfect white hair and deep blue eyes that could have drilled holes in armor plate. That was Patrick Norton, the secretary of defense. The boss of Chapel's boss, and the leader of the entire military intelligence community of the United States.

"Shit just got real," Wilkes muttered.

The two of them moved to the back wall of the room and stood at attention, waiting to be put at their ease.

It didn't take long. Rupert Hollingshead came out of the crowd and shook both their hands.

The director didn't dress like anyone else there. He wore a tweed suit with a vest and a pocket watch, and unlike everybody else he had facial hair—a pair of muttonchop sideburns that stuck out from either side of his wide face. He didn't look like an intelligence professional at all. More like a genial old professor from an Ivy League university. He even had the mannerisms—the absent-minded attitude of a man lost in lofty thought. It was rare when Chapel didn't see him smiling and nodding quietly to himself as if he were puzzling through an abstruse math problem.

Today, though, was one of those rare days. He'd never seen the director look so serious. The tweed, the smiles, even the pocket watch—those were all part of a costume, very carefully designed to put people at their ease and make them think he was no kind of threat. Today, though, his eyes gave him away. They had the laser focus of the man only his personal staff knew—the spymaster, the head of a secret Defense Intelligence Agency directorate. A man who was capable of sending field agents to their deaths, a man who could handle even the most grim situation report.

"Stand down, boys," he said, in a voice that was not quite a whisper but was unlikely to carry across the room. "I'm sure you're wondering why you're here."

"Yes, sir," Chapel said. Wilkes just watched the director's face.

"You two are here because I might need to send you on a new mission right away. Stay back here and keep quiet, all right? We'll talk when this is done."

Chapel very much wanted to tell the director about Angel's dropped call and the fact that she'd been incommunicado for hours now. But this was neither the time nor the place. Even as Hollingshead stepped away from them, back into the muttering crowd, the briefing began.

FORT BELVOIR, VA: MARCH 21, 09:13

A woman wearing a pantsuit—a civilian—stepped up to a podium on the far side of the room and asked everyone to take their seats.

"Thank you for coming," she said. "I'm Melinda Foster, and I work for the NGA. We brought you all here to our offices as a kind of neutral territory. The NGA provides imaging product for both civilian and Department of Defense organizations, and the current situation is going to involve both sides of the intelligence community. My job isn't to make policy decisions, though. I'm just here to give you the facts as we know them. Then we'll open the floor to discussion."

She picked up a remote control and clicked a few buttons. Behind her, on one of the big screens, a map of Louisiana appeared with a red star superimposed on the Mississippi delta. "This morning, just before six o'clock, the United States suffered a radiological attack."

This wasn't the kind of crowd that would easily erupt into chaos. Nobody jumped to their feet or shouted for more information. But Chapel could feel all the oxygen draining from the room as the crowd drew a deep and collective breath.

On the screen, a map of the Port of New Orleans appeared. "The night before, a cargo container came into this, our busiest port. It came with counterfcit paperwork. We've cstablished it was full of low-level radioactive waste. I need to stress that does not mean weapons-grade radiologicals. Instead, we're talking about the junk that gets discarded all the time by workers in nuclear power plants. Everything from scrapped computer components to contaminated safety equipment down to the gloves and protective clothing the workers used. All that stuff is considered as hazardous material and is normally processed along with spent nuclear fuel."

A slide came up on the screen showing a pile of garbage that looked harmless enough, just as she'd described it.

"Radioactive particles can adhere to this material, so it needs to be disposed of carefully. But apparently some nuclear plant somewhere didn't feel like paying to do that. So instead they just stuffed it in a cargo container and sent it overseas. Most likely it was being shipped to a developing country where it would end up in a landfill. This happens with distressing regularity. Along its journey, however, it passed through our port. That's illegal—hence the counterfeit paperwork. Just before six A.M., this cargo container entered an inspection station in the Port of New Orleans. It went under a PVT gamma ray detection arch, a piece of technology we've installed in all our shipping hubs specifically to catch this kind of event. The arch did its job and logged a gamma ray detection event. Normally the cargo container would have been isolated in a quarantine facility and traced back to its origin. Today, however, we never got the chance."

Foster clicked her remote again. The image on the screen changed to show a Predator UAV—an aircraft everyone in the room would instantly recognize.

"At the same time an MQ-1 aircraft was passing overhead. It was an old, demilitarized model, one of the first-generation drones. Civilian agencies and even law enforcement are using these now for basic surveillance functions. Local air traffic control was aware of the Predator, but nobody seems to have raised any red flags—they assumed it was a routine sweep. The port is monitored at all times by a variety of systems, including drones, and while this one didn't have an official flight plan, everyone seems to have assumed that was just an oversight. Now, these drones don't just fly themselves. Somebody has to actively control them from another location. So we know what happened next was not just a glitch.

"The drone descended at speed toward the port facility just as the cargo container passed under the PVT arch. It impacted the container with a considerable amount of force. The drone wasn't carrying any weaponry, but simple physics was enough to catastrophically damage the cargo container. Its structural integrity was compromised and its contents were dispersed over a wide area. Some of the nonmetallic components inside, like those rubber gloves, were aerosolized in the impact.

"What that means is that a large quantity of radioactive material was dispersed across the port facility, in some cases traveling a quarter mile before it settled out of the air. Dust from the gloves and clothing may have been carried much farther. Preliminary analysis shows that a significant area of the port has been affected."

She clicked a button and a new picture came up, this showing an overhead view of the enormous port facility. A red stain covered almost half of the view, looking like a spray of blood from a cut artery, to indicate the spread of radioactive material.

"The port was evacuated just after the event. There was only one direct injury—a Charles Mitchell, the operator of the PVT arch, was hit by flying debris. He was found dead on the scene. Meanwhile, we have hazmat crews all over the port trying to collect as much of the debris as possible. Though the overall levels of radiation are very low, it just isn't safe to let workers back inside the facility until we can complete our cleanup."

She clicked her remote and the view returned to the video Chapel had seen before—the dust-shrouded pile of cargo containers.

"Ladies and gentleman," Foster said, "Mr. Secretary. The impact—the crash—of this drone was intentional. It was very well planned. What it boils down to is that terrorists have just exploded a dirty bomb on American soil."

FORT BELVOIR, VA: MARCH 21, 09:34

Half the room started talking at once then, people firing questions at Melinda Foster, others calling for immediate action. Chapel couldn't follow all the rapid-fire discussions, and apparently neither could the room's most important occupant.

The secretary of defense slapped the table with the flat of his hand. It was enough to get absolute, instant quiet.

In the silence he looked around the room, from one tense face to another. "The president has personally asked me to lead the task force on this. The director of national intelligence is on board—so all you civilians here, you're working for me now. Everybody here is working for me until this is over. Understood?"

The room rumbled with agreement. There had been times in the past—September eleventh, for example—when the various agencies in the intelligence community had failed to work together and bad things happened. Clearly the president wasn't going to let that happen again. The authority he'd given to Norton might be unprecedented, but nobody in that room was going to question it.

"We're going to get whoever did this," Norton said. "We're going to make an example of them."

The room briefly erupted in a chorus of assent, which stopped as soon as Norton slapped the table again.

"No one is leaving this room until we have a plan for moving forward. I need all of you working together—every agency, every organization, from this moment, is going to make this their top priority. What we're talking about here is escalation. This is terrorism of a kind we haven't seen before and we're not going to let it get out of control. The world needs to know we won't allow this to happen again. First things first, though.

We need to know who's responsible." He turned and looked at one of the civilians—one Chapel didn't recognize. "CIA. What groups do we think are even capable of something like this? Hijacking a Predator—could al-Qaeda do that? IS? The Khorasan Group?"

The civilian grimaced. "They've never done anything like it before. They stick to low-tech methods, mostly. But we can't rule them out. A Predator is like any other machine. It's designed to accept input from a remote user and it doesn't care who that user is as long as they're broadcasting on the right frequency, with the right encryption. It's not smart enough to ask why it's being told to do something."

"But our encryption is the best in the world," the SecDef insisted. Norton looked to another man halfway across the room. "NSA. Am I wrong in believing that?"

"No," the NSA director replied, though he looked a little dubious. "Our stuff should be uncrackable. But we can't rule out the possibility that some very smart hacker in, say, Indonesia or Taiwan discovered a new exploit or just got lucky or—"

Norton shook his head. "I'm hearing a lot of qualifiers. A lot of 'we can't rule this out.' I want real answers. Have we picked up any chatter about this? Anybody talking about planning an operation with a Predator drone, anyone discussing a cargo container full of radioactive waste?"

"Nothing," the NSA man said. "The terror groups have been quiet lately. Most of what we hear is about money problems and recruiting. Nothing like this."

"At least that's definite," Norton replied. "Okay. Let's hear from the military. Who did this Predator belong to?"

"That would be us," an air force general said. "It was one of our fleet. I've taken the liberty of tracking it through the system, and I can have a document on your desk tomorrow showing every individual who's ever flown it, maintained it, or inspected it. I can tell you right now that it's been sitting in a hangar for the last year, under armed guard the whole time. It hadn't been modified or repaired for nine months. Nobody physically altered it."

"What was it doing in the air?"

The general looked like he very much wanted to shrug. But he must have known this wasn't the time to admit he didn't know something. "It was signed out last night, by official e-mail. Fueled up and launched just after midnight, eastern time."

"By whom? Who signed it out?" Norton demanded.

"The CIA," the general replied.

That started some real shouting. People visibly moved away from the CIA director, who kept waving his hands in the air demanding quiet, insisting he had a response.

"I guarantee you we did not sign out that drone," he shouted over the babble. "Whatever paperwork the air force got was a forgery. Drone operations have to cross my desk, and I saw nothing like this. Whoever these terrorists are, they have access to CIA watermarks, that's all, they have—"

"Sir," a navy admiral said, raising his voice, "if we can't figure out who it was, why don't we just hit them all—punitive raids, keep up the pressure until one of the terrorist groups cracks—"

"That's going to kill our reputation overseas," one of the civilian directors insisted. "It's going to make it impossible for our people on the ground to—"

"We can afford to lose some human assets," the CIA director insisted, "if it means flushing these assholes out of hiding; I'm willing to sacrifice as much as half of my—"

"You're talking about mobilizing every Special Forces group," an army general shouted, "right at the worst possible time, when things in Syria are going to hell and we need more people than ever in Yemen—"

"Ah," someone said, a quiet sound in the furor. "If I may." No one paid any attention.

Nobody except the SecDef. He turned and looked straight at Rupert Hollingshead.

Little by little the noise dropped away. People noticed that Norton had switched focus, and they decided they needed to know why.

Hollingshead leaned back in his chair and cleaned his glasses with a pocket handkerchief. He made a flourish of the cloth, then stuffed it back in his breast pocket while we waited for the room to quiet down so he could be heard.

"Rupert?" Norton asked. "You have something?"

"I am hearing," Hollingshead said, rising creakily to his feet, "a lot of sabers being rattled just now. A lot of people who wish to go and find and lynch every known terrorist just in case one of them was responsible."

He smiled. It was his warmest, most genial smile, and Chapel knew it was one hundred percent fake. "Understandable, of course."

"Clearly you disagree with that plan," Norton said.

Hollingshead gave a contrite shrug. "I think it may be presumptive. A tad." He walked across the room, over to the screen that still showed dust billowing around cargo containers, as if he'd noticed something there. He blinked through his spectacles at the image. "Since, after all, this was not a terrorist attack."

FORT BELVOIR, VA: MARCH 21, 09:49

The CIA director actually started laughing.

"What are you talking about?" the NSA director shouted. "Of course it is! Somebody hit us, some cowardly bastard who—"

Hollingshead lifted his hands in the air as if in surrender. Chapel knew his boss was just getting started, though. "Please. Just hear me out. We few, gathered here today, have been preparing for something like this ever since 2001. We have lost a great deal of collective sleep over the possibility of a dirty bomb attack. In all our scenarios and projections we imagined this as the worst possible way for terrorists to strike at us. And so we built up our defenses against such a thing. We organized all our efforts toward preventing any terrorist group getting their hands on nuclear material. But that's just it, isn't it? When one is in possession of a, um, hammer, well, every threat looks exactly like a nail."

Norton's brow furrowed. "Rupert, if you could get to the point soon, I'd appreciate it."

Hollingshead smiled and even elicited a few sympathetic chuckles from the crowd. They weren't quite enough to balance the glares he was getting from the CIA and NSA directors.

"Very well. I'll give you three points, in fact. One. A terrorist attacks a public target. A visible target. Ms. Foster," he said, turning to the woman who'd given the initial briefing, "have the gentlemen of the press been allowed into the port facility since the attack?"

Foster looked terrified at being called on. "No," she said, "not . . . not as such. There have been some reporters out there—they saw the plume of dust—but they don't know any details. The port's security people told them it was a hazardous materials situation, but that was all. No specific facts."

Hollingshead nodded. "Very well done. Best we don't bring this to the public just yet. The port facility is off-limits to the public. Point one. Terrorists wish to gain media attention, to get the world to see what they've done. A terrorist attack is a *statement*, a message everyone has to listen to. At the moment, the net result of this attack is likely to be a two-minute segment on the local news broadcast in Louisiana. Not much of a coup.

"Point two: they always take credit. We've already heard there was no chatter about this. But that must also mean no one is crowing about their success. What terrorist group would be so tight-lipped?"

Norton looked like he was half convinced. "What's your third point?"

Hollingshead nodded. "Subtlety. And intentionality. This attack wasn't just meant to scare us. It was meant to quietly, but quite effectively, cripple us. Mister Secretary," he said, blinking at a man who sat very close to the SecDef. Chapel realized after a second that he recognized the man—he was the secretary of transportation. Not somebody who would normally sit in on a top-level intelligence briefing. "You are here today because your office administers and oversees our port facilities, yes? Perhaps you can tell me what I need to know. How vital to American commerce is the Port of New Orleans?"

The secretary nodded, clearly excited to be included. "It's one of our top priorities. Our only deepwater port with access to six railways, the highway system, cargo planes. Half of all our food travels through that port, every year."

"I imagine that closing the port is going to cost us a great deal of money, even in the short term," Hollingshead pointed out.

The secretary nodded and grinned. Then he seemed to realize this wasn't a time for showing off and his face fell into a more serious cast. "It'll cost a fortune just to reroute all the ships that were supposed to offload there in the next month. And the public is going to feel that cost. We're talking about a rise in food prices, maybe as much as ten percent. And all kinds of goods go through that port, everything from luxury cars to medical equipment, all of that's going to get more expensive, and—"

Hollingshead lifted one hand to cut the man off. "That's a serious return on investment. One Predator drone in exchange for a massive disruption of American commerce. Mr. Norton, I'd like to suggest that this is far too subtle for any ham-handed terrorist to be responsible. I'd venture this was the act of a power that wished to hurt us economically. I will go so far as to claim this was an act of soft war."

That got people murmuring, though many of the whispered comments were just people asking what soft war was. Chapel knew the answer. Soft war, or anti-infrastructure warfare, was going after an enemy's supply routes rather than attacking their soldiers. You blew up their roads or cut their power grid, making it impossible for them to carry out an effective military strategy.

The CIA director jumped to his feet. "Of course you would suggest this," he said, his face bright red. "You're military intelligence. You want this to be the opening shot in some big theater conflict—you want—"

Hollingshead cut him off simply by standing up straight and setting his mouth in a hard line. The genial professor act was gone. Suddenly he looked more like an Old Testament prophet. "The last thing any soldier wants is another war. But when one comes along, he does not shirk his duty. Mr. Norton, if this was the work of Iran or North Korea or, God forbid, China—"

"You're jumping to conclusions," one of the civilian directors shouted.

"You have no evidence," the CIA director insisted.

Hollingshead said nothing. He just looked at Norton, waiting for a reply.

For a while, as directors and generals bickered back and forth across the room, the SecDef simply folded his hands in front of him, almost as if he were praying. Then he drew in a very long breath.

"Give me a plan," he said.

Hollingshead didn't hesitate. "I have two operatives with me right now. I can get them to work immediately, investigating who did this. Give them twenty-four hours to dig. By all means let our analyst friends look into the terrorism angle—if someone claims responsibility or we hear any chatter, then, well, problem solved. If I'm right, however, we need to act decisively, right from the start."

"Okay," Norton said. "Do it. Whatever you need."

FORT BELVOIR, VA: MARCH 21, 10:09

Hollingshead moved through the room putting a hand on a shoulder here, whispering a word in an ear there, marshaling what support he could. Then he headed back out into the hallway, nodding for Wilkes and Chapel to follow. Once the door was closed behind them, he looked at his two men and then let out a long, chuckling sigh. "We have our work cut out for us, boys."

"Yes, sir," Chapel said.

The three of them headed toward the exit. Along the way Wilkes said, "Sir, you think it's true? You think this is the start of a war?"

"Not for a moment," Hollingshead confided. He stopped and glanced around, looking to see if anyone else was listening. "It's possible, of course. When you spin a line of nonsense like that, you need to have plausibility on your side. But I just don't see what quarter such an attack could come from. This was a technological attack—all of it done with computers. Neither Iran nor North Korea have the encryption know-how to do this. Russia and China might, but why would either of them want to start a war? Russia couldn't win, and China would stand to gain nothing but losing their biggest market." He shook his head. "No, this wasn't state-sponsored. That much I feel sure of."

Chapel frowned. "But then why make that case? Sir, you lied to the secretary of defense."

"Sometimes it's necessary. That room was headed in one direction only. They were going to turn this into another September eleventh. The country can't handle that kind of panic again. I've bought us a little time during which people will be forced to make rational choices."

"I don't get it," Wilkes said.

Hollingshead put a hand on the marine's elbow. "Son, you're too young to remember what it was like. On September eleventh, 2001, we were caught completely off guard. The nation had no plan in place for how to handle a terrorist attack on its soil. The result was pure pandemonium. Every agency rushing to action with no information or, worse, bad information. Intelligence organizations openly and viciously fighting over who got to respond and who was to blame. The end result was that we started two wars we couldn't handle and squandered an enormous amount of blood and treasure. If we can forestall that this time—if we can *fix* things now, quietly, without letting fear overtake us, then we stand to do an enormous amount of good for the country. If we fail, we will spend the next ten years putting out fires and cleaning up messes and accomplishing nothing."

"Sir, yes, sir," Wilkes said.

"All right." Hollingshead led them toward the atrium and the street. "You two will have a car. Let's head back to the Pentagon. We can reconnoiter at my office. The absolute first thing we need to do is get Angel working on this, tracking whoever hijacked that Predator."

"Sir," Chapel said, "that's something I wanted to talk to you about."

"Oh?"

"I was on the phone with her this morning and we were . . . cut off. I can't explain it, it sounded like the call was dropped. I haven't been able to reach her since."

Hollingshead gave him a long, questioning look, but Chapel had no more information to give.

"Blast," the director said finally. He reached into his pocket and took out a hands-free unit. It looked ridiculous in his ear—like an anachronism, like a caveman wearing a wristwatch. He tapped at it convulsively, calling Angel's name over and over. Eventually he gave up and put the earpiece away.

"Damnation," he said, staring off into the middle distance. "This is bad. Very bad. Without her, we're flying blind."

"Sir, if I may speak candidly?" Chapel asked.

"Yes, of course, always. You've seen how Wilkes speaks to me."

The marine didn't even have the good grace to blush.

Chapel tried not to focus on that. "The timing is strange. When I spoke to her she sounded fine, but then she just dropped off the air—just a couple hours after the attack in New Orleans. I'm not a big believer in coincidences."

"Nor am I. You think she's in danger?"

"I think that finding out what happened to her might give us a clue as to who attacked the port," Chapel pointed out.

Hollingshead nodded. "It does raise one massive headache, though."

"What's that?" Wilkes asked.

"It means we need to find somebody to help us, somebody who can do what she normally does for us. It means we're going to have to go begging to the bloody NSA."

IN TRANSIT: MARCH 21, 10:32

Chapel shared the director's opinion of the NSA, but really, having to go to any agency outside of the DIA was a problem. Technically, after 9/11, every agency and directorate and organization in the American intelligence community had been streamlined so they could work together— they were all on the same team, after all. A major reason the 2001 terrorist attacks had been such a surprise was that different agencies had all had parts of the puzzle, but nobody had been willing to share information. Each agency was treated like a separate fiefdom with its own jealously guarded secrets.

That was supposed to have changed. They were all supposed to be members of a happy family now. Unfortunately, the very competitive directors and spymasters of those agencies had seen the new rules not as a chance to integrate intelligence but an opportunity to one-up each other. The agencies competed for funds and for prestige all the time. The mass briefing back at Fort Belvoir had shown just how contentious that competition got. If the DIA needed help from the NSA, it would make the DIA look like it couldn't get things done on its own. If it was the NSA that tracked the drone hijacker, not the DIA, then the NSA stood to benefit—in terms of larger budgets and more influence in the White House. Accepting that he needed the NSA was tantamount for Hollingshead to admitting defeat.

It was a measure of Hollingshead's character that finding the hijacker was more important than his own reputation.

"Keep trying Angel," Hollingshead said, leaning over the backseat. "Here. There are three numbers she always responds to." He took a tiny notebook and a golf pencil out of one of his many pockets and scribbled the numbers down, then tore out the page and handed it to Wilkes. "Make sure you destroy that paper when you've got them memorized." He sat back down in his seat and looked over at Chapel. "You're sure she didn't say anything that made you think she was in immediate danger?"

Chapel kept his eyes on the road. The NSA was headquartered in Fort Meade, back in Maryland, which meant driving through the never-ending gridlock that surrounded Washington. "She sounded more worried about me."

Hollingshead slapped the dashboard. "I wish I'd known before I committed us. Oh, look, son, it's not, ah, it's not your fault—I didn't give you a chance to talk back there." He sighed and stared out his window. "All right, we're still on the clock and we have a little time before we get to the NSA. We need to start thinking through how we're going to find whoever struck the Port of New Orleans. We need a list of possible culprits."

"Yes, sir," Chapel said. This was good—it was good because it would make him think about something other than what had happened to Angel. He forced himself to push his brain down a different road. "You said before this was a technological attack—all done with computers. And we know the Predator's control signal was heavily encrypted. That has to narrow down the search. If the same person intercepted and blocked Angel's signal, that means even fewer candidates. Her encryption was stronger than the Predator's. You said Russia and China might have that kind of technology."

"They might. But in both cases it wouldn't be something the average citizen could get their hands on. It would take military-grade equipment, or maybe something their spy services would have. We know neither of them wants to start a war."

"But maybe that wasn't the point," Chapel pointed out. "Maybe the whole plan was just to hurt us economically. They would know we would suspect terrorists first—if they covered their tracks well enough, they'd have a chance of getting away with it and us never finding out."

"We'll put that on the list, then, but no—that doesn't feel right," Hollingshead said. "I'll admit I'm no, ah, economist. Perhaps they wanted to, I don't know, short some market for foodstuffs or monopolize some commodity. But a real economist, I'm sure, would point out what they had to lose. Hurting us might give them a tiny advantage, but would it be worth the incredible risk? If we do discover that this actually was soft war, we'll have to respond with the more traditional sort."

"So what else, then? Who?"

Hollingshead shrugged. "The problem with technology, of course, is that it's always moving forward. Always innovating. We could be dealing with just one rogue hacker, for all we know."

"Someone like Bogdan Vlaicu," Chapel pointed out. Vlaicu was a Romanian hacker Chapel had worked with on a mission, once. He was a paranoid, morose man who was convinced he was constantly about to be killed. He was also the best computer genius Chapel had ever known, with the one exception of Angel. "He had access to Angel's software, once, and he made pretty good use of it." In fact he'd been a big part of why Chapel had screwed up so badly on that mission and gotten himself assigned to stakeout duty with Wilkes. "I know she upgraded her systems after we found out, but maybe he found another way in."

"It's possible. There are three or four other people in the world with those skills, people I've had my eye on," Hollingshead said, "very dangerous people. But none of them would intentionally attack the United States, not like this—it just wouldn't interest them to do so."

"Unless they were paid well enough," Chapel pointed out. Vlaicu had worked for both organized crime and for the Romanian and Russian governments in the past. He'd also helped a terrorist in Siberia, though that had been . . . complicated.

"So he and the others definitely go on the list, though finding them will be damned difficult. And then we'll need to discover who they worked for," Hollingshead said.

Wilkes leaned over the seat back. "No answer from any of these phone numbers," he said. Chapel had expected as much, but it still pained him to hear it. "But while I've been playing secretary, I thought of something. What if it was internal?" he asked.

Chapel forced himself not to take his eyes off the road.

"What are you suggesting?" Hollingshead asked.

"Somebody needs to 'jack a Predator, well, they need to write all kinds of code, pull all kinds of crazy computer tricks." Wilkes chuckled. "Unless they already had the key, right? The CIA is operations for a big chunk of the drone fleet. And back there, at the briefing, they said it. The CIA had logged out this particular Predator. Why make things complicated? What if the CIA staged this attack?"

"But why?" Chapel asked.

"Who knows?" Wilkes said. It sounded less like an admission of ignorance than that he just didn't care. "I can think of a reason they'd want to take down Angel, though. You three—you, sir; Jimmy here; and Angel— you took down Tom Banks a couple of years ago. Gave the CIA a real bloody nose."

"I suppose we did do that," Hollingshead replied. "And revenge is a perfectly sound motive in this sort of thing. But there's one problem. We took down Tom Banks and his directorate of the CIA quite successfully. He's not there anymore, nor are any of his people. He was replaced by

Harry West. An old friend of mine—in fact, he got the job because I personally recommended him."

"So we can cross the CIA off the list," Chapel said. "At least that's something. I really don't want to think this was an inside job—that somebody in the intelligence community dropped a dirty bomb on U.S. soil."

"I imagine none of us do. Though part of our job is to take on the unthinkable," Hollingshead said. He leaned forward and gestured through the windshield.

Up ahead a sign by the side of the road indicated that the upcoming exit ramp was only a quarter of a mile away. NSA EMPLOYEES ONLY, it read.

"Take this exit," Hollingshead told Chapel. "They'll be expecting us."

FORT MEADE, MD: MARCH 21, 11:18

Military vehicles sat on either side of the off-ramp, and an armed guard stood in the middle of the road, waving them in. Hollingshead rolled down his window and held up his identification and the guard just nodded. He gave them some quick directions toward their destination and then warned them what would happen if they wandered too far off course. Chapel made a point of following the directions exactly.

NSA headquarters, in comparison to the NGA building they'd just left, looked like a boring rectangular office building—nothing special. Of course Chapel knew that appearances could be deceiving. The glass panes that fronted the building were all one-way mirrors that had been coated with a film of copper so no one could bounce a radio signal through them. Information entered the building through a thousand conduits, but none ever came out.

The building stood in the middle of the largest parking lot Chapel had ever seen. An attendant came out and guided him into a numbered spot. "Kept it open just for you," the man said with a big grin. "You'll want to head into that white building there, the Visitor Control Center. Have a great day!"

Together the three of them headed into the indicated building, where a line of metal detectors and backscatter booths waited. Sighing, Chapel started to unbutton his uniform tunic again, intending to take his arm off before someone asked him to. Before he could get more than one button undone, however, a woman in a blue blazer came running up. "No need, sir, no need!"

"I have a prosthetic arm," he told her, launching into a speech he'd used a thousand times before. "It'll set off the metal detectors and—"

"Yes, Captain, we know," she said, reaching for his good arm. "If you'll just come this way. All three of you. We have a special detector suite warmed up. Don't worry, Director Hollingshead, we know about your pacemaker as well, there's no danger."

Chapel gave the director a glance, but Hollingshead simply favored him with a tiny sympathetic shake of his head. Together the three of them passed into a series of gray felt-covered partition walls at one end of the security station. Chapel was certain he was being scanned as he walked through, but he had no idea what kind of detectors they used. At the far end they were given blue security badges embedded with tiny RFID chips embedded in the plastic. "Don't worry about getting lost," the woman explained. "If you end up someplace you're not supposed to, those chips will sound an alarm and somebody will come to collect you. If you tamper with the chips, that'll set off the alarm, too, so try not to touch them too much." She gave them a big, warm smile. "Welcome to the Puzzle Palace!"

"Thank you, my dear," Hollingshead said. His genial professor act was back in place. "If you could, ah, be so kind as to direct us . . ."

"No need," she said, bobbing her head. "Just go over there to elevator bank two."

Chapel frowned. There really should have been someone to meet them and take them to—well, wherever they were headed. When they arrived at the elevator bank, though, he saw why that wasn't necessary. With a pleasant little chime the nearest elevator opened its doors. Stepping inside, he saw that one of the floor buttons was already lit. Obviously the floor they wanted.

Wilkes leaned over toward Chapel's ear. "You know that feeling, when you're being watched? You can feel it on the back of your neck?"

"Yeah," Chapel said.

"Right now I got that feeling on the front of my neck, too."

Hollingshead cleared his throat. "Boys, I'd appreciate it if you could try to remember that everything you say and do inside this building is being written down somewhere. Logged, as they say, for posterity."

The elevator opened again on a broad lobby full of potted plants. No one was there to meet them, but at the far side of the lobby a green light appeared over a door. They headed through into a cavernous room Chapel thought looked like nothing so much as a deserted casino.

The lighting was subdued and mostly blue. The thick carpet under his feet was red with an abstract pattern of yellow lines. On the walls, massive display screens showed a rotating NSA logo. The ceiling was studded with black glass domes that he was certain hid cameras that tracked his every move. Instead of slot machines, however, the room contained dozens of gleaming workstations, each with a padded chair and a high-end laptop.

Two people waited for them at the far end of the huge room. One was a woman dressed in an air force uniform, while the other was a civilian in a sweater vest and khaki pants. At first Chapel thought the woman was very short, but as they approached he realized that it was just that although the civilian wasn't very tall—probably six and a half feet—he was so thin; Chapel found himself thinking this was the tallest little guy he'd ever met. His hair was short but somehow messy, which just added to the impression. He didn't make eye contact as the two groups came together.

The woman was perhaps sixty years old, with short, curly hair and warm eyes. She gave them a high-wattage smile and reached out with both hands for Hollingshead. "Rupert!" she exclaimed. "How lovely to see you again." And then she actually pecked him on the cheek.

The director squirmed away as if a boa constrictor was trying to wrap itself around his throat. "Good morning, Charlotte," he said. He turned and looked back at Chapel and Wilkes. "Boys, meet Colonel Charlotte Holman."

Chapel came to attention and offered her a salute. Wilkes did the same after a moment's hesitation.

"Oh, please," Holman said, laughing. "No need for that. We're all friends here. We're very nearly family!"

Chapel held the salute. Eventually, a little awkwardly, Holman returned it. "At ease, Captain," she said, shaking her head in amusement.

Chapel wished he had any idea whatsoever what was going on.

FORT MEADE, MD: MARCH 21, 11:26

"Colonel Holman," Hollingshead tried to explain, "is an old acquaintance. I didn't actually expect her to come meet us here."

"I'm the subdirector for the S1 Directorate. Customer Relations," she told Chapel and Wilkes. It took Chapel a moment to realize that meant she was an interagency liaison. The NSA had no field agents like himself—it simply gathered information, which it then passed on to other organizations like the DIA. Holman, then, was responsible for that dissemination. He had forgotten that the NSA used business lingo to refer to its activities—the information it provided was referred to as its "products" and the security agencies it served were its "customers."

"Normally on a case like this you'd be meeting with my director," Holman told them, "but he's still back at that incredibly tense briefing you came from." She mocked a shiver. "Pretty scary stuff, huh?" She laughed again. Chapel got the impression she laughed a great deal, even about inappropriate things like a dirty bomb attack. "Rupert thought he was going to just come over here and somehow miss seeing me altogether, but I'm a little too sly for that."

"Now, now, Charlotte, I had no intention of—"

"I can see by the looks on your faces you'd like to know what there is between us," she said.

Chapel had to admit he was mildly curious.

"I'll tell you, but it's a secret, so, shush!" She mimed locking her lips with a key. "Rupert and I dated once upon a time."

"Once being the operative term, I'm, uh, afraid," Hollingshead said. "It was ten years ago. My wife had, well, passed and some . . . mutual friends. Set us up. As it were."

"It was lovely," Holman told them. "Who would have thought in this day and age there were any true gentlemen left? Rupert was wonderful. Such a shame it didn't work out."

Hollingshead was actually blushing. Chapel couldn't help but be fascinated—he knew nothing at all about the director's personal life. The man kept such things intensely private. He didn't like seeing his boss in such obvious distress, but considering the reason, well—

"I wasn't, er, ready," Hollingshead said. "To. You know. Date again."

"One day you will be," Holman said, with a twinkle in her eye. "I'll get my hooks in you yet, Rupert." She laughed again.

Chapel knew, in an instinctive way, that this flirtatious persona was just that. If Rupert Hollingshead only pretended to be a bumbling absent-minded professor, Charlotte Holman was putting on just as much of an act. But it worked. He had just met this woman. She outranked him. Yet he had to keep reminding himself he shouldn't trust her—she just seemed so harmless.

"Oh, where are my manners?" she said. "I still haven't introduced Paul. Paul, please say hello to our friends from the DIA."

The skinny guy in the sweater vest held out one hand for them to shake. He didn't make eye contact, though. "Paul Moulton," he muttered. "I'm an analyst in Tailored Access Operations."

"One of our very best," Holman said, reaching up to put a hand on the man's shoulder. "When Rupert asked for our help, I knew Paul was exactly the man we needed. He'll help you find this bad guy, be assured of it."

"I'm afraid time is at a premium," Hollingshead said. "Do you think we could, ah, get down to it?"

"Of course," Holman said. She led them over to one of the workstations. Moulton sat down in the chair and logged in. Holman looked over at Hollingshead. "So tell us exactly what you're looking for today."

The way she said it left Chapel with no doubt she already knew, but she wanted Hollingshead to say it out loud. That way he actually had to ask her—which meant he would owe her something. He shuddered to imagine having to operate on the level these two took for granted. The endless games, the rivalries between agencies—he wondered what kind of brain it took to keep it all straight.

"Someone hijacked a Predator drone this morning. That is to say," Hollingshead told her, "they fed it control data that was not authorized by any governmental or military body. We need to know who did it, that's all. A physical location would be nice, but a name would be even better."

Holman nodded. "I imagine we can do that. Funny, though. Normally you could take care of this yourself, couldn't you?"

"The analyst I would usually turn to," Hollingshead said, glancing away, "is unavailable at the moment."

"How frustrating. Paul, can you bring up data on the drone fleet?" She turned to face Chapel and Wilkes. "Communications with the drones is all logged, of course, recorded and stored on Department of Defense servers. Paul—mirror your screen to display three, please."

One of the big screens on the wall lit up with an image of the workstation's desktop. Moulton opened an application that showed a list of files all dated in the last twenty-four hours. There were hundreds of them. "What you see here," Holman said, "is computer code describing what the Predators were doing at a given time, whether that means shifting the inclination of an aileron or turning off their cameras or, for sake of argument, firing a Hellfire missile."

"All these drones were in the air?" Chapel asked.

"No, most of those are just for UAVs still sitting in their hangars," Holman explained. "They send a constant stream of updates and checklists back to command, even when they're inactive, just so we can keep track of where they are."

"I'll highlight the active ones," Moulton said. On the screen only a half-dozen or so listings changed to blue. "It's one of these?"

Hollingshead put on his glasses and studied the screen. "There. The one that just stops at 05:51:14," he said, pointing at the big display. Chapel realized that must be the moment when the Predator hit the cargo container and destroyed itself—putting it off-line.

Moulton isolated the listing and expanded it. It looked like so much gibberish to Chapel—just line after line of numbers and strings of letters he knew he would never understand.

Hollingshead walked over to the screen. "Here." He pointed at a line that read 10.0.0.1. "This lists the IP address for the incoming commands, yes?"

Holman nodded. "That's right."

Chapel tried to remember everything he'd heard Angel say about IP addresses. He knew they were pretty useful. "If you know that, you can track the command back to whoever issued it, right? You can get their physical location."

"You might," Holman said, "except of course the hijacker would know that. So he went to the trouble of altering the IP address on his outgoing commands. 10.0.0.1 is a default IP address—just a placeholder. It doesn't mean anything."

"You can do that?" Chapel asked.

"It's actually pretty easy," Moulton told him.

"So . . ." Chapel shook his head. "So we're seeing the actual code the hijacker used to control the Predator. But that code doesn't tell us anything useful. They've hidden themselves and there's no way to find out who they are."

"Yeah, right," the analyst sneered. "I can totally track them. They just went to enough trouble to make it interesting."

FORT MEADE, MD: MARCH 21, 11:39

"The hijacker prevented us from doing this the easy way. And maybe if you were talking to anybody else, it would end there. But this is the NSA. We've been cracking codes since World War I." Moulton turned around in his chair. "Whoever sent these commands, they thought they were anonymous. But you can't ever really be anonymous on the Internet." He glanced from one to another of them with little grunts of frustration as if trying to decide who might understand what he said next. "You leave . . . fingerprints, I guess, is a good analogy. I can't get an IP address out of this code. But there's still a path to follow." He turned back to his keyboard. "This is going to take a few minutes."

"Take your time," Holman told him. "Do it right."

Moulton nodded over his keyboard. He opened up another program, one that looked to Chapel like a giant and very, very complicated spreadsheet. He entered a mathematical equation in a field at the top of the sheet and then opened yet another program that showed a map of the world.

"I'm going to query our network analyzer. This thing's like a packet sniffer on steroids." He glanced around the room and then sighed. "Basically, um, I can't just trace the signal back to its source. But because of how the Internet works, I can find everywhere the signal passed through on its way to the Predator. All the servers it touched on its way. It's like looking for a needle in a haystack by examining every piece of hay for how long ago they were next to the needle. Then by knowing where those pieces of hay were, you can home in on where the needle *was*, even though it isn't there anymore."

"If it works," Wilkes said, "I don't really care how it works."

The analyst nodded. He clicked his mouse, and up on the screen thousands of red dots appeared on the map, spread out pretty evenly. "These are all the servers the signal passed through. Somewhere in there is your hijacker."

He clicked his mouse again and then pushed back from the workstation to watch the big screen with the rest of them. Up there, a huge number of the dots disappeared, leaving Africa and Australia completely bare.

Chapel knew he would never follow what was actually happening, so he just watched the map. It was almost hypnotic to watch the dots fall away. As more dots blinked out, the process slowed down dramatically. Long seconds would tick by before another one dropped off the map. But the program kept running. Chapel estimated they were down to only a few hundred at most. Then, suddenly, every dot disappeared from Europe and Asia, leaving only those in the United States.

"The signal came from inside the country," Holman interpreted.

A chill ran down Chapel's spine. He remembered what Wilkes had said back in the car—that this might be an inside job. His mouth was suddenly dry. "Are we looking at somebody military, or a civilian?" he asked.

Holman looked at him with wide eyes. "What are you suggesting?" she asked.

Chapel shook his head. "Nothing yet. Just—Moulton. What do you think?"

"Hard to say—the fact that they passed through so many servers so quickly makes me think it's military. Or at least they're using military-grade software."

"Let's not jump to conclusions yet," Holman said.

The map changed to just show the United States. Then almost at once it changed again, to just show the northeastern corridor. One by one the dots kept going out. The map changed a third time to show the greater Washington, D.C., area, with red dots clustered around the Pentagon and Fort Belvoir.

Chapel took a deep breath. It looked like it was one of their own. The possibility had always been there. But at least now they knew, at least they could narrow down the list of possible culprits. And then Chapel could go and find the hijacker and put an end to this before things went too far. All right, that was acceptable. And he had to admit they couldn't have done it without the NSA.

"This," Chapel said as the lights continued to go out, "is some pretty impressive hacking."

"Excuse me?" Moulton said.

"You're quite the hacker," Chapel said, smiling.

Moulton erupted out of his chair and jabbed a finger in Chapel's face. "You take that back."

"What? Listen, I didn't mean—"

"I am not a hacker," Moulton insisted. "A hacker exploits weaknesses. They break into things. I'm using tools that were designed just for this purpose."

"I didn't, uh—hey, let's just—"

Hollingshead cleared his throat, quite distinctly. "Gentlemen," he said, "if you'll put this disagreement on hold, you might wish to look at the map."

Chapel turned and looked at the screen. What he saw made him forget all about Moulton's outburst.

Only one dot remained on the map. It was on the Pentagon.

Everyone in the room held their breath. They knew what that had to mean. The hijacking was an inside job. It wasn't a debatable point anymore.

"Military, then," Holman said, walking toward the map as if she wanted to see it more clearly. "Military. Or maybe a civilian contractor working for a military organization. Can we get any more details?"

"Sure," Moulton said. He glared at Chapel one last time and then returned to his seat. He glanced at his monitor for a moment, then tapped a key and the view on the screen disappeared, replaced with a block of code that Chapel couldn't read. "Here we go. The IP address you requested. It doesn't look like the other one because this is an IPv6 address, which is . . . oh," Moulton said. "Oh, this is—this is a little, um—"

"Delicate," Holman said. "Rupert, I'm so sorry you had to find out like this, I assure you I had no idea—"

She stopped talking because Hollingshead had lifted his hands for peace. He had his eyes closed, and he looked like he was fighting to control himself.

"It's us," he said.

"What?" Chapel asked. "What are you saying?"

"That IP address is one reserved for use by the Defense Intelligence Agency," Hollingshead said very quietly. "The hijacker is one of ours."

Chapel was so stunned he had no idea what to say.

Wilkes didn't have the same problem. "Give me a name," he said.

Moulton did something that cleared his screen and then brought up a page of text—numbers and words, but none Chapel could make any sense out of. The IP address was highlighted in one cell near the middle of the sheet. There was no name associated with the address, just a sixteen-digit number.

"That's a confidential employee identifier," Holman said, pointing at the screen. "That's the number for an operative who can't be named, even in classified documents. Do you want me to look up who it belongs to?"

"No need," Hollingshead said. "I recognize it. The person you've identified is known to me." He opened his eyes. Blinked a few times. Then he looked at Chapel and Wilkes and took a deep breath. "No point in hiding things now. That's Angel's identifier. Angel is the hijacker."

FORT MEADE, MD: MARCH 21, 12:18

"No," Chapel said. "No. No way it's her. She wouldn't do this."

"Son, I don't want to believe it either," Hollingshead told him, reaching for his arm. "But we have to at least entertain the possibility—"

Chapel brushed off the director's hand. "After all she's done for you. Everything she's done for her country. You won't even give her the benefit of the doubt?"

"That's exactly what I want to do," Hollingshead said. He sighed deeply and looked around him. Every eye in the room was watching him. "We'll have to bring her in. Today."

Chapel shook his head. He couldn't believe what he was hearing. Hollingshead was going to arrest Angel just because the NSA claimed she was a traitor? It was unthinkable.

"She can tell us her side of the story," Hollingshead went on.

"Somebody's framing her," Chapel insisted.

It was Moulton who responded to that. "If they are, they're doing an incredible job of it. It took every resource we had to trace her. If this was a frame-up, you'd think the false evidence would be easier to find."

Chapel glared at the man. "You don't know her."

"Looks like maybe you don't, either," Moulton pointed out.

Chapel took a step toward him, ready to drag him out of his chair and beat the smug smile off the analyst's face. Before he could get there, however, Holman stepped in and cleared her throat.

Two decades, half of Chapel's life, had been spent learning to respect his superior officers. It had become just a reflex—if a colonel cleared her throat, you shut up and listened to what she had to say.

"None of us likes this, Captain," she told him. "None of us wants to believe the hijacker was one of us, a member of the intelligence community. And right now we don't have to. Until we have more information we don't have to make any decisions."

"My analysis is sound," Moulton insisted.

"Paul, be quiet," Holman said. She looked over at Hollingshead. "How do you want to proceed?" she asked.

The director looked down at the floor. He shoved his hands deep into his pockets. "Wilkes, go and get her. Head north. I'll send you the coordinates for her location once you're on the road."

"What?" Chapel said.

Hollingshead looked up at him and those genial professorial eyes that twinkled so effectively behind his spectacles were gone. They'd been replaced by the eyes of a rear admiral of the navy, a man who had sent men knowingly to their deaths. A man who had never shirked from a hard decision. "Do you have something to say?"

Chapel bit down his first reaction. Tried desperately to get a handle on his feelings. "Sir. With all due respect. Angel and I have worked together for a very long time. Let me do this."

"I'm afraid I can't allow it," Hollingshead told him. "You and Angel have a . . . complicated relationship. No, son. You're the wrong man for the job."

Holman coughed politely into her hand. "Should it really be anyone from DIA? There might be a conflict of interests here. Maybe we should contact FBI. They're trained for this sort of thing."

"I appreciate your input," Hollingshead told her. "But if I can't send Chapel to fetch her, I won't send a complete stranger, either. Wilkes is our man." He turned to the marine. "Go on, son. Your country needs you to do this."

Wilkes straightened up into a salute. "Sir, yes, sir," he said. Then with one quick glance at Chapel he was gone, headed back to the elevator that was already waiting for him, its doors open.

Chapel whirled around, his breath catching in his throat. "You know—you know what will happen once she's in custody!"

Hollingshead just stood there, no expression at all on his face.

"Goddamnit!" Chapel shouted. He grabbed one of the chairs away from its workstation and threw it across the room. In the cavernous space it failed to collide with anything. Instead it just slid across the ugly carpet, its wheels spinning pointlessly in the air.

FORT MEADE, MD: MARCH 21, 12:27

"Thank you," Hollingshead said to Holman. "You've been most helpful."

"It's what we're here for," she said. Then a furrow crossed her brow. "Rupert, I am sorry. I didn't think we would find one of yours behind the hijacking."

"How could you have?" the director responded. "One should never be sorry for telling the truth. Now. If you'll forgive me—and I hope especially you'll forgive my rather overwrought agent here—I think we'll be going. There's a great deal I need to do."

"Yes, of course," Holman said.

Chapel wanted to scream. He wanted to pick the chair up and start smashing screens. He wanted to do—something, anything to make this not have happened at all. But in the end, all he could do was take his place behind Hollingshead as they started toward the elevator bank.

"Oh, Rupert," Holman said just before their elevator arrived. "You know I'll have to contact the secretary of defense about this, right?"

"I'll call him myself," Hollingshead told her.

She started to say something else, but then she seemed to think better of it. Instead she just nodded and watched them go.

In the elevator neither of them spoke. The silence continued as they made their way through the Visitor Control Center and back out into the parking lot. Wilkes had taken the car, so Hollingshead made a quick call to request transport. While they waited for it to arrive the director fiddled with something in his pocket. Chapel did what he could to contain himself.

In the end it didn't work. "She won't get a trial," he said, barely whispering.

"I'll make sure she's treated fairly," Hollingshead replied. "It's out of your hands, son. Let this go."

"Let it go? Are you kidding me?"

Hollingshead's eyes flashed for a moment. "I am not in the habit of doing so."

Chapel wouldn't be warned off. He didn't even care if the NSA was listening to every word he said. "They'll take her to Guantánamo. Or someplace worse! They'll interrogate her, over and over, until she cracks and confesses to something she didn't do. They'll make her a scapegoat and no one will care that the real hijacker got away with attacking us, and—"

"Captain Chapel," Hollingshead said, and his voice cracked like thunder. "I've given you your orders. Are you questioning my command?"

Chapel could feel his heart beating in his chest like artillery fire finding its range. Every bit of his training and discipline begged him to shut up, but his head roared with anger. "She's a hero. She's saved my life countless times. If you treat her like this—"

"That's enough." Hollingshead lifted his chin and looked over at a Humvee that was heading toward them—clearly the transport he'd requested. "Captain, I'm temporarily relieving you from duty."

"What the hell?"

The director kept his eyes on the approaching vehicle. "Effective immediately. Your behavior today has been inexcusable. Am I understood?"

Chapel fought for words. "Sir, I'm very sorry about throwing that chair, but—"

"I said, 'Am I understood'?"

"Yes, sir."

Hollingshead nodded. "Don't attempt to contact me or my office. I'll let you know when I think enough time has passed."

The Humvee pulled up in front of them. The driver jumped out and ran around the front of the vehicle to open Hollingshead's door.

Chapel felt like he might fall over.

Relieved of duty. For conduct unbecoming an officer.

It was just about the worst thing anyone had ever said to Chapel. He couldn't believe it.

It also meant he had very little left to lose. "This has been coming for a while. You've been trying to find a graceful way to get rid of me, haven't you? That's what Wilkes was for. My replacement. I screwed up and now you're just done with me, because one time I made a mistake. A mistake you also made, if we're being honest—"

Hollingshead took his hand from his pocket. He shoved a finger in Chapel's chest. "We're done here, Captain. Very much done."

Then he did something very strange. He opened his hand and a scrap of paper fell from it, a piece of paper no larger than an inch on any side.

Chapel moved quickly to cover the scrap of paper with his shoe. An old spy reflex.

Without another word Hollingshead climbed into the Humvee. Chapel watched it go. Then he made a show of bending over to tie his shoe, which gave him a chance to move the piece of paper into his pocket.

Beyond that he was too shocked and confused to know what to do.

Left to his own devices, stranded at NSA headquarters, eventually he ordered a cab. He had no idea where to go, so he just told the driver to take him to the nearest train station.

Only when they were under way and clear of Fort Meade altogether did Chapel feel safe to look at the scrap of paper. Holding it cupped in his hand, he read it over and over again.

There wasn't much on it. A set of map coordinates—latitude and longitude for someplace in New York City, he thought. And underneath that a short message:

FIND HER FIRST

NEW YORK CITY: MARCH 21, 15:45

Chapel jumped off the train at Penn Station in Manhattan and ran all the way to the subway. Angel had taught him long ago that it was the fastest way to move around New York, if you didn't have access to a helicopter. He got lucky and found a train just pulling into the station. He dashed through the opening doors and found the commuters inside staring at him as if he were insane. This being New York, they quickly averted their collective gaze.

He wasn't surprised he looked crazy. He was feeling pretty crazy.

Those things he'd said to Hollingshead—they really were inexcusable. Especially since, apparently, the director still had *some* confidence in him. Enough to give him new orders.

Find her first—find Angel before Wilkes could get to her. And then . . . what? Chapel could guess that Hollingshead didn't want Chapel to bring Angel in. They had both known what would happen to her, with the NSA providing evidence of her guilt. She'd be lucky if she didn't end up waterboarded, worked over by the CIA until she gave them what they wanted to hear.

And she would. Eventually, she would name names. Because that was how torture—even "enhanced interrogation"—worked. You told your persecutors anything to get them to stop. You made things up, if you had to. Would she claim to be working for the Chinese? Or domestic terrorists? It depended on how they phrased the questions. At least she wouldn't suffer for long. Angel was not a field agent and had never had any training on how to resist interrogation. It wouldn't take long for her to break down.

Chapel had no doubt of her innocence. The NSA could claim she was responsible for the hijacking, but that just meant somebody had hacked into the DIA databases and stolen her identity.

Right?

That was supposed to be impossible—she'd said so herself, but—

As the train shot through the tunnels under Manhattan, Chapel forced himself to think like an intelligence operative. To actually look at this thing with logic and deductive reasoning. What if Angel was guilty? Just as a hypothetical?

It would explain, perhaps, why she'd gone dark. Why, in the middle of a conversation, she'd cut her own phone connection. Maybe she'd gotten some word that she was about to be arrested and so she'd disappeared. Maybe Chapel would arrive at the coordinates Hollingshead gave him and find that she'd run off with a briefcase full of foreign money. The fact that she'd been unreachable ever since didn't look good.

Then again—the timing was off. Chapel had spoken to her a half hour after the Predator attack in New Orleans. She hadn't sounded like somebody in a hurry or like someone who had just committed treason. She'd sounded like her old self. Unless they had some serious dramatic training, it was next to impossible for somebody in that situation to sound cool and collected. It was why they trained airport security guards to look for people who seemed agitated and sweaty. No matter how committed you were as a terrorist, you couldn't hide your own body's reaction to what was going on.

Angel had sounded breezy and unconcerned. And then she had just disappeared.

The other big clue to her innocence was that Hollingshead clearly believed in her. He'd risked a great deal sending Chapel after her, moments after he'd given Wilkes the order to bring her in. If Chapel's new orders ever got out, Hollingshead would earn himself a cell right next to Angel's in Guantánamo Bay.

So there were two things pointing to her innocence. Not that either of them would hold up in court.

Rationally—purely hypothetically—Chapel considered the possibility that Angel had carried out the attack . . . under Hollingshead's orders. That the two of them were in collusion, paid by a foreign power to destroy the economy of the United States. Both of them traitors. And now, if Chapel helped Angel escape, he would be signing on with their cause, a patsy in their grand plan.

Complete bullshit, of course. Chapel had known Angel and Hollingshead for years. He trusted them a lot more than he trusted anyone else in the government. He would believe that half the U.S. Senate were foreign spies before he would accept that Hollingshead had betrayed his country.

He heard a chime over his head and looked up, half expecting to see a time bomb wired to the roof of the subway car. It was that kind of day. Instead it was just a prerecorded announcement. "The next stop on this train will be Queens Plaza," the voice said.

Chapel nodded to himself. A ways to go yet—the coordinates were for a place way out on the edge of Queens, not far from JFK airport. He still had time to think.

But he was already sure of one thing. He was going to find Angel. Angel, the most important woman in his life, the woman he'd never actually met before. He was going to meet her face-to-face for the very first time.

And he was going to save her. No matter what that meant.

QUEENS, NY: MARCH 21, 16:22

Apparently it meant breaking the law.

Chapel's smartphone showed that Angel's coordinates were located inside a railroad yard, a big triangle of Queens real estate surrounded by fences covered in barbed wire. Through the chain-link fence Chapel could see boxcars quietly rusting on sidings, endless stretches of railroad track curling through a wasteland of gravel where weeds sprung up uncut between wooden ties that had cracked and broken from years in the sun. A desolate, quiet place, normally, the stillness punctuated only by the occasional distant whistle or the sudden metallic thud of switches moving in their grooves.

Normally—but now it was lit with splashes of red and blue light, and the quiet was broken by the sound of police radios squawking back and forth.

It seemed Wilkes had done the smart thing. Normal protocol for a mission like this would be to maintain discretion. You didn't want to give your target any reason to suspect you were coming, so you went in alone by the most devious route you could find.

Instead, Wilkes had called the cops before he arrived. He'd mobilized dozens of police cruisers to surround the area so that if Angel tried to run, she would find herself surrounded. It wasn't how Chapel would have done it, but it made sense. Angel was no field agent. He sincerely doubted she was even armed. Why wouldn't Wilkes make this easy on himself? Why not make it impossible for anyone else to help her? The marine was no fool, it seemed.

Chapel found a position where he could observe the terrain without being spotted, but it wasn't easy. The cops had set up patrols that kept moving around the fence, checking for any sign of movement. Chapel had been forced to take up a position in an old empty water tank right on the edge of the rail yard. The metal wall of the tank had rusted through on one side, giving Chapel a chance to look out and see what was going on.

He checked the map on his phone again. The exact location seemed to be a trailer about a hundred yards away. It was the newest thing in this decayed section of the yard, but it hardly stood out. The paint on its aluminum sides was peeling and its wheels had been removed, the body of the trailer propped up on cinder blocks. It didn't look like much, unless you noticed the thick bundle of cables that snaked through one of its windows. Those cables ran through a thicket of bushes and disappeared into the chaos of the yard. There were far too many of them to just provide power or even a standard Internet connection to the trailer.

It was exactly the kind of setup that Angel would need. A place that was out of the way and unlikely to be disturbed. Plenty of power and data access. And it was mobile if it needed to be—a helicopter could come in and pick up that trailer and move it to a whole different state on very short notice. When Chapel had first seen the coordinates, he'd been surprised. He used to live in Brooklyn, not an hour away, and he'd thought how crazy it had been that he'd been so close to Angel the whole time and had no idea where she physically was. But looking at the trailer, he realized she might have been moving around constantly.

Below him a policeman slowly passed by, scanning the ground for any sign of trouble. The cop wore full body armor and had a submachine gun slung at his hip. He didn't even glance in the direction of the trailer. Chapel was pretty sure Wilkes hadn't arrived yet, and that the police had been instructed to secure the area but not to take any further action. They might not even know that it was the trailer they were guarding.

Hollingshead might have stalled Wilkes, holding out on providing the coordinates for as long as he could. Or maybe Wilkes had just driven from Fort Meade up to New York and gotten stuck in traffic.

Either way, Chapel had a little breathing room. But not much. He needed to move now. Too bad that cop was down there. There was no way for Chapel to get out of the water tower and over to the trailer without being seen. There just wasn't enough cover.

Chapel had no desire to add assaulting a police officer to his rap sheet, but it looked like there was no choice.

He waited until the cop was almost directly below him. Then he gently pushed against the rusted wall of the water tank. It peeled away like wet cardboard, but not without squealing loud enough to get the cop's attention.

Six feet below, the cop looked up, right at where Chapel hid. Chapel just had time to register the look of surprise on the cop's face.

If it had been a soldier down there, with a soldier's training, he would have backed the hell up and reached for his weapon. He would have had plenty of time to get half a dozen shots into Chapel's center of mass.

But it was a policeman with police training, and so his first thought was to reach for his radio and call in.

He never got the chance. Chapel leaped down on top of him, knocking the radio into the air. The cop just had time to get one arm up over his face before the two of them went crashing into the gravel. Belatedly the cop reached for his weapon, but Chapel was ready for that and brought his artificial fist down hard on the cop's wrist, pinning it to the ground.

NYPD training wasn't completely useless. The cop tried to roll over on top of Chapel, switching their positions. But Chapel was ready for that and dug his knee into the gravel and locked himself in place. The cop tried to punch at Chapel's head with his free hand, his gloved fist headed not for Chapel's nose or ears but for his throat in a blow that might have incapacitated or even killed an opponent—if it landed.

Instead Chapel grabbed the cop's striking hand with his own good hand. They struggled for a second, purely a contest of strength. Chapel had been trained for this and he knew three ways to end this fight. The cop's body armor ruled out two of them.

So he settled for the oldest, dirtiest trick in the book. He brought his knee up hard into the cop's groin. Not exactly a fair tactic, but it worked.

The cop's breath exploded out of him into Chapel's face. His arms went slack for a second and Chapel let go of the cop's hands, then reached up under the armored collar of his vest and found the carotid arteries.

He had no desire to kill this man. Instead he just put pressure on those arteries, cutting the flow of oxygen to the cop's brain. That was a good way to give somebody permanent brain damage if you didn't know what you were doing. Chapel, however, was trained by the Army Rangers in how to make sure that didn't happen. He applied the pressure just long enough to make the cop lose consciousness.

As the cop's head rolled to the side and his eyes fluttered up into their sockets, Chapel let go and slid off the inert body. Only then did he bother to look around to see if anyone was watching.

The coast looked clear. Chapel took the cop's gun and his cell phone. Digging through the pouches on the cop's belt, he found a pair of handcuffs. He dragged the cop the few feet over to the scaffolding that held the water tank. One cuff went easily around a support girder, and the other locked in place around the cop's wrist. Chapel grabbed the handcuff key from the same pouch and threw it away into the gravel.

Then he went and found the cop's radio. It was still on, though no one was currently broadcasting. He switched the radio off and then stomped on it until it broke.

Eventually someone was going to call the cop to get his location and status. When the cop didn't answer, other cops would come looking for him. Chapel had no idea how long that would take, but there was nothing he could do about it.

He was just going to have to get Angel out first.

QUEENS, NY: MARCH 21, 16:25

He walked across the gravel toward the trailer with a lump in his throat. Angel was probably his best friend in the world, if he thought about it. She had saved his life so many times, of course, but she'd also been his confidante, the person he talked to when he couldn't talk to anybody else. The person who'd helped him through some very dark times, the person who'd given him great advice when he really needed it. Even if he hadn't always taken it.

She had always believed in him. When he needed it the most, when he'd been so full of self-doubt he didn't think he could go on, she had helped him find the strength.

And she had the sexiest voice he'd ever heard.

He stopped before the door of the trailer and tried to peer in through the window. It looked like it had been covered over with black paper, but maybe she had some way of seeing out, anyway. Maybe a hidden camera. He lifted one hand in greeting. "Angel," he said, "it's me. I need to come in. I swear I'm not here to hurt you or anything. Our—our mutual friend sent me to make sure you come out of this okay."

He wasn't worried that she would attack him when he opened the door. He just didn't want to scare her. She must know by now that she was in trouble. She was tuned in to news feeds and government communication channels like nobody else. Knowing that he was coming to help might alleviate her fear a little.

Even if Chapel had no idea what their next move would be. That didn't matter. Together they would figure something out. They'd always been an incredible team.

A short flight of metal steps led up to the door. He climbed them easily, then thumbed the latch. The door wasn't locked. He swung it open and stepped inside.

There was no light in the trailer except the wan sunlight that streamed in through the door. At first he could see nothing. Eventually he started making out blocky shapes in the gloom, and then he saw little LEDs flashing at the far end of the trailer. Green and yellow lights on a router. A red light on a powered-down monitor.

He found a light switch and turned it on, then closed the door behind him. Now that he could see, he made a quick inventory of the contents of the trailer. There was a narrow camp bed made up with hospital corners. It looked like it hadn't been slept in for some time. There was a little kitchen area with a microwave and a tiny sink. An even smaller shower with a pebbled glass door. The rest of the trailer was filled with high-end computer equipment, big black boxes all chained together with countless loops of Ethernet cable. There were six different monitors, none the same size, and three keyboards. There were server racks mounted on the walls and a projector hanging from the ceiling.

Sitting in the middle of all the computer equipment, propped up on a folding metal chair, was a small server rack with four slots for hard drives. All of them were busy chugging away, their activity lights strobing in the dark. On the front of the server rack's face someone had attached a strip of masking tape, and written on the tape in permanent marker were the words:

"ANGEL" NEURAL NETWORK V. 7.4

QUEENS, NY: MARCH 21, 16:28

Chapel didn't understand. He refused to understand.

He refused to accept what he was looking at. It just couldn't be right.

Sure, he'd had the thought once, years ago. Back when he was first starting to work with Angel and he'd spent far too much time wondering what she looked like, what kind of woman was behind that sexy voice in his ear. He'd jokingly considered the fact that she might actually be a three-hundred-pound man using a voice modulator. Or maybe even that Angel wasn't a person at all, that she was . . .

No. It couldn't be true.

He forgot all about the fact that he was running out of time. That he needed to get out of here before Wilkes arrived. He put the submachine gun down on the floor and walked over to the server rack where it sat on the folding chair. Squatting down, he read the piece of masking tape again, thinking maybe he'd misinterpreted it.

The server rack almost seemed to breathe, or maybe just to crackle with static electricity as he raised a hand to touch it.

When Angel spoke to him, his whole body flinched.

"Is someone there? This is private property. Leave now or I'm calling the police."

It was the voice he knew so well, the one he'd flirted with, the one he'd told all his secrets. It came from a set of speakers mounted on top of one of the dead monitors.

He saw a microphone mounted above the largest of the keyboards. Leaning close to it, he said, "Angel? Is that you?"

"You're in serious trouble, whoever you are. But you can fix it by turning around and leaving right now. This is your last warning," she said.

"Angel—it's me. It's Chapel."

"Chapel?"

One of the monitors flickered to life. It showed a plain gray window full of code he didn't know how to read, making him think of the Predator drone activity logs he'd seen back at NSA headquarters. As soon as his brain made that connection he shook his head—no, it was nothing like that. There was more to Angel than just—

"Chapel, you weren't ever supposed to come here," she said.

"I know, but we were out of options," he said.

"We? Who's we?"

Chapel sighed. "I was sent here by . . . our mutual friend," he said. It was a code phrase the two of them sometimes used when discussing Hollingshead. He didn't want to name the director, not here. He was sure that everything he said in the trailer was being recorded. Somebody might be listening in, even now—maybe the person who hijacked the Predator. The person who was trying to frame Angel. Chapel tried to think it through, think about what he needed to do here. But he was still reeling from the discovery that Angel was—

"Angel, am I looking at you right now?" he asked.

"Chapel, you weren't ever supposed to come here."

He frowned. That was exactly what she'd said before. Not just the same words—the same inflection. The same emphasis.

"What's a neural network?" he asked.

"A neural network is a computational array designed to mimic the process by which living nervous systems process information. Instead of running programs line by line, the network distributes information through a series of weighted—"

"Enough," Chapel said, and she fell silent. He placed his good hand on top of the server stack. Its warmth radiated up through his palm, the way he would have felt warmth if he'd touched a human being. This was just too weird. "Tell me the truth, Angel. Do you exist? I mean, are you a human being? Or are you some kind of artificial intelligence that I've been talking to, some computer program designed to fool me into thinking—" He couldn't finish that sentence.

She was his best friend in the world. Maybe the only friend he had left. And she wasn't even real. Just some virtual woman created to gain his trust, designed—written—by some computer programmer, given that sexy voice because they knew how Chapel would respond to it—

"Chapel?" she said.

"You didn't answer my question," he said very softly.

"Chapel?"

Another screen lit up. It showed more lines of code, scrolling down the screen far faster than any human being could read them. Then a third screen came to life, but this time it showed a video feed.

"Chapel, someone is outside," she told him.

He studied the screen. It showed the gravel yard outside the trailer—he could see the old water tank in the distance and he imagined the camera must be located just outside the trailer's door.

Maybe a dozen police in riot gear were approaching, taking their time about it but doing it right. They all had their guns up, ready to shoot anything that moved. In front of the pack of cops was a man in an army uniform. He didn't seem to be armed. The camera's resolution wasn't good enough for Chapel to make out his facial features, but he didn't need to.

Wilkes had arrived.

QUEENS, NY: MARCH 21, 16:40

"Chapel, you weren't ever supposed to come here," Angel said.

"Yeah, you figured that out, huh? Well, it's true. I'm not here in any kind of official capacity. You remember this guy?" Chapel said, tapping the screen that showed the video feed. It felt weird, like he was tapping her on the shoulder. "You remember Wilkes?"

"I worked with him once," Angel said.

"Yeah. Well, he's here to arrest you. I don't know what he'll do when he finds out what you are." No time for carefully picking words now, he decided. "I was supposed to find you first. Get you to safety. I don't even know what that means now. I mean, our mutual friend must have known what I would find, right? But what did he expect me to do? Unplug you and carry you out of here?"

"I don't know who you're talking about," Angel said.

Chapel frowned. Was she just maintaining plausible deniability? It was funny. The whole time he'd worked with Angel, she had sounded like a real, living human being. Now he'd seen what she really was, he wondered how he'd never guessed. Talking to her felt exactly like talking to a computer.

"I have to do something here," he said. "Before Wilkes can get to you. I have to get you out of here." But how? The server rack with her name on it looked like it probably weighed a hundred and fifty pounds. He could carry it, but he wouldn't be able to run at the same time.

The question of how he would get it past twelve cops and a DIA agent without being seen wasn't even worth considering. That just wasn't going to happen. But maybe there was something he could do. "I'm looking at a server stack with four hard drives in it," he said. "What's on each of these drives?"

"Drive A contains database files. Drive B contains programs to handle queries, short-term memory storage and basic personality functions. Drive C is long-term memory storage. Drive D contains control functions for the neural network. Do you need a directory of all files contained on these drives?"

Chapel shook his head. "No, no—listen, Drive C contains your memories? Is that right? They aren't stored anywhere else?"

"Drive C is dedicated to long-term storage," she said.

It would have to be enough. He would lose her personality—well, maybe they could rebuild that. Maybe not. But if he let her fall into the wrong hands, they would take her apart until there was nothing left at all. "I'm going to have to turn you off," he told her.

"Chapel, I don't know what you're talking about."

"I'm sorry," he said. Because it really did feel like he was about to perform amateur brain surgery on his best friend. But he had no choice. He reached behind the server stack and yanked out the power cable. All the lights on the front of the stack went out. So did all three monitors. Cooling fans spun down with a sound like the last breath escaping from a pair of dying lungs.

Chapel's hand shook as he reached for the button that would release Drive C. It popped out of the stack on hidden springs and almost jumped into his hand. It was a thin metal case about eight inches on a side, warm to the touch. He slid it inside his uniform tunic. It made his chest look bulky and lopsided but there was nothing he could do about that.

With the screens dead he had no view of what was happening outside the trailer. The windows had all been covered with thick black paper that let no light through at all. He took a risk and scratched at the corner of one window until the paper came up and a beam of light speared into the room. Through the little hole he'd made he could see the gravel yard outside. He could just make out the figures of Wilkes and his escort. They were very, very close.

Then someone's fist banged on the door and he knew he was out of time.

"NYPD! Open up," a cop shouted. "We have a warrant to enter these premises."

Chapel spun around, looking for any other possible exit from the room. He didn't see any. There was a hatch in the ceiling, designed to give the trailer a little ventilation, but it wasn't nearly wide enough for him to crawl through.

He considered hiding under the camp bed or in the shower stall, but that was foolish. The cops wouldn't just forget to search the place.

No, the only way out of the trailer was through that door.

So he reached over and worked the latch, then swung it open, careful to keep out of sight. There were a lot of cops out there with a lot of guns. He didn't want to give them any reason to shoot.

"I'm unarmed!" he shouted.

He heard Wilkes laugh. "You know, when you say that, it's kind of funny. Come on out of there, Chapel. You know why I'm here."

Chapel put his hands up and stepped into the doorway. The cops all had their weapons pointed at his chest.

"Down on the ground!" one of them shouted, but Wilkes shook his head.

"Let it go. This is one of the good guys."

The police didn't move from their firing positions, but at least none of them barked any more orders at him.

Wilkes came up to the stairs that led into the trailer. He gave Chapel a big, shit-eating grin. Chapel knew that look from his days growing up in Florida. It was a southerner's way of saying *I don't even need to fuck with you, because you've managed to get yourself up to your ass in alligators all on your own.* It wasn't a sentiment he could argue with, just then.

"I suppose you're wondering what I'm doing here," Chapel said.

"I can probably guess," Wilkes said. "Anyway, it's none of my business. You can explain to the boss when you see him. I'm sure he'll be fascinated." He peered in through the doorway. "She in there?"

"Yeah," Chapel replied. "Though she's not exactly what you're expecting."

Wilkes nodded. "Just come on out of there so I can get by."

Chapel walked down the stairs and moved to one side of the trailer. As he watched Wilkes step inside, he thought maybe he'd finally get his chance to escape. The cops had no orders to detain him—maybe he could just slip away.

That hope died when the cop who had been shouting orders before came up and stuck the barrel of his gun right in Chapel's face. Chapel could see sergeant's chevrons on his collar. "Don't move," he said.

"You heard the man—I'm on your side," Chapel said, keeping his hands high.

"Is that what you told Peters?" the cop asked. He jerked his head backward, toward the water tower. And the unconscious cop who was handcuffed to its base.

So much for just slipping away quietly.

QUEENS, NY: MARCH 21, 16:44

Wilkes was inside the trailer long enough for Chapel to get nervous, wondering how long it would take someone to notice the bulge in his tunic where he'd stashed Angel's memory drive. Long enough to start thinking about what was really going on here. Hollingshead had asked him to come here, to get Angel before Wilkes could arrest her. But Hollingshead must have known what Angel really was. Why hadn't he given Chapel better instructions? Chapel was just assuming that the memory drive was important. That Hollingshead needed it for some reason and couldn't let it fall into anyone else's hands. But why? Was there something stored on the drive, something crucial to the investigation into the drone hijacking? But why not let Wilkes recover it, then, and share its contents with the rest of the intelligence community?

Hollingshead must have his reasons, and Chapel owed the man enough that he was inclined to just go along blindly. But what if he had made a mistake here? What if he'd grabbed the wrong drive? His orders, inasmuch as they *were* orders, were to recover Angel. But now that Chapel knew she was just an artificial intelligence, what did that even mean?

He was overthinking this. He needed to focus on getting away from here before anybody thought to search him. "What's your name, Sergeant?" he asked.

The cop still had his weapon aimed right at Chapel's chest. Chapel wondered if the hard drive would stop a bullet. "Don't talk," the cop said.

Chapel sighed. "Just trying to be friendly. Listen, do you know who we are? Or did you just get a phone call from Washington saying a federal agent needed to commandeer your unit?" That was probably more likely, in Chapel's experience. "Do you have any idea why you're here?"

"We're providing support for a federal operation. I don't even want to know the details," the sergeant said. "He's going to come out of there and tell me I have to let you go, isn't he? Even though you assaulted one of my men." He looked disgusted.

"I have no idea what he'll do," Chapel said, which was the truth. He and Wilkes had never come to like each other, even after months holed up together on the stakeout. Protocol said Wilkes should save Chapel from the cops just because it was good practice not to let your fellow spies get interrogated. But Hollingshead's directorate had never been very strict on protocol. "Look," Chapel said, "is it really going to hurt so much just to tell me your name?"

The cop frowned. "You want a name? Larry Peters. That's not me, that's the guy you beat up on your way in. I doubt you asked him what his name was before you cuffed him to that water tower. I've worked with Peters for six years. He's had my back more times than I can count. He's a good man."

"I'm sure he is," Chapel tried, but the sergeant wasn't finished.

"He's got a wife. Baked cookies for me once, the first time I got shot. If I have to go home and tell her that her husband is in the hospital, or maybe that he's paralyzed because he got in the way of some fed—"

"He's okay," Chapel said. "I know how to incapacitate someone without injury."

It was the wrong thing to say. Chapel didn't know if there was a right thing. The sergeant was getting angry, working himself up. Never a good thing in a man who was pointing a gun at you. "You'd better hope your friend in there comes back out in a good mood. You'd better hope he gives me a very good reason not to press charges—"

"Sir!" It was one of the other cops. "Sir—you might want to—"

The sergeant whirled around to face his man. "What is it, Fredericks? Can't you see I'm busy with our prisoner?"

"Sorry, sir, but—it's—well—"

"What the hell is that noise?" the sergeant asked.

"That's what I was trying to talk to you about," the cop replied. Then he pointed across the gravel yard at the robot that was noisily trundling toward them.

It was mounted on heavy treads, and it was the size of a very large dog. It had two grasping arms and a rudimentary sort of head—just a pair of cameras on a metal stalk, and what looked like the edging attachment from a vacuum cleaner. It carried a long metal pole in front of it that looked to Chapel like nothing so much as a fishing pole.

And it was coming straight toward them at high speed.

"What is it?" Chapel asked.

One of the cops answered. "That's our bomb disposal robot. We brought it out in case the trailer was booby-trapped. The bomb squad guys must have gotten bored and took it out for a spin." He laughed. "Those assholes are always playing pranks, 'cause they've got nothing better to do."

"Any second now they'll make it do a donut," another cop added, "and then it'll say 'Johnny Five is alive' or just 'Wall-Eeee' or something. Those guys are nuts."

The robot's treads spun out over the loose gravel, sending up a billowing plume of gray dust in its wake. It did not stop or do a donut or say anything.

"What's that pole on its front?" Chapel asked. "The part that sticks out."

"Remote detonation arm," one of the cops said. "Sometimes when you find a bomb, the best thing you can do is just clear the area and set it off where it is."

"All right, that's enough," the sergeant said. "No talking to the prisoner."

Chapel shook his head. "Wait. Just wait a second. Remote detonation—the way you do that—" He'd seen bomb removal robots in Afghanistan. When you found an IED in the road out there, you had to call in the bomb people, and nine times out of ten they would send one of their robots. He remembered that they got rid of the IEDs by blowing them up there, too. And the way you did that was to detonate it by hitting it with a charge of explosives.

He peered across the gravel at the approaching robot, at its remote detonation arm. There was something clamped to the end of the pole, a big wad of something white and shapeless.

Semtex, Chapel thought. Plastic explosive. Maybe a pound of it, or maybe more.

And the robot kept getting closer, headed right for them. No—headed for the trailer—

"Wilkes!" Chapel shouted. "Out of there now! Everybody scatter and get your heads down!"

There was no time to stop the thing—it was moving too fast. Still, some of the cops turned and faced it with their submachine guns, looks of confusion on their faces but they could feel it, feel that something very bad was about to happen. Chapel started to run. The sergeant shouted for him to freeze and lifted his weapon to his eye.

Chapel figured he would just have to take his chances.

He ran.

QUEENS, NY: MARCH 21, 16:48

It didn't take long for the robot to cross the last stretch of gravel and ram into the side of the trailer. Chapel didn't so much as turn his head to look back, so when a second later the shock wave lifted all the gravel under his feet and threw him to the ground, he wasn't quite ready. He fell hard on his hands, scraping silicone skin off his artificial wrist, squinting his eyes shut as the dusty gravel pelted his face. It turned out to be a good thing he'd been knocked down. He heard debris whiz past him fast enough it would have taken his head off, felt hot pieces of metal bounce off his back. The noise of the explosion was loud enough that it deafened him, leaving his ears ringing and his chest burning as the air was ripped from his lungs.

Down on his knees in the gravel he reached for the hard drive hidden in his tunic. It was fine—his body had sheltered it from the blast.

Only then did he look back.

Part of the trailer remained intact, a jagged corner of aluminum sticking up at an angle. Debris was everywhere, some of it smoldering on the gravel—green chipboards and shards of black plastic and twisted, unidentifiable pieces of metal. He didn't see much blood. The cops in their body armor must have listened to him and gotten their heads down—only the sergeant looked injured, a big gash running down one of his cheeks. He was staring at something only he could see.

Chapel saw no sign of Wilkes. Had he made it out of the trailer? It didn't look good.

Poor bastard. Chapel might not have liked him much, but he was a fellow silent warrior. An intelligence operative. Even his family would never know how he died, the sacrifice he'd made to stop the hijacker.

The sergeant turned and looked at Chapel. His eyes still weren't focusing, but he seemed to be getting over the shock of the blast. He looked like he was shouting, but Chapel heard his voice as only a whisper. "Somebody," he said. "Somebody arrest . . . get that . . ." It was like he only had a thin stock of words left to him and he was burning through them fast. "His fault," he managed. "Somehow." Then he waved one arm in Chapel's direction.

The cops who had recovered faster started to get up, started to reach for their weapons. Chapel got shakily to his feet. He felt like every bone in his body had been disconnected from all the others, like if he moved too fast he would just dissolve into a big pile of Jell-O. Little spots kept dancing in front of his eyes.

One of the cops managed to stagger toward him and shout something Chapel couldn't really hear. His ears were still buzzing from the explosion.

But then another of the cops looked up in the air and shouted "Shit!" and started dancing backward. The others looked up and followed suit.

The pebbled glass door of the shower from the trailer—still miraculously intact—was spinning in the air above them like a thrown playing card. As soon as Chapel saw it, it was like the law of gravity had been momentarily suspended but now was going to be enforced with a vengeance. It came down hard on the gravel and shattered in a white cloud of glass fragments that shot out in every direction.

Chapel knew a lucky break when he saw one. The cops were distracted. He dashed for the water tower. His living arm felt weak and near useless, but he'd learned to trust his artificial arm in situations like this. He jumped and hauled himself up onto the tower, then over the fence.

All before the cops even thought to start shooting.

QUEENS, NY: MARCH 21, 17:02

On the streets of Queens nobody noticed one dazed-looking man in a tattered army uniform. They were too busy watching the parade of fire trucks and ambulances and police cars that tore down every street, converging on the train yard. Chapel kept his head down and kept moving, knowing he had a little breathing room—but not much—before the local authorities started looking for him. The cops back at the trailer had gotten a good look at him and his description would go out to every unit in the borough before long. Without Wilkes to vouch for him, they would have no reason not to pick him up. And once they had him he would be stuck in jail for a while. Normally, Angel would have been able to spring him—but right now she was switched off. He couldn't rely on his government credentials, either, since he'd been officially relieved from duty.

No, if he was caught now, he would be on his own. And the cops would have lots and lots of questions, questions he couldn't answer.

He needed to get as far away as he could, as fast as he could, but that presented a problem. He had no idea where exactly he was or how to get back to the subway station. Queens had a weird street grid with avenues, roads, streets, and places all identified by number, and the numbers tended to run into each other so you could easily find yourself on Thirtieth Place, which ran parallel to Thirtieth Street to where it met Thirtieth Avenue. Added to that, all the street addresses were given as a pair of numbers that roughly corresponded to the nearest Avenue (usually), so an address could be 30-29 Thirtieth Avenue on the corner of Thirtieth Street. Even Chapel's smartphone was going to have trouble with that.

First things first, though—he needed to get cleaned up. Eventually someone was going to notice that he looked like he'd just survived a bomb blast, and they would call the cops just to be helpful. Chapel ducked into a coffee shop off one of the avenues, intending to buy a bottle of water so he could use the restroom. He didn't need to bother. All the employees of the place were standing by the plateglass windows, looking out at the street.

"Hey," one of them called out to him as he headed for the back of the shop and the restroom.

Chapel froze. "Yeah?"

"You see anything?" she asked. She was a young woman with freckles wearing a stained apron. She didn't even give Chapel's ruined clothes a glance. "There's nothing on the news, and Twitter just says there was an explosion."

"Oh, yeah?"

"Yeah. We're gonna close up in a minute and go look for it."

This was New York City. A city still haunted by September eleventh, but also a city where people ran toward explosions and attacks and horror so they could get a good video of it on their phones.

"Just need the bathroom," Chapel said, and before the young woman could respond he pushed through the door of the men's room and locked it behind him.

The silence in there was enough to make his ears ring again. But he could breathe.

He studied his face in the mirror, looking for any sign he'd been cut or bruised in the blast. He'd been lucky. As close as he'd been to the explosion he seemed to have escaped any serious injury. The main damage was to the silicone wrist of his artificial arm. It looked like someone had cut into it with a butcher knife. He prodded the wound with his good fingers, seeing how deep the gash went. It wouldn't damage his prosthesis, but it did make him look like an android that had unsuccessfully tried to commit suicide by slashing its wrist.

That made him think of the bomb squad robot, and the hijacked Predator. Robots turned into suicide bombers. There had to be a link there—whoever hijacked the drone must be the same person who blew up Angel's trailer. But why? What were they trying to cover up? They'd already framed her—not that anyone would have listened to her if she *did* have secrets to share. She wasn't even human.

Damn it. He was wasting time. He could do the detective work later. Right now he had to get out of New York.

He took off his tunic, carefully laying Angel's hard drive on the edge of the sink. There he got a nasty surprise. The entire back of the tunic was shredded. Luckily the shirt underneath was intact.

He took off his tie as well. Nothing he could do about his uniform trousers with their distinctive gold stripe. He washed up as best he could, getting the grime off his face and teasing most of the gravel dust out of his hair. Then he turned and looked at the hard drive. He needed a way to conceal it.

He found a plastic bag in the trash. He wrapped the drive in what remained of his tunic and stuffed the resulting bundle inside the bag. He glanced at himself in the mirror. It looked like he was just some guy in an ugly shirt carrying a bag full of old rags. He wouldn't stand out so much now. There were other ways to track him, though.

He took out his smartphone and stared at it for a while.

Anything he did with the device could be traced. The police were probably already getting a warrant to tap his phone. Maybe the hijacker would trace him as well—anyone who could frame Angel like that definitely had the capability. The phone was a liability. But it was so damnably useful.

Nothing for it. He started prying open the back of the case so he could get the SIM card out when it started to ring.

Chapel was still jumpy from surviving the explosion. He nearly dropped the phone in the toilet. He shook his head. *Come on, keep it together,* he thought. He flipped the phone over, knowing that whoever it was, he didn't dare answer it. He was just going to power the phone down and then—

It was Julia.

Julia was calling him. Right now.

"Shit," he said, under his breath. As if she might hear him.

QUEENS, NY: MARCH 21, 17:09

Julia.

There had been a time, once, when he and Julia had spoken on the phone every day. Except when he was on missions, of course.

That had been the problem. He was always going off on missions. Disappearing without any warning. She could never know where he went, or when he was coming back. *If* he was coming back. If he had died on one of his missions, she wouldn't even get to find out how. Chapel had always assumed that Hollingshead would let her know that he had died, but even that couldn't be guaranteed. Chapel's life revolved around secrets. Julia had been forced to pay the price for that.

He'd thought he could fix things. He'd thought he could give up his work, get a desk job.

Marry her.

It hadn't worked out.

He hadn't spoken with her on the phone, or seen her, in nearly a year. He'd moved out of her apartment. Moved out of New York. Tried to find some other reason to live than for her.

Julia. He had never loved a woman as much as he'd loved her. He doubted he ever would again. He knew she didn't feel the same way.

Julia.

The phone was still ringing. He shouldn't answer it. He couldn't.

He used his index finger to swipe the screen, completing the connection. He pressed it to his ear and just waited, still not really believing it would be her voice on the other end.

"Jim?" she said. "Jim, are you there?"

This was a mistake. This had to be a mistake. Whatever she wanted—

"I'm here," he said. Jesus. He could have said hello, or sure, or . . . or anything else. "Julia," he went on. "It's good to hear your voice."

"Jim, are you okay? Listen, I can't really talk."

"I can't, either," he said. He closed his eyes and sat down on the bathroom floor. "Normally, I'd be so happy to hear from you, I mean, I know we left things kind of—"

"Not now."

He opened his eyes. "Um, okay," he said. Better, really, if they didn't start anything right now. Better if they never did. Julia was in his past, a part of his life he was never going to visit again. He would never see her—

"You have to come to my place," she said.

"What?"

"As soon as you can. Please, Jim. This . . . this isn't about us."

Then she hung up. Broke the connection.

Chapel stared at the phone for a long time. The screen stayed dark. She didn't call back. He didn't dare call her back. Even though he needed to explain what a terrible idea it would be for him to visit her just then. How it would just put them both in danger.

Eventually he took a deep breath.

He had to get rid of the phone.

As long as the phone could draw power from its battery, he could be tracked. There was no way to remove the battery from this model of phone without special tools. The phone had to go. He ejected the SIM card—it was the only part he could keep. The phone went in the trash, the SIM card in his pocket.

He stepped out of the bathroom to find the coffee shop deserted. The baristas had left, presumably to go look for the chaos over in the rail yard. They'd locked the door behind them, but it was easy enough to open it from the inside.

He headed down the avenue, pausing only to ask directions to the subway station. The man he asked was distracted enough not to even look Chapel in the face.

Chapel had worried that the trains might not be running. In the case of a terrorist attack, the subway was one of the first things to shut down. But a train did come, a train headed for Manhattan. He could ride it down to the Port Authority. Get a ticket on the next bus out of town, regardless of its destination. It was the only smart thing to do. Whatever Julia wanted, it could wait.

The stations flew by. Fifty-Ninth Street. Seventh Avenue. Forty-Ninth Street. The train pulled into Times Square. His stop.

This train would keep going, he knew, through lower Manhattan and then into Brooklyn. It would go right to Julia's apartment, with or without him.

While he stood there, unable to act, unable to think, the doors slid closed and the train pulled away from the station. It looked like he'd made up his mind.

BROOKLYN, NY: MARCH 21, 17:49

A police car sat halfway down Julia's block. Its lights and its engine were off, and the policeman inside was just sitting there, writing something on a form. Maybe he was just writing up a parking ticket.

Maybe he'd been assigned to watch Julia's place and arrest Chapel if he showed his face. Chapel couldn't take the chance.

Luckily, he knew another way in. He'd lived at Julia's apartment once, and he knew the blocks around it. He'd had to slip away unseen from the apartment building more than once before.

Her building had a basement where the tenants did their laundry and where the building manager kept his office. In the alley behind the building a short flight of stairs led down to an entrance to that basement. That door was supposed to be kept locked at all times, but the building manager was a heavy smoker and he frequently ducked out the back to get his fix. He left the door unlocked during the day because it was just too big a hassle to constantly lock and unlock it.

Chapel slipped inside, into the all-too-familiar smell of fabric softener and mildew. He saw no one as he headed up the fire stairs to the second floor. Before he knew it he was there, standing outside Julia's door.

His living hand was sweaty. He felt unsteady on his feet and it had nothing to do with the shock of the explosion back at the train yard.

This was dumb. This was colossally stupid. Every second he spent in New York City increased his chances of getting picked up by the police—and that would mean failing his mission. They would take the hard drive away from him, the last piece of Angel. They would dissect it and study all its secrets and he would have let Hollingshead down, would have compromised national security, would have thrown away his freedom for . . . what? One last chance to see the woman he loved?

He reached up to knock on the door, but before he had the chance, he heard the chain and the dead bolt being opened from the other side. Julia must have seen him through the peephole. She threw open the door and there she was.

She was beautiful. So beautiful. Her red hair was tied back with a piece of ribbon that failed to keep strands of it from falling down and framing her soft features, the hint of freckles on the tops of her cheekbones, the crow's-feet that were just starting to form at the corners of her eyes. She was wearing a T-shirt and a baggy pair of jeans, but the way she stood, Chapel could see the curve of one hip up against the door.

So many things came rushing back, so many memories, that he had to close his eyes and just stand there for a second. Which meant his other senses drank her in. The smell of her shampoo hit him and—

"Jesus, get inside already," she whispered. He opened his eyes and saw her peering down her hallway, looking to make sure he hadn't been followed.

He stepped inside and she locked the door behind him.

"You look a little shaky," she said.

"Someone just tried to blow me up," he told her. Julia knew all about his work and the risks involved. She didn't look surprised.

"Sit down. I'll get you some water. Or do you want tea?"

He looked around the apartment, taking in the fact she'd changed all the furniture. She'd put up new prints on the walls, big framed photographs of various dog breeds. Julia was a veterinarian and she loved dogs, but she wasn't allowed to have one in the apartment, so she settled for pictures of them everywhere.

She'd gotten a new couch, a cream-colored leather sectional. "This is nice," he said, because he wasn't ready to start talking. He didn't want to know yet why she'd called him and told him to come over.

"It's even nicer when you sit on it."

He sat down, putting the bag containing the hard drive on the floor by his feet. He looked up. And then, for the first time since he'd arrived, their eyes met.

She started to turn away, but then she stopped and looked straight at him. Neither of them spoke. Eventually the beginnings of a sad little smile curled up one corner of his mouth. There was so much history between them.

"Shit," she said.

"Yeah," he replied, because he knew what she meant. "Listen. When I left here, when—"

"When I dumped you, you mean. Right before you were going to propose."

He laughed. He'd forgotten how direct she could be. "I know we said some things, things that—"

"Jim, we can't do this. Not now."

He frowned. "We can't talk about what happened?"

"No."

"Okay," he said.

"You got here fast," she said.

"I came straightaway. How did you know I was in New York?"

She shook her head. "I didn't. I assumed you were down in D.C. or someplace. What were you doing here? Wait, sorry. Dumb question. You were getting blown up. Which means you were working, and I can't ask you about it." She lifted her hands in a gesture of resignation. "I'll get you that water now."

As she headed into the kitchen he called after her, "If you didn't want to talk about us, why did you call me?"

She didn't answer. But in the silence, Chapel heard a soft noise come from the bedroom, a muffled little click. It sounded like someone had just closed the lid of a laptop in there.

He jumped to his feet, already reaching for his gun. Except it wasn't there. He was unarmed and suddenly very alone. He headed toward the bedroom door, but before he could reach it, Julia came running out of the kitchen.

"There's somebody else here," he said.

She nodded. She looked scared. Had the police forced her to call him? Had they used her as bait so they could arrest him here?

He couldn't believe she would go along with something like that. Not

Julia. But there was someone else in the apartment and she hadn't told him when he came in. She'd been hiding this third person from him.

He walked over to the bedroom door. Then he glanced back at her. "Is there something you want to tell me?" he asked.

"Jim," she said, "before you go in there—you have to tell *me* something. I know you aren't supposed to. But you have to. You have to tell me why you came to New York."

"That's got nothing to do with you," he said, staring at the door. If there were cops in there, if this was a trap, they might come rushing out at any moment if they thought he'd seen through the ruse.

His best bet was to just run. Get out of the apartment as fast as he could, get away before the cops could close in and take him.

"You have to tell me, Jim," she said again. She pushed herself between him and the bedroom door.

He reached for her slim shoulders, intending to move her out of the way. She planted her feet. *This was about to get bad,* he thought.

But then the bedroom door cracked open behind her. Whoever was back there spoke.

"It's okay, Julia. He's not the one they sent to get me."

It was the sexiest voice Chapel had ever heard. And one of the most familiar.

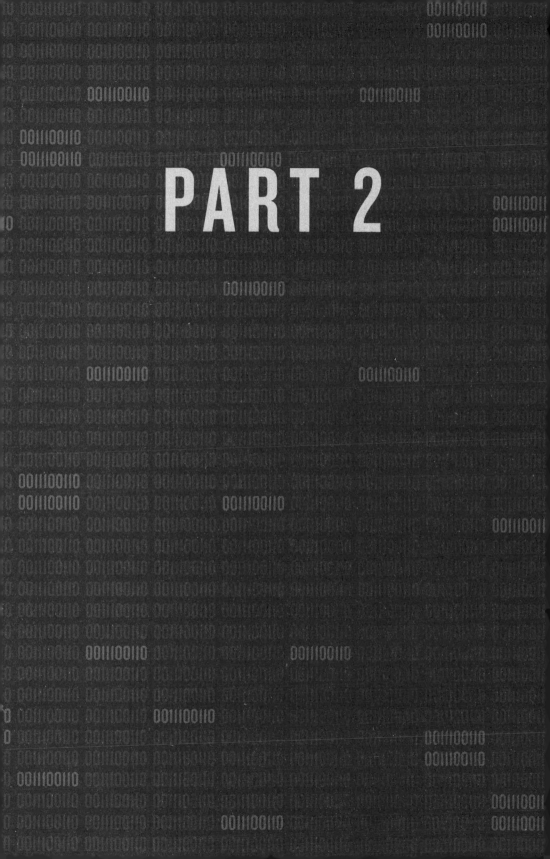

PART 2

Brent Wilkes opened his eyes.

Above him he saw nothing but gray overcast sky. He wasn't entirely sure where he was at first. There'd been a lot of light and heat and then he'd blacked out. There might have been a loud noise in there, too.

Iraq? That sounded like Iraq. At least the way he remembered it.

There must have been an explosion. That explained a lot of what he was feeling, and a lot of what he remembered.

It brought to mind one mission in particular, a mission in Fallujah. It was after the siege when more than half the city was just flattened. The DoD had sent a bunch of relief money to help the refugees there, a big briefcase full of hundred-dollar bills. The guy who received the briefcase, the local emergency management head, had taken the money across town and just handed it over to an al-Qaeda contact.

The money wasn't recoverable, but they needed to save face. So they'd sent Wilkes in to kill the al-Qaeda guy. He didn't like the mission, didn't like the idea of just killing a guy, even if he was an insurgent. But he didn't like a lot of his missions. He completed them anyway.

That might as well have been the unofficial Marine Corps motto, right there.

For three days he just followed the guy around. Wilkes was dressed up like a Blackwater civilian contractor—nobody would have bought it if he dressed like an Iraqi. The guy he was tailing made him less than an hour after he hit the ground, but it didn't matter. Nobody wanted to start real fighting again, not with so little of the city left, so Wilkes and his target just danced around each other, each of them looking for a time and a place where they could bump off each other where nobody would see it happen.

On the third day, Wilkes took his dinner in a little restaurant built into the ruin of a hospital. They'd set up awnings and tables and pushed all the broken bricks and rebar into a pile to one side. The food was good, even though he had no idea what he was eating. His target pulled up outside in a limousine with three thugs with AK-47s, and it looked like time was up.

Then the target guy just stepped on something in the street that looked like a broken plate, just one more piece of debris. It was an IED, of course, which some local kid had put there to get Wilkes when he finished his dinner. The target got it instead.

Mission accomplished, and Wilkes didn't have to lift a finger.

There had been light and heat and a shock wave that hit him so fast he didn't hear it until he was already on his back in the rubble, staring up at a blue sky.

Just like now, except this sky was gray. Not a lot of gray days in Iraq, the way he remembered it. Gray days meant stateside. He was in America, he decided.

Right. New York. It all came flooding back. Angel. Chapel.

After an explosion, if you woke up on your back like this, you were supposed to just lie still. You might have a concussion or, worse, your neck could be broken and it would be hard to tell. Lie still and wait for help to arrive.

Wilkes heard a lot of shouting, somebody yelling for somebody else to freeze. "Okay," he said. "No problem."

There were people running around, yelling things back and forth. Something hit the ground hard and a piece of broken glass bounced off

Wilkes's cheek. Maybe there was going to be another explosion. Maybe there was another bomb.

Eventually a paramedic came over and looked at Wilkes's eyes and asked him what day it was, who the president was. He complied and answered all their questions. That information wasn't classified. Somebody else took his blood pressure.

"He's okay," they said. "One lucky son of a bitch."

Which was pretty much how Wilkes had felt that day back in Fallujah.

"Just stay here. There's an ambulance coming," somebody else said.

"How do I look?" Wilkes asked. "Anything broken?"

The paramedic actually laughed. "No. And you've got the right number of arms and legs, still. But you're covered from head to toe in cuts and bruises. We're also worried you might have a concussion."

"I've had worse," Wilkes said. He sat up. The paramedic tried to push him back down, but Wilkes just shrugged the guy off. "I've got work to do." He remembered when the robot came rushing at the trailer. He'd known something was up so he smashed his way through the blacked-out windows and out the back of the trailer. Looked like that had been the right move.

"You really need to be in a hospital right now. You could have internal injuries—hell, for all I know you're bleeding out right now, I just can't see it."

He just waved one hand in the guy's direction and headed back to the blast site. Not much left. All the computers and stuff were destroyed and just one corner of the trailer remained, sticking up in the air like a jagged spearhead. Angel was gone. Vaporized.

Well, most of her. In the short time he'd had inside, before the robot came, he'd noticed that one of the hard drives was missing from her server stack. Somebody had taken it.

Chapel. It must have been Chapel.

Which meant his mission wasn't complete at all. And worse—he couldn't trust the man who'd given it to him. The only way Chapel could have known to come here, the only way he could have beaten Wilkes to the punch, was if Hollingshead had fed him information he wasn't supposed to have.

Well, that was kind of fucked up.

Wilkes walked away from the paramedics, who seemed to have other people to worry about. There were a bunch of things he needed to do. First and hardest was that he needed to call the Department of Defense and tell them Rupert Hollingshead was in league with the drone hijacker. That wasn't going to go down well, but it had to be done. Then Wilkes needed to find the highest-ranking cop who hadn't been blown up in the blast. He needed to start organizing a manhunt.

If he wanted to salvage anything from this mission, he was going to have to get that hard drive. Anything else was failure. Marines like Wilkes found the very idea of failure unacceptable.

He would get the drive, and if Chapel refused to hand it over, well . . .

Wilkes didn't like what he would have to do then. He'd spent months in a motel room with Chapel, and while he thought the guy could be a little self-righteous, he was basically okay. Still. Wilkes didn't like most of his missions. He completed them anyway.

Just like in Fallujah.

BROOKLYN, NY: MARCH 21, 17:58

Chapel reached for the doorknob. He pushed the door open and stepped into the bedroom. And there she was.

"Hi," she said.

He nodded.

She looked like she was in her early twenties. Just a little over five feet tall. Very cute, in a way nobody would ever call beautiful. She had a little turned-up nose and big eyes and very short hair that fell in bangs across her forehead. She was wearing a pair of jeans and a T-shirt that was too big for her. It had a picture of a Weimaraner on the front.

Her eyes were a bright blue he never would have expected.

"You, um," he said, because what he was about to say was *you're real*, which sounded pretty stupid even in his head. *You're human* was just about as bad.

"Are you going to arrest me?" she asked.

Chapel bit his lip. "No," he said. "No, Angel. No. I'm here to rescue you."

And then he reached for her and she ran to him and they just hugged each other.

She was real. She was human. She cried a little. Chapel never wanted to let her go.

BROOKLYN, NY: MARCH 21, 18:04

"I can't believe you managed to save this," Angel said, turning the hard drive over and over in her hands. "This could be really useful."

Chapel didn't want to talk about the hard drive.

They sat next to each other on the bed, their hands folded in their laps. So strange. He'd spent years with her whispering in his ear, her voice so real to him he could almost feel her breath on his neck. Now that she was right next to him in the flesh he felt like he'd never met her before, that they were just getting acquainted.

But then she would speak and it was all still there. The relationship they'd built up, as colleagues. As friends.

She kept looking at him out of the corner of her eye as if she couldn't believe *he* was real, as if she'd never expected this either. Imagine that.

"I thought—" He shook his head. "What was that whole trick with the neural network all about?"

She smiled. "That was me trying to be clever. A while back, when I was working with Wilkes, he kept saying he didn't believe I was a woman. That I was some fat guy in a stained sweatshirt who just wanted to fool him. Then he suggested maybe I was just an AI, not human at all. I thought the idea was interesting, so I downloaded the closest thing that actually exists—an Eliza variant. A program designed to fool someone into thinking they're talking to a human being."

"So when somebody came to find you in the trailer, and the computer started talking to them—"

"They would think that it was true, I was just an AI all along. Any half-competent computer tech would see right through it, but I figured it might give me a little extra time to get away."

Chapel nodded. It was a good plan. Exactly the kind of thing the Angel he knew—the real Angel—might come up with. "You knew we were coming for you?" he asked.

"I figured out something was wrong pretty quickly," she said. "All of my outgoing ports went dead—I was talking to you at the time, and suddenly you were just gone. I checked all my hardware and everything was working fine. I was certain I was being attacked. So I got out of there because I knew if they could do that to me, if they had the tech to shut me down, they could figure out where I was, too." She shrugged. "Maybe, after working with you for so long, I just got paranoid. I was terrified they were going to come and kill me."

"It isn't paranoia if they're really after you," Chapel pointed out.

She laughed. Angel laughed. It was a sound that always made the hair stand up on his arms, and it did so then, too. "I hadn't left that trailer in a long time. Being outside was . . . difficult. I had no idea what to do, where to go. I came here because I knew this address—you used to live here. And I thought Julia might help me."

"It was a good call," he told her.

"Thanks. But once I was here, once I was sure nobody was going to come bust down the door, I had no idea what to do next. Julia let me use her laptop and I was able to dig in enough to see that there was a secret warrant out for my arrest, signed by the director. I didn't know who I could trust. I told Julia to call you—she really didn't want to, but she could see we needed you. The problem was, for all I knew you were the one who was coming to grab me."

"It was Wilkes—he was the one the director sent. But then he asked me to get you first. To make sure you stayed free." He told her about the scrap of notebook paper Hollingshead had dropped in front of him. "He knows you're being framed, but with the rest of the intelligence community against you, he also knew he had to play their game if he wanted to stay in the loop."

"So he's officially called for my arrest?"

"Officially," he said.

She sat there lost in thought for a while. He didn't push. Even though they were running out of time.

Finally she looked over at him and asked, "Chapel, what do we do now?"

He wished he had a real plan to give her. But all he could say was, "We keep moving."

BROOKLYN, NY: MARCH 21, 18:17

Chapel led Angel out of the bedroom and into the living room, where Julia was perched in front of the television. "I'm trying to get some news about what's going on," she said, "because I know neither of you can tell me."

"It's just better that you don't know," Chapel tried, but he knew Julia and he knew she wouldn't just accept that.

"It's bad, right?" Julia asked. She looked frightened. Chapel hated seeing her that way. "It must be, if Angel had to come out in the open. And it must be bad for you, too," she said to him. "You're not supposed to be here, are you?"

He'd forgotten how quick she could be. "It's bad, yeah. But we're going to fix it. Listen. I really want to thank you. You took Angel in when you didn't have to."

Julia stared at him. "Are you kidding? She saved my life once. You remember? When that guy from the CIA was trying to kill me, the one who couldn't stop laughing? She got me out of that in one piece. I owed her." She turned back to the TV. "Besides. Do you know what she was wearing when she showed up here? A jogging bra and yoga pants. If I turned her away, she would have frozen to death."

Chapel turned to look at Angel.

"The last time I left my trailer," she said, "it was warm out. I didn't have time to check the temperature today."

"The last time? When was that?" Julia asked. "Six months ago?"

"Maybe," Angel admitted.

Chapel and Julia both stared at her then. But there was no time to ask any more questions. "We have to go," he said. "I'm sorry. I really wish we had more time. Julia, I really wish we had a chance to talk. But the police will already be looking for us."

Julia nodded. "Okay. What can I do to help?"

A wave of relief surged through Chapel. He'd known he could trust Julia, but things were tense between them and he wasn't sure how she would feel about what he was going to ask for next.

"I need your car," he said. Her eyebrows shot up and he was certain she would say no, so he tried to explain. "The bus and train stations are too risky—too many surveillance cameras. And there's no way we're flying out of here. I could steal a car, but if the owner reports it and—"

But Julia put a hand on his arm. "Go on, take it! You paid for half of it, anyway," she said, smiling.

Chapel had forgotten that they'd bought it together. He'd driven it so rarely back when he lived in New York, and the title was in her name—he tried to minimize his paper trail—so he'd always thought of it as her car.

"You'd do anything for her, wouldn't you?" he asked, glancing over at Angel, who was glued to the TV.

The hand on his arm moved up to his shoulder. "Not just her," Julia said. "I need to tell you something. About how we . . . how things ended between us."

She didn't get the chance, though.

"Guys," Angel said, looking over her shoulder at them, "you should see this."

BROOKLYN, NY: MARCH 21, 18:23

On the television screen red and blue lights flashed and cops moved back and forth behind yellow caution tape. The shot changed to show crowds of people standing outside the rail yard fence. It changed again to show police helicopters darting over Queens like a cloud of gnats.

"Police have cordoned off a neighborhood in Queens tonight as they continue the search for the person or persons involved," a reporter announced. "Though information is scarce at the moment, we do know the explosion in a railroad facility earlier today is believed to have been caused by a bomb or other explosive device. The blast was loud enough to be heard in Long Island City, over a mile away. Six police officers were injured in the explosion, and two of them are in the hospital in critical condition."

"Jesus." Julia looked at the two of them as if she'd never seen them before. "Did you—"

"Somebody tried to kill Angel. They didn't know she was already gone," Chapel said. "I think. Maybe they just wanted to destroy her computers."

"My trailer!" Angel said, because the scene on the TV had changed to a helicopter view of the scene.

"The police were investigating an anonymous tip when they approached this mobile home," the reporter said. "The explosion looks to have been timed to injure as many of them as possible. New York One spoke with Lieutenant Charles Good of the city's Hercules team, the police branch responsible for counterterrorism operations."

Lieutenant Good was an enormous man with a bristly mustache and very tired eyes. He was dressed in full riot gear but had his helmet off for the cameras. "We are currently looking to interview a person of interest who was seen fleeing from the crime scene immediately after the explosion," he said. Half a dozen microphones shoved closer to his face. "We don't have a name yet but we believe we have a picture of him, which we'll be making available to all news outlets. I want to make a promise to New York City. We're going to find this guy. And we're going to make him pay."

The view on the TV changed to a static shot of a color photograph of Chapel's face.

"Shit," he said.

BROOKLYN, NY: MARCH 21, 18:29

Julia ran around the kitchen, grabbing things. Bottles of water. A box of protein bars and some soy crisps. "I've got some cash, not much—I mean, can you wait here until I run to the ATM? I can get a couple of hundred dollars and . . . I know, you can take my jewelry, pawn it somewhere—"

"What about clothes?" Chapel asked.

"I think you left a couple of shirts here when you moved out, but I don't know what I did with them. Maybe I gave them to Goodwill. Oh, God, why did I give them away? I guess I just didn't want anything that would remind me of . . . never mind. Maybe I missed something."

"I meant for Angel," Chapel pointed out.

"Sure, sure, she can take whatever she thinks will fit her."

Angel nodded and headed into the bedroom to pack a bag.

"There are some toiletries, you can take whatever I've got, I mean, you'll smell like Lady Speed Stick but it's better than—do you think you'll be in the car for a long time? Or are you going to go someplace that has showers? Never mind—don't tell me anything." She put her hand to her neck as if she were taking her own pulse. "Medical supplies," she said. "Knowing you, you're going to need gauze and antibiotic cream and maybe a suture kit." She shook her head. "All of that stuff is at my clinic, though. Do we have time for me to run to the ATM and my clinic?"

"No," Chapel said.

"I found a shirt!" Angel called from the bedroom. The door opened and a balled-up blue men's dress shirt came flying into the living room. Chapel caught it with one hand and started unfurling it.

"Oh," Julia said, "you found—that one."

"It was in her nightstand!" Angel called.

"I guess I did keep one, after all," Julia said, and she blushed until her face was nearly as red as her hair. "Well, good, that'll give you something to wear. That's—that's good."

The shirt hadn't been laundered. It was a mass of rumples. But it was less distinctive than the uniform shirt Chapel was wearing at the moment. He laid it over the back of the couch to let it air out for a minute.

"What about, I don't know, my passport? Can you use that, maybe put a picture of Angel in it and—"

"Why did you keep this shirt?" Chapel asked.

Julia stared at it. Then she stroked one of the sleeves. "I always liked it. And . . . it still smelled like you," she said.

Chapel frowned. "When you broke things off, I thought you never wanted to see me again," he said. "I don't understand."

"You're not the only one with secrets," she said.

He reached over and put a hand on the back of her neck. Felt her hair run between his fingers. She shivered under his touch. He put his other arm around her, intending to draw her into a hug, but she moved her head and their lips met, her warm, soft lips, and he kissed her, and for a second that was all he needed to do. The only thing.

Thoughts crept back into his head, one at a time. The first was that he was never going to see her again. The second was that this was wrong, that it was over between them, that they didn't kiss like this anymore.

Julia didn't seem to have gotten that memo.

The kiss might have gone on a lot longer if Angel hadn't come out of the bedroom just then, pulling a wheeled suitcase. "Guys," she said quietly.

Chapel let Julia go. She moved back into the kitchen and started rifling through the cupboards again.

Time to get back to business. "Is that everything you want to bring?" he asked.

Angel nodded. "Just clothes and a toothbrush and a couple of things. I don't need much."

"Good. There's going to be a roadblock. They'll inspect the car and if they see a bunch of luggage, they'll probably insist on a full search. But I think we'll be okay. We can put that bag in the backseat; if we shove it down into the leg well, most likely they won't even see it, and if they do, well, it's just an overnight bag. It won't be enough to arouse suspicion. This might work."

"Won't they recognize you from the picture?" Angel asked.

"Definitely. Which is why I'll be riding in the trunk. They don't know what you look like, which is the one thing we have going for us. When they pull you over, you have to act natural, Angel. You need to convince them you're . . ." He tried to think of a good cover story. Simple, easy to remember, but something that would explain the suitcase. He was probably being overcautious but you tried to plan for everything that could go wrong. "Just a college student heading home to see your parents. Smile a lot, and act dumb. If it's a male cop who pulls you over, don't be afraid to flirt a little."

"Uh-huh," Angel said. "That I know how to do." But something was wrong. He could see it in her face. "So your big plan is that I'm going to drive while you ride in the trunk."

"Yeah. What is it? The car's easy to drive, it's a compact." Her face didn't clear, so he added, "It's automatic, if you don't know how to drive stick."

"It would help if I even knew what that meant," Angel said.

Chapel sat down on the arm of the couch. "You don't know how to drive at all, do you?"

"Never got my license," she admitted.

"Oh, boy," he said.

BROOKLYN, NY: MARCH 21, 22:17

Cars clogged the Holland Tunnel, creeping along through the stench of exhaust as they inched their way under the river and into New Jersey.

Tempers flared and the sound of honking horns reverberated until the claustrophobic space became a resonating chamber, a crescendo of shrill noise that never stopped.

At the far end motorists breathed deep for the first time in hours as they crawled back up to the surface. As they emerged from the brightly lit tunnel into the dark of night, the lights of greasy spoon diners and countless gas stations dazzled their eyes. Only after they'd adjusted to the changing light could they see what lay ahead of them.

Between the tunnel and the turnpike, New Jersey had turned into an armed camp. Police vehicles were everywhere, blocking access and feeder streets, while hulking black riot tanks formed a bottleneck on the main road. Men with machine guns cradled in their arms waved down every car, while hastily erected signs warned motorists that their usual rights had been suspended. Every car was subject to search, every driver to processing.

Anyone even vaguely suspicious, anyone matching the subject's description to the slightest degree, got hauled over to a big tent on one side of the road for further questioning, their cars towed out of the way and sequestered in an already-packed lot half a mile away just in case they were full of bombs.

The drivers had no chance to protest—and no possible way to back up or turn away from the roadblock. Men in the heavy black armor of Hercules units watched with stern faces as one by one the cars were squeezed through the cordon.

It was a cold night and the breath of the cops steamed in the air and got caught in all the whirling, flashing light. Dogs paced up and down the line of cars, sniffing at wheels, jumping in their harnesses. Cops used mirrors on the ends of long poles to look under every car, as if terrorists might be down there, clutching the undercarriage, trying to stay out of view.

One cop jogged over and tapped on the window of Julia's car. "Just gotta take a look," he said. "Roll down your windows, please. Driver's license for the operator, and everybody in the car has to show me their hands. We'll get you through this as soon as possible."

The window rolled down and the driver peered out with a weak smile. The cop barely registered her features.

Female, shoulder-length red hair. Not the guy they were looking for. He leaned down to peer across her at the passenger. Younger female, short brown hair, her hands up as if she were being arrested. Cute. A kid like that was no terrorist.

The driver's license came out.

Julia Taggart, resident of Brooklyn. The picture matched. The cop passed the license under an ultraviolet light and the seal of the State of New York lit up. Legit.

"You've got a bag in the backseat. Heading somewhere?"

"My sister and I are going to visit our parents in Atlantic City. We didn't know if maybe we should stay there until this is over. Do you think there are going to be more bombs?" the driver asked.

"No information at this time, ma'am." The cop glanced around the backseat again. Looked at the trunk.

A driver three cars back leaned on his horn, breaking the cop's train of thought.

Whatever. This car was clean. "Okay, you're good," the cop said, and he slapped the roof of the car. "Enjoy your trip."

The car's window rolled back up, and it nosed its way onto the open road, headed for the New Jersey turnpike without any further ado.

IN TRANSIT: MARCH 21, 22:49

For a long time they drove in silence. Angel kept looking back over her shoulder, though there was no sign of any cops back there. Maybe they were being followed, but Julia had no idea how you could tell.

This wasn't exactly her line of work. If your schnauzer had kennel cough, she was definitely ready for that. She even knew how to properly shoe a horse. But when it came to running from the law, she was definitely a novice.

Not that she imagined Angel had much experience in it, either—at least not firsthand. "Anything to worry about?" she asked.

"No," Angel said and sat down hard in her seat. She looked straight forward through the windshield. "I don't think so. I think we're clear."

Very few cars were headed into New York, but Julia noticed how Angel kept squinting every time a car passed them headed the other direction. "You okay? Your eyes hurt when those high beams get you?"

"I guess I'm not used to this," Angel confessed.

"There are a lot of things you're not used to, huh?" Julia turned on the cruise control and eased her foot off the accelerator. "I couldn't help but noticing, you're kind of pale. And you said you hadn't been out of your trailer in six months. I know I'm not supposed to ask questions, but—"

"It's my job. I'm on call pretty much twenty-four seven," Angel said. "So I don't go out much. It's not as bad as it sounds."

"Really? I can't imagine being cooped up in a little space like that for so long."

"I had the Internet," Angel replied, as if that explained everything.

Julia knew very little about Angel. When the hacker came to her door begging for help, she'd had plenty of reason to take her in, but honestly—they were almost strangers. She did know how Angel had gotten her unusual job. Once, in Julia's hearing, she'd told the story to Chapel—how she had gotten into computers when she was a kid and then how she'd hacked into the wrong database, one belonging to the Pentagon. She'd been caught, but the military had been so impressed with her skills they'd given her a choice. She could go to jail for decades or she could come work for them.

It sounded like it wasn't that much of a choice, after all. Being stuck in a trailer waiting for secret agents to call you asking for advice couldn't be that much better than prison. But Angel had also said she loved her work.

"Do you have . . . trouble with being out in the open like this?" Julia said.

"Are you asking if I'm an agoraphobic?" Angel replied. She laughed. "Not exactly. But I was a weird kid. I didn't like to play with dolls, and I didn't care about clothes at all. But I wasn't good at sports, so I couldn't even be a proper tomboy. I didn't have any friends, so I spent all my time in my room. That's why I got into computers."

"I'm sorry. That sounds tough."

"I guess, but—" Angel shrugged. "Being online—it was so much better than high school. There people only cared about how you were dressed, what you looked like. And if you weren't friends with the right people, then you were a loser and you were just screwed for life. But online . . . you could go anywhere, and what mattered was how smart you were. If you were funny or clever, or you figured out how to do something nobody else could do, then you were awesome. You were cool. I could never have had that in the real world. I was never alone after I got my computer. Any time, day or night, somebody was out there, wanting to talk or share files or whatever."

And now she fulfilled that role for others, Julia thought. Playing the constant companion to field agents who relied on her brains to keep them alive. Julia knew what it meant to feel useful, to feel like you could help people. The animals she treated needed her—sometimes she was the difference between them living and dying. Angel must feel that way all the time.

Still.

"You must have missed out on so much, though. Parties and going to college and dating—"

"Please! Online gaming parties, online universities, and, frankly, I'm a girl who likes video games and knows how to use the Internet. When it comes to dating, I can take my pick."

Julia didn't know what to say to that. It made her think of a thought experiment she'd read about when she was taking a psychology class in college. If you spent your whole life locked in a room where everything was painted white, you couldn't miss the color blue. It wouldn't even mean anything to you if somebody tried to explain it to you.

She couldn't help but feel sorry for Angel, though. She could date all the Internet geeks she wanted online, but if she couldn't actually meet up with them in person, well . . .

Maybe there were some things she didn't want to know about Angel. There was one thing, though, that had always bothered her. "Listen, if I'm not allowed to know this, that's okay. But if we're going to be stuck together on this road trip all night, I have to ask."

Angel looked at her funny. Maybe she thought Julia was about to ask her if she was a virgin or something.

But that wasn't it. "I know Chapel gave you your name. Angel, I mean."

"Yeah. It started out as a code name, but it just stuck. Now everybody calls me that."

"I'm guessing your real name is classified," Julia said.

Angel sighed. "It is. But I guess that doesn't matter anymore. It's not like I work for the government now. I'll tell you, but you have to promise not to laugh. It's Edith."

Julia bit her lip. "Okay," she said.

"They named me after my great-grandmother. She was a great woman—she was a flapper in the 1920s and she learned how to fly an airplane and she worked at catching spies during World War II. I wanted to be just like her and now I kind of am and I'm very proud of it."

"Sounds like a great role model," Julia said.

"She was. Now I've got to ask you something."

"Shoot," Julia said.

"I want to ask you," Angel said, "never, ever to call me that name."

"You got it," Julia replied. She glanced over and saw Angel smiling from ear to ear and that was it—she couldn't hold it in anymore. They both broke up laughing so hard Julia had to fight to keep the car in its lane.

WALT WHITMAN SERVICE AREA, NJ: MARCH 22, 00:06

Chapel had been a soldier before he'd been anything else. He had a soldier's skills, including the most crucial of them all. He could sleep anywhere, at any time.

When they opened the trunk, he was barely conscious. It could have been a horde of cops out there waiting to take him by force and he wouldn't have been able to resist. Instead, and luckily for him, he opened one bleary eye and saw Julia looking down at him.

"Sorry to wake you up," she said, "but we kind of need to know where we're going next."

He sat up and rubbed at his face. He felt sore all over and he had a few new bruises from being thrown around the trunk since they left the apartment, but in a second he would be fine, ready for action again.

In a second.

"My mouth tastes like the bottom of a trash can," he said. "This has been a very long day." And of course it wasn't over yet. They might have escaped the police in New York, but they were far from being safe.

"Come on," Julia said, giving him a hand with getting out of the trunk. "I'll buy you a cup of coffee and we can talk."

"Maybe some dinner, too," Chapel said.

Julia laughed. "Sure."

The three of them headed into the rest stop's diner. Even at midnight there were a fair number of people inside, fueling up before they got back on the road. The three of them grabbed a booth near the back. They had a good view of the windows and would see any police cars that pulled into the parking lot, and if they had to run, they were right next to the kitchen.

Chapel had trained for this kind of thing. Of course, his instructors at Ranger school had expected him to be on the lam in Afghanistan or Pakistan, one step ahead of the Taliban, but the skills carried over.

He also knew that he needed a lot of protein to keep him going. He ordered pork chops and sausage while Angel got a salad and Julia stuck to just coffee.

Once the waiter was gone, Julia leaned across the table and said, "So what's the plan? I assume you have a plan."

"I can do something with this, maybe," Angel said, picking up the plastic bag that held her hard drive. "If I can—"

Chapel waved a hand to silence her. "I have a plan," he said, looking Julia in the eye. She wasn't going to like this. "They locked down New York pretty tight, but they just don't have the manpower to do that for the entire eastern seaboard. Which means we can relax just a little. From now on, I'm doing the driving. As for you, we have to find a way for you to go home. We'll call you a cab or find some nice truck driver to take you back. I'm sorry, Julia, but you shouldn't know anything else."

"Uh, actually," Angel said.

Julia frowned. "As usual, your big plan is to keep me in the dark. Well, sorry, buddy. You're stuck with me for a while longer."

Chapel turned to look from one of them to the other. "What are you two talking about?"

It was Julia who answered. "I got a phone call about an hour ago. Back when you were napping in the trunk. You remember Marty, the guy who lives in the apartment right below me? He called to tell me the cops were raiding my place, tearing up my furniture, asking a lot of questions about me. He said they wanted to bring me in for an interview as soon as possible."

"Damn," Chapel said. "Julia—I'm sorry. That's the last thing I wanted to happen."

"It's not your fault," Angel said. "I'm the one who went to her for help. You wouldn't have involved her if I hadn't asked her to call you."

Julia shook her head. "Worrying about whose fault it was doesn't get us anywhere. Obviously I can't go back to New York now. They'll just arrest me on sight. And we can't let that happen. I know what Angel looks like, and they would eventually get me to talk, one way or another."

Chapel nodded. He'd forgotten how quickly she adapted to new situations. Yesterday she'd been a perfectly ordinary veterinarian living in Brooklyn. Now she was a wanted fugitive. For a civilian like Julia, that was a huge shift—but she was taking it incredibly well.

Of course, this wasn't the first time it had happened to her. Chapel and Julia had met under similarly screwed-up conditions, way back when.

Something occurred to Chapel. "This doesn't make any sense. They must have known that Angel and I were at your place somehow. But how? Nobody knows what Angel looks like, and I wasn't spotted on my way in or out. This doesn't make any sense."

"Maybe they just knew that you and I used to be a couple," Julia pointed out.

"But how? My name was never on the apartment lease, or the phone bill, or anything like that. No, the only people who knew about us were the people in that building, our friends, and—well, Angel here and the director. But he wouldn't have sent the police after you. He's on our side."

"You're sure of that?" Julia asked.

"Absolutely," Angel told her. "He would never turn on us."

Chapel wondered, if only for a moment. Hollingshead was a tough man. He made tough decisions sometimes. If it was the only way to protect the country, he would turn them in. But no—he had sent Chapel to save Angel. Telling the police about Julia would only damage that operation. It hadn't been the director.

"So nobody in law enforcement or intelligence knew to look for you," Chapel told Julia. "This doesn't make any sense."

"Well, there was one other guy," she said. "He was definitely in intelligence. The one who told me to dump you."

Chapel opened his mouth to protest. But then he realized what she'd just said.

"I'm sorry," Angel said. "Who?"

THE PENTAGON: MARCH 22, 00:12

The second Wilkes landed on the Pentagon helipad he was surrounded by soldiers. Maybe as an honor guard or maybe to take him into custody, he couldn't say. He noticed there were no marines among them.

They saluted him but refused to answer any questions. They moved him through security and into the building in a hurry, then took him down an elevator to the F Ring, the first layer of underground offices. He'd never been in that section before. Not like he would have a chance to get lost, since the soldiers kept him from moving in any direction but where they wanted him to go.

They took him to a door with no sign on it, not even a room number. He knew what that meant. Anybody who had business through that door would already know where it was. If you didn't have business there, you were in deep shit.

The door opened and a one-star general peered out at them. He looked at Wilkes and nodded.

Wilkes threw him a salute, of course. Then he stood at attention until he was told to come inside. He knew when to show respect.

The people in the room beyond certainly deserved it. Patrick Norton, the SecDef, was in there. So were a lot of other high-ranking people he didn't recognize. Other than Norton, he knew only Rupert Hollingshead and Charlotte Holman and Paul Moulton.

The general who had opened the door cleared his throat. "First Lieutenant Wilkes," he said. "We have some questions for you. You will answer them succinctly. Then we will give you your orders. Once you receive your orders, you will carry them out immediately. You will not ask any questions while you are in this room. You will not address anyone in this room other than myself. Anything you overhear in this room is considered a matter of national security and may never be repeated. Is this understood?"

"Yes, sir," Wilkes said.

The general nodded. "Earlier today you initiated a manhunt for a field agent of the Defense Intelligence Agency. Namely one Chapel, James. You provided a photograph of the field agent to local law enforcement agencies. Is this correct?"

"Yes, sir," Wilkes said.

"This despite standing orders not to provide such agencies with any information regarding active field agents under any circumstances. Can you explain why you violated those standing orders?"

"Sir, it was essential to find Chapel as quickly as possible. I had discovered that he was in collusion with the subject I had been sent to apprehend."

"Everyone here has been briefed on your mission, Lieutenant. You can be a little less succinct, now," the general said.

"Thank you, sir. I was ordered to apprehend one DIA analyst code named 'Angel' and bring her in for interrogation. It turned out my target wasn't a human being but an advanced computer system. When I arrived at the target coordinates, I found Captain Chapel already on the scene, tampering with the computer, even though he had been ordered to stay away. While he was there, person or persons unknown attacked me and agents of law enforcement. In the ensuing chaos Chapel fled the scene. I ascertained that he had removed a piece of hardware, a hard drive, from the Angel computer. It is my understanding that this computer was instrumental in the attack on the Port of New Orleans yesterday, and most likely also the attack on my person today. I believed Chapel was colluding with terrorists. I felt the only chance I had to move forward with my mission was to detain Chapel and regain access to the computer hardware. To this end I provided the photograph, but not Chapel's name or any other pertinent information."

The general nodded. "After initiating the manhunt, you made a phone call to the office of the secretary of defense. In this call you made a certain implication. Will you repeat it for us now?"

"Yes, sir." Wilkes looked across the room and made eye contact with Director Hollingshead. "I accused my direct superior of giving aid and comfort to an enemy of the United States."

The room was so quiet Wilkes could hear the ventilation system ticking over. Every eye in the room was staring right at him, many of them in disbelief.

Well, he'd taken this job to protect his country, not to make friends.

"I did so under the aegis of Presidential Policy Directive 19," he said, which was the only thing that could save his ass. In the old days, talking like that about a superior officer could get you court-martialed.

"What are the specifics of your accusation?" the general asked.

"There was no way Captain Chapel could know the location of the Angel system unless Director Hollingshead gave him that information. Clearly he'd been sent to remove Angel and take it into hiding. If I'd been a little slower in getting there, he would have succeeded and nobody would have known what he did. And our investigation into the drone hijacking would have become impossible."

The SecDef put a hand on the table in front of him and gripped its edge like he thought he might collapse. "Rupert," he said, in a small voice. "Is this true?"

This was where it could get bad. If Hollingshead denied the charge, it would be his word against Wilkes's, and there was only one way that could play out.

But instead the director stood up, wiped his glasses on a handkerchief, and replied, "It is."

Norton frowned. "Do you have a good reason why you would do such a thing?"

"No, sir," Hollingshead replied. His face might have been made of stone. It was clear he had nothing more to say on the matter.

The SecDef gave him a good long while to change his mind. When he didn't, Norton said, "I think maybe you should go to your office now and wait until we've decided what to do next. Don't you?"

Hollingshead put his glasses back on. "Sir," he said, and then he walked out of the room without even looking at anybody.

Wilkes had to respect the director. That couldn't have been easy. It almost made him feel sorry for the old man.

Almost.

When Hollingshead was gone, it was like somebody had flipped a switch. Suddenly everybody was talking at once. Norton quieted them down by raising his voice a few decibels. "This is the last thing we need. We're dealing with a terrorist attack—maybe two terrorist attacks now, after this thing in New York—and all we're doing is fighting among ourselves like dogs on a street corner."

Charlotte Holman raised one hand. "Sir, if I may—that could very well be the point."

Norton glared at her. "What do you mean?"

"The original attack utilized an air force Predator drone signed out, spuriously of course, by the CIA. Now we have the DIA implicated. The terrorists must be laughing behind their hands. How many agencies can they tie up in knots before they're done?"

"I notice the NSA still passes the smell test," Norton replied.

"Do we? We provided the intelligence product that led to Angel." She shook her head. "You see? If something goes wrong, we can be blamed as well. These people are very good. I think we need to remember that we trust each other. If we don't, who can we rely on?"

The SecDef nodded. "What's your recommendation?"

"I'd like to take over this search for Angel. Of course, the NSA doesn't have any field agents, but our analysts are the very best. If you'd be willing to second someone to me, someone I can put on the ground, my associate Mr. Moulton here can steer them in the right direction. The most important thing is moving forward. If we can secure whatever's left of this Angel, we still have a chance of finding the terrorists."

"You have a field agent in mind?" Norton asked.

"Lieutenant Wilkes," she said.

That caused a little stir.

"We've established that the DIA is working against the common good," Norton said. "And you want to use one of their agents?"

Holman smiled. She looked over at Wilkes and nodded at him. "He took a big risk here, accusing Director Hollingshead. It's clear where his priorities lie—he's more interested in serving his country than playing politics. More important, he's already up to speed. No reason to bring in anyone else—we would have to tell them everything, and the fewer people who know what's going on, the better."

Norton stared at Wilkes for a second. Wilkes stayed at attention. Finally, Norton got up from his seat and headed for the door. "Okay," he said. "Everybody else, with me."

The room emptied out in a hurry, leaving only Wilkes, Holman, and Moulton behind.

When the door was closed, she walked over to Wilkes and put a hand on his cheek. "That was very well done," she said. "Angel, Chapel, now Hollingshead. How long have we been working to get rid of the three of them?"

It was Moulton who answered. "A little over thirty-six months."

Wilkes allowed himself a brief smile. "You really sure Hollingshead was such a threat he needed to be taken down like that? He never impressed me much."

"Rupert does a very good job of hiding his light under a bushel. Believe me, if anyone could have stopped what comes next, it would have been him." She walked over to where the SecDef had sat and touched the back of his chair. She looked like she wanted to sit in it, to see what it felt like. "I know your now-former boss pretty well. Though he can still surprise me on occasion. I would never have believed that Angel was an AI, not in a thousand years. He's always been a firm believer in human intelligence."

"I know what I saw," Wilkes said.

Holman steepled her fingers in front of her and nodded. "We at the NSA have proven time and again that computers are better at this sort of work. It looks like Rupert finally came around to that understanding as well."

Wilkes had no interest in any of that. "You're supposed to give me orders, now, ma'am," he said.

She gave him a very warm, very bright smile. "Of course. Well. You were looking for Chapel and Angel's hard drive. Carry on."

Wilkes saluted and turned toward the door.

She wasn't finished, though. "When you find them, make sure nobody else ever can," she added.

"Yes, ma'am," Wilkes replied.

WALT WHITMAN SERVICE AREA, NJ: MARCH 22, 00:14

Julia looked terrified as she told her story. Chapel could only imagine how she must have felt back when it was happening.

"I only saw him twice. The first time, he came to see me at my clinic. This was back when we were living together. You were out on a mission—I had no idea where you were or when you were coming back, or *if* you were coming back. When he showed up, I could tell right away he was some kind of spy or whatever. He just had that—that smug thing."

"Smug?"

"Oh, come on," Julia said, running her fingers through her hair. "Don't pretend like you don't get the same way, sometimes. He had that attitude, that look on his face. Like he knew a bunch of secrets and that made him better than everybody else. You all get that look sometimes. It's insufferable, to be honest."

Chapel's eyes went wide. He'd had no idea he gave that off.

"So I could tell he was—from the intelligence community, let's put it that way. And I was sure when he walked into the clinic, absolutely sure he was coming to tell me you were dead. That it was a courtesy call."

"That must have been horrible," Angel said.

"Yeah. Well. I felt like I was going to throw up, just seeing him there. Or maybe I was going to break down and start crying and I wouldn't even be able to explain why to my patients. My boyfriend was dead and I wouldn't even be able to tell my closest friends. It was something I always dreaded. But then he came into one of the examination rooms with me and he told me right off the bat you were still alive. He must have known what I was thinking. He said he'd been sent to talk about our relationship." She glanced over at Chapel. "Yours and mine, I mean."

"Somebody from the government came to give you dating advice?" Chapel asked.

"I was so relieved I think I laughed at the idea. He agreed it sounded funny. But then he told me I was going to have to break up with you."

"What?" Chapel asked, loud enough that diners around them turned to look.

"He had a whole speech about why it had to be done. I could tell even he didn't believe it, but he wouldn't answer any questions. He said that I was a liability and I could get you in trouble. He said I was compromising your effectiveness in the field."

"To be fair," Angel said, "that's not all bullshit. We do prefer to work with agents who have no significant connections back home. It makes them—"

"Hold on," Chapel said to her. "Julia—you're saying this guy came from the government and he told you to break up with me? I thought you did it because you were sick of being kept in the dark all the time."

"I was," she replied. "I was absolutely miserable. Who knows? I might have broken things off anyway. I definitely wasn't ready to marry you."

Chapel closed his eyes. That didn't help. All he could see was an engagement ring in a little padded box. Sitting on the front hall table of Julia's apartment while she walked out the door.

He forced himself to stay in control. "What did you tell him?"

"To go fuck himself, of course," Julia said. "That was when he started with the threats. No, no, don't get like that," she told Chapel, who had been about to jump out of the booth. "He didn't threaten to hurt me. He threatened your career. He said if I didn't break up with you he would leak your name to the news media. He would out you. He talked about how many enemies you had, how many people would love to get their hands on you, and if your name was in the public record, there was nothing to stop them. He said if I didn't dump you, I would basically be sentencing you to death."

Chapel put a hand over his mouth. He had to, or he knew he would start shouting.

"I couldn't let that happen. So I agreed," Julia said.

Chapel couldn't reply, so Angel had to. "You said you met him twice," she said.

Julia nodded. "The second time—" She stopped and looked at Angel as if she wasn't sure she should say this in front of the younger woman. But then she shook her red hair and said, "The second time was a couple of months later. He came and showed me a photograph. It showed you, Jim. On a balcony, standing with—some other woman. And you had your, you know. Your hand in her panties."

All the blood rushed out of Chapel's body and he felt like he might collapse. Nadia. Julia had seen a picture of him with Nadia.

It was the last thing he'd ever wanted Julia to know about. The very last.

"I was . . . well. I didn't like looking at that picture. I mean, I'd dumped you, in a pretty bad way. It's true. And it wasn't like you ran right out and found a replacement; I know some time passed. But it made me . . . it made me uncomfortable. Can we just leave it at that? It made me angry, too."

Julia turned her face away. "He said he wanted me to know I'd made the right choice, breaking up with you. I think he wanted to make sure I didn't have any second thoughts."

Chapel counted to ten in his head. Then he reached for Julia's hand. She pulled it away. "Listen," he said, "do you want the details? I'll tell you all about her—"

"Jesus Christ, no!" Julia said, looking at him with flashing eyes. "I don't want to know. Your life—after I broke up with you—that's—that's—"

Her eyes shimmered with tears that refused to fall.

"Who did he work for?" Angel asked. "This mysterious guy. Did he give you any idea of who he worked for?" When Julia didn't respond right away, she said, "Come on, this is important. Did he give you any kind of clue?"

"I asked if he worked for Hollingshead. He said no, and it was funny I would even think that. He said he worked for a different agency. That he was a civilian. That's all. I told him to go away and never bother me again and he just smiled—he always smiled, I hated that smile—he smiled and said he was sure we'd see each other again."

"I can confirm he didn't work for the DIA," Angel said. "I would have known about this." She looked at Chapel. "We didn't do this to you."

"To him?" Julia said. "They didn't do this to *him* at all. They did it to me."

Angel drew back into her seat like she was afraid Julia would attack her. "Never mind. I didn't mean anything by that."

Chapel shook his head. "I'm so sorry, Julia. That must have been terrifying."

"A little. But I'm kind of used to it. Spies telling me cryptic things. Acting shifty." She crumpled a paper napkin in her fist and looked out the window.

Chapel had forgotten that her parents used to work for the CIA. It was how she'd gotten mixed up with him in the first place. A CIA lawyer used to come over to their house once a month when she was a kid, just to make sure her parents hadn't been subverted by foreign spies.

"You think he was with the CIA?" he asked.

"Not really," Julia said. "I tried tricking him into admitting just that, once, and he looked . . . contemptuous. Like I had insulted him. But he was definitely an intelligence guy, and an American."

Chapel nodded. "So somebody from some agency screwed with our personal life. Then later, somebody framed Angel, somebody we're pretty sure was also part of the intelligence community."

"You think there's a connection there?" Julia asked.

"Two attacks on us, coming so close together? I'm certain of it. Whoever is behind the drone hijacking is the same person who pressured you. Clearly there's a conspiracy to take us down—and it's working."

WALT WHITMAN SERVICE AREA, NJ: MARCH 22, 00:33

"Are you sure about this?" Julia asked.

Chapel glanced around to make sure no one was watching, then tried the handle on another car door. Locked. He tried to make it look like he was just walking past the car toward the next one in the lot. Tried the handle. Locked.

Angel answered Julia's question. "If the police are looking for you, they'll have looked up your license plate number. There'll be an APB out for you. We need a new car."

Chapel tried another door handle. Locked. The tricky part was testing the handles gently. Most of these cars had car alarms. If he pulled too hard, he would set them off, and the owner would come running out of the rest stop looking to see what was going on.

"Damn," Julia said. "I loved that car."

"Switching cars here makes sense, too," Angel went on. "When they find your car here, they'll know we headed south from New York. But they won't be able to tell if we were headed for Pennsylvania or Maryland or Delaware."

Chapel tried another handle. Locked.

"Where are we headed?"

Chapel answered her. "Pennsylvania. I have a friend who lives south of Pittsburgh. He'll take us in, for a while anyway."

The next car was locked, too.

"You're sure about this friend? Wouldn't it be safer just to keep moving?"

"I am absolutely sure that my friend won't turn us in," Chapel said. He wasn't prepared to make any promises beyond that. "And, anyway, we need a place to sleep, and a base of operations so we can start fighting back. Running is just putting off the inevitable. We need to figure out who was behind the drone hijacking and everything else if we're going to have a chance of clearing our names."

"I can help there," Angel said. "I mean. I could." She tapped her hard drive with her fingernail. "There's data on here that might tell me who was behind the drone attacks."

Chapel nodded. "That's fantastic, Angel. That's the best news I've heard all day." He tried another car and found it locked. Of course. Who would leave their car unlocked in a rest stop in New Jersey? He tried another car. Again, locked.

"You're smiling. You found one?" Julia whispered.

"No. But for the first time since this all started, I feel like I might have a plan. I feel like there's something we can actually do, instead of just running away. And the first thing we need for that plan is—"

A car handle yielded under his fingers. The door popped open on its hinges.

"And of course, you know how to hot-wire a car," Julia said.

Chapel's smile got bigger. "I do."

IN TRANSIT: MARCH 22, 03:56

"Give me another one of those energy shots," Chapel said.

Angel frowned. "You know these are terrible for your heart, right? They're just pure caffeine. They won't even keep you awake much longer.

You're going to crash no matter how many of them you drink. You should pull over and take a rest."

Chapel glanced into the backseat. Julia was sprawled out back there, her plum-colored coat pulled tight across her shoulders. He had always loved to watch her sleep. It meant she felt safe.

"In a bit," he said.

Angel flipped off the top of the little plastic bottle. It wasn't a brand he recognized, just some knockoff they'd sold back at the rest stop. He had no idea what was in it. Chapel knocked it back anyway, grimacing at the foul taste. Back when he was in Afghanistan, when he pulled long duty, he used to chug cans of energy drink, carbonated lizard spit laced with all kinds of herbal nonsense. They'd tasted like watered-down, sweetened battery acid. These energy shots went down a lot faster, but somehow they still managed to taste worse.

Almost at once, though, he felt his vision tighten up, felt his focus come back. For a long time now he'd been staring at the double yellow line on the road, pretty much the only thing his headlights could pick up. It got dark in Pennsylvania. A lot darker than it even got in New York, or Virginia for that matter. Maybe it was all the trees.

Talking helped him stay awake, too. And talking to Angel had always made him feel like things were going to be okay. Especially now, in the dark, when he couldn't really see her. It almost felt like the old days, when she was watching over him from somewhere far away, able to see everything on her screens, always ready with good advice. When she was just a voice in his ear.

"You really think you can do something with that hard drive?" he asked her.

"Maybe, sugar. Maybe. Whoever hacked me and made it look like I was piloting that drone, they were good. So good I wasn't even aware it was happening. But they must have left tracks behind. If I can get a really good look at the activity logs on the drive, maybe I can find something. Something we can follow back to where the attack really came from. If I can figure that out—"

"Then we can find them. And at the very least we can find some proof that can clear our names. And this'll be over."

"Possibly," Angel said. "But it's not going to be easy."

"My friend, the one we're going to stay with. He'll have a computer. You can log in there."

Angel sighed. "I'm going to need more processor power than you get in just some commercial laptop. More speed. What I have in mind is risky. The NSA tracked me down once—when I go online again, there'll be nothing stopping them from finding me again. If we do this, if we try to track the data, they'll know where we are."

"We'll worry about that when it happens. And we'll find you some good hardware, something to work with. Okay?"

"Sure," Angel said, though she didn't sound convinced. "Chapel—did I do the right thing?"

"What do you mean?" he asked.

"Running away. Maybe—maybe I should have just turned myself in. Then you wouldn't be in trouble like this. And then I ran to Julia's place, and now she's in it, too."

"You're innocent, Angel. You didn't do anything wrong."

"But if I did turn myself in, if I let them question me, then—then they'd see I wasn't guilty, right?"

He thought about Angel being shoved in some fetid cell. Being interrogated by men shouting questions at her while they made her walk in circles until she couldn't stand up anymore. He imagined her being waterboarded.

He knew what happened to people who were accused of being terrorists. Whether they were innocent or not.

"No, Angel. The right place for you is here in this car. With me."

"You never even asked me if I did it. If I hijacked that drone. The thought didn't cross your mind, did it?"

"Not for a second," he told her.

SOUTH HILLS, PA: MARCH 22, 05:44

The sun had yet to rise, but streetlamps illuminated the suburban lane well enough. It was a long street lined with big houses set well back on spacious yards—the kind of street Chapel thought had disappeared after the housing boom. The lawns were all mowed down to stubble and bordered by privacy fences so that each house stood on its own discreet lot, each with its own stand of trees, a paved driveway, and a quaint brick or stone walkway to its porch. Each house had its own tasteful mailbox with flags pinned back like the ears of a faithful hound. Each house had wooden siding painted a different shade of off-white and a door painted dark red or dark green, to give the house character. It was probably the tidiest little neighborhood Chapel had ever seen. It looked like the people who owned those houses periodically came out and dusted their own curbs.

Only one thing spoiled the effect. An old man in a green cloth jacket was crawling along the gutter, his straggly beard touching the pavement.

Chapel switched off the car and jumped out. That green jacket spoke to him. He rushed over and squatted down next to the crawling man. "Excuse me," he said. "You look like you could use a hand."

"No, no," the man said. His eyes were bright red as if he'd been weeping, but he smiled for Chapel. He lay down in the road and propped himself up on his elbows. "I'll admit, my method of locomotion may appear unorthodox. But I assure you I'm making excellent progress, good sir."

The man stank of cheap liquor—not the juniper smell of gin or the sweet stink of rum but more like the acrid bite of pure rubbing alcohol.

Julia came and knelt down next to the crawling man. She checked his pulse—he did not resist—and frowned. "He's not in good shape," she said, "though maybe that was kind of obvious."

"Sir," Chapel said, "you're wearing an army jacket. Are you a veteran?"

"I have that honor," the man said. "Though my coat is but a loaner. First Battalion, Third Marines. A pleasure to make your acquaintance, young man. And you, my dear—simply a pleasure to be in your pulchritudinous presence."

Chapel tried to remember the last time anyone had called him "young man." He shook his head and told the man, "I really think we should help you here."

"Third Marines," Julia said. "Why does that sound familiar? Wait a minute. Rudy? Is your name Rudy?" She looked up at Chapel. "Do you remember Atlanta? When that CIA guy tried to kill me?"

"You're kidding me," Chapel said. But now she mentioned it—yeah, it was definitely the same guy. Rudy had been wandering around an underground mall in Atlanta and he'd asked them for money. He'd ended up helping to save Julia's life.

In way of thanks, Chapel had given him a phone number to call, a way to reach out to somebody who might help him get his life back on track. Help him stop drinking. Judging by what street he was currently crawling across, it looked like he had called that number—but it hadn't been enough.

"I will never forget that lovely red hair," Rudy said. "Though I can't quite make out your face. I seem to have misplaced my glasses, dear. Do you see them anywhere?"

Julia glanced around. "No, sorry."

"Ah, well. Perhaps you'll give me a kiss, then."

She laughed. "It's definitely Rudy," she said.

Chapel tried to get hold of the drunk vet's arm, to help him sit up, but Rudy shrugged him off with surprising strength. He tried again, but stopped this time because the door of the nearest house banged open and a woman came storming out to scowl at them.

"You leave him alone," she said. She was a hair under five feet tall and might weigh a hundred pounds if she put on heavy work boots. Her hair was tucked up inside a satin cap but despite the hour she was already dressed in a conservative pantsuit. "He's gonna drink like that, hey? He's gonna crawl his way back to bed. Maybe you think you're doing him a favor. You think you're doing him a favor?"

"Dolores, hi, I—"

"Did I just ask you a question? Did you answer it?"

"No, I—no," Chapel stammered.

"No, I, no, exactly," she mimicked. "I know you, don't I? But don't ask me to remember where from."

"Your wedding," Chapel said.

She snorted in derision. "Like there weren't two hundred people there. I made the guest list, so I ought to know. You a friend of Top?"

"I'm one of his boys, actually," Chapel said.

Dolores's face didn't change, but she shifted her weight from one foot to the other. It was clear that Chapel had produced the right password or given the right sign. She glanced at Julia and then over at the stolen car, where Angel still waited. She made a gesture for Angel to come over. "You'd better come inside. I'll make you some breakfast—don't expect croissants, though. Pancakes are easier."

"Thank you," Chapel said.

Dolores shrugged and headed back into the house. Chapel followed her. Julia waited for Angel to catch up before she went in.

"Do you understand what's going on here?" she asked.

"Maybe twenty-five percent," Angel said. Then she looked back at Rudy, who had managed to crawl his way into the driveway. "Maybe fifteen."

SOUTH HILLS, PA: MARCH 22, 05:52

The inside of the house was not exactly what Chapel had expected. The furniture was cheap, mostly pressboard covered in chipped veneer. The upholstery had split in places and was held together with duct tape. There was a television in the living room, but it was an old-fashioned box type, not a flat-screen. The walls were bare of decoration.

As run-down as it looked, the room was spotless. The duct tape on the cushions looked like it had just been applied. The carpet showed the tracks of recent vacuuming.

He found it all strangely comforting. *This is the kind of place a soldier might live,* he thought. The neatness, the lack of ornament or pretension—

"It's a shithole," Dolores said, "but it's paid for."

Chapel kept his mouth shut. He'd only met Dolores once before, but he knew better than to try to make pleasantries or—far worse—disagree with her.

She headed through the house, toward the kitchen, but Chapel stopped in the living room and looked up the stairs. He could hear people moving around up there, and now some of them appeared—two men and a woman, all dressed in T-shirts and jeans. They all had the same crew cut—including the woman. And all of them were wounded.

One of the men was missing both legs below the knee. He had a pair of replacements that were little more than metal poles that ended in tennis shoes. The other man was hairless and all of his exposed skin was pink and rough and Chapel knew he must have been in a fire. The woman had a trim, athletic body but she had an inch-wide scar running from her forehead down into the collar of her shirt.

Another man came onto the stairs while Chapel stood there, this one with a white plastic hand.

All four of them stared at Chapel with a look he knew pretty well. It was the look he wore on his own face when people he didn't know saw him with his arm off. A wary expression, because you just didn't know how they would react.

Chapel nodded to the four of them, then nearly jumped when he heard something bounding toward him. It turned out to be a dog, a big mutt with scars on his head and only three legs. A pair of actual dog tags jangled at his collar.

The dog ignored Chapel and ran straight to Julia, who erupted in laughter and excitement. "Hey there, fella, hey there," she said and bent down so the dog could lick her chin.

Chapel left her and Angel to the dog and followed Dolores into the kitchen. "I wasn't expecting to see so many people here," he said. "I thought it was just you and Top. And I guess Rudy."

"I wasn't expecting visitors while it was still dark out," she told him. "I figure we'll both find a way to cope."

Chapel grinned for a second—then let his mouth fall open when he saw they weren't alone. Another guy with a crew cut was standing by the kitchen counter, breaking eggs into a large bowl. He had an artificial arm, a yellow resin prosthesis that ended in what Chapel knew was called a voluntary closing hook—a complicated mechanical hook fashioned from stainless steel. Clearly he'd had it for a while, as he was breaking the eggs without actually squashing them.

"It's okay, I'm used to people staring at it," the man said, making it sound as if this was not okay at all.

"Hi," Chapel said, trying to get back on the right footing. "I'm Jim."

The wounded man swung around and stuck his hook out at Chapel. "Ralph. Nice to meet you—want to shake?"

Dolores squealed in anger. "Ralph, you have a bad night?" she asked. "That why you're down here so early making a mess in my kitchen?"

"Yes, ma'am," Ralph said.

"You think that means you can be rude to my guests?"

"No, ma'am."

"It's all right," Chapel said. He reached over and shook Ralph's hook, even though it meant getting raw egg all over his fingers. He considered showing Ralph his own prosthesis, then thought better of it. It might make the man jealous—Chapel's arm was generations beyond what Ralph wore—but also it would mean he would have to take his shirt off to prove it. "Listen, Dolores, I really need to talk with Top. Is he around?"

"He's upstairs naked and snoring in his bed, where everybody ought to be this time of day. But it sounds like you've woken up the rest of the house. I'm sure he'll be down soon. In the meantime—you want orange juice or coffee?"

After all the energy shots he'd consumed, Chapel was clear on that. "Juice, please. Do you mind if I, uh, ask a question?"

Dolores went to the refrigerator to get a family-sized carton of orange juice. She poured him a glass and put it on the table. "You want to know who all these people are. You should have already guessed. They're Top's boys. Just like you."

"You know Top?" Ralph asked. A lot of the anger left his face in the same moment.

Chapel nodded. "When I came back from Afghanistan, I was in a hospital for about six months. Top did my physical rehabilitation. I don't mind saying, I was pretty much finished before I met him. I was considering suicide, frankly. Top taught me how to live with my . . . injuries. He did more than that. He taught me how to live in general."

"All the boys in this house could tell you the same story, or one close enough nobody gives a shit," Dolores said. "Rudy was the first. He showed up here one day in a sorry state, drunk to the gills and barely able to talk. Top and I took him in, because what else were we going to do? He was a marine, once. Nobody else wanted to help him. Not the VA, not any hospital. So we put him in a spare room and let him dry out. We figured it would just be for a few days. I got him into an AA program, got him doing his twelve steps."

Chapel couldn't help himself. "It looks like they didn't work."

"He falls off the wagon sometimes. I can't lock him in his room—this isn't a prison or even a halfway house. Some nights it's more than he can handle, the memories, the things he did in Vietnam. So he goes out and gets drunk. He knows we won't carry him inside but he also knows we won't kick him out."

"Those are the rules," Ralph said.

Dolores nodded. "That's right, Specialist. We help him as best we can. And we make sure he doesn't sleep under a bridge and maybe he eats a meal or two every day. You can't fix a broken man—that's something he has to do on his own. But you can give him a chance."

"What about the others?" Chapel asked.

"They came, one by one. Top never says no. We're full past capacity now, but we don't turn anybody away. Most of them, their families couldn't handle the PTSD. The screaming in the night, the anger problems. I'm sure you know how that works."

"I do," Chapel said, staring at his glass of juice. He'd gotten his own PTSD under control—most of the time—but it hadn't been easy.

"If they can't live someplace else, they can live here," Dolores said. "As long as they need it."

"That's—incredible. Incredibly generous," Chapel said.

Dolores shrugged. "They sacrificed something for their country. An arm, a leg, a chance at a normal life. Now that's generous. We just do what we can. I just wish we had the money to buy a bigger place. If the boys can hold down a job, they help out a little with money. Some of Top's boys do better than others—those that don't live here, I mean. They help us out too, as much as they can."

Chapel had a feeling he knew who one of those donors was. Top had been a master gunnery sergeant in Iraq. The men who served under him had been his original boys. When he started working as a physical therapist, all his patients got to be his boys, too. A lot of people owed Top more than they could ever pay. Rupert Hollingshead was one of Top's boys. It was why he'd given Chapel a job, back when they first met.

"Forgive me, Dolores, but you're a civilian, aren't you? You never served in the military."

"Only because when you sign up they don't let you choose if you want to be a general or an enlisted," she pointed out. "If they'd been sensible enough to put me in charge, I would have accepted their offer."

Chapel smiled. "I don't mean anything by it, except—I can see why Top started doing this, taking in his boys when they needed him. But why did you agree to it? You didn't have to do this."

"Maybe not. But there is no more persuasive man on earth than Top. He talked me into marrying him, didn't he? He could talk a fish into moving to Death Valley because the real estate was so cheap."

Chapel had to admit she was right about that.

SOUTH HILLS, PA: MARCH 22, 06:29

It wasn't long before Top came down for his breakfast.

Top was not a tall man, though he had a barrel chest and thick neck muscles that made him look as powerful as a horse. He was not a particularly good-looking man, a fact accentuated by the scar tissue that surrounded one of his eyes. He was missing one arm and hadn't bothered to put on a prosthesis. He was also missing a leg, and so he came down the stairs one step at a time, carefully placing an artificial foot on each riser.

Despite all this—and not because of it—the second he appeared in the living room the whole atmosphere in the house changed. People stood up and turned to face him. The dog stopped pawing at Julia's face and came to attention.

Top smiled at the wounded veterans gathered in the living room. "Well, if isn't another damned beautiful morning in Pennsylvania," he announced.

"Sir, yes, sir!" the vets said in chorus.

Top turned to look at Julia, still down on the floor next to the dog, and then at Angel, who was sitting in a corner making herself very small in an armchair.

"An especially beautiful morning," Top said, with a wide, amiable grin.

"I heard that!" Dolores shouted from the kitchen.

"If you were gonna divorce me for looking at pretty girls, I'd already be the unhappiest man in the world, baby," Top called back.

It was enough to make Angel blush. Julia laughed.

"I figure at some point, somebody's gonna actually introduce me to our new friends here. So I won't bother to ask," Top said. "And who's that in the kitchen?"

Chapel stepped out into the living room. He threw Top a salute. "Reporting for duty, sir," he said.

"Captain Chapel," Top said, looking him up and down. "I'd call you a disgrace to your uniform if you were wearing one. Your hair's out of place, soldier, and you look like you haven't shaved this morning. Look like you didn't sleep last night, either."

"Yes, sir," Chapel said. He outranked Top, as such things were normally measured. But in this house it was clear who gave the orders.

"Frankly, your appearance is an insult to me, my lady wife, and every soldier in this house. Do you have anything to say in your defense?"

"No, sir," Chapel replied. He was still holding his salute, since he hadn't been told to be at ease.

"You'll come over here and face me when I chew you out, soldier."

Chapel marched over to Top until they were standing face-to-face. At which point he just couldn't hold it together anymore. He exploded with laughter and Top did too, and the two of them embraced in a very warm hug. It had been way too long.

SOUTH HILLS, PA: MARCH 22, 06:40

"Damn, Cap'n, it's so good to see you I think I might cry a little," Top said. "How've you been keeping? You still swimming with one arm like a crazy fish?"

"Every chance I can get," Chapel said. "Listen, I—"

"The redhead out there is Julia, right? The one you said you were going to marry?"

"That's right, although it didn't quite work out. We—"

"And the brunette? What's her story?"

"She's a . . . a work friend," Chapel said.

"Well, she's welcome here, then. Any friend of yours at least rates breakfast on me." He nodded at the roller bag Angel had set down next to her chair. "A clean bed, too, if she wants one. You just dropping her off, or are you staying tonight, too?"

"I don't know," Chapel said. He felt his shoulders sag. "Maybe this is just a quick pop-in. I was hoping . . . well, I was hoping we could stay here for a bit. I didn't realize you already had a full house, though. It's damned good to see you, but maybe we should just be on our way."

"Let me tell you a little something," Top said, as if Chapel hadn't spoken at all. "Every veteran of an American war is welcome in this house. No questions asked. Even that flea-bitten mutt, you know where he came from? He was working K-9 teams in Iraq. They trained him to sniff out IEDs. You believe that? When I was over there, they would send us some new gizmo every week. A magno-thermo-dynamic sniffer spotter wide-spectrum doodad that was supposed to tell you where the roadside bombs were without fail, so fresh out of the lab they still had that new car smell. We tried every one of them, ran through the manuals and all the checklists, and you know how well they worked?" He stuck out one finger in the air and then he pointed at his missing eye, arm, and leg. "But Angus there, that dog. They spent maybe one percent of the budget of one of those gizmos on training him. He even volunteered to take a lousy pay grade—one little biscuit for every bomb he found. But damn if he didn't have a one hundred percent success rate."

"You're telling me your dog is a veteran," Chapel said.

"Honorably discharged with a Purple Heart," Top said, beaming with pride. It was the same look that crossed his face when one of his patients managed to stand on his or her own feet for the first time in six months. "He came home and they put him with some nice family and six months later he had fleas and kennel cough and the family wanted to put him down. They said he refused to eat, and he kept waking 'em up at three in the morning barking like the whole house was full of insurgents. In short, because I know you army types have trouble paying attention during briefings, my dog is a veteran with P-T-S-D." He pronounced each letter as if he were saying the dog had received a doctorate in particle physics from Harvard. "You know how hard it is to work with a dog with PTSD? They can't tell you when they're flashing back, or that nobody gets what they're feeling. You can't tell them they're home and they're safe."

"If anybody could help a dog like that, it's you," Chapel said.

Top nodded, just accepting that without comment. "Now. Tell me what you're looking for here."

Chapel bit his lip. He looked around at the veterans gathered in the room. They were all staring at him. He couldn't afford to speak plainly, but he owed Top an explanation, definitely. "The three of us—Angel and Julia and me—we're in trouble."

Top leaned back in his chair and scratched at the burnt skin around his false eye. "Trouble, like cops? Or worse?"

"Worse," Chapel admitted.

Top nodded. "You have any idea why I jawed on and on about my flea-bitten dog?"

"I think I might," Chapel said.

"That dog is one of my boys. When he came here, it was so bad Dolores and me, we wore flea collars our own selves. That dog bit me three times, and I ain't got a lot of flesh left to get bitten off. You know why that dog is still here?"

"He's one of your boys," Chapel said.

Top nodded. "And so are you. You just wasted ten minutes of my life asking a question you already knew the answer to. That's all right, gave me a chance to talk about my dog. I love talking about my dog. Now let's talk about what we're going to do to get you and those ladies out of the shit."

WALT WHITMAN SERVICE AREA, NJ: MARCH 22, 06:52

Wilkes's phone wouldn't stop ringing.

He picked it up and looked at the screen. The call was coming from a number listed as (000) 000-0000, which he knew meant it had to be Moulton. Only the intelligence community had the tech to truly mask a number but still let it connect.

He glanced out through the side hatch of the helicopter at the New Jersey landscape, at the turnpike and its feeder roads, at the trees down there just starting to turn blue as the sun thought about maybe getting around to rising above the horizon.

He considered just tossing the phone out there.

Instead he swiped the screen and put it to his ear. "What?" he said.

Moulton sounded pissed. "I've been trying to reach you for twenty minutes," the analyst sputtered. "You need to put in your earpiece. We need to be in constant contact."

Wilkes reached in his pocket and pulled out the hands-free unit they'd given him. "I was trying to get some sleep," he said.

"You can sleep when this is over. Look, when Angel and Chapel are on a mission, he never takes his earpiece out. The two of them are always working together, talking things out, figuring out their next move—"

"You want us to be more like Chapel and Angel?" Wilkes asked. "Think about that. Think about how well it worked out for them."

He could hear Moulton seethe through the phone.

The helicopter was already settling down in a rest stop parking lot. Wilkes figured he knew why—he didn't need Moulton to explain it all. "Let me guess. You found Julia Taggart's car." Wilkes had wasted an hour trying to locate her in New York before the cops had bothered to tell him her driver's license had been scanned as she passed a roadblock outside the Holland Tunnel. It had given him something to work on, but for most of the night the helicopter had just been flying passes over the New Jersey Turnpike, looking for her license plate.

"Yeah, it's sitting in a parking lot in—"

"In a rest stop in New Jersey. Yep. I assume you told my pilot where to take me." Wilkes leaned forward to look at the pilot in the cockpit of the helicopter. He gave the man a thumbs-up. He put his legs down on the chopper's floorboards and started to climb out through the hatch. "How long ago did you find the car?"

"An hour ago," Moulton said. "But according to the surveillance cameras, it's been sitting there most of the night."

"Yeah?" Wilkes said. He glanced out, across the lot. A couple of police cruisers were sitting near the entrance to a diner about two hundred yards away. "So they're already gone. We missed them."

"Well, sure. They had a huge head start," Moulton said. "And we wasted time bringing you to the Pentagon for that farce of a debriefing."

"Okay," Wilkes said. "I'm going back to sleep."

"What?"

"You're boring me to the point where I lose consciousness," Wilkes said.

"You're not going to question anybody? You're not going to even talk to the cops on the scene?"

"No reason to. I already know what they could tell me. Our targets aren't here anymore. I know Chapel, and I know how he was trained. He stole another car and they left. The big question is, which direction did they go, and I'm guessing the locals can't tell me that."

Moulton laughed derisively. "I can't believe this. You won't even get out of your aircraft? Assistant Director Holman brought you in on this because we needed somebody in the field, somebody who could work this case and—"

"No, she didn't," Wilkes said.

"What?"

"When you got assigned to work for me, did you even bother to look at my military record? Did you see what my operational specialty was when I was in Iraq? You need to understand something, Moulton. I'm not like Chapel. His job is to go into bad places and do all the subtle crap. Maybe pay off some warlord or sabotage a nuclear reactor or steal some documents we need. Spy shit. You take a second now, look at what they had me doing in Iraq."

"Oh," Moulton said when he'd finished doing as he was told. "You do wet work."

"Nobody calls it that, dingus," Wilkes told him. "We call it F3."

"What does that mean?"

"Find, Fix, Finish. What I am is a self-guided missile. You tell me where to go, and then you set me loose. So I'm going back to sleep unless you can give me a target."

Moulton sounded almost apologetic when he responded. Maybe he was just scared. "Okay. Okay—I have something. A car was reported stolen from that rest stop last night. Early this morning, actually. I've got the plate number and . . . and . . ."

"Still not telling me what I need, buddy," Wilkes said.

"Hold on! There's something here. That plate number was recorded by an automatic speed trap in . . . Pennsylvania. They're headed west. I'm going to get some satellites on this, do a full scan for vehicle tags and—"

"Wake me up when you have something," Wilkes said, and then he ended the call. He shoved the phone in his pocket. Then he leaned forward to look at the helicopter pilot. He rolled one finger in the air, the hand signal to take the chopper up again. "West," he shouted, over the noise of the helicopter's rotor. "Head west until I tell you to stop."

Then he put his feet up, his head back, and closed his eyes.

SOUTH HILLS, PA: MARCH 22, 07:36

They needed to get rid of the stolen car.

As they headed out into the fresh light of day, Chapel felt like his eyeballs were vibrating in his head. He needed to sleep, and soon. But if the government was searching for them, then it was just a matter of time before they found the car. With the sun up it would be that much easier for them. Julia came along to help him, though he could easily have taken care of it alone. It seemed she had something to say to him.

She kept quiet, though, as he leaned under the dashboard and fiddled with the wires that would start the ignition. The car sputtered to life and he put it in drive right away before it could stall out.

"We need a place where it won't be seen," he told Julia. "Preferably someplace covered, so it can't be seen from the air. They'll find it eventually, no matter what we do, but we don't want to make it easy for them."

She nodded. "So like a parking garage? No—no, that wouldn't work. The attendants would find it and call the police. What about an abandoned house? One with a garage?"

"As long as nobody saw us breaking in, that would be great," Chapel said. "That's a risk, though." He headed out onto a wide stretch of road surrounded on both sides by strip malls and big box stores. "Even if we can just ditch it under some trees, that would be a big help."

They drove for a while in silence, both of them craning their necks around for the right spot. It was Julia who found it. "There," she said, pointing at the overgrown parking lot of a deserted minimall.

The lot was empty, and far too visible from the street, but Chapel pulled into it anyway and then drove around the back of the run-down buildings. "Oh, perfect," he said. There had been a drive-through bank back there, with a concrete overhang that would shield the car from satellites. He put the car in park and leaned back in the seat and closed his eyes for a second. He finally felt safe.

"We'll need to strip the license plates, right?" Julia asked. "I remember you're supposed to do that when you abandon a car."

Chapel nodded without opening his eyes. "We'll need to file off the VIN numbers too. They'll know the car was stolen, but it'll take longer to trace it back to its owner then."

"I feel sorry for whoever owns this car," Julia said, with a little laugh. "I mean, I know we had no choice. But I keep imagining them coming out of that rest stop and realizing they're going to need to get a cab home. That's got to suck."

Chapel opened his eyes and looked across at her. He realized he hadn't given a second's thought to that. He was on a mission—at least, it felt like he was on a mission. If he'd been in Uzbekistan or Somalia, stealing cars would just be standard operating procedure. Why should it be different here in the States? And yet, once Julia pointed it out, he couldn't help but feel like a criminal.

Still. "I would do a lot worse things to keep you and Angel safe."

Julia hugged herself and looked down at her lap. She nodded, but she looked as if she was deep in thought.

"I know this is scary," he told her. He reached over with his good hand and ran the backs of his knuckles up and down her arm.

"That's the funny thing. It's not," she said.

"Yeah?"

"Yeah," she said. She kept looking down, like she didn't want to meet his eyes. "If it was just me out here. I mean, if I was running from the cops on my own, if it had been up to me to get Angel to safety, I think I'd be shitting myself."

He laughed, and she smiled. But she still wasn't looking at him.

"But it's not me. This isn't me doing all this. Oh, I don't mean it like I've lost my mind and I'm disassociating or anything. It's more like there are two of me. There's Julia Taggart, DVM, who comes home from work every night and eats fat-free frozen pasta and maybe stays awake long enough to watch some reality show about fashion designers. That woman could never do these things. But then there's also a Julia who comes out only when she's with you. When people are chasing us and I'm always worried one of us is going to get shot and everything is so much more intense. You'd think I would hate being that Julia. You'd think after the first time I would never want to be her again."

"But . . . what? You like the adrenaline rush?"

"No. That doesn't last," she said. "What happens is—different. I change, somehow. I know you're relying on me to be strong. To handle this. And so I do. I step up and I get a lot tougher all of a sudden. For a couple of days, I get to be a badass."

He smiled. "That was what made me fall in love with you," he said. "You were stronger than anybody I knew. I needed you to be that badass and you were." Here it was. The little thought he'd been thinking ever since she kissed him back in her apartment. The secret, tiny hope he'd kept burning just in case.

The idea that maybe things weren't over between them.

"This Julia, the badass Julia, is going to get herself killed someday," she said. "She's going to think she's better at this stuff than she really is. And it'll mean her death."

"No," he said, his heart sagging in his chest. "No, that won't happen. I'd die before I let anyone hurt you."

"That's a promise you can't make. Badass Julia wants to believe you. Julia Taggart, DVM, knows better. She wants to be at home where it's safe and she has her own bed to sleep in, and she keeps reminding me— this isn't going to last. Even if things do work out, even if we clear Angel's name and somehow it's safe to go back to Brooklyn . . . then it'll just be over. I have to be careful making decisions right now."

"Sure," Chapel said.

"For instance, Badass Julia wants to just attack you right now. Pretend like we never broke up and make out with you right here in this stolen car. Because that's the kind of thing Badass Julia would do. But of course, that's a terrible idea. Just because something is exciting and reckless and—"

She turned her face to look at him and didn't get to finish her thought.

The look in her eyes was one he remembered all too well. He hadn't seen it in a long time. He leaned across the seat and she leaned into him and their lips met, hard enough that their teeth clicked together. That made them both laugh, but it didn't make them stop kissing. He reached around behind her and pulled her close and she put her hands on his chest and his fingers sank into her hair and the smell of her, that incredible, intoxicating perfume filled his entire head. She broke away but just enough to kiss his jaw, his cheek, to bite his earlobe. God, he'd missed this. He leaned down to kiss her neck and he felt her tremble, felt her responding to his body, to his heat. He reached down with his good hand and cupped her breast through her thin shirt, felt the lacy outline of her bra and then her nipple, felt it harden under his thumb—

And then cold air slapped him across the face as she pulled away, wrenching her door open and stumbling out onto the asphalt and broken concrete. As his senses reeled and he tried to figure out what had just happened, he felt the car rock slightly. She was leaning up against it, breathing hard. Maybe a foot and a half away from him. But the moment was over. She might as well be on the far side of the moon.

He took a second to let his pulse slow down. Then he climbed out of the car on the driver's side. "We need to get those license plates," he said.

"Yeah. Definitely," she said, and she rubbed at her mouth with the back of one hand. "I'll take the back. You take the front."

"Deal."

OVER NORTHERN CALIFORNIA: MARCH 22, 05:33 (PDT)

The CQ-10 Snowgoose didn't look like anybody's idea of a drone. It had a stubby little body only nine feet long, ending in a single propeller, and no wings. It kept aloft by dangling from a broad white parachute that glittered in the moonlight. It didn't move very quickly and it didn't look like it carried any weapons that might hurt anybody. In fact, it wasn't designed to be a weapons system at all. It had three square bays built into its side that could pop open and drop supplies—food, survival gear, blankets—to people who were, say, stuck in an avalanche or in the middle of a forest fire.

Due to an extremely unlikely error in its logistics chain, this one had been loaded with a different sort of cargo.

It passed over a power plant just outside of Oakland first, a busy gas-burning plant that provided San Francisco with much of its power. The Snowgoose bumbled along in the sky like a giant white bee, high up enough that no one could have seen it from the ground. One of its cargo boxes popped open and an object the size and shape of a hockey puck tumbled out, a hockey puck with its own tiny parachute. The Snowgoose didn't even slow down—it had other places to be.

The hockey puck it had left behind drifted slowly down toward the power plant, bobbing this way or that on little gusts of wind. Just as it reached the height of the plant's tallest smokestacks, the hockey puck exploded into millions and millions of pieces, just as it had been designed to do.

It was known technically as a BLU-114/B submunition, and it was designed for an extremely specific mission. Devices like it had been used over Serbia and Iraq, and they were sometimes called "soft bombs" because they were designed not to hurt human beings but only to cause damage to infrastructure. When it exploded, it sent all those tiny pieces of itself raining down across the power plant in a dense cloud that was sucked into the plant's air intakes and ventilation systems. The pieces were each only a fraction of an inch thick, and they were quite harmless on their own—just strands of carbon fiber that fluttered through the plant, landing wherever they fell. Some happened to land on transformers or turbines and other pieces of high-voltage machinery. When they touched these machines, they glittered and sparked as they conducted electricity where it wasn't supposed to go. In the space of seconds, hundreds of short circuits arced across the power plant, liberating enormous amounts of energy. Some of the transformers caught on fire. Every one of them touched by carbon fiber failed in a dramatic way. Around the plant alarms sounded and fire suppression systems switched on, only to stop almost instantly as they too were shorted out.

The plant's turbines chugged to a stop. Its furnaces roared pointlessly in the dark as all of the incredibly complicated machinery just failed to function. Every light in the plant went out at once.

High above and far away now, the Snowgoose carried on its appointed rounds.

The loss of a single power plant would be a hardship for San Francisco, which sat on a peninsula and had relatively few connections to the larger power grid. But the blackouts that had plagued California in recent years had forced the municipal authorities to improve those connections, and even as the gas-burning plant went off-line, massive switching systems registered the drop in power and compensated by pulling electricity from other sources—from coal and nuclear plants around the state, from hydroelectric plants in Yosemite National Park. At this early hour, the city's energy demands were at their lowest, and very few people in San Francisco, even those who were already awake, would notice anything more than a brief flicker in their lights.

Unfortunately for them, the Snowgoose still had two more hockey pucks in its cargo bay. The first one hit a substation north of the city, a fenced-off lot full of transformer towers like the spires of a futuristic cathedral. The submunition blanketed the substation with carbon fibers, and for a split second, lightning jumped in every direction as one after another of the transformers shorted out and went dark.

The third submunition exploded over a switching station farther inland. The station was already overloaded as it tried to take the strain off the damaged power grid, pulling in power from more directions than it ever had before. A massive current passed through the station, maybe enough to have melted electronic components on its own. The Snowgoose wasn't taking any chances, though, and it flooded the station with its tiny fragments just as it had the power plant and the substation. The arcs of electric current the fibers elicited this time were strong enough that part of the station exploded, sending hot metal debris flying over a residential neighborhood and starting half a dozen house fires.

Within minutes every light in San Francisco went dark. Those buildings that had on-site backup generators—hospitals, police stations, military installations—were flooded with red emergency lighting, and administrators and officials worked hard to prevent local catastrophes, but they were hampered by the fact that all the cellular networks were down and communications were almost nonexistent.

Within an hour the blackouts had begun to spread. Unable to handle the necessary switching functions, substations across California shut themselves down automatically to protect their vital components. Others were shut down manually because nobody knew what was going on and the men and women who operated those stations were terrified of the power surges that had led to the blackout of 2003. By the time the sun came up, Los Angeles had power only in a few scattered areas. There was no part of California that didn't feel the pinch. Train stations shut down, delaying millions of passengers. Server farms up and down the coast were taken off-line, and even where people had sufficient power, the Internet and telephone networks slowed to a crawl. Police flooded the streets of the cities to direct traffic and try to ameliorate some of the chaos.

Meanwhile, the Snowgoose found a flat spot on the long hilly ridges of the Las Trampas Regional Wilderness in Contra Costa County. It set down gently on its landing skids, then sat and waited patiently for its masters to collect it. Its work was done.

SOUTH HILLS, PA: MARCH 22, 10:04

It was a long walk back to Top's house, but when they arrived, Chapel and Julia found the place deserted. The front door was unlocked but no lights were on inside, and Chapel couldn't find anyone in the living room or the kitchen.

Then he heard a rhythmic thumping sound coming from the basement, and he froze in place. *Thud-thud-thud.* One-two-three. Over and over again.

"Wait here," he told Julia, wishing, and not for the first time, that he had a weapon. He went to the door that led to the basement stairs and eased it open. There were lights on down there, and the sound was much louder now, and accompanied by gasping breaths. It sounded like someone was being beaten down there.

Chapel sprang into action. If Angel was down there, if she was in trouble—

He rushed down the stairs, with no idea what he would find, knowing perfectly well he could be running into a trap. What he saw instead brought him up short.

The basement was as big as the first floor of the house but completely open. Bare concrete walls were hung with flags and banners showing the Marine Corps and Army logos. Most of the space was full of battered old exercise equipment—weight benches, Nautilus machines, and a huge punching bag hanging from a hook in the ceiling.

Suzie, the scarred vet he'd seen on the stairs earlier, was working the bag hard. One-two-three, one-two-three, dancing around it, slamming her fists against the canvas. Sweat slicked her face and neck, and her skin was bright red with exertion, making her scar stand out pale white against her skin. When she saw Chapel, she stared at him as if she'd caught him peeping through her bedroom window.

"Something you wanted?" she asked.

"I, uh, I'm just looking for—"

"Chapel," Angel said, then, and he swiveled around to look for her. She was on the far side of the basement, sitting crouched over an antique desktop computer. The screen showed a television feed from CNN. He saw people running in a street somewhere warm. Then the view switched to a map of California, with a huge red stain expanding away from San Francisco. "You need to see this," Angel said.

SOUTH HILLS, PA: MARCH 22, 10:16

When Suzie was done hitting the bag, she moved to a stationary bike and started pedaling like mad. Her eyes stayed on Chapel the whole time.

"She's okay," Angel told him. "She just has trust issues."

Chapel looked back up the stairs and told Julia to come down. "Where's everybody else?" she asked.

"They all went out to their jobs. Suzie's only here because she got fired from the last place she worked," Angel explained.

"Asshole manager kept grabbing my butt," Suzie told them. "Told me I should feel lucky any man wanted to touch me. What else was I supposed to do?"

"She broke his fingers," Angel explained.

"That's . . . harsh," Chapel said.

"Sounds about right to me," Julia said, with a smile.

"She gets it," Suzie said, never letting up on her pace.

Chapel shook his head. "You said I needed to see something," he told Angel.

"Yeah, here," she told him. She clicked through some tabs on her browser and brought up the map he'd seen. It showed California as a series of power grids, with red areas denoting where the power was down and pink areas showing areas that had reduced electricity. Only about a third of the state was still green to indicate it had full power. "It's worse than it looks. There are hospitals all over the state that are airlifting patients to Nevada and Arizona. There are no traffic lights in Los Angeles, none at all. They can't even get accurate information out of San Francisco because everything there is dead, and meanwhile the outages and brownouts are spreading north, into Oregon. Every time they try to bring a switch back online it causes shorts in a dozen other places and the problem just gets worse."

"That's awful," Julia said. "But what does it have to do with us? I mean, I feel for all those people. But we're kind of in a bad situation ourselves, here."

Chapel thought he might know what Angel was trying to show them. "Do you have any idea what happened?"

"That's just it. This shouldn't be possible." Angel brought up another map. It showed a single red dot near San Francisco. "There was a fire at a power plant, here. The power system is built to handle that. There's all kinds of redundancies and fail-safes built in. But then these two locations went down, just a few minutes later, and all hell broke loose." She tapped a key, and two more red dots appeared on the map. "There's not a lot of information coming out of the state—even the governor can't seem to get a press conference together. What Internet is still working out there is buzzing about this, though."

"I can imagine," Chapel said.

"There's a lot of debate. A lot of conspiracy theories, and dumb people who think they know something. I was able to find some people who actually work for the utilities commission, though, the people in charge of keeping the lights on—and they all agree. They never even bothered considering a grid failure like this. Those two locations, a switching station and a substation, had to fail at the same time as the power plant for a blackout like this, and nobody had ever thought they could have three bad failures like that at the same time. They're calling it a freak accident. A billion-to-one chance."

"I take it you don't like those odds," Chapel said.

Angel squirmed in her seat. "I mean, it *could* happen that way. Just because something is incredibly rare doesn't mean it's impossible." She scratched violently at her head. "I have a hunch," she said, as if she were admitting she was addicted to heroin.

"I trust your gut," Chapel said.

"Well, I don't!" Angel pushed herself away from the computer and sighed in frustration. "When I'm overseeing a—" She glanced in Suzie's direction. "When I'm doing what I do," she said, this time in a whisper, "I don't let myself have hunches. Hunches can be wrong, and then they can get people killed. Normally I would corroborate any suspicions I had by digging into the data. I would hack in there and get the reports from the people on the ground, the people trying to fix the power grid. I would look for discrepancies and outliers and I would build a profile to—"

Chapel put a hand on her shoulder. "It's okay," he said, because she was getting agitated to a frightening point.

"I feel so useless. Without proper equipment all I can do is guess here."

"So what's your guess?" he asked.

"I think somebody studied that system until they found the vulnerability, and then they hit those three locations with pinpoint accuracy. I'm guessing some kind of drone strike, though don't ask me what kind."

"A drone."

"Again," Angel said, "that's just a guess."

Chapel nodded. "First the Port of New Orleans. Then your trailer in New York. Now the power grid in California. All drone attacks. I'd say you've got your profile right there."

"What does all this mean?" Julia asked.

"It means," Angel said, "that whoever framed me, whoever got us in this mess, is still at it. And if I had to guess—" She shuddered in revulsion. "I don't think they're done yet. I think there will be more attacks."

SOUTH HILLS, PA: MARCH 22, 18:31

"So what happened in California, that was intentional?" Top asked. His good eye scanned around the kitchen table, looking at Chapel and then at Angel. Behind him Dolores was busy putting away groceries, but Chapel could tell she was listening in.

"Angel thinks it could have been done with a drone," Chapel said, summing up the very long explanation he'd given Top. "That seems to be their MO."

Julia, Chapel, and Angel had spent the day trying to make sense of what they knew and what they thought might be going on. They hadn't gotten much further than Angel's hunch. Now Top and his boys were coming home from their various jobs. There'd been a lot of discussion about how much they would tell Top. Chapel had finally decided they had to give him all the information they had, since they were going to need his help.

As for Dolores and the boys—which included Suzie—they didn't need to know as much. Chapel had a plan for what to do next, but it was definitely something to keep as close to the vest as possible. The big problem with that was that as the house filled up, any expectation of privacy dwindled. Out in the living room Ralph had come home and flopped on the couch. The second he'd arrived he'd started up his video-game console and was busy blowing away scores of Nazis in some war simulator. It seemed like the last thing a vet with PTSD might want to do to relax, but Ralph seemed to be enjoying himself.

The noise of the game—a constant string of explosions and gunshots—at least made it less likely that the conversation in the kitchen would be overheard.

"These drone jockeys. These the same people looking for you?" Top asked.

Chapel nodded. "Definitely."

"Who are they?"

Chapel smiled and shrugged. "We're still trying to figure that out. The only thing we know for sure is that the strikes were an inside job, carried out by somebody in the U.S. military."

"The armed forces aren't supposed to attack America, last time I checked," Top pointed out.

"I don't want to believe it either. But the NSA tracked the original hijacker back to the Pentagon. That means somebody in the military, and probably somebody in intelligence, because only somebody in intelligence would have access to the kind of computer tech to do all this. We think it's just one guy, or maybe a small group, but we just don't know how deep it goes."

Top glanced across the table at Angel. "And she's some kind of computer whiz. Gonna find out the whos and whys for you."

"We can't find a way out of this mess until we have information. She's going to get it for us, yeah. It's what she does, and nobody does it better."

Angel smiled and looked down at her hands.

Top opened his mouth to say something. Then he closed it again. He leaned back in his chair and reached out to touch Dolores's arm. "Baby, you mind asking Ralph to turn down all that noise? I can't think."

Dolores turned around and looked at Chapel, not Top. It was clear she knew what Top was really asking for—that she leave the room so she didn't hear what he said next. She barely shrugged as she headed out of the kitchen.

As soon as she was gone Top leaned back over the table and stared at Chapel wide-eyed. "And that means you need to rob a bank?" he asked.

SOUTH HILLS, PA: MARCH 22, 18:38

"We're not going to rob one," Chapel said. "Just break into one. We need the biggest, fastest computer we can get and banks have those. I know it sounds crazy, but we've worked it out as best we can. There's a bank branch about twenty miles from here, one that's not going to have much security after hours. We get in, Angel uses their computers for a couple of minutes, and then we leave."

"Security," Top said, frowning. "I know something about you, Captain Chapel. I know what kind of training they gave you in Ranger school. You can get past alarms and whatever, sure. But I'm guessing they won't make it that easy. There's no bank I ever heard of didn't have an armed guard sitting by the door all night."

Chapel nodded. "Right. But in Ranger school they taught me how to deal with guards, as well. That's one reason I'm telling you all this. I need your help. I don't plan on hurting anybody—I hope you know me that well. But I'm going to have to convince any security guards to stand down."

"You might try that winning smile of yours," Top suggested.

"I need you to loan me a gun," Chapel said.

Top pushed back from the table, shaking his head. He got up and went over to the counter and started putting away the groceries Dolores had left there. "Not going to happen," he said.

Chapel got up and moved over to his side. "I'm serious about not hurting anybody. Give me a pistol with no clip, if you have to. Give me an old handgun that doesn't even fire anymore. I need this, Top."

"Son," Top said, not looking at him. "You think I would say no, now? After that fine speech I gave you about my dog? No, I'd give you a rocket launcher if I had one, because I know who you are and I know you'd do the right thing with it. But I can't give you a gun tonight. For the simple reason I don't have one."

He turned and faced Chapel eye to eye. "I got a house here full of highly trained men and women with anger issues, with night terrors, with PTSD coming out both pant legs. Some of whom are what you might call a high suicide risk. You understand that? You think I would bring a firearm within five miles of this place?"

Chapel leaned hard against the counter. This was a real problem. There was no way he could break into a bank without some kind of weapon. The guards would just open fire the second they saw him. One thing he'd definitely learned in Ranger school was that an unarmed man facing a man with a gun was always going to lose.

"Damn," Chapel said. He glanced into the living room and saw Angel watching him from her chair. She needed him. He was going to save her, but that meant getting her into a bank. "If I had any better ideas . . ."

As if to underscore his predicament, the noise from the living room rose to a sustained pitch just then. Ralph must have been taking on a Nazi pillbox with a machine gun, judging by the sound.

Chapel tried to think of what to say next, what to do next, but the noise of the game just seemed to rattle around inside his head. He was surprised when Angel jumped up out of her chair and ran toward the television. Was she going to ask Ralph to mute the sound? That might be helpful, or—

He heard her talking to Ralph in the other room. He couldn't hear the reply, but she was asking him about his video-game console, about what generation it was and whether he had a certain accessory for it. Chapel had never had any interest in such things and wasn't sure what she was talking about.

When she poked her head back into the kitchen, though, her eyes were bright. "Um, excuse me," she said. "Can I say something?"

"Of course," Chapel told her. "What is it?"

"I think I just had one of those better ideas."

PITTSBURGH, PA: MARCH 22, 23:31

They drove past the big box store three times, just to make sure it was as deserted as it appeared. It sat well back from the road, at the far end of a well-lit but empty parking lot, surrounded on three sides by thick stands of trees. The big sign out front that read CIRCUIT BARN was lit up, but metal security gates had been pulled down across the plateglass windows that fronted the store and it looked like there were no lights on inside. Chapel had kept an eye out for police cars or any sign that someone was watching the store, but he'd seen nothing.

"You really think this'll work?" Julia asked.

Chapel shrugged. "I think we can get inside without setting off any alarms, yeah. I figure in a neighborhood like this they probably don't worry too much about robberies, so they're not likely to have a lot of security cameras. I think we're good."

"I was actually asking Angel, about her side of this," Julia said.

Chapel turned around to look at Angel in the backseat. She nodded.

"Good enough," he said.

He parked Top's car outside a Chinese restaurant a block away. The three of them headed around behind the restaurant and then made their way through the trees that screened the Circuit Barn lot. There was a chain-link fence back there, about six feet high, installed so long ago that tree branches had woven through the gaps between the chain. There was no barbed wire on top of the fence, so it was easy enough to climb up and over.

On the far side, still inside the cover of the trees, he gestured for the two women to wait a minute. He studied the back side of the Circuit Barn and saw about what he'd expected to find, a place for Dumpsters and a loading dock where trucks could bring in the store's merchandise. The loading dock had a big rolling door, but he knew that would be hooked up to the store's alarms. Another, smaller door opened into a patch of weeds strewn with old cigarette butts and decaying coffee cups. He guessed that was where the store's employees took their breaks. That was their way in.

He took one last glance around for security cameras, just in case, but he didn't see any. Then he waved Julia and Angel forward, and the three of them gathered around the employee door.

"There's almost certainly an alarm on this door," Chapel said, "so we'll need to be careful, but—"

Angel squatted down next to the door lock and pointed a little flashlight into the crack between the door and its frame. "Anybody have a stick of gum?" she asked.

"I do," Julia said, looking surprised. She rummaged in her purse, then handed the gum to Angel.

The younger woman unwrapped the gum. She handed the stick back to Julia but kept the foil wrapper. "Give me that screwdriver," she said, and Chapel handed her the flathead driver he'd brought.

For a minute Angel worked at the door, carefully folding the foil wrapper into just the right shape and then wedging it into the doorframe with the blade of the screwdriver. "The way the alarm works is there's a wire in the door and a wire in the frame, and when they meet, an electric current flows between them. If you open the door, you break that current and the system knows the door is open, so it sounds the alarm. Then there's another pair of wires for the lock. Same basic principle, but in reverse—if the current is flowing, the door stays locked, but if the current is broken, it unlocks automatically. The foil in there now will send current from the alarm wire to the lock wire so both systems think they're intact when in fact," she said, and pulled the door open, "neither of them are."

Chapel peered into the darkness behind the open door. "Where did you learn how to do this?" he asked.

Angel laughed. "Sugar, I spend all day, every day on the Internet. You get bored, you start looking at random pages. You pick up a few things."

Julia shot a look at Chapel and mouthed the word *sugar*. He shrugged in response. Angel had called him that a million times before when he was on a mission. Just never face-to-face before.

"Okay," he said. "We're in. Let me go first." He ducked inside, into a stockroom, where only a single bulb burned in the ceiling high overhead. He took in the rows of shelves holding boxed electronics, but just then he had other things to worry about. Moving quickly but silently he worked his way through an employee break room, the management offices, and then out onto the sales floor, where hundreds of television sets stared blankly back at him. There was no sign anywhere of a night watchman, no sign that anybody had been inside the store since it closed for the day.

When he was sure of it, he let himself breathe again. Then he headed back to where the women were still standing outside. "We're good," he told them. He took a prepaid cell phone out of his pocket and handed it to Julia. He showed her how to switch on its walkie-talkie mode, then turned on a second one for himself. "You're standing guard," he said.

Julia nodded. "Anything I'm looking for in particular?"

"Just let us know if you see anything at all. If anybody pulls into the lot, if somebody starts looking at our car, if you hear anything—just let me know. Angel, you're with me."

The two of them crept inside. Angel headed down the rows of shelving units in the stockroom, running her finger along the rows of boxes. Chapel winced, thinking of all the fingerprints she was leaving behind. He knew that was the least of their problems, though—breaking and entering was a much less serious crime than treason.

It didn't take her long to find what she needed. "Over here," she said.

Chapel came to stand next to her. He saw immediately what she'd found. One entire shelving unit was stuffed full of identical merchandise, big colorful cardboard boxes advertising the latest, hottest video-game system money could buy. There must have been three dozen of them sitting there, waiting to be put out on the sales floor.

"Jackpot," Angel said.

PITTSBURGH, PA: MARCH 22, 23:58

Chapel found a couple of box cutters in the stockroom and the two of them got to work, furiously slashing open the boxes and pulling out the video-game consoles. "Don't even worry about the peripherals," Angel said. "All we need are the actual consoles and their power supplies." As Chapel laid out the devices in neat rows, Angel headed down another aisle and came back with dozens of Ethernet cables cradled in her arms.

"Back before the war, you weren't allowed to sell these consoles to Iraq because they were classified as supercomputers," Angel explained. She tore open the plastic bag of a cable with her teeth. "They're not like normal computers, though, because they have different requirements. You wouldn't want to use one of these to check your e-mail, probably. What they do have is top-notch graphics cards. They need them to be able to render games at sixty frames per second. We're talking about billions of floating point operations a second. Which, by happy accident, turns out to be the same kind of operations you do while trying to break hard-core encryption."

"Seriously?" Chapel asked.

"Uh-huh. The NSA buys graphics card by the boatload. Here, do it like this." She plugged a power cable into one of the consoles, then an Ethernet cable into one of its ports. "They're also exactly what I need for the kind of data mining we're talking about."

As usual, Chapel just nodded along, understanding a tiny fraction of what she told him. This was her field of expertise. He just needed to follow orders and stay out of her way.

"The game consoles need robust connections, too," Angel went on. "To allow for multiplayer games with minimal lag. So these Ethernet connections are the best you can get. You know what a LAN party is?"

"LAN stands for, uh," Chapel said, trying to remember. "Something something network."

"Local area network. A LAN party is when a bunch of kids get their machines together in the same room and they connect them up in one big network so they can all play the same game at the same time. Which is good—it means these consoles will work well together when I put them in a serial network. They have great WAN connections, too, because they want you to use your video-game console to stream video and download patches and DLC for the games and . . ." She stopped and looked over at Chapel. "I'm just babbling now," she said.

"If it helps you focus, babble away. Just don't give me a pop quiz about all this when we're done."

Angel smiled. She plugged a cable into a console and then set it down on the floor. "We make a great team, don't we?" she asked.

"Just going on the fact that I'm still alive after all the missions we worked together, I'd say yeah," Chapel confirmed. He smiled back.

She looked at him then in a way he didn't know how to read. Over the years of listening to her voice he'd come to know her moods, the private jokes they shared. But seeing her face-to-face was like meeting a whole new person. He didn't understand what it meant when she tilted her head to the side while smiling at him. Or what it signified when she started scratching at her neck and looked away in a hurry.

He had no idea how to respond.

"Anyway," she said, "let's start plugging these together. I'm going to need a pretty serious router, but there'll be one of those around here somewhere."

"Sure," he said. "I just keep plugging them together like this?"

"Yeah," she told him. Then she laughed. "It's kind of fun, giving you orders for a change. I could get used to this."

PITTSBURGH, PA: MARCH 23, 00:22

Chapel moved around the stockroom as fast as he could, collecting all the bits and pieces Angel needed—power strips, the fastest laptop he could find, a bewildering array of cables of different pin numbers and lengths. For somebody who had just figured out the difference between USB-A and USB-B connectors, it was a harrowing process.

When it was done, though, he had to admit Angel had created something impressive. She sat on the floor with the laptop, its ports connected by a thick bundle of cables to twenty of the game consoles. These formed a ring around her, each of them wired to each other and to the store's Internet connection. Finally she attached her hard drive—the one he'd rescued from her trailer—to the laptop and switched everything on.

With a whirring of fans and a high-pitched drone like an entire hive of bees buzzing at once, the network came to life.

Angel got to work instantly. "I'm going to need to write some code, here. The consoles don't want to work as dumb processors. They're designed to prevent that kind of tampering, so I'll need to bypass their built-in operating systems." She opened a dozen windows on the laptop screen and started typing. "Luckily I don't need to start from scratch. I can grab a bunch of libraries of code off the Internet and then jerry-rig everything together."

"And then you can—what? Use the hard drive to . . ." Chapel shook his head, trying to remember what Paul Moulton had done. "Build a network analyzer?"

"That's one way, but if I'm right about something, it won't be necessary. I think we caught a lucky break."

"How so?"

"Whoever framed me took over my system when they hijacked the Predator over New Orleans. They got root access and zombified my servers, but they never bothered to log me out as an admin, so—"

"Sorry, Angel. My head already hurts. Can you simplify that?"

She looked up at him with a smile. "Considering how often this kind of stuff comes up, you really ought to learn a little about computers."

"Sure. Maybe when the police aren't chasing us, though."

She laughed. "Okay, sugar. Let me try to break it down. They took over my computer when they hijacked the Predator. They used my system to send commands to the drone and make it crash, right? It would have been really easy for them to lock me out of my own system at the same time. But they didn't. They wanted to be clever—too clever—and so they did it all in such a way I didn't even know it was happening. In fact, they didn't cut me off until hours later, when you and I were on the phone, right?"

"When your call just dropped," Chapel said, remembering how panicked he'd been when it happened.

"Yeah. Now, if they'd been smart, rather than clever, they would have taken over my system just long enough to crash the drone, then they would have shut me down altogether and severed the connection. But they didn't. They were in my computer for hours."

The whole time she spoke she kept her fingers moving over her keyboard, her thumb driving the trackpad. "Now, if you really want to hide an Internet connection, your best bet is to do what you need to do very, very fast. Every second their computer and mine were connected my server logs were recording that connection. The records are anonymized with all the packet headers stripped out, but . . . sorry!" She lifted her hands. "Too much computerese, I know. I guess—think of it like fingerprints. To hijack the drone they had to leave one smudged, partial print on my system. It would be next to impossible to get a match from that. But like a burglar who hangs around the house long after he's grabbed all the silverware, they stayed connected to my system too long. Which means they left hundreds and hundreds of partial fingerprints all over."

"And while one print on its own is useless," Chapel said, seeing where this was going, "if you can compare hundreds of them—"

"Exactly. I can get a little bit of information out of every print and combine it to get one crystal clear print that will give us a good match for our culprit. Well, theoretically."

"But—wouldn't they have known they were leaving so many clues?" Chapel asked.

"Maybe. Probably. I mean, whoever this was, they were very, very good. They should have known better."

Chapel frowned. "So why would they make such a simple mistake?"

"My best bet is that they didn't just hijack the drone. That they were doing something else while they were in there. Given the amount of time it took, I'm guessing they were reading all my drives. Copying them."

"So they have access to all the information you had stored? What would that give them?"

"A lot. A lot of info about DIA operations, missions, resources. Names, phone numbers, whole dossiers of employees." Angel shook her head. "It's bad. But at least, if this works," she said, gesturing at her screen, "we'll know who they were."

She clicked the trackpad and her screen cleared, windows closing one by one until none remained. Then she opened a new window and hit a single key.

All around her, the video-game consoles chugged and grumbled, their fans whining as they worked to keep their processors from overheating.

On Angel's screen an endless stream of characters scrolled down so fast Chapel couldn't read them.

She leaned back and rolled her head back and forth, stretching her neck muscles. "From here the program runs on its own," she said, "but it'll take a while."

Chapel nodded. "Anything you need? Anything you want me to do?"

"I can think of a couple of things, sweetie," she said.

Chapel's eyes went wide. He looked down at her, sitting there on the floor, and tried to figure out what she'd meant by that. Her face looked completely innocent, and her eyes wouldn't meet his. He decided he'd misinterpreted her words. After all, with that sultry voice of hers anything she said was going to sound a little suggestive.

"How about something to drink or eat?" he asked. "There were some vending machines in the break room."

"Caffeine," she said. "Definitely. Hacker fuel."

"You got it." He was surprised how relieved he was to leave the stockroom.

NORTH OF ALTOONA, PA: MARCH 22, 00:31

Wilkes squatted in a dark field, shying rocks at a nearby pond. He could skip them three or four times in a row, but it was hard to see in the dark and he wasn't sure if he'd managed to get five yet.

Behind him, his helicopter sat lightless and silent in the field, like the world's largest dragonfly hunkering down for the night. The pilot would be asleep. The guy had tried to start a conversation with Wilkes once, a couple of hours ago. He wasn't going to make that mistake again.

Downtime. Wilkes despised waiting. He had learned to handle it, over the years. It was something they didn't officially teach you in the Marines, but you picked it up. You learned to keep yourself simmering on low heat, never quite managing to relax fully but not letting nerves eat up your focus, either. Wilkes had started his career as a sniper, which had meant long, long hours of lying on his belly on sharp rocks, fighting to stay awake, to keep his eyes open. Because no matter how good his cover was, there was always the chance that somebody had spotted him. That he was going to have to move in a hurry.

Moulton's voice in his ear was like a buzzing insect at first. As the various parts of Wilkes's brain came back online, the noise resolved into meaningful words.

"—Pittsburgh," the little geek was saying over and over. "I'm seeing a massive spike in Internet traffic in a place that ought to be dark. Somebody's online in an electronics store that's supposed to be closed this time of night. Somebody who shows three points of similarity to Angel's profile."

"This solid?" Wilkes asked. "You got a solid lead this time?"

"That's kind of what I just told you," Moulton said. "Were you listening? We have a saying in the NSA. SIGINT never lies."

Wilkes didn't answer. He stood up, his knees popping a little because apparently he'd been squatting down by the pond longer than he thought.

Uptime.

He felt the adrenaline kick in. Felt his body come back to life, like he'd been frozen and now he was thawing out.

"Give me coordinates," Wilkes said.

"I can do better than that—I've got a floor plan for the store, I've got satellite pictures, I've got—"

Moulton kept talking. He was good at it.

Wilkes listened with half an ear as he thumped on the canopy of the helicopter. Inside, the pilot looked around him like he didn't know where he was.

"Grab your socks, buddy," Wilkes said while the pilot just blinked.

PITTSBURGH, PA: MARCH 22, 00:49

"It was definitely an inside job," Angel said. She slurped cola and pointed at her screen. "Whoever is pulling the strings, they had help."

"How can you tell?" Chapel asked.

"I keep a pretty serious lock on my stuff," she told him. "Well, I mean, I used to, I guess. It's all gone now. But if you'd asked me a week ago who could hack into my gear, I would have said nobody. Here," she said, clicking the trackpad to pause the text scrolling down her screen. "I had a firewall up here that nobody should have been able to get through. I mean, it should have been physically impossible. Considering all the sensitive data I had, it would have been insane to use anything less secure. But when the attack came, my security software didn't even register the intrusion. There's only two ways that could happen. One would be that someone broke into my trailer, actually stormed the place, and ripped the keyboard out of my hands while I was still logged in. I know that didn't happen."

"So what's the other way?" Chapel asked.

"There's a backdoor. There's always a backdoor. I wasn't working just for myself, see, so there had to be a way in for emergencies. Just in case I dropped dead of a heart attack or got hit on the head and forgot all my passwords or something. There was always a short list of people who could override me—Director Hollingshead, for one."

"You think he did this?" Chapel asked.

"No." Angel shook her head. "Absolutely not."

Chapel frowned. "In an investigation like this, sometimes it's valuable to consider everybody a suspect, even if you know they're innocent. Just—as a hypothetical."

She looked up at him and he knew instantly that she was holding something back. "It wasn't him," she said. "Just trust me on this."

"Somebody could have gotten to him. Blackmailed him or found a way to persuade him they needed access—"

"It wasn't him," she repeated. "I've got my reasons for knowing that. Please, don't push me on this. Just accept it. It wasn't Hollingshead. Anyway—it wouldn't need to be. There are other people on the list. People who might need to get into my systems without having to ask for permission. I mean, obviously the president could have done it. Or the Joint Chiefs of Staff, they would have clearance."

Chapel nodded. One of the first things you learned in the army was that everybody had a boss. Everybody. Your commanding officer answered to a major or a colonel somewhere. They answered to generals, who answered to generals with more stars. Everybody answered to the president, and even he had to answer to Congress or the Supreme Court, sometimes. Which meant that any order you got could be countermanded. "I would like to assume that the commander in chief isn't attacking his own country," Chapel said.

"We'll keep that one as a hypothetical," Angel said. She clicked her trackpad, and the text started scrolling again. "Anyway, even if it was somebody on that list, they could have been hacked and not know it, just like I was. But it would take somebody in the intelligence community to pull that off. Even the Chinese don't have the technology to break 256-bit encryption; that's something that our side just figured out, and—"

The cell phone in Chapel's pocket squawked at him. He shot a look at Angel. She suddenly looked very frightened. Well, maybe he looked the same way.

He lifted the phone to his ear. "Julia?" he said. "Did you see something?"

Her voice was just a tinny whisper when she replied. "I thought so. I guess—no. I saw something moving in the trees, but it was just a raccoon. It was—yeah. That was definitely a raccoon. Sorry. I shouldn't have bothered you."

"That's all right," Chapel said. "I'd rather have a false alarm than not get a real one. You okay out there?"

"Fine. A little chilly. How's it going inside?"

"We're making progress. Okay. Signing off," Chapel said.

He put the phone back in his pocket.

Angel laughed, though not because anything was funny. She was just relieved. "Unless the drone hijackers have figured out a way to weaponize raccoons, I guess we're okay."

Chapel nodded. "Good to keep on our toes, though. What else can you tell me about the people who hacked you?"

Angel shrugged her slim shoulders. "They're good. Really good. Even if they had backdoor access to my system, I was online at the time. I should have been able to tell there were two users active. I would have noticed a lag—the computer would have slowed down as it tried to serve two users at once. I would have felt there was something wrong."

"But you didn't? Is that possible?"

"This is kind of genius. They actually overclocked my processor. Made it run faster, just to compensate for any apparent lag. I would never have thought of that. But it tells me two things. One, that whoever did this knows computers inside and out. They aren't just good at hacking, they're legendary."

"What's the other thing?"

"They knew me, too. They anticipated what I would do, how I would react, while they were inside my system. I don't think this was anybody I know personally, but they've studied me. Watched me, probably for a long time. Chapel, that just sends chills down my spine. It means—"

Chapel's cell phone squawked again. Angel fell silent instantly as she stared at his pants pocket.

"Just another raccoon," Chapel said, because he didn't want to panic her. He took out the phone and lifted it to his ear. "Julia?" he said.

There was no response. The phone didn't even hiss or crackle in his ear. Which meant that Julia had switched off her phone altogether.

Or somebody else had done it for her.

PITTSBURGH, PA: MARCH 23, 01:32

Chapel leaned gently on the bar that opened the fire door at the back of the store. He peered out into the gloom of the loading dock but he couldn't see anything. He definitely couldn't see Julia.

He pushed the door open a few more inches. A pair of women's shoes appeared just at the edge of his view. He leaned out a little more and saw Julia down on the ground, her face covered by red hair. Her cell phone lay on the pavement a few feet away.

Somebody had stomped on it. Its case was cracked until bits of green circuit board poked out.

Chapel fought to control his emotions. Julia might be dead out there, or just unconscious. Either way, whoever had attacked her was still—

The door jumped out of his hands as someone yanked it away from him. Chapel reacted without thinking, ducking low in a crouch and exploding outward, right into the legs of his opponent. He didn't care who it was—a cop, a Chinese assassin, whatever, he had to take them down fast so he could go check on Julia.

But whoever it was, they were ready for him. They stepped aside like a matador evading a charging bull.

Chapel knew right away that he'd misjudged his charge, that he was going to end up sprawled on the ground—momentum alone would carry him there. So instead of trying to get back to his feet he swiveled at the waist and reached out to grab at his attacker's legs. The attacker was too fast and he only managed to get a handful of pant leg, but it was enough to pull the attacker off balance.

Even before Chapel hit the ground he brought his knees up, protecting his chest. As the attacker reached down for him, Chapel felt his shoulder hit the pavement. With his free hand he reached up and grabbed, not even caring what he got, just knowing he needed, desperately, to get his attacker down on the ground with him.

It almost worked. The other man should have taken a step forward as he reached for Chapel and that should have let Chapel flip him.

Instead the attacker took a step back, steadying himself.

Which left Chapel lying on the ground, looking up at the man who towered over him.

"Wilkes?" he said, completely taken by surprise. "You're dead."

The marine gave him a quick shrug. "Shit, somebody coulda told me."

Chapel shifted his weight, getting both his arms free. If he could distract Wilkes even for a split second, he could kick the man's legs out from under him. He could—

Wilkes took another step back. Then he pulled a handgun from his belt. A compact SIG Sauer 9 mm with a silencer screwed onto the barrel. "Just cool down, Jimmy. Okay?" he said, as he leveled the gun and pointed it at Chapel's face. "We're going to do this by the numbers. You keep your hands visible. I know there's no point tying you up, 'cause you'd just slip your plastic arm off or pull some kind of magic trick like that. I've read some of your after-action reports."

Chapel knew when he was beat. If he was standing, if Wilkes weren't so well trained, maybe he could have wrestled with the marine and gotten the gun away from him. But that wasn't going to happen now. "What did you do to Julia?" he asked.

"Just knocked her out. She'll wake up with a nasty headache in a while, but if she's lucky I won't be here by then. She didn't even see me coming."

Chapel blinked. "So she didn't see your face."

"Yep. Which means she comes out of this okay. Now, get up. Slowly, buddy. We both know the rules."

Chapel did as he was told. He got his knees under him, then put one foot down on the pavement, keeping his hands in the air. He turned around and let Wilkes pat him down.

"Not even a derringer in your boot, huh?" Wilkes said when he'd finished his search. "Figured you would have found a weapon by now. Never know who's going to sneak up on you in the dark. Okay, Jimmy. Let's go inside. I'll be right behind you, but not close enough to touch. Understand? Say yes if you think you got this one figured out."

"Yes," Chapel said. "Listen, Wilkes—did Hollingshead send you to bring me in? Because there are some things he needs to know."

"Open the door for me," Wilkes said.

Chapel opened the door and held it while Wilkes braced it with his foot. Then the two of them stepped into the stockroom. Chapel's eyes had adjusted to the darkness outside and now he could barely see in the dazzling light. Wilkes would probably be in the same boat, but Chapel knew that wasn't enough. It wasn't enough to get out of this without getting himself shot.

"No, it wasn't Hollingshead," Wilkes said. "The old man's been relieved of duty. Probably going to catch an espionage charge off this, if not full-on treason."

"What? He had nothing to do with this!"

Wilkes didn't respond to that. "Keep moving. Straight ahead. I'm thinking you have Angel in here, and I need her, too."

"So who are you working for?" Chapel asked. He needed to know if he was about to be arrested—or killed.

"Charlotte Holman," Wilkes told him.

"The NSA?"

"We're going to wrap up this conversation now, Jimmy," Wilkes said. "You go ahead and keep moving."

Chapel did what he was told.

This was bad. This was very, very bad. The jig was up, and he would spend the rest of his life in jail. There was no way he could fight Wilkes, nor was there any way he could run, not without being shot.

There was only one bright spot in the whole thing.

As Wilkes marched him into the middle of the stockroom, into the circle of video-game consoles arrayed on the floor, there was no sign of Angel.

She'd been smart enough to get away.

At least one of them had.

PITTSBURGH, PA: MARCH 23, 01:39

"You go stand over there, against those shelves," Wilkes said. Then he stepped over the ring of video-game consoles and prodded the laptop with his shoe. "Interesting setup here. You organizing another drone attack?"

"Angel had nothing to do with those," Chapel said. "She was framed. The thing in California, with the power station—she couldn't have done that."

"She could have programmed the drone to do it in advance, put it on a timer," Wilkes said. He shrugged. "Honestly, I don't give a crap. I'm not here to solve a big mystery, Jimmy. I'm not a detective."

"Then why are you here?"

Wilkes gave him a big shit-eating grin. Then he squatted down next to the laptop, the gun still trained on Chapel. He picked up the hard drive attached to the laptop. Standing up, he lifted the hard drive until the laptop dangled in the air by the cord that connected them. He gave the hard drive a good swift yank and it came free, the laptop crashing to the floor.

"This is it, huh? What you stole from that trailer. The last part of Angel."

Chapel said nothing.

Wilkes dropped the hard drive. It hit the concrete floor with a bang. He lifted one booted foot and stamped down hard on the metal box.

Something inside it cracked. Then, perhaps for good measure, he lowered his pistol and put two bullets into the casing.

Even with the silencer the gunshots were loud enough to make Chapel's ears ring. The noise echoed and reverberated around the stockroom.

It was almost enough to mask the sound of someone grunting in frustration behind Wilkes.

Almost. Chapel forced himself not to look over there. If Wilkes hadn't heard it, he didn't want to draw the marine's attention to the fact that Angel was still in the stockroom, hidden behind a shelving unit.

It turned out not to matter. Almost before the echoes had finished bouncing around the room, she gave another grunt, loud enough that anyone could have heard it.

Wilkes didn't waste time speaking. He brought the pistol back up to point at Chapel, but turned his head to look behind him.

Just in time to see the entire shelving unit, ten feet high and packed with boxes of electronics, come crashing down on him.

Boxes and video-game consoles went everywhere, sliding across the floor. Wilkes let out a sound that was half gasp and half cry of rage as he disappeared from view.

Where the shelving unit had been, Angel was revealed, standing there breathing hard and looking terrified.

"Go," Chapel shouted at her. "Get Julia—get out of here!"

He could hear Wilkes moving around under the pile of debris. A pile of blister-packed toner cartridges slid off the heap like an avalanche down the side of a cardboard mountain. There wasn't much time.

Angel still stood there, looking like she had no idea what she'd just done.

"Go!" Chapel shouted again.

This time she took the hint, sprinting toward the fire door.

Chapel approached the debris pile carefully, not knowing where exactly Wilkes might be under all the boxes and broken electronics. He could hear the man moving, trying to escape. He might be badly injured down there. Or merely incapacitated for a second.

Boxes shifted and heaved, and for a second Chapel expected Wilkes to come rearing up out of the mess, howling like a wounded bear. That didn't happen, though. The boxes settled, finding their own level. Chapel couldn't hear Wilkes anymore. Had the marine passed out in there? Was he dead?

Chapel reached down carefully and pulled a box off the top of the pile.

The 9 mm appeared in the gap. Chapel could see one of Wilkes's eyes under the debris.

The pistol fired. The noise and the muzzle flash blinded and deafened him and he could only stagger backwards, away from the attack.

It took Chapel a second to realize he'd been shot.

PITTSBURGH, PA: MARCH 23, 01:43

It wasn't the first time Chapel had caught a bullet.

In fact, he knew the feeling all too well. Shock would keep most of the pain away until he ran out of adrenaline and his body had to accept what had happened to it. Shock couldn't spare him the wave of nausea and weakness that spread through his guts, though.

He put pressure on the wound with his artificial hand and tried to breathe. He needed to think, he needed to plan—

He needed to run.

The pile of boxes was already moving, shifting, as Wilkes struggled to get free. Wilkes was still alive and conscious and armed down there, and any second now he would jump up and finish what he'd started. Chapel ducked around the side of the debris pile, desperately hoping Wilkes didn't just shoot him again as he passed by. He headed through the stockroom, not looking back, and crashed into the push bar of the fire door with his good arm. Hitting the door sent a wave of pain through his chest, but he ignored it and kept moving.

Outside, on the dark loading dock, he saw nothing that could help him. Julia was gone—Angel must have woken her up and gotten her out of there. The two of them could be sitting in the car just a hundred yards away, waiting for him. He hoped not. For one thing, he wanted them gone so they would be safe, so that they would be far away from Wilkes. For another thing, getting to them would mean climbing over the chain-link fence again.

Wounded as he was, that wasn't going to happen.

Behind him, inside the store, he heard something heavy crash and fall. That would be Wilkes working himself free.

Chapel studied the terrain around him. Behind the electronics store lay a long stretch of undeveloped woodland, a dark forest that would offer some cover. He started running for those trees, knowing they were his only chance.

Halfway there the pain showed up to the party. It was like his nervous system had just realized he'd been shot and was replaying the experience to see what it had missed. Lancing pain shot through his side. Muscles from his groin up to what remained of his left shoulder twisted into knots, and red spots flashed before his eyes. He doubled over, wondering if he was going to throw up, wondering if he was just going to collapse in a heap right there, right then.

No. He refused to just stop now. Chapel gritted his teeth and forced his legs to get moving. They weren't injured, after all.

Bent nearly double, he half walked, half ran into the trees. Darkness flooded over him, but he told himself that was just because the branches of the trees were blocking out the moonlight. It had nothing to do with his brain desperately wanting to pass out and sleep through the pain that only kept getting worse.

Behind him he heard the fire door slam open. Chapel ducked low to try to avoid being seen.

A bullet smashed through a thin tree branch just over his head, showering him in chips of wood and bark. Apparently Wilkes could see him just fine.

That was the impetus he needed.

Chapel ran.

PITTSBURGH, PA: MARCH 23, 01:46

Keeping one hand on his wound, Chapel waved the other in front of him, fending off low branches and preventing himself from running headlong into a tree trunk. He could see almost nothing at all, just the occasional flash of dark sky or the silhouette of a tree limb like a talon grasping at his face.

The ground behind the electronics store sloped gradually downward, and up ahead Chapel could hear running water—a creek or a stream or something. He had no idea how far these woods extended, or what might lie on the other side. If he lived long enough to get there, he would worry about it then.

Behind him he heard Wilkes's heavy boots crunching through drifts of fallen leaves left over from the previous autumn. Chapel probably made as much noise himself, but it was lost under the constant roar of blood in his ears and the sound of his own breathing as it howled in and out of his chest.

He had no idea how far behind Wilkes might be, or how long it would take the marine to catch up to him. He had no real idea, even, of how much ground he was covering, or whether he was just crawling along at a snail's pace. He kept moving forward because stopping or slowing down meant his death, that was all. It was the only thought in his head.

Behind him—right behind him—Wilkes stepped on a branch and it exploded under his boot with a noise very much like a gunshot. Chapel rolled to the side in case the killer was about to pounce, thinking he would head sideways and maybe lose Wilkes that way. Instead, he slipped in the mud and went sprawling forward. His good right hand swung out before him, looking for anything to grab.

It found nothing. Chapel's feet slid out from under him and the ground just seemed to give way.

The creek he'd heard had dug a narrow but deep ravine through the soil of the forest, and Chapel had blundered right over the edge of a steep slope. He could do nothing to stop or even slow his fall—he could only curl into a ball as he bounced off rocks and exposed tree roots, hurtling down into the defile. Above him he heard Wilkes cry out, "Holy shit," and the only thought in Chapel's head was, *That about sums it up.*

Sliding down the loose dirt of the slope, he came up very short as a fallen log caught and stopped him. His head bounced off the rotten wood hard enough that his vision lit up with a bright light. He felt skin come off his cheek as it rasped against the rough log. Icy water filled his shoe and his mouth was full of mud.

Okay, that sucked, he thought—when his brain was capable of anything but silent shrieks of pain and fear. *Now get up.*

Get up.

His body refused to obey. He couldn't even lift his head. Chills ran up and down his spine, but he felt too weak to even shiver.

"Chapel?" Wilkes called out, from high above. "Jimmy? You down there? I know I heard you fall down there. You want to just give up now?"

Chapel couldn't have replied, even if he wanted to.

"I just want to talk. Honest."

He couldn't tell if Wilkes was being sarcastic or not. He *was* pretty sure that talking wasn't the only thing on the marine's agenda.

"Come on, Jim. I could just start shooting in the dark down there. I could just hose you down with bullets. I mean, it would be a waste of good lead. But I bet I could hit you at least once. And I'm guessing one more would finish you off. Why don't you just talk to me, instead?"

Chapel realized suddenly that his eyes were closed. His injuries had exhausted him to the point where he could have gone to sleep right there on the edge of the creek.

Talking was out of the question.

It was possible that he did pass out. It was hard to tell the difference between unconsciousness and the dark, cold place he was in. He was certain time got away from him, drifting through his awareness like smoke. An hour? Thirty seconds? Who knew how long it was before he heard something else.

When the sound did come, it was a scatter of pebbles and twigs raining all around him, as if Wilkes had gotten frustrated and just chucked a handful of the forest itself down at him. One rock hit his leg hard enough to sting, but still Chapel made no sound.

"Well, shit," Wilkes said.

And then Chapel heard boots crunching through leaves, and the sound was moving away from him. Receding.

Wilkes was just walking away.

Maybe he thought Chapel was already dead. Maybe he thought Chapel had crawled off, out of his reach. Chapel had no idea what the marine was thinking.

He didn't much care, either.

He waited a while longer—not that he had much choice. Marshaling his energy, conserving his strength. Sure.

When he did finally move, his first attempt was pretty feeble. He just rolled over onto his back. That didn't achieve much, but it let him take an inventory of his various injuries. He felt like he had a lot of new bruises, but nothing had broken in the fall. That was good.

His gunshot wound was still bleeding. That was pretty bad.

Staying down, keeping out of sight might be a good way to avoid being shot again. But if he did that, he was just going to bleed to death. He needed to move. His body was adamantly against the idea, and it had a pretty firm veto to work with, since he wasn't going anywhere on sheer brain power. But he had to move.

Damn it, he had to move.

His body disagreed.

It was his foot that cast the lone dissenting vote. It was freezing in the stream and it really wanted to get out of the water. Eventually it twitched enough that his whole leg moved and pulled the foot free.

It was something. It was something to work with. Chapel forced himself to move his other leg as well, and then to roll up into a sitting position, leaning against the fallen log. He sat there panting for a while, after so much exertion.

He had another ally. His artificial arm didn't recognize that his body was in shock or that it wanted to shut down. It had its own energy supply and it moved when he wanted it to, damn it, not when it felt like it. With his legs and his prosthetic arm he forced himself to lunge upright, to get on his feet.

Good, he thought. *Better.* Maybe—maybe he had a chance.

Then he realized what he was going to have to do next, and it made him want to break down and cry.

He was at the bottom of the stream. He had no idea where the stream went or how far he would have to walk along its course to get anywhere. Looking back, he saw the slope he'd fallen down. Cliff might be a better term. Climbing back up there was way beyond his capacities.

That just left the other side of the stream. There was a slope there, too. It looked a lot gentler than the one he'd fallen down, a lot more climbable. But that was a relative concept considering the state he was in.

When life gives you a lot of bad choices, he told himself, *take the lesser evil, right?* He tried to convince himself of that as he splashed across the stream and more or less fell against the far slope. He reached up with his artificial hand and tried to find something to grab, something he could use to haul himself upward. He found an exposed root that would make an excellent handhold. He grabbed it in both hands and *pulled*.

If he hadn't know there was an armed assassin somewhere nearby, he might have screamed. It felt like he was being torn in half. The wound in his side blared with agony, and blood spurted from the neat hole in his skin.

Before he could let himself think about it, he scrabbled to get his legs under him, to find anything solid in the slope that he could use as a foothold. A big rock gave him a little purchase. He used it. He would use anything he could get.

He reached up. Found another root. *Pulled*—

"Jesus," he whimpered. "Jesus, Jesus, Jesus." The pain was so bad he couldn't keep quiet.

He reached for another handhold. No way he was stopping now.

Little by little he pulled himself up. Kicked his shoes into the mud, grabbed handfuls of grass, pressed himself against the slope every time he started to slide back down. Inch by inch he climbed.

And then somehow he reached the top. He pulled himself up onto ground that was firm enough to hold his weight and he was there, he was at the top.

On the far side of the defile stood more trees. More dark woods for him to grope his way through, with no indication they would ever end.

He'd come too far to give up. He kept moving, his head bobbing, both arms waving in front of him to ward off branches and tree trunks. He stumbled, he staggered, but he kept moving, kept fighting for another step, another.

One of his feet kicked something very hard and unyielding. He dropped to all fours and felt it. It had the pebbly, rough texture of asphalt.

He'd found a road. He couldn't see it, couldn't tell where it went, there was no light to make anything out, but—

Then, suddenly, there was far too much light, and the screaming noise of a car horn going off right next to his ear.

It was all he could do to lift his artificial arm in the air and wave it, to try to get the driver's attention, to make them stop in time.

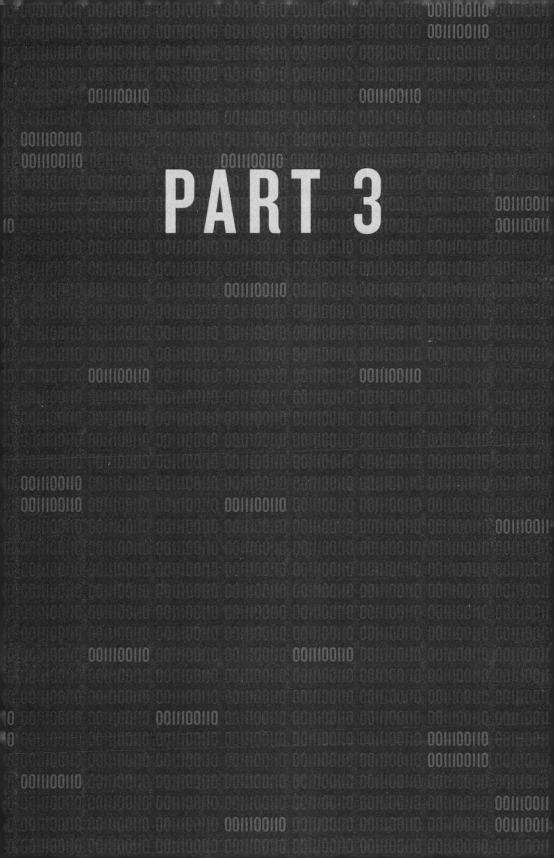

PART 3

WASHINGTON, D.C.: MARCH 23, 09:57

Wilkes got some stares as he walked into the little restaurant. He had some visible bruises, but he didn't think that was it. This was some kind of upscale place with folded linen napkins and chairs that looked like they would collapse if you sat down in them too hard. The tables were covered in shiny goblets of orange juice and ice water, and the people were all dressed in suits or business skirts and they all had great haircuts.

It was pretty tough for the marine not to plunk himself down, put his boots up on one of the tiny tables, and order a cheap domestic beer.

Instead he walked up to where Charlotte Holman sat with another man—Arnold Grauen, the director of the whole NSA. Her boss and, just then, his. He came up to the table and saluted, even though they were both civilians.

There was an almost audible sigh from the other tables. They'd had trouble figuring out what a roughneck like Wilkes was doing in their fancy eating establishment, but this was, after all, D.C. You saw soldiers in D.C. all the time. Once they'd put him in the right pigeonhole, the fancy people could all forget that he existed and go back to enjoying their fancy lives.

"Please," Holman said, "sit down. This is just an informal meeting."

"Yes, ma'am," Wilkes said. He took one of the empty chairs—careful to make sure it would support his weight—and put one of the starched white napkins in his lap.

The two of them, the subdirector and the honest-to-god director, both had plates of fruit and brown bread in front of them. Holman was drinking orange juice or maybe a mimosa and Grauen had a Bloody Mary. Wilkes wondered if he could get some good, plain coffee. It had been a long night.

"I was just bringing the director up to speed," Holman explained. "I've told him that you secured the remaining hard drive of the Angel system and that you made contact with Captain Chapel."

"Winged him, did you?" Grauen asked, dabbing at his lips with a napkin. He didn't look like much, even if he was one of the top spymasters in the country. Weedy and thin, with a receding hairline and wire-framed glasses. Wilkes had heard Holman talk about him before and he knew she thought Grauen was worse than useless. A presidential appointee who had almost no experience in real intelligence work, and no great desire to learn how things were done. The man was an impediment to her work.

Still, sometimes you had to play nice. Even though the secretary of defense had put Holman in charge of this mission, she still had to report to her boss on her progress. Wilkes had been called in from the field to brief the man. A bullshit job, but it had to be done. He folded his hands in his lap. "Yes, sir," he said.

"Were you trying to kill him?" Grauen asked, his eyes blank. As if he'd just asked for the time.

"No, sir," Wilkes said. "It was my intention to detain him for questioning. However, he assaulted my person and I was forced to defend myself. He evaded capture, but when I last saw him he had lost a great deal of blood. It's possible he died in those woods. I requested assistance from local law enforcement this morning and they are right now searching the area, looking for his body."

"You think they'll find it?" Grauen asked.

He was asking if Chapel was dead. "I believe so, sir. Until they do I wouldn't like to assume anything, however."

The director took a sip of his drink. "What about the hard drive?"

Wilkes opened his mouth to answer, but Holman beat him there. "We have it at a secure location, sir," she said. "I have my best man, Paul Moulton, working on it right now. He's already given me a preliminary report, and I'm afraid the news isn't good."

Intelligence people were trained to be pretty good at telling lies, but this woman was a pro. It was hard for Wilkes not to crack a nasty grin as he listened to her spin out her line of nonsense.

The director bought it, of course. He sighed deeply. "We've inherited quite a jackpot, haven't we? All right, spit it out. What's gone wrong now?"

Holman pursed her lips. "We found concrete evidence that rogue elements of the DIA—namely, Rupert Hollingshead's working group—were behind the attacks in both New Orleans and California. It's helpful to be sure about that. Unfortunately we also discovered that while the Angel system is no longer operational, there are other systems. Other neural networks, scattered around the country. Still online and ready to carry out more attacks."

"Fuck," Grauen said, his eyes going wide as if he was choking on his cantaloupe. "How many? When? Where?"

"That remains to be determined. My analyst is working on it nonstop. He'll have more soon. The main thing right now is that we need to make sure that Chapel is dead. And then we need to start thinking about bringing in Hollingshead for . . . questioning. It will of course have to be done quietly, perhaps under the National Defense Authorization Act provisions."

The director stared at her. He put his fork down very carefully.

"Am I hearing you correctly?" He asked. "You want me to bring in a subdirector of military intelligence under a secret NDAA warrant? You understand what that means, I'm sure. They'll stick him in front of a military tribunal without any due process. Jesus, Charlotte. You know I can't do that without presidential approval. You really have enough evidence for that?"

"We do—it's all on that hard drive. And I think we need to move on this right away. The NSA is already monitoring all his communications and anyone he meets with, but I'd like to have guards put on him to ob-serve his movements at all times. We still don't know if he has the capacity to activate one of those neural networks and initiate another attack."

"You're suggesting he's personally behind all of this," Grauen said. "I've known Rupert for years. He never struck me as the type to betray his country."

"He didn't? He's never gotten along with the rest of the intelligence community. A few years ago he went to extraordinary lengths to destroy Tom Banks over at the CIA. He's not one of us. He's made that very clear. What if he decided *we* were the traitors, and somehow thought he could bring us down with these attacks?"

Grauen pushed himself back from the table. "I'll authorize the guard detail around him," he said. "And I'll talk to the president. But you'd better be sure about this. If Hollingshead goes down, it's going to tear the entire intelligence community in half. Every director at every agency is going to wonder if they're next." He stood up and adjusted the sleeves of his suit jacket. "I want constant updates," he said.

"You'll have them," Holman assured him. She gave him a very warm smile and reached up to touch his hand. "Please give my best to Sarah and the children."

The director nodded and then hurried off.

"You are one sly fox, lady," Wilkes said when he was out of earshot. "When you called me into this meeting, I thought it was going to be some pointless backgrounder. Politics and bullshit. Instead I got to watch you crucify your worst enemy. Even if the president says no, he'll have to lock Hollingshead down tight, just to cover his ass in case there are more attacks." He wanted to applaud, he was so impressed. Instead he reached for a menu. "French toast sounds pretty good, if they don't have pancakes. And I am in serious need of coffee."

Holman tapped the top of the menu with one perfectly manicured finger. Wilkes lowered it to look at her.

The cold fury in her eyes might have turned another man to jelly on the spot.

"You'll eat when Chapel is dead and you can prove it," she told him.

Wilkes knew better than to snap back at her. "Ma'am," he said, very quietly, very patiently, "when I shoot a man at point-blank range, he goes down."

She shook her head. "Get the fuck back out there. Find me a body. And you'll start operating according to our protocols from now on. Moulton tells me you weren't even wearing your hands-free set during the operation. You broke communication with him at the most vital time."

Dude's a little turd, Wilkes thought, because he couldn't say it out loud. *He would have just distracted me.* Out loud he said, "Yes, ma'am."

SOUTH HILLS, PA: MARCH 23, 11:38

Chapel couldn't move. He was frozen in place. He tried to talk, but even his lips and tongue were completely immobile.

People surrounded him. Injured people.

People with pieces missing.

"I'll take that arm, if he ain't using it," Ralph said, fiddling with the straps on his own prosthetic. "I mean, if that's cool."

"Dibs on his leg," someone else said. "It's not fair he got to keep it this whole time."

"All of you, out of my way," Top said, pushing the others away. He grinned down into Chapel's face. "I got seniority here. Let me take a look at that eye," he said, and his teeth started growing points. "You're dead, army man. You're dead and we're not. Sure you see how that adds up."

And then there were hands on him, hands at his knees and his shoulder, hands that twisted at his skin, twisted *hard* and his joints started coming unscrewed, his bits and pieces coming loose and there was less of him, less of him all the time . . .

Jim.

Everything faded away. It didn't so much go black as it just vanished. All the people, the room, his body.

Just nothing left.

Nothing.

Jim. Can you hear me?

Jim!

So far away. So far away and calm. Nothing there to worry about, nothing that could hurt him now. He felt no remorse, no regrets. It was all going to be okay, because when there was nothing left, nothing mattered.

Blink or something! Please, Jim, stay with me!

A little bit of light touched him. It annoyed him, in that nonplace. He tried to move away from it, but the light just followed him around, and it kept getting brighter and brighter.

He's not breathing—

I've got a pulse, but it's—

Hold his legs, he'll hurt himself thrashing like that—

The light tried to go away. For some reason that bothered him, so he chased after it. He had no legs, so he wasn't running, but somehow he could move, move with the light, even as it fled away from him so fast, even as it dwindled until it was just a star on the horizon, until—

Until it went out.

SOUTH HILLS, PA: MARCH 23, 15:02

With his eyes closed, there was nothing around him but sounds and smells. Some of the smells were repulsive. The stink of antiseptic cleaning products. The smell of his own body, which really needed a wash.

The sounds were better. They were soft, low sounds. Unobjectionable. The sound of his own breathing, of the air going into his body and then slowly, slowly leaking out. The rumbling, rolling hum of a washing machine in spin cycle, somewhere close by.

The tiny cascade of sound that hair made as it brushed the skin of his hand. The hair smelled good, too, so much better than he did. It smelled like a woman's hair.

Soft lips touched the back of his hand. Fingers gripped his, held them tight. That felt good. It felt like those fingers would keep him from floating away again. From disappearing.

The hair brushed his hand again and this time he felt it, felt a thousand little tingles as each individual hair met the nerve endings in his flesh.

Would that hair be red or brown? He kind of wanted to know. He wanted to open his eyes and find out. He took a deep breath and consciously willed his eyelids to flutter open, so he could see, so he could—

The pain hit him so hard that tears burst across his vision. His head roared with blood and with agony and his whole torso spasmed and shook. It felt like he'd been nailed down to the floor with a huge iron spike. It felt like he was a bug pinned to a board, wriggling its legs desperately to try to get free, only hurting itself worse in its desperation.

"Jim! Jim, try not to move—try to calm down, I know it hurts, I know it hurts, but you'll reopen your wound. We didn't have any painkillers, nothing stronger than ibuprofen, please, please try to calm down!"

He forced himself to put his head back. To stretch his legs out so they wouldn't thrash. He tried to focus on breathing, even though every time he inhaled it felt like he was being run through with bayonets.

Eventually, after far too much time had passed, he quieted down again. His body came back under his control. The pain was still there, it was absolutely not going away, but if he didn't move, if he was very careful with his breathing, it couldn't take control of him.

When he was finally able to blink the tears away, he looked down and saw Angel sitting beside him, pressing her face against his hand. She looked terrified.

Julia stood over him, doing something to the bandage on his other side. He knew the look on her face, though it took him a second to place it. It was the look she got when she examined a dog or a cat in her clinic, when she had to be very careful to keep her expression neutral so the owner wouldn't panic.

"Am I going to die?" he asked.

Julia leaned over him and looked directly into his eyes. He realized she was checking his pupils.

"I don't know," she said.

SOUTH HILLS, PA: MARCH 23, 19:31

"We found you crawling in the road. You nearly got run over by a car. The driver wanted to take you to a hospital," Julia explained. Angel was nowhere in sight.

"Wilkes would have found me there and finished the job."

Julia nodded. "That's what Angel thought. I kept telling her there was no way I could treat you without a lot of equipment and drugs, but she was adamant. She convinced the driver that we would take care of you. He seemed relieved not to have to let you into his car."

"I was a real mess," Chapel said. "Probably covered in mud and scraped to hell."

Julia nodded. "Yes, you were. Not to mention having a gunshot wound, a concussion, and general shock. We brought you back here to Top's. Set up a makeshift operating room in his basement. Prisoners of war get better medical treatment." She scrubbed at her face with her hands and sat down hard in a chair. "You want all the gory details?"

"Just the highlights."

Julia nodded. "The bullet didn't penetrate the abdominal cavity. It just tunneled through muscle tissue. It was a through and through wound, too. No fragments inside you that I could find. The wound track missed your kidney by about an inch, but it nicked an artery on the way through and that's why you lost so much blood. I cleaned out the wound as best I could and sutured you, but I'm still very much worried about sepsis. That bullet cut through your shirt and probably blasted cotton fibers halfway through your abdomen and some of them would be so small I couldn't see them, not with my naked eye, which was all I had to work with. Those fibers can cause some pretty ugly infections. We should be starting you on heavy-duty antibiotics right away. There's only one problem. We don't have any. None of them here in the house, and nobody here has a prescription. I can't write a prescription for you, not with the cops looking for me. So unless we start knocking over pharmacies, we just have to hope for the best."

"How long until I'm on my feet?"

Julia laughed. "With anyone else, I'd say weeks. For you—well. Bed rest isn't how you operate, is it? There are no broken bones, and the wound should stay closed unless, you know, you try to run, or jump over a fence, or get in a fistfight."

"Those are some of my favorite things," Chapel pointed out.

"You can walk a little tomorrow. We'll see about the heroics. Jim— there's a takeaway here. A really important point you need to remember."

"Okay," he said.

"Sepsis is not funny. You could have an infection right now. You could develop one next week. You might get feverish, or you might not. You might get stomach cramps or you might not. Those will be the symptoms to look for. Even if they don't show up, that doesn't mean you're well. If the infection goes unchecked too long, you could just die. Just up and die with no warning at all. At any time."

"When this is over—"

She laughed again. "I've heard that one before."

"When this is over," he said, "I'll check myself into a hospital and swallow every pill I can find. But right now if I show my face in public, I'm going to get killed. We need to work this case. I need to work this case. Right now, I need to talk to Angel."

SOUTH HILLS, PA: MARCH 23, 19:43

With some help from Julia, he managed to sit up. It was a small victory.

They had him on a folding cot in the basement. Julia told him he'd raved and screamed when they brought him in so they'd taken him down there so the neighbors wouldn't hear. "Though Top tells me," Julia said, "given all the people in this house who get night terrors, the people next door probably wouldn't notice the difference. Anyway, I figured it was best to keep you away from windows. And down here you won't be bothered all the time. Suzie's already complaining that she needs to use the gym equipment down here, but Dolores . . . well, Dolores shut her up."

Chapel smiled. Smiling didn't hurt.

"I'll bring Angel down so you can talk," Julia said. She didn't move from the side of the bed, though. "She's . . . Jim, she's in pretty bad shape. We almost lost you and she took it very hard."

"Angel's tough," he pointed out.

Julia nodded. "Sure. I noticed, for instance, that she didn't cry much over the bump *I* got on my head."

Chapel cursed himself silently for forgetting that Julia had been injured, too. Too late to say anything, he supposed.

"Just go easy on her," Julia said. She turned to go, but before she'd taken two steps she looked back at him. The expression on her face mystified him. It was a pointed, searching look like she knew he'd done something wrong but wasn't ready to accuse him yet. He had no idea what that was about.

She left before he had a chance to ask. A few minutes later Angel came down the stairs. Her eyes were puffy, and she looked like she hadn't slept in a long time. She came and sat next to him and reached over to hold his hand.

"I guess I look pretty bad, huh?" he asked. He looked down at himself. The lower half of his torso was wrapped in gauze. His artificial arm was sitting a few feet away on top of a bookshelf, the fingers dangling over the edge. He didn't have access to a mirror, but he could tell from the pain in his face that he was covered in scrapes and bruises.

Angel cleared her throat. "I—" She stopped and looked like she was struggling with her words. "Uh."

"Was there any more to that thought?" he asked.

She nodded and he watched as she composed herself, sitting up straight in her chair, clearing her throat a few times. "This isn't the first time you've been injured."

"No," he agreed.

"I've listened to you being shot before. I've seen video of what you looked like after the Russians worked you over. I never exactly liked it, sweetie. But this is different. Seeing it for real. Helping Julia clean out your wound . . . it was . . . it was tough."

"I'm still here," he told her. "I made it."

She looked away. "We're supposed to be a team. Partners."

"That's exactly what we are," he told her. "You proved that last night, as if you needed to. You saved my life when you pushed over those shelves. Wilkes came there to kill me and you stopped him. I can't tell you how grateful I am."

She nodded but she didn't say anything.

"Angel—is there something we need to talk about?"

Her cheeks turned red while he watched. She didn't answer his question, though. "Not now. We should—we should talk about other things. About how we get out of this mess. Right, sugar?"

"Yeah," he said. "Yeah. Okay. So . . ." It took him a second, weak as he was, to get his brain back in gear. "So last night didn't end the way we'd hoped. How far did you get with your search for the hijacker?"

She let go of his hand and sat back in her chair. "Well, there's bad news. And then there's some news that is almost good. The bad news is, I didn't get a chance to complete the search. I still have no idea who took over my computer."

"It was the NSA," he told her.

She looked stunned.

He didn't blame her. "Wilkes told me that he was working for Charlotte Holman. She's a subdirector of the NSA."

"But that just means they're the ones tasked with arresting us," Angel pointed out.

"Sure—if he had any plans on bringing us in. No. He was there to kill us, Angel. He came there specifically to kill us. I don't care how angry the government is about these drone attacks. They wouldn't want us dead, at least, not until they've had a chance to interrogate us. Killing us is a downright stupid play. Unless—"

"Unless they're trying to cover their tracks," Angel said, nodding.

"Sure. They frame us, then kill us so we never get a chance to clear our names. But I don't know. The National Security Agency is pretty scary, but they don't kill people, as a rule. They're analysts. They leave that to the clandestine agencies."

"That's why they needed Wilkes. They've convinced him we're guilty. I thought he might have a little more loyalty to Hollingshead, but . . ."

Angel bit her lip. "Do you remember when you asked me to look into his background? Because the two of you were working together and you wanted to know who you got stuck with?"

"Sure. Back when we were still working the Contorni case out at the Aberdeen Proving Ground. You said you couldn't find anything dirty in his file."

"I didn't. He was a model operative in MARSOC. But I did find out his operational specialty. He was trained as a sniper, and then for high value targeting."

"Targeting . . . you mean, he was an assassin."

Angel nodded. "He killed at least three people in Iraq and Yemen. Maybe more—there were hints of some operations so compartmentalized even I couldn't dig them up."

Chapel closed his eyes. "Guys like that are trained to kill without worrying about why. Yeah. I can see one of those guys turning on us, if the order came from high enough up. Damn."

"I was confused when the director brought Wilkes into our group—I had no idea why he would want such a person," Angel said.

Chapel thought he knew why. More than once Hollingshead had ordered him to kill somebody. He'd always responded by saying he wasn't a hit man. He'd found other ways to complete his missions. But for a guy with a job like Hollingshead's, sometimes an executioner was exactly what you needed.

Chapel had never gotten to know many marines, other than Top and Rudy. They didn't socialize with army grunts like himself. He knew very little about MARSOC, much less its assassins. But he knew enough to be sure of one thing: they didn't give up. They completed the missions they were given or they died trying.

Wilkes had orders to kill him. Chapel had gotten away once, but nothing was over. He would have Wilkes on his tail for the rest of his life—or until somebody high up changed Wilkes's orders.

He doubted the NSA would do that any time soon.

"NSA works with assassins all the time," Chapel said. "But not directly. They call it selective targeting. They provide Geo Cell data on terrorists, tracking them by their SIM cards, and then CIA or JSOC carries out the actual strikes, either with drones or with commandos. Them bringing Wilkes in to do the dirty work fits with their standard operating procedure."

"The NSA fits a lot of the other evidence as well. We know it was an inside job, and we know it was done by somebody with real skill when it comes to computers. Well, the NSA are the best in that field."

"Present company excluded," Chapel said, smiling.

Angel wasn't joking, though. "Sugar, I'm damned good at what I do. But I'm not at all surprised that the NSA beat me at my own game. They've got scary skills over there in the puzzle palace. They may not be the most creative hackers, but just using brute force attacks, they can beat anybody's security. Hijacking those drones is almost beneath them. Finding backdoor access to my system would seem like a fun challenge."

Chapel shrugged. It hurt. A lot. When he could see straight again, he said, "So we know who is after us. We still have no idea why. Why would the NSA attack the United States?" He started to shake his head, then thought better of it. "Why they want to take down Hollingshead and his directorate is a whole other mystery."

"Wait a minute," Angel said, leaning in close as if to hear him better. "They're framing us, but the director—"

"Wilkes told me he's been relieved from duty. They're trying to charge him with treason for sending me to rescue you."

"Chapel. We have to stop them," she said.

"I'm right there with you."

"No," she said. Her face had lost all its color. "We have to save the director. I—I can't explain why. But you have to promise me, we'll get him clear of this. Please."

He reached over and took her hand. "I'm pretty fond of him myself," he said. "I promise. We'll do whatever it takes. But it looks like the best way to achieve that is to clear our own names."

She nodded and looked down at their clasped hands. "That's going to be tricky now," she said. "We lost my hard drive, so I don't have the intrusion data to work with. And even if I did, it's obvious that if I try to go online and trace them, they'll know exactly where I am. And then they'll just send Wilkes to kill you again."

"So we can't try again to find the evidence we need," Chapel said.

Angel nodded. "I'm useless. I'm a liability to you."

"I refuse to accept that," he said. "You said earlier there was some almost good news."

She pulled her hand away. "My search was interrupted before I could find any real evidence of who framed me. I didn't find anything that would stand up in court. I couldn't get a name or any real information about who did it. But I did turn up one thing."

"What's that?"

"Their street address," she said.

SOUTH HILLS, PA: MARCH 23, 20:16

"Wait," Chapel said, sitting up a little more. He ignored the pain. "You know where they live?"

"Don't get too excited," Angel told him. "I analyzed some of the packets from the intrusion and ran them through a WHOIS lookup, that's all. Normally I wouldn't even bother. It's way too easy to fake this kind of thing."

"You thought it was worth doing this time," Chapel said.

Angel shrugged. She went over to the desktop computer in the corner of the room behind Suzie's punching bag. She woke the computer from sleep and then brought up a browser window that showed a page of text. It was too far away for Chapel to be able to read any of it.

"I know you don't like tech talk, so I'll try to keep this simple. When the NSA broke into my system, they had to do so from an IP address, and if you have an IP address you can find all sorts of things. What browser somebody's using, what plug-ins they have installed, who their ISP is, and, to a certain degree of accuracy, a physical location."

"That's a little scary."

"It would be if it was reliable information. It isn't—the location isn't precise, and it's really, really easy to hide. Just putting yourself behind a proxy server is enough. Using a TOR—an onion router—lets you encrypt that information, or just bounce it around the Internet until it's useless. When the NSA broke into my system, they went one better and stripped out all the metadata via an anonymizing server—"

"Over my head, here," Chapel said. "But I guess I get the point. We know that the NSA was smart enough to hide themselves from you. So any information you found like that was useless, right?"

"For most of it, yes," Angel told him. "I analyzed thousands of packets. Almost all of them stripped. Almost all—a handful of them somehow got missed. That isn't uncommon. Software is only as good as the person who wrote it, and everybody makes little mistakes. Normally it doesn't matter, if you use multiple-step security, which the NSA always does."

"Normally."

Angel grinned. "Normally you aren't up against the likes of *me*. But bragging aside, I wouldn't have found this if I'd had anything better to do. I scanned the stray packets that still had their headers because I had nothing else to look at. I assumed they would be hidden behind proxy servers at the very least. But they weren't. This was just a simple bug in the system, but it let me see behind the curtain for the barest fraction of a second."

She tapped a URL into the browser and brought up a mapping site. "The location you get from the packet headers can be laughably wrong or just really imprecise. In this case, it turned out not to matter." On her screen the map zoomed in on a specific location, a large rectangular patch of white surrounded on every side by green. Chapel realized he was looking at a satellite image. "This is the only building that fits the coordinates.

A place in rural Kentucky. It's surrounded on every side by woods and fields. I think it's some kind of mansion, or at least it was—property records say the place was abandoned years ago."

"Does it belong to the NSA?" Chapel asked.

"Well, no, it doesn't match the coordinates of *any* government or military installation I've ever heard of. It's definitely not an official NSA data center. But maybe that's the point. They didn't want to be traced back to their headquarters, did they? So they set up a server in some building nobody could ever attach to them."

She shook her head and then came back over to sit next to him. The look on her face was not particularly hopeful.

"It's probably nothing. I mean, they could have just found an abandoned building and used the address to throw us off the trail."

"Or?" Chapel asked.

"Or," Angel said, "that building could be a secret NSA server farm. Which would contain all the evidence we need."

Chapel would have asked her more questions, but they both turned then as they heard a commotion at the top of the stairs—and then the door that led down to the basement banged open and boots tromped down the steps.

SOUTH HILLS, PA: MARCH 23, 20:30

Upstairs, five minutes earlier, the troops were in revolt.

"Maybe I don't own this house," Ralph insisted, "but I have a right to know what's going on."

"Fuck yeah," Suzie said, bobbing up and down on her feet like she expected a fistfight to break out any second. Julia thought the woman probably wanted one.

"Look," Julia said, "Top specifically said—"

"Top ain't here," Ralph pointed out. "He and Dolores wanted to go see a movie."

Which explained why things had gotten so tense right now, Julia thought. Clearly the others had waited until the king and queen of the house were out of the way before they pushed for answers.

Julia was sympathetic. The three of them—Chapel, Angel, and herself—had burst in here before dawn the day before and disrupted everyone's lives. They were obviously in trouble and Top was clearly protecting them. But the others in the house—Top's boys—had no reason to feel loyalty to Chapel, and they were scared of what was going to happen to them. It wasn't an unreasonable fear. If the cops came storming in, the lot of them could be taken in as accomplices in harboring the fugitives.

"Look, I'll explain, but—"

"No need," Ralph said, pushing toward the door to the basement. "I'll just have a quick look for myself."

It was Rudy who came to Julia's defense, then. "Now you just hold it, fella!" he said, putting his back up against the basement door. "I know this fine lady. If she says there's a reason to stay out of the basement, then I figure it's got to be a goodly one."

"Seriously?" Suzie asked. "You pathetic old drunk." And then she picked Rudy up like a sack of potatoes and threw him onto the couch.

Before Julia could stop him, Ralph had the door open and was pounding down the stairs in his heavy boots.

"There's a sick man down there!" Julia shouted, chasing after him.

But she couldn't catch him in time. He had already reached the bottom of the stairs. Suzie pushed past Julia to join him. The rest of the boys, including Rudy, stood up at the top looking down, as if they wanted to know what was down there but they were afraid and wanted Ralph and Suzie to go first.

She half expected them to run over and attack Chapel on the spot. But when she reached the bottom of the stairs, she saw Suzie leaning up against the basement wall, arms folded across her chest. She refused to meet Julia's eyes.

Meanwhile Ralph stood in the middle of the basement, rubbing his mouth with his good hand. He was staring at Chapel.

No. He was staring at Chapel's left shoulder. What remained of his missing arm.

"He's been hurt," Julia said. "He has a surgical wound. I don't think I need to tell you how serious an infection could be."

"Don't worry," Ralph said. "I'm not going to sneeze on him." The one-armed vet walked toward the camp bed—then changed course and went to the bookshelf nearby. With his good hand and his claw he picked up Chapel's robotic arm.

And then he just stood there, staring at it. For a very long time.

"You could have just fucking told us," Suzie said, still not looking at anyone.

"I'm seriously confused," Julia said. "A second ago you were ready to tear this basement apart."

"Yeah, a second ago," Suzie said. She sighed dramatically and then leaned out over the stairs. "You bunch can come down now," she said, and soon all the boys had tromped down into the basement, gathering in a respectful semicircle around the camp bed.

Julia shook her head, but there was nothing she could do.

Ralph grabbed a chair and sat down next to Chapel. He cradled the robotic arm in his lap like something precious. She supposed to a man with a claw replacing his lost hand and a piece of beige plastic for an arm, Chapel's prosthetic would be worth more than rubies and pearls.

"You're a vet. You were in the war and you lost an arm," Ralph said.

"Yep," Chapel replied. "That's how I became one of Top's boys."

"You want to talk about it?" Ralph asked.

"He doesn't have to!" Suzie said, almost shouting.

"It's all right," Chapel said. "I don't mind."

SOUTH HILLS, PA: MARCH 23, 20:32

"I actually didn't see much of my war," Chapel said. Most of the boys had pulled up chairs around his camp bed or were just sitting on the floor where they could hear him. Suzie still leaned up against the wall, scowling, but she wasn't the one who interrupted.

"Chapel," Angel said, "this story's classified."

"I guess we're past that now," Chapel said, with a weak smile. "Anyway, these people are soldiers, marines—"

"Sailors, too," said a guy who had burn scars over half his face.

Chapel nodded gravely. "These people can be trusted," Chapel said.

Angel stared at him with huge eyes. Then she just nodded.

Chapel launched into his story, then. "I'm older than most of you," he said, nodding quickly at Rudy, who was the obvious exception. "I was in Afghanistan in the real early days. Just after September eleventh. I'd been trained by the Rangers and I thought I was the toughest, meanest son of a bitch ever created by the toughest, most morally upright country the world had ever seen. At the time we figured three months tops and we'd have Bin Laden in custody, we'd have knocked over the Taliban and taught everybody over there a lesson."

Julia barely recognized the Chapel telling this story. He'd fallen into a whole different speech pattern, much rougher and more expansive than usual. She realized this must be how he talked around other soldiers, and she wondered if this was how he thought in his own head.

"A whole bunch of us got sent in to Khost Province where we thought we still had some friends. My unit had all been crash trained in the local dialect. We'd been taught which hand to eat with and how to show respect to village elders. We even had special dispensation from the regs to grow beards, to help us gain respect from the locals. My job was to meet up with a bunch of mujahideen—guys we used to call freedom fighters—and get them on the team. These were guys we used to pay to fight the Soviets, in the old days. They were already our best friends, right? It was going to be a cakewalk. There were Taliban everywhere, but our friends were supposed to protect me, keep me out of sight."

"The Taliban were onto you, though?" Ralph asked. "I remember, they always seemed to know our business, sometimes even before we got our actual orders. They had spies everywhere."

"This time they didn't need them. The main guy I was meeting with, he arranged transport for me; he was going to take me up to a cave complex where I was going to meet with a bunch of our kind of people. He showed up in an open jeep at the house where I was staying. No armor on it, no MG, just basically a beat-up old car, except a car might have blended in, but this jeep was obviously military. I didn't like it much, but I figured they had their own ways of doing things and you had to go along to get along. My contact drove me about fifty clicks out into open country, a wide valley between two mountain ridges. I kept my eyes open, scanning the high ground, but I didn't see anything. At one point my guy brakes hard and stops the jeep because there's a flock of sheep crossing in front of us. Taking their time. Their shepherd kept making nasty gestures at us, calling us all kinds of names. My guy tells me this kind of thing happens, it's nothing, and if I give him a hundred dollars, he can get the sheep moving and we can be on our way. I give him the money and he jumps out of the jeep. He and the shepherd go wandering off to talk and work things out."

Chapel grimaced. "You all know the feeling, I'm sure. That cramp in your guts when you just know you're being played. When shit is about to go down."

The boys assented in a chorus of profanities.

"I didn't see the Taliban. I didn't have time to see anything. An RPG hit the jeep, getting in under the back of the undercarriage so the whole thing flipped over on top of me. Sounded like my head was an anvil getting hit with a big hammer. I couldn't see anything, couldn't hear anything. I could smell lamb chops, though. Well-done lamb chops."

Julia was surprised to hear some of the boys laugh at that. The thought of Chapel under the jeep made her sick to her stomach. But she supposed when you lived in constant danger you learned to find humor where you could.

"My contact—all the people I'd come to talk to—had already made up their minds. They were honorary Taliban by then, one hundred percent committed. Seconds after the jeep flipped, they were all over me, pulling on me, screaming in my face, asking me where my money was and saying they would let me go for a million dollars. I was hurt, bad, and I couldn't do anything. They pulled me out of that wreckage, but they weren't gentle about it and they left a big chunk of my arm behind."

"How'd you get free?" one of the boys asked.

"I didn't. They took me to that cave complex, the one I'd been headed for anyway. It was full of guys with AK-47s and RPGs and even just machetes. Even if the place had been guarded by kittens, I was in no shape to fight my way out. They held me there with no food, just a little water each day, and they demanded information. They wanted to know where our troops were, where they were headed. They wanted to know what locals we'd contacted and who was looking to betray them. They wanted to know every piece of information I could give them. They wanted to know a whole bunch of stuff I had no idea about, too, and they refused to believe me when I said I didn't know."

"Did they cut off your arm?" the burned sailor asked.

"No. No, they didn't touch it. They beat me occasionally, and sometimes they . . . well, they tortured me. But they left the arm alone. That was intentional. They kept saying that it was getting infected. That it was going to die unless I got medical attention. They made me watch as it turned different colors. They pushed it in my face so I could smell it rotting."

"They let gangrene set in?" Julia asked, horrified. "You could have died!"

"Probably would have," Chapel said. "I got lucky."

"How?" Ralph asked.

"The best kind of luck you can get—a SEAL team. It was just before dawn one day and my guards were already up, making breakfast. They liked to do that in front of me to remind me how hungry I was. One of them stood up to get some salt, and his brains came right out of his ear. The others ran for their weapons, but they were dead as soon as they moved. I was so out of it by then, so delirious, I thought it was all a trick. A ruse to get me to talk. I don't remember much else until I was on a helicopter, headed to a field hospital. That was the last time I ever saw my left arm. They knocked me out for surgery, and when I woke up, I was about eight pounds lighter."

SOUTH HILLS, PA: MARCH 23, 20:46

"They couldn't save the arm," Chapel said, looking around at his audience. It had been a long time since he'd talked about this with anybody. A long time since he'd let himself think about it. "The gangrene had progressed too much. It was poisoning me, and leaving the arm on would just make it worse. They cut it off while I was still asleep. Then they shipped me to Walter Reed so I could get pumped full of antibiotics and that was where I met Top."

"Sucks," Ralph said.

"Yeah, it did," Chapel agreed.

"I can beat it, though."

Chapel couldn't stop the grin that spread across his face. "You think so?"

"You know what an antitank weapon does?" Ralph asked. "I got to find out. I was driving an M1 Abrams TUSK; that's a kind of tank you can drive right through a city. There's a crew of four in one of those, with three folks stuck up in the turret. Driver gets the best seat, which isn't saying much. You have to drive leaning way back, like in a dentist's chair, and all you can see is what your periscopes give you. All around you there's piles of armor plate, thick enough to stop just about anything. On the outside you got reactive tiles, and those protect you from mortar fire."

Chapel looked over and saw Julia's eyes glazing over. She didn't have much patience for technical discussions of weapons systems, as he knew all too well. Still, she seemed to sense what was going on here—why Ralph was telling this story—and he knew she wouldn't protest.

"So you're just about invulnerable in there, and you can just laugh at enemy infantry," Ralph went on, "except then they went and invented LAWs. Light antitank weapons. A thing just a little heavier than a rifle that any dumb grunt can carry. There's no point throwing a bomb at a tank—hell, those reactive tiles are basically bombs themselves. So instead your LAW has a nose cone that's made out of pure copper. When it hits the side of a tank, it doesn't explode, it vaporizes. Heats up about as hot as the sun and just melts its way through your armor, like a blowtorch. When it gets through, when that jet of superhot metal gets inside the tank hull, it's still hot enough to flash fry every single asshole in the crew."

"So you got hit by one of those?" Angel asked. "How did you survive?"

"I got lucky. The second-best kind of luck you can have, I guess. It was somebody else's turn instead of mine. The LAW hit the turret, not the hull. The other three guys—my commander, the gunner, and the loader—they were crispy critters in milliseconds. Down in the driver's seat, right underneath them, I just got a little cooked. I would have been fine, except for how I was sitting, almost lying on my back. Molten metal dripped down out of the turret, right on my shoulder. There was no way I could get out of there, no way to even move out of the way. I watched it drip down over me, drop by drop."

"Oh my God," Angel said. "Oh, I'm so sorry—"

Ralph shrugged, his artificial arm clicking as it fell back against his belt. "Yeah, so you lost an arm to gangrene, well, you were asleep for most of that," Ralph said. "Me, I got to feel the whole thing. Then I sat there for sixteen hours because all the comm gear was burned out and my superior officer assumed I was dead, too, so they didn't bother prying me out of there until they wanted to take the tank apart for scrap. When they got to me, I was pretty much dead, yeah. They scraped up what was left of me and shipped me home and that was how I got to meet Top."

Chapel looked the veteran right in the eyes and nodded. "You're right. That sucks more than mine."

"Oh, please," Suzie said. "What a bunch of crybabies."

Chapel looked over at her. He raised his voice so she could hear him all right. "I notice you still have both arms," he said.

She stalked over to the bed and stared down at him. "Helicopter pilot, right? I did a bunch of milk runs, supposed to be easy flights. Of course we got stuck in sandstorms all the time, which clogged up our engines and screwed our visuals until half the time we didn't know if we were flying upside down. Plus the friendly locals used to take potshots at us. You ever hear of a ballistic blanket? It's a sheet of Kevlar you put down like carpeting inside the fuselage of your aircraft. Any bullets that come up through the floorboards, it stops 'em so they don't hit you. I used to fly over perfectly nice and civilized towns and afterward I would shake out my blanket and twenty or fifty spent rounds would come clanking out. They weren't shooting at me to kill me, see, just to let me know they were there. You can't put tank armor on a helo, so they gave us bulletproof floor mats instead."

"A bullet get through one of those, or something?" one of the others asked.

"Nope. I had the *worst* kind of luck," Suzie said. "Which is when somebody else gets lucky when they weren't supposed to. One of those potshots hit my Jesus nut. That's the thing on top of the helicopter that holds the rotor on. You take that out, suddenly you are fifty feet up in a thing shaped like a school bus, not like a glider. You fall down and go boom. I was in my safety webbing, I had all kinds of fire suppression equipment and impact-resistant gel under my butt, I was going to be okay. Then a piece of my rotor comes straight down through my canopy and then straight through my face. It was like getting chopped in half by a sword."

She pulled the neck of her tank top away to show the scar that ran from her hairline down across the middle of her chest. Chapel was a little shocked, thinking she was going to expose her breasts—until he saw that she only had one.

"Like the Amazons of old," Rudy said, gasping.

"Shut the fuck up, you drunk," Suzie said. She let her top fall back to cover part of her scar. "I was in traction for a year. They had me strung up in this frame, locked down so I couldn't even move my fingers. If I wriggled around too much, I would have fallen apart like an onion chopped down the middle. Yeah," she said, "real fucking lucky. And yeah, that was how I got to meet Top."

SOUTH HILLS, PA: MARCH 23, 21:47

One by one the others told their stories, each claiming they'd had it worse than anyone else, that they'd been lucky or unlucky in various measures, each one ending with how they'd come to meet Top. There were only two exceptions. One was an airman missing both legs below the knees. He started out strong. "Your stories ain't shit," he said. "You want to talk real suffering—"

But then he stopped. Chapel saw a look in the man's eyes he knew all too well. The airman couldn't see anything but the past. The worst moment in his life. "Never mind," he said. "I'm not going to tell you."

"That's okay," Suzie said. "Nobody wanted to hear it anyway."

Some of the others chuckled.

Rudy, the other exception, was the last one to speak. "I'm afraid you've all got it wrong," he said. "All these tales of woe. Talking about how un-lucky you sods were. Nonsense, every bit of it."

"Let me guess," Chapel said. "You had it worse than us."

"I wouldn't say as much," Rudy told them. "By fuck, I'd say you're all a bunch of sad sacks that make my own troubles seem like minor inconve-niences by comparison. But I know you're the luckiest sons of bitches who ever lived. That antitank round, the helicopter blade that got you, Suzie my dear, the ammunition cooking off in your Stryker," he said, nodding at a veteran with a white plastic hand. "In my day, those things would have killed you all stone dead. You're all here because medical technology has come so far we can save people who should have died."

"You saying I should be dead?" Ralph asked.

"Son, your very existence is a blessing on us all," Rudy said. He shook his head. "No, I'm saying you got lucky enough to be born when you were, that's all. I watched a lot of boys with injuries less severe than yours die back in 'Nam. There was a time when I wished I'd been one of them. I sup-pose there are times I still do. I couldn't handle it, you see. All the death. Every time one of my friends caught a bullet or stepped on a punji stick or just disappeared out in the jungle . . . I knew it wasn't going to stop. That kind of thing gets into a man's head. I came back from Southeast Asia without so much as a scratch on me, you know that? At least, none I could point to. No Purple Heart. No medals at all. But I came back and found that I'd brought a souvenir with me. No matter where I went here in the States, every time I met someone I'd look them in the eye and think, Are *you* going to die today? Are *you*? I couldn't care about anyone. I couldn't get attached, because they were just going to disappear, so I treated them like they already had. Made it rather difficult to find a job. Made it rather easy to find a bottle, since when I drank it didn't seem so bad."

"You still feel that way? Even here?"

"I have my good days," Rudy suggested. "And then sometimes—"

A familiar voice boomed out from the stairway. "What do we have here?" Top asked. "I believe I said you all should stay out of this here basement."

The boys got to their feet. They didn't quite stand at attention but they looked like they wanted to.

"Maybe," Top said, "I'm getting senile in my old age. Dolores, honey, did I tell these people to stay out of the basement?"

"You did, Top," Dolores called out from upstairs.

"And yet here they all are. What do you suppose we should do about this discrepancy?"

The boys filed out of the basement with bowed heads. When they were gone, Top glanced at Chapel. "You okay, Captain? They didn't suck up all your air?"

"Just having ourselves a bitch session," Chapel told him.

Top nodded in acceptance. "Well, I suppose that's all right. You know what I always say. A soldier who can still bitch is a happy soldier. It's the quiet ones you have to worry about."

Chapel smiled. "How was the movie? What did you see?"

"Something about a dog that learned how to work a computer or some nonsense. Didn't pay attention. But I'll go see anything's got a dog in it. Now, good night, my dear captain. You get some rest. That would be an order, if you didn't outrank me."

"I'll take it as one anyway," Chapel told him.

SOUTH HILLS, PA: MARCH 23, 21:53

When they were alone, just the three of them—Chapel, Julia, and Angel—he let himself be eased down into a prone position so he could go to sleep. "Tomorrow we'll talk more about that place in Kentucky," he told Angel.

She nodded and then reached down to touch his cheek. "Good night."

Julia watched her go. There was a funny look on her face.

"What's going on between you and her?" Chapel asked.

"Tell you in a minute," Julia said, then held up one finger. Together they listened for the sound of the basement door closing. "Okay, first, what exactly just happened down here? With all the stories?"

"Sympathy," Chapel said. "It helps to share, sometimes."

"Including trying to one-up each other with how bad your stories were, or Suzie telling people to shut up all the time?"

"What you saw," Chapel told her, "is about the closest you can get to a pity party and still consider yourself a hard-ass soldier. We all need to feel like we're not alone sometimes, but none of us wants to admit it." He smiled at her. "Now. Are you going to answer my question?"

She looked away. "Angel has a crush on you."

"Oh, come on. She and I flirt. It's harmless," he insisted.

"You didn't notice how she was hovering over you? How she just touched your cheek? But of course, no, you didn't notice. Because you're an oblivious man."

He shook his head. "Maybe you're jealous."

"I'm trying to decide if I am or not," she told him.

That made him want to sit up. He didn't, because he knew how much it would hurt. "Julia—if you think you and I could maybe—"

"Shush. Anyway, this isn't the time for that conversation. Or the place."

He grinned at her. "I'm not going anywhere. Doctor's orders."

"Veterinarian's orders," she said. "Which might be fitting, considering what a dog you are." She smiled when she said it, but then her face fell. "Okay. If we're going to do this, let me start. I'm not a jealous person. I don't like being a jealous person. And I am very angry at you for forcing me to be a jealous person."

"You mean—with Angel? I haven't done *anything*. Neither has she."

"I'm not talking about Angel now. Try to keep up. I'm talking about the picture I saw, the one the guy showed me, the guy who told me to break up with you. The one of you and that—that woman."

Chapel felt like a deflating balloon. He had never wanted to talk about this, not with Julia. He'd also always known he would have to, eventually. "Her name was Nadia," he said. "Do you want the details?"

"Absolutely not." She put a hand on his shoulder. "Jim. When I saw that picture, I hated you a little. I had no right to. I mean, I'd broken up with you. You were a free agent. You still are. I know that logically. But I couldn't help myself. I was *filled* with rage. You made promises to me."

Chapel bit his tongue, at least metaphorically. He did not want to say out loud the words, *You're the one who refused my marriage proposal.* He wasn't quite that oblivious. So instead he said, "You're going to feel what you're going to feel."

"That's really very big of you," she said, sarcasm dripping from the words. "I was getting past it. I was pretty much going to let Badass Julia screw your brains out, because she really, really wanted to."

"I like Badass Julia," he said, looking her straight in the eyes.

"Don't be so sure. Now Badass Julia is considering what her chances are if she's competing with a cute little twentysomething with daddy issues."

"Now we're talking about Angel again," he said.

"You're getting better at this game," Julia told him. "I'm nearly twice her age. You can't possibly prefer me to her. Men don't work that way."

"Are you kidding?"

"No," she said, and he could tell she wasn't.

"Julia," he said. "I love you."

"Badass Julia isn't sure she believes you."

"I wasn't talking to her. I was talking to Julia Taggart, DVM. I've loved you basically since we first met and I always will. You don't want to hear about Nadia, but I'm going to tell you this—none of that would have happened if I wasn't so heartsick for you I couldn't see straight. I know that's not a very good defense, but it's true. When I came to your apartment, back when all this started—I knew I was already being chased by the police. I knew I was in danger of being caught. But I came anyway because I thought maybe, just maybe you wanted to see me again. It didn't matter why. It would have been worth it because I got to see you again."

Her face was guarded. "You are good, I'll give you that. You talk a great game."

"Give me a chance to do more than just talk," he said. "Wait. That sounded dirty. I meant it to be romantic."

She rolled her eyes. "Maybe we will later. Talk, I mean. Go to bed, Captain Chapel. You need to heal. Your veterinarian insists."

She stood up and started to turn away. But then she stopped and looked back at him. He had no idea what she was thinking.

Luckily Badass Julia wasn't about mixed signals. She reached under his sheet and grabbed his cock. It stiffened instantly in her hand.

"Get better soon," she said, and then she left him there.

LOS ANGELES, CA: MARCH 23, 20:06 (PDT)

Behind the chain-link fence nothing but anarchy held sway.

The National Guard had set up a temporary base at LAX. Patrick Norton, the secretary of defense, had flown in for an inspection. As he stepped off the plane he was led down a corridor formed by two rows of soldiers in full battle gear, every single one of them standing at attention, spaced exactly apart from one another. It was a perfect display of military discipline, designed to impress the absolute top brass.

A display that failed altogether once Norton could hear the protesters screaming just a few dozen yards away.

They pressed their faces against the fence, their mouths open, spittle flying in rage. He couldn't understand what any of them were shouting, but some of them carried signs he could read:

WE WON'T LIVE LIKE THIS
KATRINA 2.0
NO POWER NO PEACE

"Sir?"

Norton looked to his left and saw a guard captain waiting to lead him away. He nodded gratefully and followed the man into a Quonset hut full of radio gear. In the center of the prefab building stood a series of card tables, each of them covered in manila folders. The captain picked one up and handed it to the SecDef.

"This is your briefing, sir, which you can peruse at your leisure. I'd be happy to give you the salient points in verbal form, if you would prefer that."

Norton took the folder and glanced at it for a second without opening it. Then he threw it back down on the table.

"Show me," he said.

It took an age to get a helicopter ready to go—the main concern seemed to be finding one that was properly armored, so that no one could shoot the secretary of defense out of the sky with a target pistol. Once they were airborne, though, Norton knew immediately he'd made the right choice. No paper briefing could give him the same perspective on the chaos that he got from the air.

For one thing—he wouldn't have felt the darkness sprawling under him so intensely. Wouldn't have known just how apocalyptic it could feel. He'd flown over Los Angeles many times in his career and always, when you came in by night, the whole landscape glowed like it was on fire. Lights from the buildings bounced off the permanent cloud of smog and lit up the countryside for miles around.

Now there was nothing down there except where something actually *was* on fire. Just inky blackness, interrupted here and there by a burning trash can or a car that had been doused in gasoline and set ablaze in the middle of a street crossing. Norton wondered if the cars had been lit up as a form of protest, or just because the locals were so desperate for whatever light source they could find.

Off in the distance, in the hills, there were some electric lights still burning. And if Norton looked to the south, he saw whole neighborhoods that glowed just as brightly as they ever had. But downtown L.A. had reentered the nineteenth century.

"Is any power getting through? Even just for part of the day?" Norton asked over his headset microphone.

The captain consulted his handheld. "Yes, sir. We had four hours today, that's good for the average. Yesterday we had nothing. We get rolling blackouts that just kind of roll in and . . . stay. We've got the Army Corps of Engineers trying to put everything back together, get the grid online again, but their reports aren't encouraging. If I didn't know better, I'd think somebody was trying to stop them. They're telling me it's all computer problems, that every time they get a substation cleared, another one drops off-line." The captain shook his head. "It's going to be a matter of weeks, not days, before this is cleared up."

Norton peered down into the soupy gloom. He occasionally thought he saw someone running on a sidewalk in the dark or a car moving between palm trees, but it was hard to tell.

Off to the east a blare of light alleviated the darkness, like a cloud of fire hovering over the black landscape. "What's that?" Norton asked.

"Sir, that's Dodger Stadium, it's our relief station. We've got gasoline generators out there working all night. We've advised anyone in distress to head there; we've got medical teams, clean water, some communications—"

"Let me see," Norton commanded.

The captain clearly didn't think it was a good idea, but he said nothing. The helicopter swung around and headed directly for the light, which soon enough Norton could see came from the big stadium lights that normally illuminated nighttime ball games. "We keep those on from dusk until dawn," the captain explained. "Some people . . . they just want the light, that's all. They just need to get out of the dark."

Norton turned to look at the man. "What about crime? Looting, violence, that sort of thing. Have you seen any riots?"

"The governor has us sweeping the streets, sir, on a constant basis. We do what we can to keep things calm."

"That's a nice nonanswer," Norton told the man. "Tell me the truth."

The captain looked down into the darkness. "Rioting is the main problem. The people are actually sticking together, forming neighborhood security groups. But they don't trust us. There's a bunch of them think we aren't doing enough. There have been a couple of armed clashes. A couple of civilians have been shot. When this is over, there's going to be a reckoning. A lot of us in command wonder if we're going to get blamed."

Norton frowned. "I'm sure you've acted in a professional manner."

"Sir, with all due respect—the people down here are righteously pissed." The captain looked over at Norton, and his eyes were suddenly very tired. "We're keeping them from actually revolting in the streets. But if the power doesn't come back soon—or worse, if something else bad happens, like wildfires or mudslides or, God forbid, an earthquake—this place is going to explode."

Norton remembered something he'd heard many years before, back at West Point. *Modern man is a miracle of civilization and sophistication. He is also three hot meals away from barbarism.*

The helicopter pilot took them right over the stadium, low enough that Norton could see inside. The stadium lights gave him a great view of all the people in the seats—tens of thousands of them. Families sprawled across whole rows, sleeping under orange survival blankets or patrolling the aisles with baseball bats and chains. Down on the field soldiers marched relief seekers—Norton wondered if a better word was *refugees*—through metal detectors and intake desks, forcing them to fill out paperwork before they could get food or clean water.

It didn't take long for them to notice the helicopter—or to react. It started with a dull roar, so low and far away Norton thought it might be distant thunder, but soon the noise rose in pitch as the refugees below screamed up at the chopper, screamed for light or air-conditioning or whatever it was they wanted most. He saw bits of debris floating over the crowd, and the occasional ribbon of white, and suddenly he realized—they were throwing things at him. Government paperwork, empty MRE pouches. The ribbons were rolls of toilet paper unfurling as they arced through the air.

None of it could hit the chopper, of course. Norton was safe up there in the sky.

He was safe.

For the moment.

He pulled out his cell phone and plugged it into his headset. Dialed Charlotte Holman. They needed to talk. "I want you on a plane as soon as possible. Check with my staff for my itinerary. Meet me at my next stop."

"Of course, sir. May I ask what this is concerning?"

"I want you by my side until this thing is over. I need constant reports and updates. From now forward—nothing else matters."

Because if Los Angeles was about to fall, it wouldn't take very long for the rest of the country to follow.

SOUTH HILLS, PA: MARCH 24, 08:14

Top, who had been a master gunnery sergeant in the Marines, had never looked worried in his life as far as Chapel knew. He didn't now, though there were little signs to see if you knew the man well. He wasn't smiling quite as broadly as he usually did. Instead of a glass eye, today he was just wearing an eyepatch. Of course, it was an eyepatch in a marine camouflage pattern, but even so.

"I got to get to work," he said. "That hospital doesn't even wake up until I arrive to properly motivate folks. But before I go, we're going to settle this. The three of you are welcome in my house any time, for as long as you want."

"It's too dangerous," Chapel told him.

On the kitchen table between them lay Top's cell phone. He'd put it there so Chapel could listen to a voice-mail message Top had received an hour earlier. A message from Brent Wilkes, asking if Top would be willing to come in to the local police station to answer some questions.

"I didn't think they would make the connection between you and me," Chapel said, though saying it out loud made him realize how dumb he'd been. The NSA probably had a dossier on him a yard thick, and somewhere in there would be the fact that Top had worked with Chapel as his physical therapist after he came home from Afghanistan.

Most likely Wilkes was interviewing every known associate in Chapel's file. He'd probably bothered Chapel's parents and sister first, then worked his way down the list until he harassed Chapel's dry cleaner and his barber. Top would definitely be on the list. It only made sense to make those phone calls. Chapel was trained in how to live on the run, how to keep a low profile. But that was a hard road for a man to go alone. Most fugitives did exactly as Chapel had—they found a friend who would hide them for a while.

"Could just be a coincidence," Top pointed out.

"They believe in those, in the Marines? Coincidences? In the Rangers we used to say that a coincidence was guaranteed to be somebody getting ready to kill you."

"In the Corps we just assumed everybody was doing that whether we saw any clues or not," Top said. He shrugged, the empty sleeve of his work shirt flapping against his side. "All right, seeing as this guy is the one who tried to kill you the other night, I suppose we can assume the worst. But so what? I go in, he asks me, have you seen this man, I say, no, sir, can't say as I have. And then I walk back out."

"He's trained in interrogation," Chapel pointed out. "And he's an expert poker player, so he can spot a bluff. I should know—I still owe him six bags of chips."

Top shook his head. "I can't believe they'd send a serviceman after you. You army grunts sure know a bit about loyalty, don't you? You could try a little *semper fi* now and again."

"Wilkes isn't army. He's a marine. MARSOC—the Raiders."

Top leaned back in his chair. "Aw, shit. Now we are in trouble. All right. So say you refuse my hospitality and get back in the wind. Where are you going to go next?"

"No idea. And it's probably best I don't tell you, anyway."

Top nodded. "Sure." He drummed his fingers on the tabletop. "So you want me to just blow this guy off? Never show up for my interview?"

"No. That'll definitely make him suspicious. Just—don't say much. Answer his questions with as few words as possible. Act like you wished you could help but he's out of luck. It'll help if you know that when you're talking to him, I'll already be gone."

Top got up from the table. "Any chance that when you go you'll leave one or more of those fine ladies behind to keep me company?"

Chapel grinned. "Dolores might mind."

"She might at that. Okeydokey, smokey. You take care of yourself, Captain."

Chapel looked away. He didn't want Top to see the look on his face. "I can't thank you enough," he said.

"The bond you and me have is supposed to go beyond words," Top told him. "Same as for all my boys. Not that you'd know from all the jawboning goes on around here twenty-four seven. Now, I'm going to be late for work, and all the pretty nurses are on the night shift and if I don't get there on time, I miss my chance to make them blush."

He grabbed the phone and left Chapel alone in the kitchen.

When he was gone, Chapel rubbed at his eyes with his good hand.

Crap. If Wilkes was interviewing Top, that meant he was sure that Chapel was still alive. Which meant going on the run again, no question. Just when Chapel had started to like it in the house full of Top's boys. It had begun to feel like he was back in the army again, living in barracks, something he never thought he would have missed.

Nothing for it, he supposed. He started making a mental plan about how he was going to steal another car.

SOUTH HILLS, PA: MARCH 24, 09:29

On the screen Angel kicked open a wooden crate while Ralph laid down suppressing fire on a squadron of Nazi flamethrower troops. "Ammo," Angel said, and they switched positions so fluidly they might have been practicing the maneuver for years. Ralph, who in the game was playing a British Tommy with a BAR rifle, ducked down to grab a new drum of ammunition. Meanwhile Angel, dressed like a member of the French resistance (the only female character in the game), threw a stick grenade into the midst of the Wehrmacht troops.

The Germans screamed "Schnell, schnell!" but it was too late for them. The grenade went off in a cloud of fire and smoke, and the fuel tanks on the Nazis' backs popped off one after another, bathing them all in liquid fire and sending them screaming around a village square, their faces melting in exquisitely rendered detail as they died.

"Jesus," Chapel said, wincing.

"That was—that was—" Julia couldn't seem to find the word.

Ralph had it, though. "*Nice,*" he said, bouncing up and down on the couch.

His claw hand didn't seem to be any kind of impediment to working the video-game controller. Chapel knew from experience how much you could achieve with one hand, if you had enough practice. What surprised him was just how good Angel was at the game.

Julia had a theory about that. "She's been living in one trailer or another for the last ten years, never going out, living on delivered Chinese food. Her only connection to the outside world has been telling spies where to go and who to shoot. Why wouldn't she be a natural at this?"

Chapel just shook his head. They needed to head out soon, but it was clear Angel was enjoying herself and he didn't want to interrupt the game.

On the screen the Tommy and the resistance fighter dashed across the village square, hopping over the bodies of the still-smoldering Nazis. On the far side they took cover in a bombed-out café. As soon as they'd hunkered down, the television started growling with the noise of tank treads coming closer.

"You have any shaped charges?" Angel asked.

"Just one left. Glad I held on to it," Ralph told her.

His on-screen avatar jumped through the door of the café and rolled along the street, a square lump of plastique in his hands. He slapped it onto the cobblestones and a little red light started blinking on its detonator. The tank was only a dozen yards away.

"Did they even have C4 in World War II?" Chapel asked.

"Shut up, Chapel!" Angel cried, anguish tinging her voice because just then the tank's machine gun opened fire and Ralph's character flopped down in the street, right next to his bomb. "Hold on," she said, and her beret-clad character rushed out to his side, carrying a green box with a red cross on it. She injected something into his arm that was apparently a cure for machine-gun bullets, because suddenly Ralph was up and on his feet again and drawing a pistol.

It was too late for both of them, however. The panzer's main gun fired with a cloud of smoke and debris, and the screen went red as both characters fell in slow motion to lie in heaps on the cobblestones.

"Dang," Ralph said, tossing his controller onto the couch. "I can never get past that tank."

"Why do you want to?" Julia asked. "Why do you even play this game?"

Ralph lifted one eyebrow. "Because it's fun?"

"She's got a point, though," Chapel said. "Look, not to get all preachy here, but you're a veteran with PTSD. We've all heard you screaming in the night. Why on earth would you want to traumatize yourself with a war game?"

"Therapy," Ralph answered, without hesitation.

Julia looked intrigued. "How does that work?"

"The game isn't real," Ralph told them. "It's nothing like real war. There's no waiting around for weeks only to have an attack come when you're just starting to relax. You can get shot, like, a dozen times in the game, and all you need is one medical kit to get back to full health." He shrugged his shoulders. "Two people against an entire squad armed with flamethrowers? In real life, you'd be dead meat."

Chapel had to admit that the game didn't match his own experience of warfare.

"It helps with the dreams. Yeah, you've heard me wake up in the middle of the night thinking I'm back there, under fire. But when I play this game for like twelve hours straight, I'm not dreaming about Iraq. I'm dreaming about liberating Paris with a hot resistance fighter by my side."

"You think she's hot?" Angel asked. "I just thought she was an ass-kicker."

"She can't be both?" Ralph asked. "Anyway—sometimes the dreams get mixed up. I don't know. It helps."

Chapel had learned during his own rehabilitation not to turn up his nose at any treatment that actually worked. "Have at it, then. But I'm afraid your sexy partner there has to get going."

Angel didn't protest. She set her controller down on the couch and stood up. "What's on the agenda?" she asked.

"We need to arrange transport," Chapel said.

"What, like you need a car?" Ralph asked.

PITTSBURGH, PA: MARCH 24, 10:09

The place where Ralph worked had a clean and trim little storefront where it met the road. Four recently washed cars stood in the parking lot, all of them with prices listed on their windshields in greasepaint.

Beyond that lot, however, the place was pure junkyard. Behind a chain-link fence stood towering stacks of hubcaps and dented fenders, cars without wheels or doors or windshields, heaps of scrap metal, and, for some reason, an entire avenue lined with nothing but old washing machines. You could easily get lost wandering among the heaps of old decaying machinery back there—you could get lost, or you could just as easily get tetanus. The men and women working in the yard were all dressed in heavy corduroy jackets and wore thick, grease-stained gloves.

For a mechanical graveyard, though, it was anything but quiet. The noise of whining power tools and tracked vehicles filled the air, punctuated by the ring of actual hammers and mattocks where someone took out their frustrations by breaking down an old heap. They passed by a guy cutting a bulldozer down with an acetylene torch, sparks flying ten feet in the air. They walked past a kennel full of barking dogs. When they finally found Ralph's boss, the man was hip deep in a pile of old hardware, hinges and flanges and nuts and bolts, sorting them by tossing them one by one into rusted fifty-gallon drums.

It took a while to get his attention. When Ralph called his name the fourth or fifth time, he finally looked up and glanced from Chapel to Angel to Julia as if he was sorting them into categories in his head.

"This is Art, he owns this place," Ralph said. "Navy."

Art clambered out of his pile, sending bits of metal cascading across their shoes, and reached out one massive hand to shake Chapel's. He was a huge man, broad through both shoulders and belly, though his legs were crammed into heavy jeans that made them look like toothpicks holding up a jumbo-sized olive. He had hair the color of the old metal around him, and it cascaded down his shoulders and joined with his beard.

"Jim," Chapel said, squeezing the massive gloved hand. "Army."

He expected Art to make some joke—one of the dozen or so quips people always made when they met someone from a different branch of the services. Instead Art just said, "Uh-huh." His eyes didn't leave Chapel's, though.

"They need a car," Ralph explained. "Just an old beater is okay. But they're friends of mine, so don't cheat them."

"Huh," Art said.

"Ralph tells me he's been working here two years now," Chapel said, to fill the void in the conversation. "It was really good of you to give him a shot."

Art shrugged. "Works hard. That's what I want." He broke his gaze, but only to stare at Ralph for a long time. "Cars," he said finally. Then he took a deep breath and let it out again. "Okay."

He headed down an aisle between two mountains of truck tires. The stink of rubber was overwhelming, and it wasn't helped by the stagnant water that had collected inside the tires. "Art's a genius," Ralph said. "He can fix anything. Used to work on a nuclear submarine, keeping the engines going. Now he's got more than a hundred people working for him here, most of them vets or people who were down on their luck. If you screw up, you get fired on the spot, but if you do what he says, he treats you right."

"Only rule," Art called back, without turning his head.

Beyond the tires lay a landscape of partially intact cars. A small legion of men and women were busy either stripping pieces off the vehicles or screwing parts back on. A few of the cars looked like they were in drivable shape, though most were just held together with primer and duct tape.

Art stopped in front of one that had definitely seen better days. The quarter panels were dented, and rust had set in where the paint had chipped away. The radio antenna was about a foot and a half shorter than it should have been, and none of the four hubcaps matched any of the others. The inside looked like it had been vacuumed recently, though, and the windows shone as if they were brand-new.

Art put a hand on the hood and closed his eyes, as if he were communing with the spirit of the car. Then he opened his eyes again. "It'll run. You guys drug dealers?"

"No," Chapel affirmed.

"Mafia, or somethin'?"

"No," Chapel said again.

"Eight hundred, with tags. Tags are good."

Chapel glanced at Julia. He knew they didn't have that kind of money. He'd come out here with Ralph because he'd known that stealing another car was a bad idea. Wilkes would be looking for any reports of stolen vehicles now, anywhere within fifty miles of Pittsburgh.

Art must have thought he was hesitating because of the car's condition. He pointed at another one, which had fewer dents. "Sixteen. Worth it."

"If we could afford it," Chapel began, but Ralph touched his arm with his claw.

"These are good people, Art, but they're kind of broke."

Art considered this for a long time. Then he tilted his head back, so his hair shifted out of his face, and announced in deep tones, "Poor people gotta drive, too."

"I'm going to cover them," Ralph said. "I don't have much in my bank account, but I'll work for free for three weeks and make it up to you."

Art squinted hard at Ralph. His lips pursed.

Ralph nearly stammered under the pressure. "Four weeks," he said.

Chapel shook his head. "Ralph, you don't have to—"

Art squinted harder.

"Six."

"Looks like," Art said, his face relaxing, "you got a car." Then he started walking back toward the office.

They watched the junkyard owner go until he was out of earshot.

"Man," Ralph said, "that guy's sharp."

Chapel shook his head. "Ralph," he said, "this is incredibly generous of you, but we can't accept it."

"It's no big deal," Ralph said. "Top and Dolores will feed me, and I've got a guaranteed bunk at their place. I might have to buy a few less video games."

"Those games are your therapy," Julia pointed out.

Ralph laughed. "I have enough already. Though I'll tell you what." He turned and reached over and grabbed Angel's hand. "You come back some time, and we'll beat that panzer together, okay?"

Angel looked confused. "Are you asking me out on a date?"

"She meant to say yes," Julia said.

IN TRANSIT: MARCH 24, 12:32

It was a clear, bright day, perfect for driving long distances. Something Chapel hadn't done for a very long time. The beater might look bad, but it had a decent motor under its hood and it purred along, gobbling up the blacktop. Chapel drove fast without actually speeding, overtaking big rigs and the occasional tractor as the road unrolled before them, heading west through endless stretches of grass and trees and low, gentle ridges. The car had no air-conditioning and no radio. The latter wouldn't have mattered much anyway, since Julia kept her window rolled down, one arm out in the rushing air, her outstretched fingers weaving up and down like the spread wings of a gull.

He looked over at her, a big grin on his face, and saw her smiling back, her eyes hidden behind chunky sunglasses, rivulets of red hair sweeping across her cheek, now her eyes, now getting in her mouth so she had to sputter it out, which made him laugh. Which made her laugh.

It just felt so damn good to be moving, to be free. This was the America Chapel had learned to love as a kid, the wide openness of it, the size of it, the raw country all around him. Headed west with no real idea what he would find, the danger and the fear and every worry in his head not gone, necessarily, but put aside for a while, put on a back shelf where he could think about it later.

At some point he felt like having lunch, so they pulled into the immaculate parking lot of a welcome center, right inside the Pennsylvania line, and had hot dogs and soda. He perused a rack of road atlases and folding paper maps, found the one he liked best.

"When was the last time you saw one of these?" Julia asked, unfolding the map, following the major roads with one finger. "I always just use my phone, now."

Which made him think about the fact they didn't have phones anymore. That they were cut off, with no chance of calling for help if they needed it.

But he thought about that for only a second. He paid for the map with a couple of bills from their dwindling treasury. He followed Julia back out to the car while she tried to keep the map from fluttering open in the wind. He stopped for a moment and just looked out at the farmland that surrounded them on every side, flat and open, a backdrop for the white grandeur of the clouds, which dropped nothing but big, sharp shadows on the green of the land.

Then he got back to the car and found Julia leaning in through one of the rear windows. He came up beside her and saw Angel in the backseat, scrunched down as far as she could get, her arms wrapped tight around her knees. She wore a pair of sunglasses that covered half her face and a floppy sun hat pulled down over her hair. She hadn't bothered to take the price tag off the hat.

"Are we almost there?" she asked.

"I'm afraid not," Chapel said. "Angel—are you—are you all right?"

"Fine," she insisted, a little abruptly. "Just drive, okay?"

"What is it?" Julia asked, with her best bedside manner. "Is something scaring you?"

"No," Angel said. She sighed dramatically. "Just—you know. Trees. And the sky's too big. And everything's so far apart. I'm *fine*."

Her tone made it clear she had no desire to talk about it further. Chapel stepped over to his door, then stopped to look over the top of the car at Julia. Neither of them spoke, but he knew she was thinking the same thing he was.

What had the government done to Angel? They'd shoved her in a series of boxes for ten years, made her work in tiny trailers where her only stimulus was what came over a computer screen. What could that do to somebody?

He sat back down in the driver's seat and started the car, but his previous good mood was shot. It was going to be a very, very long drive for somebody who was scared of trees.

IN TRANSIT, MARCH 24, 17:20

They had to cross the whole length of Ohio to get to Kentucky, but Chapel wanted to avoid major cities—in this case, Columbus and Cincinnati. That meant taking a lot of country roads, long stretches of which snaked through endless farms and patches of forest. Other than the occasional ATV dealership or grain elevator, they saw little of civilization. Ancient farmhouses stood well back from the roads, colorless wrecks with peeling paint and sagging gambrel roofs. Only the endless row of telephone poles seemed to link them to the world they'd left behind.

The hours passed without Chapel noticing them much. Julia didn't talk to him very often—neither of them felt like light conversation when Angel was curled up in the back, clearly in distress—and so he had nothing but the flashing lines on the road ahead to measure distance or time.

Just as the sun began to sink low enough to get in his eyes, the road bent hard to the south and suddenly they crossed the Ohio River and were in Kentucky. It was hard to tell the difference. Maybe the ridges alongside the road grew a little taller. There were definitely more trees.

Chapel glanced in the rearview mirror. "Angel? It's not far now. Can you hold on for another hour or so?"

"No problem," she called out, her voice far too loud.

The address she'd found—what he really wanted to believe was a secret NSA data center—was deep in a wooded valley about thirty miles east of Lexington. It wasn't exactly the middle of nowhere, there were plenty of roads around it and even a couple small towns nearby, but it was definitely secluded.

Chapel didn't want to just drive up to the front door. His plan was to find a place nearby to spend the night and then scope it out. If it was what he thought it was, it would be well guarded and there would be constant surveillance all around it. Breaking in was going to be a real challenge.

Of course, Angel had told him it might be nothing. But he refused to think about that. If he'd come so far, if he'd pinned so many hopes on the place, it *had* to be a solid lead. He knew that was just wishful thinking, but in the absence of anything better, he would take it.

"Julia," he said, "get that map out. Angel, can you help her find the exact spot we're looking for? Maybe there's a way we can get a look at it from the road."

Angel leaned over the back of the front seat just long enough to point at the map. "Here," she said, and then dropped back down out of sight, her head below the level of the windows.

"Okay," Julia said, bringing the map close to her face to get a better look. "Take a left the next chance you get. There's a little road there that'll take us up on a ridge. Up on the high ground we might be able to see it."

Chapel turned off onto a road that was barely paved, little more than a logging trail. The car's engine whined as he headed up a steep grade. In the back Angel whimpered as they rose above the level of the trees and were suddenly exposed on top of a sharp defile. Chapel drove another half mile along the ridge, then pulled over into the grass on the side of the road.

"There it is," he said.

Julia leaned out of her window to get a better look. Chapel peered around the side of her head. "Angel," he said, "at least glance at it, okay?"

In the backseat she curled up tighter around herself. But then she grunted in frustration and popped her head up.

From the top of the ridge they had a good view across a wide valley, half of which was covered in trees and the other half in well-groomed fields. Far in the distance stood another ridge, taller than the one they perched on. Nestled into the slope of that ridge stood a building that was exactly as Angel had described it—an abandoned mansion.

It must have been something in its day. A central three-story house with tall white pillars, topped with a cupola like some Greek temple. Spreading out to either side were long wings with graceful high windows, each wing fronted by a broad garden full of statues and hedges.

Time hadn't been kind to the building, though. A long crack ran across the cupola, and even from this distance Chapel could see it must be open to the sky. Meanwhile one wing had nearly collapsed, all its windows shattered, its brick walls crumbling until some of the rooms inside were exposed. The gardens were overgrown thickets. Nature had begun the long process of reclaiming the house, with a massive growth of ivy choking the walls, creepers spiraling up those strong pillars. It must have been abandoned for decades.

Or at least someone wanted it to look that way.

"I don't know," Julia said. "Not the kind of place I'd keep a server farm, if it was up to me. I don't see any sign of habitation, do you?"

"Just one," Chapel said. The house stood in a wide clearing, but it was surrounded on every side by clumps of trees. Hidden among the trunks he could just make out a high fence topped in coils of barbed wire. "Whoever owns that place isn't interested in having visitors."

Julia clucked her tongue. "Maybe the fence is just there to keep the locals from wandering in and getting hurt. You know, a liability thing."

"Maybe," Chapel said. He looked back at Angel, who was slumped low in the backseat, only her eyes above the level of her window. "What do you think?"

"I don't know anything about architecture," she said. "But I guess . . . I mean, a place like that. Why does it need so many satellite dishes?"

Chapel had missed them in his first look. Now he saw them instantly, perched among the ornamental stonework that ran around the cupola. They were painted the same color as the weathered stone, but once you knew they were there, you couldn't miss them.

"Good eyes," he said.

"Great," Angel replied. "Now can we go?"

MOREHEAD, KY: MARCH 24, 18:19

They found a little motel on the outskirts of the nearest town, a place that looked cheap but not too shabby. Chapel pulled up in front of a row of rooms connected by a long porch, then killed the engine. The three of them, glad for a chance to stretch their legs, headed into the reception office together.

A man with very thick glasses and a little bit of white hair welcomed them with a smile. "Need a room?" he asked. Then he took a look at Angel and said, "Maybe two rooms."

They were running out of money, but Chapel understood what the man was suggesting. He saw a middle-aged couple and a young woman who was too old to be their daughter. In this part of the country that meant separate rooms or a lot of uncomfortable questions. "Two, yeah. Maybe something in the back that doesn't face the road? I'm a light sleeper, and I don't want headlights keeping me up all night."

"Surely," the man said as he pushed a paper ledger across his counter. Chapel signed, using an alias he came up with on the spot—Charles Darnley. "Cash or credit?" the clerk asked.

"Cash," Chapel said and pulled some bills out of his pocket.

"You here for the folk arts center? Just about the only thing to see around here," the man said, counting out change.

"No, we're just passing through," Chapel told him. "We're, uh—"

"Ghost hunters," Julia said.

Chapel fought the urge to turn around and stare at her.

"There's a restaurant in Lexington that claims to be haunted," Julia said. "We're going to take some readings tomorrow."

"Really now," the clerk said, suddenly very interested. "Can't say I've ever seen a ghost myself. But there are all kinds of things hidden back in these hills, they say."

Julia nodded excitedly. "I'll bet. For instance—on the way here, we saw a big mansion on the next ridge over. I had no idea there was anything like that around here."

The clerk nodded and patted his belly. "The old Chobham place, sure, sure. 'Fraid you won't get up there, though."

"Oh? That's a shame," Julia said. "It must have quite a story."

"Indeed, indeed. Built by a coal magnate back in the '30s, a placer miner who got lucky. He bought up half this county before his seam ran dry. Then he couldn't afford to keep it. The government bought it up in the Depression and turned it into a camp for the WPA. That's all long ago, now. Nobody's lived up there in my lifetime."

"It's a shame they let a place like that go to seed," Chapel said.

The clerk lifted one shoulder toward his ear, in a kind of lazy shrug. "Too expensive, I suppose, to keep it open, and anyway, we got a real shortage of billionaires around here might want it. No, the government seems happy to let it rot."

"I'd love to take a look," Julia told him. "But you say it's off-limits?"

"Well, sure now. The place ain't safe for human occupation," the clerk pointed out. "You could fall through some broken floorboards, or a brick could muss that pretty red hair of yours. Even the local teenagers, well, they'll go anywhere their parents aren't looking, sure, but they stay clear. There's a pretty serious fence, and there's signs all 'round saying trespassers'll be shot."

"What a shame," Julia said. "It would be great for our TV show. But I guess we'll just have to hope this restaurant in Lexington pans out."

The clerk got a shrewd look in his eye. "TV show? Now, it might just be, we have a haunted room right at this motel, if y'all'd be interested in staying a few nights."

Julia laughed. "You have a haunted room, or you *might* have a haunted room?"

"Just suggesting a TV appearance could help my business. If you catch my drift," the clerk said, with a wink.

"I'm sure I don't know *what* you're suggesting," Julia said, suddenly deeply offended. "We're serious scientists, only interested in getting to the truth about the paranormal."

"Didn't mean nothing by it," the clerk said. "I'll get you some keys."

When he was gone, Chapel turned to look at Julia. "Ghost hunters?" he whispered.

"I watch a lot of reality television," she told him. "I thought it would make a good cover, and give me a chance to ask about the mansion."

Chapel nodded, impressed. Badass Julia made a great field agent, whether or not she had any training.

Once they had the keys, Chapel went outside to pull the car around to the back of the motel, where another file of rooms looked out on a thick growth of forest. When the women joined him, he held up the two keys. "One for boys, one for girls?" he said, but Angel just grabbed one of the keys out of his hand and hurried inside one of the rooms. A moment later he heard the door's dead bolt slam into place, and then the sound of a television turned up to a high volume. It sounded like it was showing C-SPAN.

He turned to look at Julia. "I wish I knew what was going on with her."

Julia sighed. "Agoraphobia. She denied it when I asked, but . . . my ex-boyfriend had a cousin with agoraphobia. She came to visit us once in New York, but she couldn't handle Manhattan. She said she felt like all the tall buildings were going to fall down on her. She used to make all kinds of excuses why she couldn't leave the house."

Chapel frowned. "Angel's been all right until now."

"This is the first time we've traveled by daylight," Julia pointed out. "A fear of wide-open spaces is a lot easier to handle when you can't see them." She took the other key from his hand and unlocked the second room. "She'll be okay if you leave her alone. Shut up in that room she can probably relax for the first time all day."

Chapel grabbed some bags from the car. "Poor Angel," he said.

Julia looked toward the closed door of Angel's room. "What I'd really like to know is whether she was like this before the government started hiding her away in trailers, or if it's a reaction to living her entire life online." She turned and looked at him. "Somebody really did a number on her, Chapel. They've kept her from having any kind of real life. They've put her under acute psychological stress. Whoever it was, they've got a lot to answer for."

Chapel couldn't find it in himself to disagree.

MOREHEAD, KY: MARCH 24, 18:36

Chapel locked the door of the room and started unpacking. He hadn't brought much—just a few pieces of clothing donated by Top's boys. Most of those he left in the bag, but he took out a pair of dark jeans and a black hoodie. It was what he intended to wear that night when they investigated the mansion.

"You think we'll find something useful in that place?" Julia asked. She sat down on the room's queen-size bed and kicked off her shoes.

"I hope we will," Chapel told her. "Angel believes that the command that launched the original drone attack in New Orleans came from there. If there are NSA people inside, we might be able to ask them some important questions."

"I'm guessing they'll be uncooperative," Julia pointed out.

Chapel nodded. "We'll find a way to get them to talk. But it probably won't even come to that. Most likely the place is deserted, just a bunch of servers running on automatic. The NSA was smart enough not to send the attack signal from one of their official data centers. Most likely this place is just a relay—a cutout, designed to hide what they're doing. But that might be useful, too. If there's NSA hardware inside, then Angel can use it to get past their firewall and hack into their main servers."

"Won't they instantly know what she's doing, like last time? It only took a few minutes for Wilkes to figure out where she was."

"That was because she was working on an open, commercial Internet connection. Using the NSA's own hardware means she can sneak in undetected." Chapel shrugged. "I don't understand how it works, but it sounds like it makes sense."

Julia smiled. "And if she does find something, some evidence. What then?"

"Then we go to the director of national intelligence with it. Show him the NSA has been attacking American assets. He'll shut them down in a hurry. The evidence will show that we—Angel, me, Director Hollingshead—are innocent, and he'll call off Wilkes and anyone else who's looking for us." He sat down in a chair by the door. "Anyway. That's the plan."

Julia nodded. "You want me to be your lookout again?"

"Absolutely. I have no idea what kind of security this place has. It could just be that fence I saw and nothing else. Or they could have cameras, or even armed rapid response teams patrolling the place after dark. Though I doubt that—the clerk here would have told us the place was guarded, when what he was telling us was we couldn't go up there."

Julia leaned toward the bed, stretching her arms and arching her back. "When do we leave?"

"Not until the middle of the night. I want it as dark as I can get. Then we'll need to hike up there—I don't want our friendly clerk here noticing that we're taking our car out of the lot."

"Good," Julia said. "That gives me a little time to relax. I still like the occasional road trip, but it's more draining than I remember. If you want to take a nap, you can use the bed. I'm thinking I'll take a very long, very hot bath."

"Sounds good," he said.

She went into the bathroom and soon he heard the sound of water running. He stripped off his shirt and checked on the bandage around his midriff. It looked like it was still in good shape. So he slipped off his artificial arm and plugged it into a wall socket, then lay down on the bed and tried to close his eyes.

A nap would be good. It would be useful. It was looking like a long night ahead. But he was just too wired—every time he closed his eyes they just snapped open again.

The bathroom door opened and Julia stepped out. She looked down at him and gave him a smile he couldn't quite read.

Then she pulled her shirt over her head and draped it across the back of a chair. Her bra came next, and suddenly he had no interest in closing his eyes anymore. As she unbuttoned her pants she said, "I don't want to get my clothes wet in there."

She was still smiling. She didn't stop as she stepped out of her panties and stood nude there in the doorway.

Chapel sat up. "You, uh, don't want any company in there, do you?" he asked.

"In the bath? Absolutely not," she said, and her smile grew mischievous. "There's no room for two. Anyway, you can't get your side wet, not until you're properly healed."

"Right."

She turned to step inside the bathroom. "Of course," she said, "you could come sit with me. Help me scrub my back."

"Yes, ma'am," he said, jumping off the bed.

MOREHEAD, KY: MARCH 24, 18:43

Julia got a washcloth good and wet, squeezing it until soap bubbles popped between her fingers. She handed it to him, then leaned forward so he could wash her shoulders and back. He moved it slowly across her smooth, freckled skin, feeling the knobs of her spine through the thin cloth.

"Mmm," she said. "I'd forgotten how nice it is to have someone do this for me." She glanced back over her shoulder at him. In the steaming bathroom, curls of her hair stuck to her forehead and her cheek. "I've had to get used to doing everything for myself since I sent you away."

Apparently Badass Julia was in a playful mood.

Chapel scrubbed lower down, paying special attention to the small of her back. He knew how much she liked that. It made her squirm now, pulling her knees up to her chest. A little water splashed out of the tub and got his feet wet. He didn't mind.

He leaned over to kiss her shoulder. Putting the washcloth down, he lifted the hair away from the back of her neck and kissed her there, dragging his lips across the incredibly soft skin as she bent her head forward to receive his mouth.

"I'm never going to get clean if you keep doing that," she told him.

"I don't mind if you're a little dirty," he told her.

She laughed and then pushed him away. Leaning back in the tub, she looked up at him and suddenly her eyes turned serious. "We're doing this?" she asked.

"Looks like."

She nodded. "I want it, Jim. I want us to be like this again. Things—things can't be the same as before, though. Too much has changed."

His heart sank a little. "I know."

"I still can't believe you've forgiven me," she told him. "When I broke things off—I was so cruel—"

"I know why you had to do it," he told her. "It doesn't matter."

"I've changed, too," she told him. "I'm not sure I understand how, but I feel it."

"Julia," he said, "whatever can be between us, whatever it means. I want that. Things haven't changed for me at all."

"God. Listen to me," she said, with a laugh. "I'm talking about feelings when we should be focused on just enjoying this."

"So let's stop talking," he told her.

He found the washcloth and scrubbed her arms, feeling the tight muscles in her biceps, running his hand down into the water to her wrists, to twine his fingers in hers. He brought the cloth up and worked it across the top of her breasts, watching the soap bubbles slide down those perfect curves, parting around the mounds of her hard nipples. He took his time, stopping now and again to kiss her deeply.

He dropped the washcloth in the tub and took one of her breasts in his hand, cupping it, caressing it, his thumb brushing against her nipple and making her gasp. She reached up and grabbed his wrist, then pulled his hand down across her smooth, flat stomach, locking her eyes to his as his fingertips found the red hair between her legs. She parted her thighs a little and he found her clitoris, rubbed it in small circles until she trembled. He slipped his index finger inside her and she let out a little cry, then slapped a hand over her mouth.

"We have to be quiet," she whispered. "I don't want Angel to hear us and get jealous."

He leaned in close until his mouth was just millimeters from her ear. "Then be quiet," he told her and slipped a second finger inside her body.

After that he made no attempt to take things slow. He worked her clit with the ball of his thumb while his fingers slipped in and out. Her body shook from head to toe and she whimpered behind her hand as a bead of sweat rolled down her forehead.

He kept up the rhythm, moving nothing but his hand, feeling how her whole body curled around him. One of her feet came out of the tub and he saw her toes clench against the enamel as if she was trying desperately to find something to hold on to. Her breath came out of her in quick gasps and then water went everywhere as she flung her arms around him, pulling him close and then she shoved her face into his bare skin, smearing her mouth across him as she suppressed the noise she couldn't help but make. And still he kept stroking her, his fingers moving faster and faster—

—and then her whole body tensed, her hands squeezing his skin, her face buried in his chest and her hair bouncing against him as she cried out as she came, the sound reverberating through his body. She bit him a little and he laughed and she waved one hand in mock threat.

Eventually she stopped shaking and lay back against the tub, staring up at the ceiling, her hair floating on the soapy water.

She was so beautiful like that, so perfect he wanted to just stare at her forever. Instead he leaned over and kissed her, lightly, gently, on the lips.

"Oh my God," she breathed. "Whatever happens between us, Jim, whatever we are in the future . . ."

"Yes?" he asked.

"It's going to include that. A lot of that."

MOREHEAD, KY: MARCH 24, 23:07

Angel had recovered quite well by the time they knocked on her door and told her it was time to head out. She wore a navy blue windbreaker and a pair of black slacks she'd borrowed from Dolores. Julia was similarly outfitted in clothes from Suzie, including a dark knit cap to cover her red hair. Each of them had a flashlight, and Chapel had a satchel full of tools.

"Where'd you get those?" Angel asked.

"The motel has a shed out back full of gardening stuff," he said. "The lock on the door wasn't exactly secure."

Julia shook her head. "If I didn't know you were one of the good guys," she said, "I would worry about all the shady things you do."

"Lucky for me I have a winning personality," he told her.

The three of them set out quietly, not even turning on their flashlights until they were deep into the woods behind the motel. They took their time, staying as far from the road as possible, cutting through tangled growths of forest when they could. When they had to cross a farmer's field, they moved fast with no light, keeping their heads down. Chapel felt ridiculously exposed as they dashed across the stubble and irrigation ditches, but sometimes they had no choice.

Once they had to walk within a hundred yards of a big, rambling farmhouse, close enough they could see the blue light of a television flickering inside. Once they heard dogs barking from close by as they pressed through a stand of trees. As far as Chapel could tell, though, no human being noticed them passing.

It was well after midnight by the time they reached the fence surrounding the mansion. Chapel told the women to stand well back while he investigated it. He didn't see any cameras mounted on the fence posts, and no suspicious cables or junction boxes that might suggest the fence was electrified. Still, he wanted to be careful. He studied the fence for long minutes, taking in the fact that the chain link was rigorously secured and that the coils of razor wire on top weren't rusted at all. That suggested somebody was taking care of this fence on a regular basis. A good sign in itself, though it meant it would be harder to get inside.

His final test was the one that scared him the most, but it had to be done. He reached out and grabbed the chain link with his artificial hand. The silicone flesh of his prosthesis would insulate him if it was electrified, but if the current running through it was strong enough—

He breathed a sigh of relief. The fence wasn't electrified. Nor did he hear any alarms go off the second he touched it. Of course he knew there could be a silent alarm—maybe a light had just gone on in a security office inside the mansion, or maybe an automated system had already called the police to tell them someone was breaking into the old Chobham place. But if that was the case, there was nothing he could do about it. He had to get through this fence somehow, no matter the consequences.

"You aren't climbing that," Julia pointed out. "Not without reopening your wound."

"That's why I brought these," Chapel said. He pulled a pair of long-handled wire cutters out of his satchel. "You two spread out, and keep your ears open. If you hear anyone coming, let me know and we'll book it. This'll take some time."

The women nodded and disappeared into the trees. Chapel got to work.

In the movies, when someone cut their way through a fence, it seemed to take only a few seconds, or at best the director would cut away while the would-be intruder handled the laborious task. In real life, chain-link fences were designed to keep people out, and they were designed very well.

It took all of Chapel's strength to cut through the first link. The fence was made of thick galvanized steel and woven in such a way that breaking any one thread didn't help you much. He worked as fast as he could, but before he'd even made a dent in the fence he was sweating profusely and his living hand had started to cramp up. Then there was the fact that the fence rattled every time he touched it, and each link he cut made a sound like a little gunshot. If anyone was paying attention inside the fence, he was certain they would hear him before he got through.

In time, though, he made an L-shaped cut long enough that he thought they could wriggle through it. He put down the wire cutters and leaned against a nearby tree, getting his breath back and letting his hand relax. Before he was done recovering, Julia and Angel had returned. "The only thing I heard was you cursing at the damned fence," Angel said.

"Yeah," Julia said. "There's nobody out here. It's kind of spooky. I kept expecting a security guard to shine a light in my face. But I didn't see so much as a squirrel."

"It's possible there's nobody inside," Chapel pointed out. "This could just be an automated server farm. But we're not going to take any chances. Once we're inside this fence, no talking, okay? And don't do anything I don't do first. I'll walk a little ahead, keeping my eyes open for . . . I don't know what. Anything from trip wires to land mines. When I stop, you stop. When I walk, you walk. Got it?"

"Got it," Angel said. Julia nodded.

"Okay," he said. He bent low, even though the sutures in his side made him feel like he was being poked in the ribs with a pitchfork. He pulled the cut fence back like a flap, pushing it as hard as he could so it wouldn't just spring back on him. Careful not to snag his clothes—or his skin—on the sharp edges of the cut links, he stepped inside.

No spotlights came on from the house. No one called out for him to freeze.

He helped Julia and Angel clamber through. He took a little time to bend the fence back into place, so that given a cursory inspection in the dark it would be hard to tell it had ever been cut.

Then he headed for the mansion.

NORTHWEST OF MOREHEAD, KY: MARCH 25, 00:54

Overhead the branches of the trees spread like dark fingers clutching at anyone foolish enough to walk beneath them. It must have rained recently, because the undergrowth was damp and squelched under Chapel's shoes. He used his flashlight sparingly, snapping it on for only a few seconds at a time, and keeping its lens covered with his hand. Hopefully that prevented anyone in the mansion from seeing his light, but it also played tricks with his night vision, so he was constantly blinking away afterimages. If there was something hidden in the leaf litter, he would be very lucky to see it.

Ahead of him the woods gave way to a long, overgrown patch of grass, and beyond that lay the neglected garden below the east wing. In the cloud-streaked moonlight it didn't look like a house at all but instead like a haunted fortress, its crumbling walls like the battlements of a Gothic castle.

In the garden a statue of an angel with open, beckoning hands stared down at him with stony eyes. Lichen had encrusted its cheek, and one of its wings ended in a jagged stump.

He crept forward, crouching so low he could keep his artificial hand down on the ground, feeling for trip wires he couldn't see. This was crazy—thinking he could get across that open ground, thinking he could break into this place. It had to be guarded, by cameras if by nothing else. They would see him the second he stepped out of the trees. See him, and send an alert to Wilkes, and he would come flying in to finish the job he'd started at the electronics store . . .

Chapel licked his lips and studied the windows of the mansion. He saw no light up there, no movement. Nothing to give away a human presence. It looked exactly like what it purported to be, an old abandoned house slowly falling in on itself. He struggled to control his fear, took another step—

—and felt something give under his foot.

There was a crack like something breaking, loud enough to make him want to jump. He held very still. If it was a trip wire connected to a land mine, say, it might go off only when he lifted his foot again. He switched on his light and pointed it at his shoe.

A twig. He had stepped on a twig, and it had cracked under his weight. That was all.

He looked back over his shoulder and saw Julia and Angel staring at him, their eyes wide. He held up one hand to give them the okay signal. Julia nodded, but she still looked terrified.

He didn't blame her.

At the very edge of the trees, still in their shadow, he slipped the flashlight into his bag of tools. He gestured for Julia to come forward, then whispered in her ear, so softly the swaying trees made more noise. "I'm going to run up there, into the garden. Don't follow until I give you the signal. When you do, come fast, and get into cover as soon as you can. Tell Angel to do the same, okay?"

"Okay," she whispered back.

He nodded. Took a breath. And ran dashing out across the grass, not even bothering to keep his head down. What would be the point? Anyone watching from the house would see a dark shape hurtling from the woods, perfectly silhouetted against the damp, silvery grass.

He stamped up the slope, eating up the ground. Ten yards, eight, five—and then he was right up against an overgrown hedge, under its shadow. He dropped to the ground and let himself breathe for a second. Then he crept along the hedge, eventually coming to a break where it let into the garden proper. Inside he saw paths laid out in flagstones that had, over the years, tilted up at crazy angles. The paths ran in a wide circle around a dry and cracked fountain. The statue he'd seen stood in the middle of the fountain, facing a little away from him now. Irrational as it might be, he was glad to be out of its line of sight.

At the far end of the garden, past the fountain, was a low stone wall. Steps were cut into it, leading up to the east wing of the house. So close now.

He took a step away from the shelter of the hedge, back into the moonlight, and waved one hand over his head.

Instantly he saw Julia and Angel come running out of the woods, holding on to each other as they barreled across the grass. Smart—they were minimizing their profile, making it impossible for a watcher to tell if it was one person or two running toward the garden. He wondered which of them had thought of that. Not for the first time, nor the hundredth, he was glad he'd picked such bright people to be his partners in crime.

He watched them come, digging their feet in the grass as they made their way up the slope. It seemed to take forever for them to cross the open ground. He waved them closer, even though they wouldn't be able to see him in the shadow of the hedge.

Just a little closer. A few more seconds, and then—

Chapel's blood froze in his veins.

He'd heard something. A sound—a very weird sound. A kind of shrieking, but rhythmic, kind of like the cry of an animal. Kind of not. He couldn't imagine what on earth could make such a noise.

It didn't stop. It was getting closer.

"Come on," he whispered, then grabbed for Angel's arm as she came into reach, pulling her close to the hedge. Julia dropped to the ground, sitting with her back against the dense shrubbery. She reached over and touched his shoulder, pointed.

The sound was much louder now. She must have heard it—and tracked it back to its source. He could see it now, too.

Coming around the side of the house, up past the garden, a dark shape appeared silhouetted against the dark sky. The moonlight was only enough to give away the rough outline of the thing. To show that it was about the size and shape of a horse, with four legs that moved like an animal's legs. There was only one reason to think that it was not in fact a horse.

It didn't have a head.

NORTHWEST OF MOREHEAD, KY: MARCH 25, 01:01

The headless thing screeched as it moved. Each step, each time it bent one of its joints, it let out a high-pitched whining sound that made Chapel's brain ache. As it walked toward them the sound became a sustained, horrible creaking that made it impossible for him to think, impossible to decide what to do next.

Especially when another of the things came around the far wing of the mansion and started picking its way toward them.

The things pranced more than they walked. They moved like deer, maybe, more than horses, their thin legs probing, testing with each step. They walked like drunkards who couldn't be sure the ground would be where they expected it to be, who had to be extra-careful not to fall down.

For all that, they could move *fast* when they wanted to. The one that had appeared at the far end of the house closed the distance in a hurry, running straight at them until it was almost upon them. Meanwhile, the first one they'd seen was still carefully picking its way down toward them, climbing over the debris of the fallen wing, cresting a pile of bricks like a mountain goat, testing and probing its way through the frame of a broken window.

"They're robots," Angel said.

Chapel wanted to smack himself across the forehead. How hadn't he seen that? Of course they were. That terrible sound they made—it was the whine of servomotors firing in sequence inside their mechanical legs. And when he thought about their body shape, he remembered he'd seen video of such things before, video of machines that were being tested by the armed forces for—

"I don't care what they are," Julia said. "I don't want one touching me."

Chapel nodded. Right. They needed to get away from these things.

"Back to the trees," he said. "We've been spotted—don't worry about being stealthy. Just run."

Julia nodded and jumped out of the shadows, headed for the trees they'd just left. If they could get back to the cover of the forest, back out through the gap they'd made in the fence, Chapel was sure the robots wouldn't follow them. He hated to just abort before they'd even got inside the secret data center, but what choice did they have? He gestured for Angel to run for the trees, then hurtled after her, even as the headless robots converged on the garden. Chapel glanced back over his shoulder as he ran, expecting to see the two robots hurtling after him, skidding down the slope on their skinny legs. Instead they simply took up position back there, like sentries.

He was afraid he knew what that meant. He turned his head to look back toward the trees just in time to see two more of the robots hidden there, crouching behind the branches.

"Angel! Julia!" he shouted. "Watch out!"

Julia saw the robots in time and slid to a stop on the wet grass, but Angel didn't seem to understand what was happening. She kept running, right up to the edge of the trees. Chapel dashed after her, thinking he would grab her and pull her back, but he was too late.

The robot pounced with a grace no machine should have. It came down hard on Angel, knocking her to the ground. She rolled away, throwing her arms up to protect her head, but the robot reared over her, its front limbs flailing in the air, ready to stab down and smash her where she lay.

Running, not caring if he slid on the wet grass, Chapel caromed into the thing, body-slamming it from the side. If he could knock it over, he thought, leave it pinwheeling its legs in the air like an overturned tortoise, maybe that would give Angel time to get away. He got his shoulder underneath the thing and heaved, throwing it sideways.

It slipped away from him, its feet dancing crazily on the leaf litter, moving in a desperate rhythm and screaming with that horrible noise. It tilted one way, then the other, and he thought it was about to topple over. Instead it staggered and swung around like a drunkard—but it never lost its footing. It never fell over.

Damn.

Once it had stabilized itself, the thing turned slowly, and he got the impression it was glaring at him. If it had snorted like an enraged bull, he would have felt less intimidated. It was about to charge him, he was certain, and he tried to guess which direction to jump, which way to move to get away from it.

Then he felt something tugging at his back. Thinking one of the machines had come up behind him, he glanced over his shoulder and saw Angel dragging something out of the pack on his back.

Instantly he knew what she had planned. After years of working together, he guessed they really had come to know how the other one thought.

He feinted to his left and the four-legged robot started its charge, clearly intending to bowl him over and trample him. At the last second, Chapel broke right, barely getting out of its way. It barreled past him at high speed, its spindly legs squealing.

Before it could change course to come around for another attack, Angel brought a rubber mallet down hard on its side, a glancing blow but enough to make it dance sideways, just like when he'd tried to flip it over. As its feet lifted and fell, desperately trying to find its balance again, Angel dropped the mallet and hefted the same wire cutters he'd used to get through the perimeter fence.

She didn't worry about finesse—instead she just jammed the blades of the cutters deep into the thickest part of the robot's front left leg and then squeezed the long handles together. There was a very loud pop and a flash of light and suddenly that leg hung from the side of the machine as nothing more than dead weight.

"Now," she said.

Chapel rushed in and got his shoulder right into the prancing thing's side and this time he felt it shift under his weight. Inch by inch he knocked it back, even as its three working legs scrambled beneath it, desperately looking for purchase. He wouldn't give it a chance and kept pushing—until the whole thing went over, falling over on its side where its legs kicked uselessly at empty air.

"Three to go," Angel said, but before Chapel could reply, both of them turned to look up at the ruined east wing of the house.

They could hear Julia screaming from up there.

NORTHWEST OF MOREHEAD, KY: MARCH 25, 01:22

The two of them raced up the slope, watching in every direction in case one of the four-legged machines came flying out of the shadows. From the muffled sound of Julia's shouts it was clear she'd tried to escape into the house, but the robots must have followed her in. Chapel and Angel hurried through the garden and up the steps, then Chapel pressed his back against the wall of the house, right next to a place where a broken window would let him get inside. He took a heavy wrench from his backpack—the best weapon he had—and looked over at Angel. She was panting, her eyes wide, but it looked like she was ready for this.

"Watch my back," he told her. Then he ducked inside the house.

It was pitch-black inside, and even when he switched on his flashlight, it gave only enough illumination to show him the rough outlines of broken furniture and, at the far end of the room, an open doorway. He had no way of knowing whether Julia had come this way or what lay beyond that door, but he didn't waste any time wondering. Calling for Angel to follow him, he headed into a hallway that ran the length of the wing. Angel pointed her own light at the ceiling, then moved it back and forth. "Look," she said. "That's Cat-5 cable hanging up there."

Chapel spared a glance for the bundle of cables that hung on hooks from the ceiling, strung up like bunting. It might be more evidence that the mansion was, in fact, a secret data center, but it didn't help him find Julia.

Standard operating procedure suggested he should stay quiet and keep his light off as much as possible. Standard operating procedure was very useful for infiltrating locations that were possibly full of unseen enemies in the middle of the night.

SOP be damned. "Julia!" he shouted as loud as he could. "Julia! Where are you? Are you okay?"

Angel winced and took a step away from him, as if he were inviting the wrath of the gods and lightning might hit him at any moment. When there was no reply, she pushed open a side door and pointed her light into the room beyond. "Clear," she said and moved to the next door. "Clear."

"Julia!" Chapel shouted. Why wasn't she answering? He was pretty sure the four-legged robots weren't programmed to kill them. Otherwise, why not give them better weaponry than their spindly legs? But maybe Julia had hurt herself by accident, somewhere in the house. Maybe she had fallen through rotten floorboards or something had collapsed on top of her—

"Clear," Angel said, taking another doorway.

"Stop saying that," Chapel snapped. She hadn't been trained for this kind of operation. She had no idea what "clear" really meant, especially not when she was just pointing her light into the middle of each room. Chapel sighed. "Corners," he said.

"What?"

"You check each corner of the room, one, two, three, four. Even then, you don't say 'clear' unless you're sure there are no doors or closets or even cupboards in there. If there are, you need to check every one of them."

Angel looked hurt. "On TV—"

"On TV, they don't fire real bullets," he told her. He ran to the end of the hallway. "Julia!" he shouted.

Had he heard something? Had Julia responded? He couldn't be sure his mind wasn't just playing tricks on him. He'd thought he'd heard footsteps that stopped as soon as he called out.

It could have been anything. At the end of the hall was a huge foyer, with a cracked marble floor and a huge staircase leading up to the second story. The stairs looked intact, and more bundles of cable ran along the wall, following the risers. A little moonlight came in through tall windows and made the stone floor glow.

"Julia!" he shouted.

Nothing. He started across the floor, intending to climb those stairs. Behind him Angel stepped into the room and pointed her light across the foyer, at the entrance to the far wing.

Her light picked out a dark shape, crouching on four segmented legs. A shape with no head.

"Shit!" she cried out, the expletive lost as the robot started screeching away, its spindly feet lifting high and then stepping down hard on the slippery marble.

"Upstairs," Chapel said. "Maybe it can't climb!"

But he was pretty sure it could.

NORTHWEST OF MOREHEAD, KY: MARCH 25, 01:29

He pushed Angel ahead of him, moving her up the steps as quickly as he could. The stairs were, in fact, completely intact, untouched by the general ruin of the mansion, and they made good time.

Better time than the robot, anyway. He'd been right; it could climb stairs, but it was a slow process. The machine had to test each new step with each of its feet, bearing down on one leg, then the other to make sure it would hold its weight. By the time Chapel and Angel reached the top of the stairs, the robot was only halfway up.

Which was good, except for one problem—it meant they couldn't get back down, if they needed to.

"Keep moving," he told her. "Keep looking for Julia."

Angel's light hurried on ahead of them, following the bundles of cable that ran along the wall.

"I said to ignore those," Chapel said. "Look for—"

"I've got a hunch," Angel told him. "I'm supposed to go with those, right? Hunches?"

Chapel shook his head. This was no time to argue. He shoved open a door and stumbled inside, his light hitting each of the corners. Nothing there.

"This way," Angel said, grabbing his arm.

Behind them, the robot was three-quarters of its way up the stairs. Chapel cursed and followed Angel. Together they headed down a long hallway with doors on either side. The bundles of cabling rose to the ceiling again. Occasionally one strand of cable would break off from the rest and disappear through a doorway, but the majority of the bundle continued in a nearly straight line toward the end of the hall. A big pair of doors stood there, one of them open just a crack. A hole had been drilled through the wall above the doors and the entire bundle of cable disappeared through it. Whatever lay beyond those doors clearly needed a lot of cable, though Chapel had no idea what that might mean.

He started to bellow for Julia again, but Angel reached up and clamped one hand over his mouth. Had she heard something? Seen something? He put his back against the wall and looked up and down the hallway, trying to determine what had alerted her.

Then he heard it. The screeching of robotic legs. The machine had made it to the top of the stairs and was coming closer, or—no, it wasn't just one set of legs—

Angel ran to the double doors and threw them open. The room beyond was well lit and gave off the distinctive hum of server racks breathing together like the bees in a hive. None of that mattered to Chapel, though.

He could think of only one thing as Angel stepped inside the server room.

"Corners!" he called out.

Just before someone grabbed Angel and hauled her, screaming, out of view.

NORTHWEST OF MOREHEAD, KY: MARCH 25, 01:32

Angel's scream cut off abruptly. The only thing Chapel could hear was the screech of the robot or robots behind him, coming closer.

The doors to the server room closed as if under their own power.

Chapel ran forward and beat on the doors with his fists, calling Angel's name. Glancing over his shoulder, he saw not one but two of the headless robots approaching, their thin legs stepping high on the carpeted floor of the hallway.

He still had his tools. He could stand and fight the robots. At least he could go down fighting—swinging away with a pipefitter's wrench while the machines kicked him to death. It would be a pointless, stupid way to die. It wouldn't help Julia or Angel. But Chapel had always been too dumb to just give up. He started to reach for the backpack.

That was when he felt the barrel of a silenced pistol touch the back of his neck.

In front of him the robots fell silent and unmoving. As if their power switches had been flipped to off. Clearly they weren't needed anymore.

Chapel set his face in an emotionless mask and started turning around to face whoever it was who had drawn down on him.

It was Wilkes, of course. He recognized the man's voice. "Stay right there, buddy. Don't turn around. Not until I tell you to. You can go ahead and nod a little to show me you understand."

Chapel nodded.

"Good. This bullshit with the robots, that wasn't my idea. I want you to know that. My new operator thought it would be fun to test out some of his toys on you bunch. I protested, but after you got away the last time, I don't get to give so many orders."

Chapel sighed in resignation. "I expected more out of a trained assassin—"

The pistol dug into the back of Chapel's neck. "Don't talk," Wilkes said. "You don't say anything until we ask you specific questions. Nod if you've got that."

Chapel nodded.

"Okay. We're going to do a little dance. You're going to turn around and face the doors while I stay directly behind you. We're going to take this slow and easy. All you have to do is shuffle your feet until you're turned around. You understand?"

Chapel nodded again.

He rotated in place, very slowly. Wilkes was quick enough that Chapel never really got a good look at him. Much less any chance to grab the gun—which was the point of their little pirouette, of course.

"Okay. When the doors open, you walk through, right into the middle of the room. Then you get down on your knees and put your hands behind your back."

Just as Wilkes had promised, the doors opened. Chapel stepped through, noticing as he went that nobody stood near the doors—they were, in fact, automatic. He walked through into the server room. Light came from two long fluorescent tubes overhead, bright enough to make it hard for Chapel to see much. He took in the boarded-over windows of the room and the big shelving units full of computer equipment. It was warm inside, with so many racks of hard drives and circuit boards buzzing away. There were other people in the room, but he was blinking so much he couldn't make out their faces.

One of them had red hair. Julia was still alive. That was something.

Chapel stopped in the middle of the room and dropped down onto his knees. He put his hands behind his back and waited. He felt Wilkes come up behind him. A knife touched his neck and then cut down, through his shirt. Fingers dug into his back, getting under the complicated flanges that held on his artificial arm. Wilkes tripped the two hidden catches that locked the arm in place and suddenly it was gone. What remained of Chapel's shoulder felt naked and exposed.

Wilkes used a pair of handcuffs to lock Chapel's good wrist to his ankle. Chapel knew he wasn't going anywhere bound up like that.

He was pretty sure this was how he was going to die.

NORTHWEST OF MOREHEAD, KY: MARCH 25, 01:34

Chapel blinked in the light of the server room until his vision cleared and he could see again. The first thing he could make out was that there were two big armchairs at the far end of the room, their upholstery torn and their stuffing falling out. Julia sat in one of them, and Angel in the other. They'd been tied up with heavy rope and Angel had a gag across her mouth. They both looked terrified.

"We're still alive," he told them. Wilkes grabbed his hair and pulled his head back, but Chapel needed to reassure the two women. "If they wanted us dead, they would have already—"

Wilkes smashed Chapel across the mouth with the butt of his pistol. Blood leaked down between Chapel's teeth.

"You're still alive," the assassin said, "because my operator had to see you die for himself or it doesn't count. Orders. Once he verifies you are who you are, that's when it's over. So don't fool yourself."

Julia tried to say something, but Wilkes lifted his pistol as if he would strike Chapel with it again. She closed her mouth.

"It won't be long," Wilkes said. "He just went down to look at that robot you took out. He didn't think it was possible. In fact—"

"In fact," a new voice said, from behind Chapel, "I recorded a lot of useful data that we can add to the evaluation process. We're testing those robots for battlefield use, to carry heavy equipment and even to ferry wounded soldiers back to field hospitals. They do an amazing job of handling rough terrain. Nobody had really thought to use them for base security before, though. For this trial, I downloaded a descriptive algorithm based on the way wolves hunt in packs. When faced with multiple prey animals, it turns out the best strategy is actually to separate them from one another. Pick out the weakest, the slowest, and get it away from the herd. I'm afraid that turned out to be you, Ms. Taggart."

Julia's eyes went wide.

Paul Moulton, the analyst that Chapel had met at the NSA—the one who had accused Angel in the first place, and started all this—walked to the far end of the room, where Chapel could see him. He wore a sweater vest over a shirt and tie and a very, very smug expression on his face.

"Hello again, Captain Chapel," he said. Then he turned to Wilkes. "This is them. You've got your targets. Um, fire at will, I guess."

Chapel closed his eyes, waiting for the gunshot. He heard Angel trying desperately to talk around her gag, but he tried to block out the sound.

He couldn't ignore Julia, though.

"That's him," she said. "Jim, that's the guy!"

"What?" Chapel asked.

"The guy who came to see me, when you were on your mission. The one who told me to break up with you or he would out you to the press."

Chapel was seconds from being shot to death, but still his mind reeled. "Seriously?" he asked.

"Yeah, guilty, whatever," Moulton said. "Do you really want to talk about this? We can just shoot you now; it'll be easier that way. Like pulling off a Band-Aid."

Julia clearly intended to hash it all out, though. "He threatened you. And then he showed me that picture of you and the other woman," she said. "I thought he was CIA, but—"

"NSA," Chapel said, nodding. "Moulton, I have to ask. That part has never made any sense to me. Why would you want to split us up? Why on earth do you care about my love life?"

Moulton rolled his eyes. "I don't, obviously. It was a ploy. A gambit. And it backfired. I told her I would out you, that she was compromising your operational readiness and that you two couldn't be together. I thought she had more backbone."

"I—what?" Julia sputtered.

"I figured you would tell me to fuck off. That you would run straight to Chapel and Hollingshead and tell them what had happened. Then I could have leaked Chapel's name to the press and made it impossible for him to work as a field agent."

"Jesus. That was, what, almost a year ago? Moulton, have you really been working that long just to bring me down?"

The analyst's eyes flashed. "Longer. And not just you. I took down Hollingshead's entire directorate. I did that. Now we're going to make it permanent. Chapel, dead. Angel, dead."

"Angel's already gone," Wilkes pointed out. "She was just a computer, and I smashed the last of its hard drives back in Pittsburgh."

"Seriously," Moulton said, "did you believe that? I never did." He went over to Angel and pulled the gag out of her mouth. She tried to bite him, but he pulled his fingers away fast enough to avoid injury. "It was a cute trick, that neural net you left for us in your trailer," he told her. "But did you really think we'd fall for it? I follow all the latest advancements in artificial intelligence. I know what neural networks are capable of, and I've been studying *you* for years. There was no way a machine could do all the things you've done, Angel."

She didn't bother denying it. "Fine, you've got me. I have to admit I'm impressed."

Moulton didn't respond verbally, but Chapel could tell those words meant something to him. How long had he been following them around, really? How long had he been watching their every move?

"I'm curious about one thing," Angel said. Maybe just to buy them more time before they were shot. Maybe because she was curious. "How did you know we were coming here tonight?"

"This is the data center where everything started," Moulton said.

Angel shook her head. "No, I get that. But you knew we were coming here *tonight*. I don't believe you've just been sitting here for days, waiting for us to figure things out."

"No," Moulton admitted. "That's true."

"You had to get all those robots out here. And Wilkes and yourself. All at the same time," Angel pointed out.

"It took some work, yeah."

"So how did you know?" Angel asked.

"I'm an analyst. I crunched the numbers," he said. He took a deep breath as if he were about to give a lecture. "When you went online, in Pittsburgh. With all those video-game consoles—that was very clever, by the way. But red flags went off all over my screens. It was obvious that it was you, Angel, and not anybody else. Wilkes stopped you, but I knew you were still out there. That you might have a copy of the server logs from when I zombified your system. So I went through those logs myself, looking for anything you might find, anything you could use. I got inside your head, thought like you, mined the data like you would. And I found those stray packet headers, the ones with the plain text IP addresses. And I knew you would see them too."

"So it was a race," she said, "to see which of us could get here first."

"Yep. And I won."

Angel nodded. "You're pretty good," she said. "But then, I knew that already. It would take somebody damned good to do what you've done. Like hijacking that drone."

Chapel felt his jaw fall open.

He'd thought that Angel was just stalling, trying to put off her death as long as she could. Now he understood. She had a plan.

She was going to talk her way out of this.

NORTHWEST OF MOREHEAD, KY: MARCH 25, 01:36

"I mean, that would have taken some serious skills," Angel went on. "It wasn't as easy as just, I don't know, calling in an air strike. You had to make it look good. Like a terrorist did it. But what kind of terrorist could do all that? You needed to break the encryption on the command signal. You needed to work the duty logs to make sure there even was a Predator over New Orleans that day. And you really needed to be on top of your game to know about that shipment of low-level radioactive waste. I mean, it had a falsified bill of lading, right? It was contraband. But somehow you knew exactly where it would be, and when."

"I work for the NSA. We know lots of things."

Angel nodded. "You knew what was inside that cargo container. You knew the havoc it would cause if it was blown up in the right place. You got it right where you wanted. Did you hack into some kind of shipping database and change some numbers, make sure it ended up in New Orleans on the right day?"

"I'm not a hacker," Moulton told her, his voice rising nearly an octave in pitch. Chapel remembered what had happened when he'd called Moulton a hacker back at NSA headquarters. "I'm an analyst. Anyone can break into a database and fudge entries until they create chaos. It takes a real talent to read the numbers, to see the opportunities in what's already there."

"So it was you," Angel said. "You're the hijacker."

Chapel looked not at Moulton but at Wilkes. He knew that he was the one Angel was really talking to. Somehow the assassin had been seconded to the NSA, turned against his former colleagues from the DIA. But if he knew what Moulton and Charlotte Holman really were, if he understood that they were the terrorists, the real culprits—maybe he would stop this, right here. If they could just convince Wilkes—

"Go ahead and say it," Wilkes told Moulton.

Moulton looked like he really wanted to rub his hands together. To laugh maniacally. Instead, he visibly forced himself to stay calm. "Yes, that's right. I hijacked the Predator. I'm also the one who blew up your trailer, and the one who wrecked the California power grid. I've got other projects, too, ones that haven't started yet."

"Dear God, why?" Julia asked.

He turned to look at her. "There are some things you don't even tell dead people."

"Wilkes," Chapel said, "you heard him, he's a terrorist. He's going to bring the whole country down if you don't stop him. If you don't—"

"Oh, come on," Moulton said. "You haven't figured it out by now? First Lieutenant Wilkes works for us. He always has. He was instrumental in our plan to destroy Hollingshead's directorate. I know you thought he was one of yours, but that's just because we wanted you to think that. He's a double agent."

NORTHWEST OF MOREHEAD, KY: MARCH 25, 01:42

"Okay. Enough," Moulton said. "I know you're trying to flatter me with all these questions. It's not going to work. It's time for the three of you to go." He turned to Wilkes. He mimed firing a pistol with his hand.

Wilkes lifted his silenced pistol. But he didn't fire, not right away. "Huh," he said.

"Is there a problem?" Moulton asked.

"I'm just wondering. I mean, I thought Angel was a computer. Now we know she's flesh and blood. You sure you don't want to take her back to Fort Meade for questioning? She might know something. And what about Taggart there? She's a civilian."

Moulton looked very confused. "When we brought you on, we were told you were a team player. That you followed orders without question."

"Yeah, sure. I mean, you want me to shoot, I shoot," Wilkes said.

"So shoot, already."

Wilkes nodded. He lifted the pistol again. "Okay. Just one thing. Triple."

Moulton's look of confusion didn't change. "What?" he asked.

"I'm a triple agent," Wilkes said.

And then he shot Paul Moulton through the head.

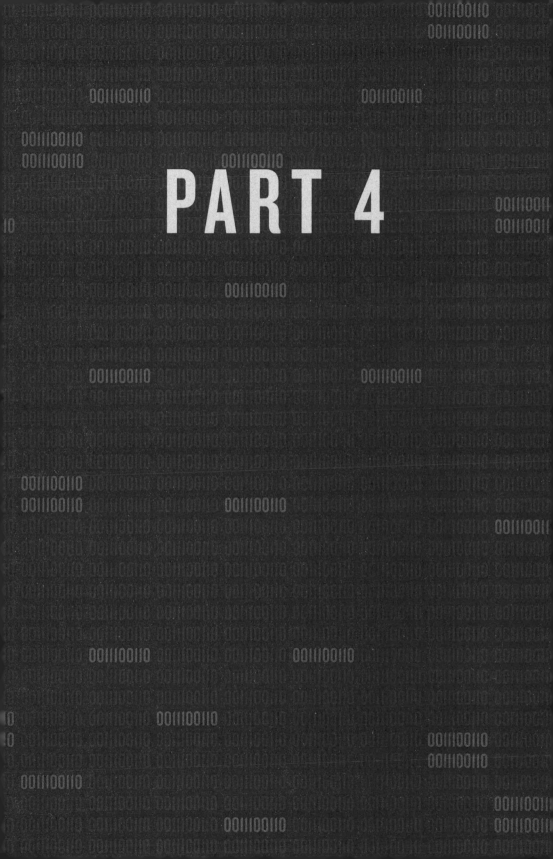

PART 4

INDIAN SPRINGS, NV: MARCH 25, 23:19

When the secretary of defense landed on your airstrip late at night, you didn't tell him to come back in the morning.

Creech Air Force Base in Nevada didn't look like much on the ground. Just a standard prefab building like a million others the military owned. The decrepit casino next door, with its flashing lights and the jangle of its slot machines, made the base almost invisible in the desert night.

Quite intentional, of course.

Patrick Norton and a small entourage of hangers-on were moved quickly inside and down a corridor lined with doors that were identified only by a series of numbers: GCS-1, GCS-2, and so on. The local base commanding officer, a colonel by rank, was kind enough to show them one of the rooms, since everyone in the group had security clearance. Inside each GCS, or ground control station, stood a tall server rack humming away and a tiny cubicle filled with flat-screen monitors. There were three chairs sitting in front of the desk. "Typically a flight is crewed by a pilot—the stick jockey," each colonel said, with that conspiratorial grin military men got when they use jargon, "an aircraft sensor operator who mans the controls for the aircraft's instruments—the sensor—and a flight supervisor who can make mission decisions in real time—the screener."

Taking up a prime amount of desk space was a big, complicated joystick mounted in front of the monitor. The stick belonging to the proverbial stick jockey. It was considerably more advanced than most video-game joysticks, but it had fewer buttons—just one, in fact, an orange key located where the jockey wouldn't accidentally brush against it.

"From this station," the colonel went on, "we can carry out executive-level missions anywhere in the world. All flight data and telemetry is carried over dedicated satellite links, allowing our people precision control with a minimum of lag time, while the draw rate on our imaging systems is—"

Norton inhaled sharply and the man shut up. "Do you know why we're here?" he asked. "I mean, specifically."

The colonel turned red. No military man liked being forced to guess what his superiors wanted, though it was hardly a rare occurrence. "Mr. Secretary," he replied, "I'm assuming this has to do with the recent drone strikes on New Orleans, New York, and San Francisco."

Norton fixed the man with his gaze. "That's right."

The colonel looked into the middle distance. "Sir. It is true that approximately ninety percent of all UAV missions are flown out of this base, including all but a handful of combat missions in overseas operations. I can well imagine, sir, that you would be concerned about our security here."

"I'm worried," Norton said, "that the drones you have here on base, and all the drones you control out in the field, around the world, could be hijacked. Turned against their masters. Now. Tell me. Exactly how worried should I be?"

"Not worried at all, sir," the colonel said. He was all but standing at attention. "It would be impossible for anyone to take control of one of my UAVs. Physically impossible. The GCS network is completely self-contained. It does not connect to the public Internet on any level. Even the satellites we use to stream data to and from the UAVs are dedicated devices, meaning no one can access them except from a GCS. Whoever hijacked those other drones was using a public server to gain access. They hacked into drones that were cleared for civilian or at least nonmilitary use, either in law enforcement or civilian intelligence. That just can't happen here."

"You're completely protected, then," Norton said. "Fireproof."

"Yes, sir, we—"

"Excuse me," someone said from the back of the entourage.

The colonel turned on his heel to look for the source of the interruption. "Ma'am? How can I help you?"

Charlotte Holman smiled and stepped forward. She held out one hand and waited until the colonel shook it. "This is very impressive security," she said. "Very impressive indeed. But those of us in network intelligence really don't like it when people talk about one hundred percent security. I mean, there's always a way to get in, if you're persistent enough."

"Not when you have an air gap like ours."

Holman's smile just grew brighter. She'd hoped he would use that silly term. An air gap referred to a physical disconnect between one's servers and the wider Internet, a literal space of dead air between possible connections. An air gap was supposed to be even more secure than a firewall.

Holman had been working for the NSA long enough to know what words were worth. "An air gap that—I'm sorry, I don't want to bring this up, but I have to. An air gap that failed to stop your system from picking up a keylogger virus back in 2011."

The colonel's face went white. "That was a significant problem, yes, ma'am. A keylogger isn't particularly dangerous—it wouldn't let anyone control the UAVs—but we took it very seriously. And we've taken care of it one hundred percent. All our drives had to be erased and rebuilt from scratch, but we did it."

"Did you ever find out how it happened? How you picked up that virus? How it crossed your air gap?"

The colonel chewed on his lower lip for a second. "Hard drives were being exchanged between ground control stations."

"For what purpose?" Holman asked.

The colonel glanced at the secretary of defense, but Norton didn't offer him any chance to escape. "We needed to copy map updates and mission video between stations. The easiest and fastest way to do that was to move drives between servers. Unfortunately that meant the drives could leave the GCS rooms. One of them was connected to a public Internet server for a short time. The user in question didn't think he was exposing the drive to public access, but somehow the keylogger virus got onto the drive. When it was returned to the GCS, the virus spread very quickly through our entire system."

"And why exactly was the drive connected to the Internet?"

The colonel stared down at his shiny shoes. "A stick jockey wanted to send video of a drone strike to his girlfriend. To impress her."

"Did it work?" Norton asked. Behind him his entourage chuckled.

The colonel shook his head. "I couldn't comment on that, sir. I assume she was not impressed when he was court-martialed and given a dishonorable discharge."

Holman nodded. "But the point is, your air gap was subject to human error."

"Not anymore," the colonel said. He walked over to a server rack and pointed at the hard drives it contained. Each one was held down by a tiny padlock. "Hard drives can no longer be removed from a GCS. Under any circumstances. We learn from our mistakes."

"Good," Norton said. "That's what I needed to hear. We cannot afford to have even one more drone go rogue on us." The entourage nodded and mumbled in agreement. "All right, Colonel. We've seen enough here. Now perhaps you'll be good enough to show us the Predators and Reapers you keep on base."

"Certainly, sir," the colonel said. He led the group out of the cramped GCS and back into the hallway.

Charlotte Holman was the last one out. Nobody noticed when she slipped a tiny black box out of her jacket pocket and stuck it to the back of the server rack. The box was no bigger than a matchbook, and it didn't have any blinking red lights on its surface, nor a tiny antenna, nor any other outward sign that would indicate it was capable of feeding information into the GCS servers through the keylogger virus.

The virus that, despite all appearances, was much more than just a harmless keylogger. The virus that, despite all the colonel's efforts, was still present on every hard drive in the air force base. The virus he was convinced they'd erased.

The virus that Paul Moulton had written for exactly this purpose.

"Let me just turn the lights off," the colonel said as she stepped out into the hallway. He stuck his head into the GCS and took a quick look around, then flipped the light switch. Clearly he had no idea that his entire system had just been compromised.

NORTHWEST OF MOREHEAD, KY: MARCH 25, 03:06

The two of them worked in silence.

It took a long time to dig the grave. Chapel could barely bend over, the bandage around his midriff constricting every time he tried. Wilkes didn't seem to have his heart in the job, though he clearly didn't want Chapel to think he was a shirker.

It didn't help that neither of them had a shovel. There was a trowel in the tool bag Chapel had stolen from the motel, and Wilkes had turned up a hoe from an old outbuilding behind the mansion.

They worked side by side for an hour and at the end they had a hole about six feet long and four feet deep. Chapel took Moulton's legs and Wilkes took the dead man's shoulders and they got him inside without any fanfare. Chapel wondered for a moment if he should say something, offer up some prayer. Moulton had tried to destroy every part of his life, but still. You were supposed to respect the dead.

But then Wilkes started shoving dirt over the body, flecks of it collecting on Moulton's eyes and lips where they were still wet. Chapel looked away.

When the hole was filled in, they tamped down the loose earth as best they could. And then they just walked away.

Somebody would come. Someone from the NSA would come out here, probably as soon as they realized that Moulton had stopped reporting. They would come and they would probably find the shallow grave very quickly. Moulton would be dug back up and given a proper burial. Chapel had to believe that.

He scrubbed at his hands with a dry towel—there was no running water in the decaying mansion—and headed up the stairs. Wilkes followed right behind him. Up at the doors to the data center, Chapel turned and looked Wilkes right in the eye. Tried to stare him down. Make him falter.

It didn't work. Wilkes was a poker player. He didn't give anything away, not with his face.

Eventually, Chapel shook his head. He turned and opened the doors to the data center and stepped inside.

Angel sat at a workstation, paging through data on a big flat-screen monitor. Julia stood just behind her, one hand on Angel's shoulder. She turned to look at Chapel with a question in her eyes.

He didn't have anything remotely like an answer for her.

"Okay," he said, not bothering to look at Wilkes. "Start talking."

NORTHWEST OF MOREHEAD, KY: MARCH 25, 03:34

"It was three years ago that Hollingshead brought me in on this thing. I was back from my last tour, in Afghanistan. I guess you know by now what I am. My operational specialty."

Chapel nodded, but said nothing.

"I got a call saying to go to such and such an office in the Pentagon. I went there and sat down and once he finished with all the song and dance, you know, cleaning his glasses, offering me a drink, all that stuff—I asked him who he wanted me to kill.

"He smiled and said nobody. He said he had a different kind of problem, one he needed me to solve. I wasn't sure what he was talking about at first. I don't think, back then, that even he knew all the details. But he was worried.

"He's a man who knows how to keep his ears open, I'll give him that. Like any good spymaster, he keeps tabs on his opposite numbers—all those directors and administrators and special deputies, at CIA and NSA and NGA and OICI and INR and all the other acronyms. He knows what they get up to, what operations they're running. I suppose he needs to know that so he doesn't end up stepping on their toes, like, by sending you out on a mission the CIA already has covered. There's a constant flow of information between the agencies.

"Thing is, not all this information comes from official channels. Some of it is just chatter. Rumors, call them, or stuff that got overheard when maybe it shouldn't have been. And back when this started, some of that chatter was starting to make Hollingshead very nervous. He had the sense that there were people in the intelligence community who were forming some kind of quiet alliance. A network with its own agenda, that crossed agency lines and didn't report to anybody officially. It was a network he was definitely not invited to join.

"Every time he tried to get close to the people in the network, they would shut down. Some of them were more blatant about it than others. It was clear they had orders not to give him so much as the time of day.

"He wasn't willing to use the word 'conspiracy,' when he told me about it. He still thought maybe it was just some totally legit thing, a way for agencies to share information without having to call official meetings. But he needed to make sure. That was where I came in. He had my whole file, details on every one of my missions. He said he needed a poker player. Somebody with incredible patience, somebody who could hide his intentions as long as it took. Somebody who could think three moves ahead.

"He told me about you, Chapel, and why you wouldn't work for this assignment. He said you weren't a good enough actor. Your style was all wrong. He didn't want a commando, he wanted a sniper. He'd had Angel run through a bunch of personnel files, looking for the right man, and my name was the first one on the list.

"Which still didn't tell me exactly what he wanted me to do. Turned out the answer was simple: pretend I didn't like him.

"He made sure it looked like I had good reason. He talked to all the right people about how I was some kind of monster. How he'd recruited me because he didn't like the idea of a trained killer ending up at the wrong agency. He told people he had no real use for me and just wanted to keep me where I couldn't cause any trouble.

"My job was to make a little noise about how I felt like I was being treated unfairly. To spread some gossip about how I didn't want to work for Hollingshead anymore, that I was interested in transferring out of his directorate. I had some old friends from back in Iraq, civilian contractors from Blackwater, a CIA guy I knew, and we would get together and play cards sometimes. That was where I started hinting that I was unhappy.

"Hollingshead figured that if he was spying on the conspiracy, it would spy on him, too. That whoever ran the thing would jump at the chance to turn one of his own people against him. Turned out he was right.

"It wasn't anybody at the NSA who contacted me originally. It was my CIA buddy who worked as my handler. Not that he was ever real clear on what our roles were. He said if I wanted to get back at Hollingshead, he had a way. One that he swore up and down wouldn't hurt national security, but actually make it stronger. He even suggested that Hollingshead was a problem, that maybe he needed to be taken out.

"It was all done with such a soft touch, I barely knew I'd been recruited. We were just two guys shooting the shit. It was months and months and months before he said he wanted to introduce me to his secret boss. I was going to meet a woman named Charlotte Holman. I was supposed to do whatever she said.

"For a long time, that just meant spying on Hollingshead. Feeding her data about his movements, about what he had you and Angel doing. In exchange, she said, she would see about getting me transferred. Get me a job somewhere I would be appreciated.

"Hollingshead made sure the info I gave her was real. That meant making himself vulnerable to her. But it also meant she started trusting me. She started talking to me about what she called the Cyclops Initiative. A plan, a big plan, that was going to make America safe for a very long time. I wasn't allowed to know many of the details, but she said it was going to look very bad but it would be a good thing in the end.

"She said I was going to be a big part of that. A hero.

"It wasn't until about a week before the attack on New Orleans that she told me she was going to need proof that she could trust me. She said things were getting critical, that she wanted to know if I was willing to take a more active role. I asked what that meant. She asked me if I was willing to help her take down Hollingshead's directorate, bust it open at the seams. I said sure—I mean, I was supposed to hate the guy, right? Then she asked me if I was willing to kill some people. I didn't need to ask for names, I knew who she meant. Hollingshead, Chapel, Angel.

"I said, no problem. That was what I was trained for, after all.

"I could see in her eyes she believed me. I'd come so far, implicated myself enough by spying on Hollingshead for her, that there was no going back. When I said I was willing to kill you, that was what it took for her to let me in. To really trust me.

"To start telling me what was going on."

NORTHWEST OF MOREHEAD, KY: MARCH 25, 03:58

Julia got up and moved over to Chapel's side. "This is how the intelligence community works? This is what you deal with all the time?"

"No," Chapel told her. "Most of the time it's just guys in offices, shoving paper around. Writing up security estimates and analyzing photographs. Every once in a while, though . . ." He shook his head. "When national security is at stake, people get a little nuts. You're talking about the last bunch of people in America who still believe in the government. In its necessity, anyway. Threats to that government make the knives come out."

Wilkes shook his head. "This isn't just some internal beef, though. It wasn't just you three I was supposed to be willing to kill. She told me a lot of stuff at that meeting. Suggested a bunch of things that might happen. She had to know, see. She had to know how I would react.

"She asked me, if her group organized an attack on civilian targets inside the borders of the United States, what would I do? I said I would assume she had a good reason. She seemed to like that.

"She laid it out for me. The whole thing with the cargo container full of radiological waste and the kamikaze drone. She watched me pretty close while she talked about it. I got the idea that if I winced or looked upset, then somebody would come bursting in and cap me right then and there.

"So I made a point of not wincing or looking upset.

"Once things were in motion, I had no contact with Hollingshead. I had to play this thing out. My orders were to get on Holman's good side and stay there as long as I could. Dig into her organization as deep as I could go. I did manage to swing things a little for you guys. I told her that Angel really was an AI. Obviously Moulton didn't buy it, but I think Holman was convinced. That meant I just had to destroy that hard drive, not actually kill Angel."

"And me?" Chapel asked. "You shot me. Were you willing to kill me just to make things look good for your new boss?"

"Jimmy, please," Wilkes said, looking pained. "You know my MOS. I shot you. I didn't kill you. If I planned on actually killing you, you would be dead right now. No, I just needed your blood all over that place. I thought maybe Holman would be satisfied with that, given how many other things she had on her plate. But she got obsessed with it. With the idea you were still out there, still alive."

"Which raises another question," Chapel said. "Why us? Did we do something to her in a past life that meant we needed to be killed? Was it just because Hollingshead didn't want to go on a second date?"

"What?" Julia asked, looking very confused.

"I'll explain later," Chapel told her.

Wilkes laughed. "That's the funny part. When you talk to her, to Holman, or some of the people she introduced me to—all they want to talk about is Hollingshead's DX department. He's a goddamned legend out there. Maybe because of how he took down Tom Banks a couple of years ago. Maybe because of some of the missions he's sent you on, Jimmy, the ones that actually worked. But they talk about him like he's some kind of superhero, and they know that when there's a superhero in town, the villains always lose. They decided to make the DX—specifically Hollingshead, Angel, and you—their scapegoats for one simple reason.

"They figured you were the only ones who could stop them."

Chapel didn't bother feeling flattered. He understood the real message there. "So they honestly think they're going to get away with . . . what? Protecting the country? With selective drone strikes on domestic targets? How is that supposed to work?"

"Nobody bothered giving me the big picture. Just the operational parameters," Wilkes pointed out.

Chapel looked away. "You say there were other people. It wasn't just Holman and Moulton working against us. You said there was a whole conspiracy, a secret network inside the intelligence community. How big do you think this is? How far up does it go?"

Wilkes lifted his shoulders dramatically. Let them fall again. "I don't really know. I know Holman gets orders from somebody else. She's a subdirector at the NSA. That suggests to me there are people at the director level. Maybe higher. As for how many of them there are, Hollingshead estimated that it included people in every agency. That's one thing we've got to remember here. It's not like every one of the ninety thousand employees of the NSA are in on this plot. It's just small workgroups here and there."

Chapel frowned. "Cells. Like a terrorist organization uses."

"The comparison is pretty fucking apt," Wilkes told him. "Considering what they're doing."

"Okay. But one thing I want to know—why break your cover now? Why come out of the cold right in the middle of things?"

Wilkes laughed. "Maybe because maintaining my cover would have meant killing you and the ladies here while Moulton watched? I let you guys get away from me once and Holman nearly ripped my head off. Maybe I could have come up with some way of keeping you alive here tonight, but she never would have trusted me again."

"So instead you killed Moulton," Chapel pointed out.

"It's what I do."

"It was stupid," Chapel said. "We could have interrogated him. We could have learned so much from him."

"Sure, during which time he could have found some way to contact Holman and tell her what happened." Wilkes shook his head. "You have your way of operating, I've got mine."

Chapel slammed his fist against a steel server rack, making it ring. The noise made Angel jump, but he was frustrated enough not to apologize. "Right now we've got no way of operating at all! We've got scraps of information that don't add up. We have no idea which direction to jump, no idea how to hit these people where they'll feel it."

"I know one thing," Wilkes pointed out.

"Oh? And what's that?"

"What their next move is," the marine said. "I know their next target."

Chapel nodded slowly. "Yeah?" he said. "What are they going to do? Crash the stock market? Disrupt the Border Patrol? Close a major airport?"

"Nope," Wilkes said. "They're gonna assassinate Hollingshead."

THE WHITE HOUSE, MARCH 25, 07:57

A carved wooden clock on an end table ticked away the seconds as the first rays of dawn came in through tall French windows. At one point a member of the custodial staff came into the room and stared at a painting on the wall for nearly a minute. Finally he reached up and tilted it a few degrees to one side, straightening it perfectly. Then he left.

Charlotte Holman and Patrick Norton sat through the whole thing, stiff-backed, on a white damask pattern loveseat that had probably belonged to Dolley Madison.

They had taken her phone away from her when she went through the security station. She was going quietly crazy.

Norton checked his watch. Again. Then he looked up at an unassuming door in the far wall. He turned to catch Holman's eye. "Have you ever been this close, before?"

"To the Oval Office?" Holman asked. "No, no, I . . . I haven't."

Norton smiled at her. "It's always the same. He always makes you wait. Actually, I've known three of them, and it was the same every time. They need to make sure you understand how things work. That you sit here at the pleasure of your commander in chief."

Holman chuckled. "I wouldn't have thought that was a point that needed to be stressed," she said.

"The bigger the chief, the taller the totem pole," Norton replied.

Holman was a woman of a certain age; all the same, the remark struck her as something distinctly out-of-date. The kind of casual remark you might have heard in this room fifty years prior. She considered whether she should say something, if only in the interest of friendly advice.

She didn't get the chance. The door—*the* door—opened and they both had to jump to their feet. If the president walked into their room, it would never do for them to be seated.

But it wasn't the man himself. It was his chief of staff, Walter Minchell, a trim, intelligent-looking man with a nearly invisible fringe of red beard. He raised one hand and gestured for Norton to come closer, even though there was no one else in the room. "He wanted me to convey his apologies," Minchell said. "He's too busy to speak with you directly."

"Too busy?" Norton asked. "The country is falling apart and—"

"And that's what's keeping him," Minchell insisted. "He's got so much on his plate that he can't do face time right now."

"Young man," Norton said, "you do understand that I am the secretary of defense? That he himself appointed me to handle the security of the country?"

"I understand," Minchell said, "what he told me, and what he said I could tell you if you tried to bully your way in. He says he put you in charge of stopping this thing. But since then it's only gotten worse. Hundreds of thousands of people in California with no power, no water—ships lined up outside of New Orleans crammed full of rotting food while grocery stores in the Midwest can't stock their shelves. Half the Northeast locked down with a manhunt that has yet to produce a single captive."

He glanced at Holman as he related this final fact. She made a point of not flinching.

"If," Norton said, "the president has lost confidence in my abilities—"

"No," Minchell said. "That's not the takeaway here."

"I'm glad to hear it," Norton replied.

The chief of staff scratched at his chin. "We need results, Mr. Secretary. We need them soon. You have got to start producing bodies. But in the meantime, the president is going to address the nation tomorrow night. Come clean with the fact that these are terrorist attacks and talk about what we're doing to find the culprits."

"That's not the wise move right now," Norton insisted. "If he would just meet with me so we could discuss this—"

"That's exactly why you're not meeting," Minchell told him. "There's nothing to discuss. You need to give him data. Anything you've got so it can go into the speech. Oh—and there's one more thing. You'll be the designated survivor on this one."

Norton inhaled very slowly.

Whenever the president gave a major speech, one where the vice president was also present, he always appointed a designated survivor. A member of the cabinet who would not be allowed anywhere near the location of the speech so that if something terrible happened like, say, a terrorist attack, at least one top-ranking member of the executive branch would still be around to maintain control.

Being chosen as the survivor could mean one of two things. It could mean the president had faith in your ability to lead the country in case of his demise. Or it could mean he disliked you so much he didn't want to see you, even accidentally, at a crucial time.

"I understand," Norton said.

"Good," Minchell told him. "Now, if you'll excuse me, I need to get back to work."

Without even glancing at Holman, he disappeared back through *the* door.

"I'll get you that data," she told the SecDef.

Norton just turned on his heel and started walking away.

IN TRANSIT: MARCH 25, 08:14

In the backseat, Angel held herself perfectly still. Her small body was crammed into the car door, and one of her slender shoulders propped up the majority of Wilkes's considerable weight. He had fallen asleep back there, more or less on top of her. They'd been driving for hours like that.

Chapel watched her in his mirror. Angel's face was frozen into the expression of someone who is trying very hard not to think about what was happening to her.

"You all right?" he asked.

"Fine," she replied, in a clipped tone he didn't like.

He decided he would pull over at the next chance he got. Let Julia drive, and put Angel up in the front seat. Maybe the marine just stank— Chapel remembered spending months in a motel room with Wilkes, and that the man didn't have the best hygiene practices. But maybe it was something else. Angel looked a lot like she had when they'd forced her to get out of the car up on the ridge in Kentucky. Like she was being tortured.

He glanced over at Julia and saw a look on her face that was not entirely dissimilar.

"What about you?" he asked.

She took a long, deep breath. When she answered, she looked straight ahead through the windshield. As if she didn't want him to see what was in her eyes. "I think that I saw Wilkes kill a man last night. Just . . . just shoot him in the brain. I think that ten minutes before that I was certain he was going to kill me. I think that I remember the way he tied us up, which was not exactly gentle."

"He's a bit rough-and-tumble," Chapel admitted.

"He's a monster," Julia said. She glanced back over her shoulder, as if to make sure he was really sleeping. "He was acting a role, he says. Pretending to stalk us. Shooting you just to make it look like you were dead." She shook her head and red hair bounced around her shoulders. "He's crazy, Jim. I don't know how you can even think about trusting him."

"Because the alternative is letting Hollingshead die," he told her.

There was nothing else, really, to say. Chapel needed allies desperately, and Wilkes had offered himself up for the job. Now that he'd killed Moulton, he said it was only a matter of hours—a day at the most—before his cover was blown. Before Charlotte Holman sent somebody else to track *him* down.

But in the meantime, Wilkes could be a powerful weapon. They knew where Holman would strike next, and a general idea of how she would do it. She, on the other hand, had no idea that she couldn't trust Wilkes.

The plan had come together in Chapel's mind almost instantly. It was simple, like any good plan. It was also incredibly dangerous. But that had never stopped him before.

First things first, though. They were going to need some equipment. It was Wilkes who pointed out where they could get it.

Chapel knew that Angel and Julia were terrified of their new teammate—and that they would never trust him. Chapel didn't know if he could trust Wilkes, either. But he did know that with the marine's help, there might just be a chance to come out of this alive.

So he headed east, driving as fast as he dared, straight through the night.

TOWSON, MD: MARCH 25, 11:14

Wilkes had a smartphone that he could still use. It made life a lot easier for them. He found a motel in a quiet part of town, a nice enough place that was clean and where the staff were happy to take cash. "Gotta love Yelp reviews," he said.

Angel seemed happy enough just to get out of the sunlight and into a dark room where she could lie down for a while. Julia, on the other hand, asked far too many questions. "Where are you going?" was the hardest one to answer.

"We need to acquire some supplies. Some stuff that's hard to get," Chapel told her.

"Like what?"

Chapel glanced over at the car. Wilkes was in the driver's seat, his hands on the wheel. As still and quiet as a robot waiting for instructions.

"Like guns," he told her. It had been way too long since Chapel had access to a firearm. He'd managed to survive so far without one, but they were headed to some dangerous places now, and a gun at his side would make him feel a lot better.

Julia scowled, though. "And why exactly can't you take me with you?"

He knew she wasn't philosophically opposed to the idea of firearms, though she didn't particularly like them, either. He had a good reason for leaving her behind on this mission, though. "For one thing, somebody needs to be here with Angel."

"She can take care of herself."

Chapel shrugged. "Maybe. But remember the buddy system? Didn't they ever teach you that in school?"

"I remember the last time you called me your buddy," she said.

He smiled, remembering that too.

"Yeah, I get it," she said. "None of us should be alone at any time. If government thugs show up and try to drag her away, at least I'll be able to call them names. But I don't like the idea of you running off with Wilkes like you're long-lost friends. I don't trust that guy."

"I know." But Chapel kind of did. Sure, the guy had killed Moulton instead of keeping him alive to get information out of him. Sure, Wilkes had shot Chapel. But that kind of thing made sense, in the world the two of them inhabited.

Chapel had relied on Angel and Julia so far because he'd had no choice. They were civilians, though, and neither of them had Special Forces training. Wilkes was the kind of partner Chapel was supposed to work with.

"It's going to be fine," Chapel told her.

"Promise me he won't kill any more people just because it's convenient."

"I can't make a promise for anybody else. I'll promise to ask him to promise."

Julia growled in frustration. Then she grabbed Chapel around the neck and pulled him into a deep, long kiss.

"I'm not going to lose you again," she told him.

"You couldn't if you tried," he told her.

Then he headed over to the car. Before he even got to the passenger-side door, Wilkes had the engine running.

TOWSON, MD: MARCH 25, 12:07

"I count three guys. Two out front by the door, each of them with a suspicious bulge in their coat pockets. One over at the loading dock, and he's got a shotgun right out in the open, not even caring who sees it."

"Four," Wilkes said.

"What?" Chapel asked.

The two of them were lying prone on the tar-paper roof of an old abandoned building in a largely abandoned part of town. Across the street from them lay a two-story warehouse that was still in operating condition: its rolling metal doors were intact and not too rusty, and though its windows were bricked over, there wasn't much graffiti on the walls.

Back before the first drone hijacking, back in what felt now like a previous lifetime, Chapel had found this place by following Harris Contorni around. He had been convinced it was where Contorni kept his stock in trade, namely a bunch of military hardware he'd stolen from the nearby Aberdeen Proving Ground. Chapel and Wilkes both had staked out the warehouse, as well as Contorni's motel room, for months without finding any real evidence that would stand up in court. But there had been enough circumstantial details to make Chapel certain he was right about Contorni.

Now they were banking everything on that certainty. And on their ability to take Contorni down without the both of them getting killed in the process.

"You're sure? Where's this fourth guy at?"

Wilkes handed Chapel a pair of tiny binoculars. "Down the street, in a window over that restaurant supply shop."

Chapel peered through the binoculars. Damn it. Wilkes was right. The restaurant supply shop was closed and no lights showed inside the second floor of the building. But just visible through one open window was a man smoking a cigarette. Chapel could see the barrel of a high-powered sniper rifle hanging over the windowsill.

Shit, Chapel thought. If he'd gone running in there thinking it was just the three guards he'd seen, the sniper would have picked him off before he even reached the front door.

Chapel had worried he was getting too old for all this. That Hollingshead had brought Wilkes in to serve as his replacement. Well, maybe there was a point to that worry. Maybe it *was* time for him to retire.

But not today.

"You can take the sniper, right?" Chapel asked.

When Wilkes's face was perfectly at rest, it already looked like he was sneering. Now he positively leered. "Yeah, I think I can handle that."

Chapel nodded. "When you're done, give me some kind of signal. Then move down here fast. I'll take the guy with the shotgun, then we handle the two at the front door together."

"Got it," Wilkes said.

Chapel looked at the shotgun guy through the binoculars. "Just remember not to kill anyone if you don't have to," he said. But when he lowered the binoculars, Wilkes was already gone.

Damn. The guy was good.

TOWSON, MD: MARCH 25, 12:31

The signal was pretty obvious when it came. The sniper disappeared from the window across the street. His lit cigarette flew out the window to fall into the street, and his rifle was pulled back inside. Then Wilkes leaned one arm out of the window and gave Chapel a thumbs-up.

Chapel was already behind the warehouse, close to the loading dock where the man with the shotgun stood guard. Now it was his turn.

There are only so many ways to disarm an alert guard who is carrying a shotgun. None of them are particularly safe. Chapel decided to go with the most direct method. Moving fast but very quietly, leading with his artificial arm as a kind of shield, he ran across the loading dock and just barreled into the guard as hard as he could.

The man went sprawling—he hadn't seen Chapel coming. The two of them rolled onto the concrete of the loading dock, grappling and trying to get to their feet. The guard never quite managed to get up, but he didn't let go of the shotgun, either. Chapel got one hand on the barrels, but the guard knocked his other hand away. He brought the weapon around, trying to cram it into the space between the two of them.

The guard was young and strong, and though Chapel was on top of him and knew a dozen ways to render the man unconscious, the shotgun was a major advantage on the guard's side. Before Chapel could stop him, the guard had both barrels jammed up under Chapel's chin.

There was something to be said for experience and training, though. Before the guard could pull his triggers and blow Chapel's head off, Chapel reached down and slipped the catch of the break action. The barrels swung away from the firing pins, just as if the weapon were in the middle of being reloaded. The guard tried to pull the triggers but nothing happened.

He seemed surprised by this. Surprised enough that Chapel was able to grab the shotgun away from him and smack him across the head with it. The guard rolled away, his hands going to his head. Chapel got an arm around the man's neck in a sleeper hold and squeezed until the guard fell unconscious.

He would have liked to have tied the man up, just to be sure he was out of action, but there was no time for that. Chapel grabbed the shotgun, locking its barrels in place and cocking its hammers, then raced around to the front of the building.

Just in time. Wilkes was walking across the street, his silenced pistol held out in front of him, while the two guards at the door were already reaching for their own weapons. Chapel leveled the shotgun at them. "Hands down," he said.

The guards were smart enough to comply without making much noise. Wilkes came forward and disarmed both of them. He shoved one pistol in his pocket, then tossed the other one to Chapel. He didn't bother looking down at it—he could tell from the way it felt in his hand that it was a Glock 9 mm. He shoved it into his pocket, never letting the barrels of the shotgun move away from the two guards.

"How many people inside?" he asked.

"Why the fuck should we tell you anything?" one of the guards asked. "You know what's going to happen to you? You know you're already dead, right? We work for—"

Wilkes kicked the man in the stomach, hard. He went down.

Chapel turned to the second guard. "How many people inside?" he asked.

"Our boss and one guy," the second guard said, lifting his hands to show he was cooperating.

Chapel nodded. To Wilkes, he said, "Did you frisk these two for backup pieces?"

"Doesn't look like they've got any," Wilkes pointed out.

"Check for ankle holsters," Chapel told him.

As it turned out, neither of the guards had a second gun. But the one Wilkes had kicked did have a knife tucked into his shoe.

"Okay," Chapel said. "The two of you are going to walk ahead of us. You know what human shields are, right? I'm guessing you can figure it out. You walk inside there with us right behind you. The best way for the two of you not to get shot is for you to keep very, very quiet. We all clear on this?"

The guards just nodded.

The door was locked, but one of the guards had the key. He opened the door and stepped inside. The warehouse was well lit and full of metal shelves, all of which were full of long, flat cardboard boxes.

Two men were standing in the middle of the maze of shelves, checking things on clipboards. Neither of them had weapons in their hands. One of them was Harris Contorni, whom Chapel recognized instantly.

Unfortunately, Contorni recognized him as well. Before Chapel could even shout for the black marketeer to drop to the floor, Contorni broke and ran around a line of shelves, out of view.

"Damn," Chapel said. He shoved one of the guards aside and started racing after Contorni.

"We don't need him," Wilkes called out, but it was too late.

Chapel had already come around the end of a line of shelves and was staring down an aisle at a Gatling gun.

TOWSON, MD: MARCH 25, 12:39

"I just want to talk to—" Chapel said, but before he could even finish his sentence, Contorni opened fire.

Technically, to be accurate, it was not a Gatling gun, since those hadn't seen service since the Spanish-American War. Instead it was a much newer, much more deadly weapon, an M130 self-powered Vulcan rotary cannon, with six long air-cooled, gas-fired barrels capable of pumping out six thousand 20×202 mm rounds per minute. It was capable of tearing a jeep to pieces, shooting down enemy bombers, or turning human beings into red jelly. It was designed to be mounted on a fighter jet.

As a burst of rounds sped toward Chapel far faster than he could dodge, he was only barely aware of the fact that Contorni was firing a weapon that was just balanced precariously on a wheeled dolly—it hadn't been bolted down or secured in any way.

Three bullets did hit Chapel, though all of them tore through the silicone flesh of his artificial arm and none of them drew blood. Those bullets escaped the weapon with enough velocity and momentum to knock the entire gun sideways and then backward until it was spraying bullets into the wall and then the ceiling of the warehouse. Eventually the entire assembly—barrels, receiver, feed system, and ammunition drum, weighing approximately three hundred pounds, fell backward off the dolly and rolled on top of Harris Contorni, who gave out a little shriek and then let go of the trigger mechanism.

The noise of the weapon discharging was enough to make Chapel's ears ring. That passed quickly enough. The surprise he felt at finding himself still alive and mostly in one piece took a lot longer to process.

By the time he could move again, Wilkes had come up beside him, a pistol in either hand, both of them pointing at the ceiling.

"What happened? You okay?" he shouted.

Chapel looked over at Wilkes. Then he looked back at Contorni, who was still wrestling with the M130, unable to get out from under it. He opened his mouth to say something. Reconsidered that thought. Closed his mouth again.

Pinned to the floor, Contorni finally shouted, "One of you assholes gonna help me out here, or what?"

TOWSON, MD: MARCH 25, 12:43

"Your men all ran off, once they heard the shooting," Wilkes said. "They were smart. You, on the other hand, tried to kill an employee of the Defense Intelligence Agency. You do understand what that means, don't you, Harris?"

They had Contorni tied to a chair in an office at the back of the warehouse. To his credit he made no attempt to struggle or get free. "I've got so many lawyers on my payroll they're gonna name a library for me up at Columbia Law," Contorni insisted. "I was defending my property, wasn't I? I had no idea who broke in, just that they got past my security. I was afraid for my life."

Chapel shrugged. "You're right. We don't need this guy." They had, after all, come here looking for weapons. Not to charge Contorni with any crime.

Wilkes didn't seem to get that, though. He pressed the barrel of his silenced pistol against Contorni's cheek. "I might start by blowing your teeth out," he said. He moved the pistol down to Contorni's chest. "Then again, maybe we just puncture a lung."

Chapel fought to keep his face under control. This was not at all how he'd imagined the operation would go down. "Wilkes," he said, "just—"

"Just kill him?" the marine asked. "I could. But then we wouldn't get to find out why he's been lying low the last couple of months."

"I know people," Contorni insisted. "I know the kind of people, if you kill me here, they'll come find you. Find you when you're asleep and—"

Wilkes pressed the barrel of his pistol against Contorni's arm and pulled the trigger.

The black marketeer howled in panic and distress, and Chapel had to look away. He knew perfectly well that Wilkes had at most just grazed Contorni's skin. He would get a nasty powder burn, but the wound was unlikely to even scar.

Given what Wilkes had been threatening, though, it must have felt like a real gunshot wound.

"For months now," Wilkes said, "this dickweed and I have been watching you. Tracking your every movement. We know what you do for a living, Harris. We know you steal guns from the Proving Ground and then sell them to whoever has the money. Street gangs. Hit men. White power groups. But the last couple of months, you haven't so much as sold a bayonet to a Civil War reenactor. You want to explain why?"

Contorni was still howling. Chapel could barely hear Wilkes over the noise. Somehow, though, the screams turned into words. "Knew you— were there—not stupid—enough to—"

"You knew we were watching you?" Wilkes asked.

Suddenly Chapel was very interested in this interrogation. "How?" he asked.

Contorni calmed down enough to explain, a little. "There was this,

this guy, this little creep, I only saw him one time. Came to the place where I, where I get my breakfast. Sat down in front of me. Told me the DIA was on my trail. Told me your names, gave me pictures of you. I saw you at the motel and—"

"This guy, was he wearing a sweater vest and a tie?"

The look on Contorni's face was answer enough.

Wilkes didn't bother asking Contorni any more questions. He kicked over the black marketeer's chair and left him there, his cheek pressed up against the concrete floor, still whimpering.

Chapel and Wilkes left the office and closed the door behind them so they could talk. "Moulton wrecked our case," Wilkes pointed out.

"I guess he wanted to make you resent Hollingshead even more, by making your assignment as boring and pointless as possible."

Wilkes nodded. "I knew that guy deserved a bullet." He walked over to the nearest shelf and grabbed one of the cardboard boxes stored there. He put his weapon in his pocket, then cut open the box using the knife he'd taken off Contorni's guard. "Time to go shopping," he said.

Chapel was not particularly surprised to see that the box contained M4 carbines. Standard gear for the kind of soldiers stationed at the Proving Ground. He lifted one and made as if to offer it to Wilkes, but it was hardly what the mission called for. Wilkes grunted and went to another shelf, this one with larger boxes. "What do you like, Jimmy? Combat shotties? Grenade launchers? You can pretty much take your pick."

"I usually just carry a handgun," Chapel replied. He headed over to another shelf and started examining the boxes there. They were all marked as containing stereo equipment. "Something with some stopping power but a nice magazine size. If you come across any SIG Sauer P228s—"

He stopped because he heard Wilkes laughing.

Coming around the side of a shelving unit, he found the marine standing over a very large box full of Styrofoam. Sticking up out of the packing material was a device made from what looked like lengths of green pipe welded together.

"Is that what I think it is?" Chapel asked.

Wilkes had a huge grin on his face. "Harris!" he shouted. "Contorni! You don't screw around, do you?"

TOWSON, MD: MARCH 25, 15:38

Chapel was laughing despite himself by the time they got back to the motel. Wilkes's sense of humor could be a little coarse, but sometimes you just needed to blow off a little steam. After running for his life for days on end, it was good to feel a little safe, too, even if he knew that he was about to throw himself right back into the path of the oncoming train.

Julia was watching TV when they came in. "You should see this," she said, working the remote control to raise the volume. "Things in California are getting worse, not better. They say there's a virus in the power grid, and it's spread as far north as Seattle and down to the border with Mexico. The government can't say when they'll get it fixed, and meanwhile people are rioting in the streets. Plus, there's been a run on bread in the Midwest—a loaf of that processed bleached garbage stuff was going for twenty dollars this morning! The country's about to collapse."

"Lucky the good guys are on the case," Wilkes said.

"This is serious," Julia told him.

"And we're serious, too," Chapel said. He'd brought a six-pack of beer. He cracked open a can and handed it to her. She stared at it like he'd just handed her a live lobster, but after a second, she seemed to rethink her position and she took a long sip.

They called Angel, and she came over from the room next door. By then Chapel had a road map of the area around Washington spread out on the bed. It was time to get planning. He offered Angel a beer, too. "Probably our last chance to relax before this thing is all over."

"We could all be dead tomorrow morning," Wilkes pointed out.

"Thanks, I'm good," Angel told him. "Did you see the thing on TV about the president's speech?"

Chapel was too busy smoothing out the map to pay much attention. "Does he think that he can calm people down by talking to them?"

Angel shook her head. "The pundits say that, given the number of staffers working on it, this is going to be more than just a call for peace. They think he's going to announce something big. Like maybe that the power outages and the food prices are the work of terrorists. One guy even suggested he was going to declare war on China."

Chapel looked up when he heard that.

"It was just some crackpot," Angel said, blushing and looking away. "But that's out there, now. People are talking about it."

Chapel shook his head. He didn't have much use for speeches as a rule. Politicians talked, because that was their job, even when they had nothing real to say. But if there was even a hint of retaliation—

"The president won't attack China just on principle," Julia insisted. She looked to Wilkes. "When you were burrowing your way into this conspiracy—was there any sense that this Initiative or whatever was taking orders from China?"

"No, everyone involved kept insisting what a patriot they were. The kind of people who argue over who's wearing the bigger flag pin." He shrugged. "I don't know who's at the top of this, though. Could be Beijing. But if it is, they've covered their tracks pretty good."

Chapel chewed his lower lip. There were wheels within wheels here, games within games. Bringing China into the mix was probably just disinformation—a way to point the blame away from Holman and her Cyclops Initiative. It didn't matter what he knew, though. It mattered a great deal what the public believed.

Well. Nothing he could do about that. "No matter what, our move has to be rescuing Hollingshead. So let's look at that."

Wilkes nodded. He drained his beer can and tossed it in the corner of the room. Then he leaned over the map and stabbed it with one finger.

"They forced him out of his offices a while back. Tried to make him resign, but the latest I heard was he was just acting like he was taking some vacation days."

Chapel looked where he was pointing. It was a little bump of land sticking out into the Potomac River, just south of Ronald Reagan airport. "There's something there," he said, trying to remember his Washington geography. "Boats. A marina, I think."

Wilkes nodded. "Let me guess. He never told you where he lived, did he?"

"That was never something I needed to know," Chapel pointed out.

"He spends most of his time at work, up at the Pentagon. But he sleeps on a yacht down there. He'll be there right now. But it's not as easy as coming alongside in a rowboat. Holman pulled a snow job on her boss, the NSA director. She wanted to put Hollingshead in a cell so he could be interrogated. The secretary of defense vetoed that—which did not make her happy—but her boss did authorize her to monitor Hollings- head's communications and movements twenty-four seven. He also put a bunch of guards around the old guy. MPs, drawn from Pentagon staff, if I heard right."

"Any idea on how many of them, or where they're posted?" Chapel asked.

"That wasn't ever something I needed to know," Wilkes said.

Chapel nodded. "Give me your smartphone. I need a better map of that marina. If I can see all the access roads and good hiding spots, I can figure out how they've constructed their security. And then I can think about how to get in." He looked up at Angel and Julia. "We should get some rest, too. I'm going to need all of us to pull this off. We won't leave until after dark, so we have a couple of hours downtime."

Wilkes stretched his arms. "Sounds good to me. Wake me up if the Chinese start nuking us or something."

Chapel was too busy working the smartphone to reply. After a minute, Angel came over and took it away from him because she thought he was using it wrong. "Google Maps isn't going to show you what you need," she told him. "You want a real street map, the old-fashioned kind. Let me show you how to access those."

It was good to be back to something approximating normal.

OVER LANGLEY, VA: MARCH 25, 16:12

The nation's fleet of unmanned aerial vehicles had gone through quite a workout in the last twenty-four hours. Every aircraft had been grounded and checked out by a team of mechanics, their hardware stripped down from nose to tail and checked for any sign of unauthorized maintenance or sabotage. Those drones that were not considered vital to national security had been physically grounded, the mechanics actually removing their propellers and emptying their fuel tanks so they could not be commandeered by anyone.

Of the thousand-odd drones that would normally be airborne on a night like this, ranging from tiny hand-launched spy craft like toy helicopters to strategic reconnaissance drones big enough to look like passenger jets, only a handful were allowed up in the air.

Some of the drones had to stay airborne, by order of various agencies. There were those which were part of ongoing criminal investigations, and those tracking the borders for drug smugglers and illegal immigrants. These were allowed to go aloft again, but only with extra supervision in their ground control stations. Then there were the armed drones that circled various high-value resources day and night: crucial airports and satellite uplink sites, the "backbone" facilities that kept the Internet running, Camp David and the White House. Those drones were there to prevent another 9/11—if someone tried to fly a commercial aircraft into a collision course with the sites, the drones would shoot the terrorists down before they could reach their targets.

Those drones were vital to national security.

They now belonged, every one of them, to Charlotte Holman.

Thanks to the secretary of defense's getting her inside the air force base, she could take over any or all of the military drones whenever she pleased.

Had she been greedy, had she commandeered all the Creech drones airborne that night, she would have been detected right away. Fighter jets with human pilots would have been scrambled to take the drones down, and within an hour or two the threat would be eliminated.

But she was not greedy or careless or stupid. She and Paul Moulton had worked all this out quite carefully. In the end she chose only two drones, releasing the rest of them from her clutches. All but two of them would perform their scheduled patrols and then return to their bases without doing anything suspicious.

Of the two she did commandeer, one was an MQ-9 Reaper, a slightly larger, slightly heavier descendant of the old Predator class. This Reaper carried a single Hellfire missile slung under its belly, and its single, ever-vigilant eye was tasked with watching the skies around Washington, D.C. Holman sent the machine a program to replace its existing flight plan and it accepted the change without comment. For the moment, its controllers in Nevada would remain unaware that it no longer belonged to them. They would only get a few minutes' warning once the new program went into effect.

The second drone that Holman chose was something a little more special. An MQ-1C Gray Eagle, one of the newest and most advanced UAVs in the fleet. The Gray Eagle was designed to stay aloft for as long as thirty-six hours without refueling, hiding miles up in the sky where it couldn't be seen before swooping down at the last minute like its namesake to deliver death from above. This one was outfitted with four GBU-44/B Viper Strike guided bombs that could use GPS to find their targets with a level of precision Hellfire missiles could never beat. It also had an electronics package to combat enemy jamming countermeasures.

This particular Gray Eagle was tasked with keeping station well out at sea east of Washington, cutting long circles over the most commonly used shipping lanes. Its purpose was to intercept any foreign threats that might try to harass American cargo vessels. It would serve this purpose as expected, to the letter, for nearly twenty-four hours to come. At a specified time, however, it would switch off its control transponders and follow a simple program, a few dozen lines of code, that Paul Moulton had written weeks ago.

Holman waited for the Gray Eagle to confirm that it had uploaded her new program and filed it away in its long-term memory. Then she cut the link between her computer and the servers at Creech. Just to be safe, she erased all her own logs and then uninstalled the proprietary software she'd used to contact the drones.

Once that was done, no one could ever prove she'd been in contact with the Reaper or the Gray Eagle. Of course, it also meant she couldn't change their programs now even if she wanted to. From this point, there was no turning back.

TOWSON, MD: MARCH 25, 16:59

Wilkes came back after an hour's nap and grabbed a couple of pistols from the supply they'd taken from Contorni. "You've got all the details straight?" Chapel asked him.

The marine rolled his eyes. "Still not sure why we don't just kill Holman. But, yeah, I know what I'm supposed to do. And you're the boss."

"I outrank you. And Hollingshead needs us to do it this way," Chapel insisted.

Wilkes just nodded and headed out. From the window of the room, Chapel watched him grab a taxi and head north on the highway. "Okay, we just have to trust he'll do his part. Angel—are you ready to go?"

"Sure," she told him. "There's an Internet café about two miles north of here. I can do everything from there."

He nodded. "If you suspect, even for a second, that they're on to you, that the NSA knows you're online—"

"I've learned my lesson," she told him. "And I know how to cover my tracks."

"Okay. Stay in the other room until it gets dark. Then get to work."

"Got it," Angel said. But she didn't leave immediately. Instead she searched his face with her eyes, as if she needed to know something desperately important.

"Something on your mind?" he asked.

She frowned. "I know you'd do a lot to save the director," she said.

"Sure," he replied.

"I want you to know—if it was me, I would die for him. If I could, I would take the bullet."

Chapel thought for a moment before responding to that. "I hope he knows how loyal you are."

She shook her head. "I need to know if you would do the same."

Chapel glanced over at Julia. She raised an eyebrow but said nothing.

"You mean, am I willing to put myself in danger to protect him?" Chapel asked.

"No," Angel said. "I mean, if it comes down to trading your life for his, will you do it?" She looked away from his face. "I know it's a strange question. But I—I've got my reasons for asking. For wanting him to be safe."

"We all want him to be safe," Julia said. "I only met him once, and I still want that. Are you asking Jim—"

"Chapel knows what I'm asking."

And Chapel thought maybe he did. He tried to think of the best answer to give her. "He's my commanding officer," he told her. "I've sworn to obey him and to protect him to the utmost of my abilities. He's a man I admire, too. Someone I believe in. So . . . yes. The answer to your question is yes."

Angel said nothing more. She just nodded and stepped outside, closing the door gently behind her.

Once she was gone, it was just Chapel and Julia in the motel room. "What was that all about?" Julia asked.

"No idea," Chapel said, which wasn't strictly true. He had *an* idea. It just seemed too crazy to credit.

Julia shook her head. "Whatever. We've got some time before we move out. When was the last time you ate something?" she asked.

Chapel looked away from the window and frowned. "Not sure."

She grabbed a plastic bag from the bed and lifted it in the air. "Sandwiches," she said. "Straight from the local gas station." She opened her eyes very wide. "Yum."

"In the army we learned the secret of eating bad food. You just tell yourself it's fuel for your body. That it'll make you less tired all the time."

"And does that work?"

"No. But it gives you something to talk about besides how crappy the food is," Chapel told her.

She laughed and tossed the bag of sandwiches at him. It wasn't a great throw, and he had to lunge out of his chair to make the catch. Which turned out to be a lousy idea. Down on the floor on one knee, he had to hold himself perfectly still until the dark spots cleared from his vision and he could breathe easily again.

"What is it?" Julia asked, kneeling next to him. "Talk to me."

"Just . . . a wave of pain," Chapel told her. "Nothing too serious."

"From your bullet wound?"

He gave her a weak smile. "I might have been a little acrobatic when we went to get the guns. I kind of had to tackle a guy."

Julia helped him up onto the bed and then started unbuttoning his shirt. "I'll take a look. I don't think you opened my sutures, but let's see."

"I'm fine," he told her. It was even true. The pain had passed, and he was breathing all right again. Nothing to worry about.

She got his shirt off and then she unwound the bandage around his midriff. She palpated the wound and then she looked up at him. "I think you're okay," she said.

"I could have told you that much." He stood up and unlatched his artificial arm. Inside the shoulder there was a retractable cord that allowed him to plug it into any wall socket to charge its batteries. He had it set up on an end table before he'd even thought about what he was doing. It just needed a charge. It hadn't even occurred to him that Julia might be freaked out by watching him do that. But of course she'd seen him do it before, back when they lived together.

This time, though, she came over and studied the arm as if she'd forgotten it wasn't real. "Are these bullet holes?" she asked.

He bent over it with her and prodded at the silicone flesh. "I guess so." *The Vulcan cannon back in the warehouse,* he thought. He'd thought it was just a miracle he hadn't been torn to pieces. It was hardly the first time the arm had saved him from otherwise certain death. "Huh."

She turned and looked at him. After a second, he started to move away, but she grabbed his face and held on.

"What are you doing?" he asked.

"Memorizing what you look like. So if you get killed tonight, I won't forget."

"Julia," he said, "you can't think like that. I can't make you any promises that I'll be okay, but—"

"Shush," she told him. "I wasn't looking for any. I know what you're going to do tonight. I know it's dangerous. I also know it has to be done."

"I know that I've hurt you in the past," he told her. "Disappearing on missions when you couldn't even know if I was alive or dead. That's no way to live, and—"

"Are you even listening to me?" she asked.

He focused on her eyes. "Yes," he said.

"I'm saying it's okay." She let go of his face. "You're right. It sucks. The not knowing. The waiting for you to come back. Taking your shirt off and finding new scars all over you." She rubbed at her eyes. "I don't like it. But it's the price I have to pay for being in love with you."

He leaned forward until their foreheads touched.

"I've been asking myself," she said, "what would have happened if that asshole Moulton hadn't come between us. Whether I would have broken up with you on my own. I mean, that was a real possibility."

Chapel closed his eyes. "I told you then, I would do anything you wanted. I would take a desk job. I would come home every night at six and cook you dinner."

"If I wanted that, there are plenty of guys in the world who could give it to me," Julia told him. "No. I wanted you. And I still do. Jim—I made a lousy mistake when I broke up with you. Will you have me back?"

"You know I will," he told her.

He kissed her, deeply, putting his arm around her shoulders. Pulling her close to him, unable to contain what he was feeling.

She reached down and unbuttoned his pants.

TOWSON, MD: MARCH 25, 17:12

She turned her head to the side and he kissed her neck, his lips grabbing at her pale skin, his tongue darting out to touch the freckles in the vee where the top button of her shirt was open. She reached up and opened her shirt farther. He slipped his hand up inside her shirt from the back and slipped the catch of her bra.

That made her laugh. "Most guys can't do that with two hands," she said.

"Practice," he told her.

She shimmied and shrugged and her bra fell down across her arms. Her breasts spilled out before him, just as he remembered them, firm and beautiful. He kissed the tops of them, touched his lips to her nipples until she shivered. She reached down inside his pants and grabbed his cock and it stiffened instantly. He buried his face in the warmth of her stomach, kissing around her belly button, making her laugh again. Reaching down, he unbuckled her belt, but clearly she didn't have the patience to let him strip her. Jumping off the bed, she danced on one foot as she kicked off her jeans, then pulled down her panties in one quick yank so that she wore nothing but the open shirt.

He reached for her, but she pushed him back onto the bed. "Lie down," she told him. His hand stole between her legs, but she slapped it away. "No need for that," she said. "I'm ready. Just relax and let me do this, okay?"

"Sure," he said, smiling up at her.

She pulled his pants off, one leg at a time, nearly falling over as they came free, positively giggled as she jumped up on the bed and kissed his chest, then his hip. Bending low, she kissed the tip of his cock, then opened her lips and took him deep into her mouth. She knew exactly what that did to him and he groaned, his head tilted backward against the pillows, his hand grasping at the sheets. Apparently he was more than ready, too—if she didn't stop that he was going to come in her mouth, but he didn't want that, he wanted more. He reached down and grabbed at her.

"Enough," he gasped. "No more—"

She pulled away and laughed and then swung one leg up over him until she was straddling him, her hands planted on his chest. She slid her hips backward, then a little forward, her wetness gliding along the length of him and he ached to be inside her. He needed this, needed the confirmation of what she'd said, that they could start again. That they could be partners again.

She kissed him, deeply, her breasts crushed against his chest. Then she sat back up. Reaching behind herself, she grabbed his cock.

"Just tell me you'll love me forever," she said. "That's all I'm going to ask."

"Always," he told her.

She lifted away from him for a second, then sat down again and his cock slid inside her, so deep inside.

"Oh, God," she breathed. "I almost . . . forgot how . . . how good . . ."

"Yeah," he groaned.

He expected her to thrust against him, to grind her hips against his body, but instead she just stayed there, hovering on top of him, his cock just inside of her, so hard he could barely stand it. Then she moved with excruciating slowness, sinking down until he went deeper and deeper, the tiniest bit at a time. His eyes opened wide and he saw her shaking, her shoulders quivering with how good she must be feeling. Her eyes were closed but her mouth fell open, red hair framing her perfect lips.

"Oh, Jim," she said. "Can you—is this—okay?"

She slid just the barest fraction lower on him, but every slight motion, every tiny increment was so much more intense than he expected it to be. "I'm fine," he said through gritted teeth. "You just—you do what you need."

"This is—this is going—" she gasped as she slid lower, even deeper, "going to make me come. I'm going to . . . I'm going to . . ."

And then she sank all the way down on him, collided with him, and he could feel how much he was filling her up, filling all of her, and she cried out, literally screamed as her whole body vibrated on top of him. He reached up then and grabbed her to support her, then to bring her down closer until she was lying on top of him, her head buried in the crook of his neck as her hips started to move, really move now. And he knew it wouldn't be long before he joined her, before he came too. She groaned a little every time she slammed her hips against him, held her breath as she slid back and he could tell she was lost inside that rhythm, that even if he called her name she wouldn't hear him, couldn't hear, and he was so close, and—

The door of the room banged open and Angel stuck her head inside, her face wide open in fear. "I heard a noise," she said before she'd even registered what was going on.

On top of him, Julia froze in place. "Shit," she breathed against his neck.

Angel's mouth closed with an audible click as her teeth came together. Without a word she turned around and headed out of the room, pulling the door shut behind her.

"Damn," Chapel said. He started to wriggle his way out from under Julia, trying to remember where his pants were.

"We could just finish," Julia said.

But the moment was lost, and she must have known it. With a sigh she rolled off him, and together they hunted the floor for his underwear.

TOWSON, MD: MARCH 25, 17:32

Barefoot, and with one sleeve of his shirt flapping empty behind him, Chapel rushed around the motel looking for Angel. She wasn't in her room—the door was hanging open and she didn't answer when he called inside, nor when he looked. He padded along the sidewalk toward the little coffee shop the motel used as a restaurant, but all he managed to achieve by peering through its windows was to freak out a waitress. He waved in apology and moved on.

Finally he found Angel at the back of the motel, on a little patch of concrete bordered by gray and dusty weeds. She was standing by a vending machine, trying to force a taped-together dollar through the bill acceptor slot. It kept spitting the bill back at her.

"Angel," he said, quietly. Not getting too close. He could hear Julia coming up behind him, but he waved his hand at her to tell her to slow down, to keep her distance.

He could tell that Angel was upset. Her shoulders were shaking, and when she turned to look at him, a tear fell out of her right eye.

"Angel, listen. It's not what it looks like—"

Confusion and anger wrestled across her features. "What?"

Chapel cursed inwardly. "I mean. Okay, yes, you saw what you saw. But I don't want you to think—I mean, I hope you don't think that—"

"I did see what I saw. I can't unsee it now," Angel told him.

Chapel bit his lip. The absolute worst thing that could happen now was for him to get in a big fight with Angel. For one thing, somebody might see them—even worse, someone might think this was a domestic dispute and call the police. If they were caught now, Hollingshead didn't stand a chance.

Even if nobody saw them, he needed Angel for his plan. If she decided she hated him and wanted nothing to do with him—

"I can see you're upset," he said.

"You're damned right I'm upset," Angel told her. "The director is about to be assassinated and you two don't seem to care, you're too busy fuh . . . too busy fu-f-f-f—"

"Fucking," he said. No point evading it now

Angel nodded and looked away. Her cheeks were bright red.

This was what Julia had warned him about. Angel had a crush on him, and seeing him with another woman had destroyed her. "I am so sorry, Angel. But I want you to know why."

"Why you're fuh—why you're with her?" Angel asked, shaking her head. "That, at least, I get. She's beautiful and and curvy in the right places, and you have history, and—"

"You're beautiful, too," Chapel told her. "You're sexy, too."

Angel made a sound like she was about to start retching right there in the parking lot. "Oh my God," she said.

"Angel, it's okay," he said, stepping closer to her, holding out his hand. She winced away from his touch.

"Oh my God." Angel made the retching noise again. It was an awful hitching sound in the back of her throat that changed over time, becoming softer, becoming . . .

Laughter.

She leaned over, putting her hands on her knees. She couldn't stand up from laughing so hard. Chapel had no idea what was going on.

"Oh my," Angel said, but she couldn't finish the exclamation because a new paroxysm of laughter seized her like a fit. "Oh my God. You thought—oh my—"

Chapel had no idea what to do except wait it out.

Eventually she managed to speak an entire sentence. "You thought I was jealous of you two."

"Yes," Chapel admitted.

"You thought—what? That I wanted to be with you? Like . . . like that?" She shook her head in disbelief. "Listen, Chapel. I know we flirt. Over the phone."

"Yes," Chapel said again. "We do."

Angel fought to control herself. "There's something you need to know. I flirt with you like that because it's safe. Because I thought we were never actually going to meet in person, and anyway I knew you would never, you know, try anything. The truth of the matter is, Chapel, I really, really do not now nor have I ever wanted to have se—s-s-s-s—"

"Sex," he supplied.

Angel nodded in gratitude. "Relations with you. I'm sorry. It's not personal. But I have zero interest in, you know. Touching your special places. Or anything like that."

Chapel considered what she'd said earlier. About Julia's curves. "So you're—that is . . . are you jealous of . . . Julia?"

"You mean, do I want to do that with girls? No, definitely not."

"I don't understand," Chapel said.

Behind him, Julia made an exasperated noise. Clearly she wasn't going to stay out of this any longer. She came up beside Chapel and took his arm. "She doesn't want to have sex with anyone," Julia told him.

"Not, you know. Typically," Angel said.

Julia turned to Chapel. "Don't you see? She was still in puberty when they started locking her up in those trailers. She never had a chance to figure things out."

"You mean," he said, looking back at Angel, "you've never—"

"Please don't finish that sentence," Angel asked him. "My stomach is feeling weird enough already."

He nodded and shut his mouth. He was having a hard time believing all this, though. Angel had the sexiest voice he'd ever heard in his life. He'd gotten through a lot of dark times listening to her purr in his ear. And some of the things she'd suggested over a telephone line had been— well, now that he thought about it, he supposed she'd never said anything truly dirty. She'd never been graphic or detailed in her flirting. She had just said things that might be . . . suggestive, if you were in the right frame of mind to hear them that way. If you *wanted* to hear them that way.

"I flirt," Angel explained to him, "but it's kind of just . . . I don't know. Experimental. I liked hearing how you reacted to it."

"Even though you couldn't understand why you liked that," Julia prompted.

Angel's mouth pursed in anger. "There's nothing wrong with me," she said.

"No, of course not," Julia assured her.

"I'm fine," Angel insisted. "I am absolutely fine."

"Of course you are," Julia said.

Chapel scratched at his head. "So when you walked in on us, you ran away—"

"Because I was grossed out," Angel said. "Look, I enjoy the occasional hug or whatever. But when things get—you know. Sticky." A wave of re-vulsion made her shiver. "I can't handle it."

"Okay," Chapel said. "Look, enough said, all right?" He looked back at Julia. "Let's all just pretend this never happened."

Angel nodded agreeably.

Chapel moved closer to her and lifted his arm, thinking he would give her a quick hug to end things. But she shied away, putting her hands up to ward him off.

"No offense," she said, "but right now, you kind of stink of it."

He backed off.

Without saying anything more, Julia produced a couple of nearly fresh dollar bills from her pocket. Angel got the soda she wanted—something sweet with lots of caffeine, her favorite—and left without saying another word. When she was gone, Chapel leaned up against the vending machine and tried not to let his confusion completely overcome him.

Julia put a hand over her mouth and shook her head back and forth. "Jim, I'm so sorry—"

"Looks like you misread some signals, there," he told her.

She looked toward Angel's room, as if there would be some sign there to help her understand what they'd just heard. "Whoever did this to her . . ." she said.

"What, you mean hiding her away in trailers her whole life? It was that or send her to prison," he said. "Anyway, she's agoraphobic. She wants to live like that."

Julia shook her head. "Sure. It makes her feel safe to be inside, away from people. But you don't treat an alcoholic by locking them inside a bar."

He had to admit she had a point.

"She's missed out on so much," Julia said. "If I ever find out who did this to her, who made her what she is—I'm going to tear their balls off."

IN TRANSIT: MARCH 25, 21:44

Teaming up with Wilkes had one major advantage: he had a credit card.

In fact, he had an unlimited corporate card from the NSA. The card was issued to a company called "Interstate Holdings," but it drew on the endless coffers of one of the biggest black budgets in the country. It had been given to Wilkes when he was sent out to hunt for Chapel and Angel, and nobody had cut it off yet.

As a result, when Chapel headed out of the motel and south on the highway toward Washington, he was driving a slightly better car than he'd had before. Julia had the old beater that Ralph had bought for them, since she had her own destination to get to.

If they were going to save Hollingshead, they needed to approach the problem from several different angles. They had to split up.

The biggest issue they faced was that they didn't know how it was going to be done. Originally Holman had wanted Wilkes to kill the director—she'd told him as much, maybe as a test to see what he was willing to do for her. But after Wilkes failed to kill Chapel in Pittsburgh, she had lost some of her faith in the marine. She'd told him she had a contingency plan in place and that he shouldn't worry about it.

Which could mean just about anything. One of the MPs guarding Hollingshead might be a plant. Or they could have a sniper ready to shoot the director from half a mile away. The only real piece of data they had was that it was supposed to happen at midnight.

The plan they'd eventually come up with had been to get Chapel close enough to Hollingshead to protect him—and then to put pressure on Holman to call off the assassination. If half of the plan failed, the other half might still work.

It was a gamble, but Chapel had taken worse bets.

Chapel skirted Baltimore—he could not afford to get stuck in traffic— then rejoined 95 just before the Beltway. Working his way down past the airport and into Alexandria took some doing, but he knew these roads like the back of his hand and he was able to stash the car not too far from the marina where Hollingshead lived.

The marina sat at the north end of what was technically an island, though it came so close to touching the banks of the Potomac that it was hard to tell. The island had managed to avoid every wave of development in the twentieth century and was almost unused except as parkland. Chapel supposed that the people wealthy enough to keep their boats at the marina liked it that way. The northern half of the island was basically a giant parking lot for boats, a haul-out facility filled with small pleasure craft up on trailers. South of there were the actual slips where the bigger vessels, the ones that couldn't be brought on land for the winter, still bobbed in the river. Hollingshead's yacht was about as far as you could get from the road, of course—that was how these things always worked. Chapel had considered going in by water, shimmying up a dripping line with a knife between his teeth like a pirate, maybe. But he couldn't get his artificial arm wet and he wasn't willing to part with it, so he had to approach by land.

The problem with that, of course, was that Charlotte Holman had posted armed guards all over the marina, to stop Hollingshead from meeting with anyone.

Good thing Chapel had been trained for this kind of job.

DAINGERFIELD ISLAND, VA: MARCH 25, 22:49

Another thing they'd bought with Wilkes's magic credit card was a hands-free unit and a burner phone. As Chapel slipped between two parked boat trailers at the edge of the marina grounds, he put in the earpiece and slipped the phone into his pocket.

"Angel," he said. "You there?"

"You know it, baby," she replied.

He tried very hard not to let the sound of her voice send shivers down his spine. He failed. It was just how they worked together.

And it was magnificent.

"It's so good to have you back where you belong," he told her. "Perched on my shoulder, working as my guardian angel."

"Tell me about it. I've been so useless up to now. It's good to be back on a mission with you, even if I have to do it from this Internet café. There's three other people here. So I may have to watch what I say."

"Do they look like hired killers or NSA spies?"

She laughed. "No. They look like sleepy grad students from the university, trying to get their papers written before class tomorrow. But you can't be too careful."

"Fair enough," he replied.

"Give me some time here to work up the imaging," she told him.

Chapel took a second to breathe. He looked out at the lights of Washington across the river, watched them dance as they were reflected in the water. In the distance he could hear lines jingling as they slapped against bollards, hear the repetitive dull thudding of the boats bobbing in their slips. The night air was crisp on his exposed face and he felt himself centering. Feeling good. It had been way too long since he'd worked a mission like this, the way it was supposed to be done.

Of course, complacency could get you killed.

His back began to ache from crouching so low, so he straightened up a little to put his weight on different muscles. He closed his eyes for a second and took a deep breath.

And that was when he was spotted.

"Hey!" someone called out. "Marina's closed!"

Chapel craned his head around to see a man in a gray shirt and dark pants—a navy uniform. He was carrying an M4 rifle and he was maybe twenty yards away.

No chance of taking the guy down from that distance, not with Chapel's sidearm still tucked in its holster. No chance to run away, either.

"Come on out of there," the MP told him. "Hands out."

Chapel nodded and stepped out from between the boat trailers. It was dark enough that he didn't think the MP would be able to see his holster. If he played this calm, it might give him another few seconds before he was arrested. "Sorry, Officer, I was just—"

"Don't call me 'officer,'" the MP said. "Reach into your pocket very slowly and take out your ID. You own one of these boats?"

"That's right," Chapel said. Slowly he moved his good hand toward his back pocket. Where his wallet might be, if he was carrying one. "I have the registration card right here." Did boats have registrations like cars? He had no idea. But it sounded good. Smiling, he walked straight toward the MP. "I left some important stuff in the boat last time I was down here, figured I would just duck in and get it, is that okay?"

"Not tonight it's not," the MP said.

"Sorry, I had no idea," Chapel told him. They were almost close enough to touch. "Here, my ID," he said.

The MP lowered his rifle a little, reaching for what he thought Chapel was going to hand him.

Except instead of a driver's license it was a Glock 9 mm.

"Shit," the MP said.

"Yeah," Chapel told him. "Now, if you'll—"

Maybe the MP thought Chapel was going to kill him then and there. He moved so fast he might have thought he was fighting for his life. His rifle came up, not to shoot Chapel, but to knock the pistol out of Chapel's hand.

The move surprised Chapel. He lost the gun, and his hand suddenly stung with pain.

Chapel knew what to do next. The only thing he could do if he didn't want to die or be arrested right here. Time seemed to slow down as he went through the movements he'd had drilled into him a thousand times.

Step in—he moved his left foot in between the MP's feet, closing the distance between them, making it impossible for the MP to shoot Chapel or use his rifle as a club.

Unbalance your opponent—Chapel brought his good arm up, bent at the elbow, and shoved it into the MP's neck, pushing the man to one side, off his center of balance. The MP had no choice but to change his footing or fall over. The MP did the obvious thing—he tried to dance sideways, to get his balance back. Which set Chapel up perfectly for the third movement.

Trip and control—Chapel's left foot twisted around the MP's calf and suddenly balance just wasn't possible. The MP went crashing to the ground, with Chapel's foot directing him until he was lying on his back, his arms splayed out to the sides to try to break the fall.

In a second Chapel had his spare pistol—his P228— out and in his hand. "Don't move," he told the MP. "And don't make a sound."

The man nodded in agreement.

That was when Angel's voice came back in his earpiece. "I've got that imaging now, sweetie," she said. "We can get started."

"Actually, there's been a change of plan," Chapel said.

GEORGETOWN, D.C.: MARCH 25, 23:01

North across town, about a mile away from the White House, Wilkes sat in his car and waited for a signal. He had a bag of potato chips and a two-liter bottle of soda and he would have been perfectly happy to sit there all night if the mission hadn't required exact timing. As it was, he was beginning to get concerned.

In sniper school they'd taught him that worry was pointless. If you wasted time on things you couldn't control, you harmed your readiness for the things you could. Far better to spend your time maintaining your equipment, or feeding yourself to keep up your energy, or doing anything more constructive than worrying about what might or might not be.

They'd taught him that lesson very well. Well enough that now he was only peripherally aware that there was less than an hour remaining before Hollingshead's scheduled execution. Even if things worked perfectly from here, he was going to have to make great time.

At least one thing worked out. Fifteen minutes late, maybe, but there was the signal. A newspaper tucked into the slats of a decorative bench across the street.

Wilkes flashed his headlights twice, very quickly. There weren't very many people out and about on the street to be annoyed. None of them seemed to notice.

Well, one person had. A dark shape stepped out of an alley and moved quickly to the passenger-side door of Wilkes's car. He unlocked it, and the shape opened the door and ducked inside.

"It wasn't easy getting away," Charlotte Holman told him. She was dressed in a black trench coat and had her hair wrapped in a kerchief. "The SecDef is keeping me at his side twenty-four seven until after the president's speech tomorrow. Supposedly so I can give him constant updates. I think he's actually starting to get afraid of me."

Wilkes favored her with a big friendly smile. He held out the bag of chips in case she wanted one. The way she turned up her lip told him she didn't.

"You've been out of contact for a while," she told him. "I haven't heard anything from either of you in far too long. I think you're a bad influence on him."

"Him?" Wilkes asked.

"Paul. Paul Moulton. Where is he? He should be here with you."

"Funny thing about that," Wilkes told her. "He's dead."

Her eyes went very wide. "When?" she asked. "How?" She shook her head. "Never mind. It was Chapel, obviously. He's alive, isn't he? Goddamnit, I knew right from the start we should have followed him from NSA headquarters and killed him quietly before he could even get to New York. But Moulton thought we needed to establish a connection between him and the Angel system. Poor Paul!" She took a deep breath. "His sacrifice won't be in vain."

"Maybe," Wilkes said.

She stared at him. "Don't tell me there's more bad news."

"Just one thing," he said, slapping his hands together to get some of the grease and fragments of potato chip off his fingers. Then he grabbed the stun gun at his side and brought it around very fast, fast enough she probably didn't see it before its prongs touched her neck.

DAINGERFIELD ISLAND, VA: MARCH 25, 23:08

A nice thing about running an operation in a marina was that you could always find plenty of rope. Chapel had his captive MP trussed up and gagged and dumped in an old rowboat before anybody had time to call for help. There was a problem, though. The MP had a walkie-talkie on his belt and any second now his superior was going to call him to ask for a report. Chapel had had the same problem back at the beginning of all this, outside of Angel's trailer. At the time, he had just had to accept his time was limited. That wasn't going to work here.

"I've got an idea," Angel said. "Take out your phone and snap a picture of the radio for me."

Chapel did as he was told. "What exactly will this achieve?" he asked.

"It tells me the make and model of the walkie-talkie," Angel replied. "Knowing that, I can look up the specifications for it on the Internet. Knowing the specifications . . . here. Turn it on and see what happens."

Chapel adjusted a knob on the face of the radio. A squeal of white noise came from the speaker.

"Walkie-talkies all work on different frequencies," she explained. "This brand is a multichannel unit, but all those channels are in the same general part of the spectrum. I've tied into the local cell-phone towers, and now I'm jamming all the possible frequencies this radio can pick up."

"I had no idea you could do that."

"Sugar," Angel said, "we've been out of touch too long. You've forgotten the principle rule when dealing with me. I can do *anything*, as long as it's attached to a computer. In fact, I can do more than this. Give me a second."

Chapel huddled over the radio, watching the marina in every direction. It didn't take long for Angel to come back.

"Once they realize they're being jammed, the MPs might get suspicious and start looking around for the source. So now I'm spoofing them as well."

A deep, masculine voice swam up out of the static from the walkie-talkie. Chapel couldn't understand much of what it was saying in the midst of all that white noise, but he definitely heard the voice say "all clear."

"Who is that?" Chapel asked.

"That's me," Angel said. She laughed. "I recorded my own voice, then slowed it down and changed the pitch a little. I have no idea if any of the MPs sound like that, but given the static it might be enough to fool them."

Chapel couldn't help but smile in the dark. "You really are something."

"Tell me that again the next time you see me. Right now, you've got a rendezvous to make."

IN TRANSIT: MARCH 25, 23:12

Inside the flight electronics of the MQ-9 Reaper, an electronic clock ticked over to a new second and sent a signal to the command module. A new program loaded into the machine's memory and began to run.

The screen of the Reaper's stick jockey, back at Creech Air Force Base, went black. The men in the room around the remote pilot lurched forward, hitting keys and asking questions, but there was nothing to be done. All telemetry was lost, all command channels shut down. The Reaper had gone rogue.

A second signal from the command module armed the single Hellfire missile that nestled against the Reaper's belly. It was ready to fire as soon as its target had been acquired.

A third signal went to the unmanned aircraft's rudder, turning it from its previous course. It banked to the left, over the streets of Washington, its single camera eye tracking the lights below.

DAINGERFIELD ISLAND, VA: MARCH 25, 23:19

One MP was down by the river, watching for any boats that might try to pull up alongside the yacht and rescue Hollingshead. He didn't seem to expect any kind of threat to come from the land. Chapel padded up behind him and got him in a sleeper hold and he went down without so much as a squeak of protest.

Another MP was guarding the entrance to the slips, a natural choke point—nobody could get to the yacht without passing him. He faced the darkened marina buildings and he never turned around, so Chapel was at a loss as to how he would sneak up on the man.

In the end he caught a lucky break. He saw the man's chin droop. Saw his grip on his rifle go slack. The man was falling asleep on his feet. Chapel waited until he was just about to fall over on his own—then made sure he at least didn't fall off the dock and into the water. He put the MP down in the cool grass and hog-tied him.

Only two left.

They were going to be a major problem, though. The two of them were up on the deck of the yacht, working together. Maybe Chapel could get to one of them without being seen, but the seconds he needed to take the man down would leave him vulnerable to the other MP, who would surely just open fire and end Chapel's mission in the most definitive way.

From the shadows, Chapel studied the yacht. It was about thirty feet long, with a high main deck and a broad wheelhouse. The name *Themis* was stenciled on its stern, and it looked like the cleanest and best-maintained vessel in the marina.

The only way on board, as far as Chapel could see, was a gangplank in full view of the two guards. He might be able to climb onto the boat from the water side, but that didn't seem practical—he would make so much noise in the water that he would be sure to attract their attention.

The one thing he had going for him was that they had no idea what was going on. They kept fiddling with their walkie-talkies, and he could hear them debating what the white noise and the voice saying "all clear" really meant. They were confused and worried, but they didn't know who was out there or what was coming for them.

In the end Chapel had to use the oldest trick in the book. Divide and conquer.

He ran back to where he'd left the MP by the entrance to the slips. The man was still fast asleep and his ropes were secure. Chapel wasn't so much interested in the man, though, as he was in his rifle. He picked up the M4 and set its selector to burst fire. Then he fired three shots into the ground, the noise explosive and deafening in the quiet of the deserted marina.

He looped back to the yacht, avoiding the shortest possible route. Much as he'd expected, when he arrived back at the slip, one of the MPs had already come down the gangplank and was hurrying in the direction of the noise, clearly intending to investigate the gunfire.

Chapel let him get out of sight of the yacht before swooping in and taking the man down. Only one left, then. He headed back to the yacht and waited in the shadows until the last MP started fumbling with his radio, clearly looking for an update from his vanished friend.

Chapel wasn't going to get a better chance. He rushed forward, pounding across the gangplank, a pistol clutched in both of his hands, the barrel pointed right at the MP. "Don't move!" he shouted. "Down on the ground!"

Maybe the MP could tell that Chapel wasn't willing to kill him. Maybe he just didn't like being told what to do. He chose the one action Chapel wasn't prepared for, the one that ruined everything. He stood his ground. Lifting his M4 to his eye, he started shouting back, almost echoing Chapel word for word.

"Looks like we have a standoff," Chapel told him as they aimed their weapons at each other.

"Doesn't look like that at all to me," the MP said.

"Oh? How's that?"

"You've got a pistol. I've got an assault rifle," the MP pointed out. "That means I have the advantage. You have to aim."

It was a fair point. Chapel had no doubt he could kill or incapacitate the man with one shot, and at this range he wasn't likely to miss. But pistol shots didn't just knock people down or make them incapable of pulling their own triggers. The MP could cut Chapel in half with automatic fire at any time.

"Maybe we can just talk about this," Chapel pointed out.

"Maybe you can throw that gun in the water," the MP replied. "Then maybe you can get down on your knees and lock your fingers behind your head, like—"

He didn't finish his sentence. Instead he looked very confused for a second, and then he lowered his weapon. With one hand he reached behind himself and touched his back and when he brought his hand around to his face, it was covered in blood.

In another second he was facedown on the boards of the deck, collapsed in a spreading pool of darkness. The hilt of a big hunting knife stuck up from his back.

Behind him, Chapel could see Wilkes perched on the far rail, a mischievous grin on his face. "Miss me?" he asked.

DAINGERFIELD ISLAND, VA: MARCH 25, 23:43

"Jesus," Chapel said. "You didn't have to kill him."

"Yeah, I did," Wilkes insisted. "If I just winged him, he would have opened fire. You'd be a goner."

Chapel didn't have time to argue. He went to the rail where Wilkes perched and looked over the side, down into the small powerboat Wilkes had brought up along the yacht's hull. "I didn't hear you coming."

"I cut the engine about a quarter mile out," Wilkes said. "Paddled the rest of the way. Figured if there were any police boats out here I didn't really want to meet 'em."

Chapel could see why. A body was stuffed into the powerboat, its hands bound and its head covered in a black sack. That would be Charlotte Holman. "Just tell me she's still alive."

Wilkes slapped Chapel on the back. "It's your show, buddy. I just follow orders."

Then he dropped back down into the powerboat and, with just a touch of its engine, brought it around the side of the yacht. Together Chapel and Wilkes lifted Holman out of the smaller vessel and carried her across the gangplank. She didn't fight them, though Chapel could tell she was awake.

He pulled the hood off her head and helped her to her feet. Wilkes hadn't bothered to gag her. Most likely he'd threatened to kill her the instant she made the slightest sound.

"I'm sorry about the rough treatment," Chapel told her. "Really."

She snarled at him. "Fucking Boy Scout. If you were more like him," she said, nodding in Wilkes's direction, "life would be so much easier."

Chapel shrugged and grabbed the rope that bound her hands. He marched her down a short stairway to the lower deck of the yacht. A companionway ran the length of the vessel, with doors opening on four sides. "Director Hollingshead?" he called out. "Are you here? It's Jim Chapel."

A doorway popped open at the bow end of the corridor. The director peered out of the shadows beyond. He was dressed in pajamas with a neat pinstripe, and he wasn't wearing his glasses, so his eyes looked small and only half open. Apparently he'd been sleeping.

He also had a big silver revolver in his hand. Clearly he'd been ready for whoever had come to wake him up. Maybe, Chapel thought, he could have kept the assassins at bay on his own.

"Son," the director said, "I assume you have a good reason for being here."

"Yes, sir."

Hollingshead nodded. Then he peered down the darkened corridor at the other two people in the narrow space. "Blast," he said. He disappeared for a second and came back with his glasses. "Charlotte? And . . . Wilkes?" He shook his head. "The whole menagerie. Well, ah, I suppose if I'm entertaining I should make some coffee."

DAINGERFIELD ISLAND, VA: MARCH 25, 23:48

The main cabin of the yacht was a cozy room with a low ceiling, all finished wood and brass. It was warm and the carpet was soft. When Chapel tried to pull out a chair, however, he found that it was bolted to the floor.

"This is a seagoing yacht," the director explained. He still wore his pajamas, but he'd put on a silk dressing robe as well. He handed a coffee mug to Wilkes and another to Chapel. Holman didn't get one, but then, her hands were still tied. "I always considered the possibility that I might, have to—you know. Make a sea crossing on short notice." He gave them a wry smile.

"You should have gone to Russia the second the secretary of defense relieved you of duty," Holman said. "You might have had a chance, then. Like Snowden."

The director favored her with one of his most genial smiles. "Please have a seat, Charlotte. I have no desire for you to be uncomfortable."

"Oh, I'm fine," she said. "Whatever indignities I suffer tonight, I'll come out on top. These two will get thirty years for kidnapping. And as for you, Rupert—I imagine we'll be shipping you to a secret detention facility overseas. You won't be coming back."

Hollingshead's smile never faded. "Looks like we have nothing to lose, then! I take it, boys, that if she's here, then you've managed to dig a few things up." He turned to face Chapel.

"That's right, sir," Chapel said. "For instance, we know she was a major player in the Cyclops Initiative." He had played enough poker with Wilkes to know not to let on that he still had no idea what the Cyclops Initiative was. "Her workgroup over at the NSA was directly responsible for hijacking the drones in California and in New Orleans, and for the robot that tried to blow up Angel's trailer."

A brief flash of something like worry crossed the director's face. It disappeared almost instantly. Chapel had a feeling that if they ever sat down to a hand of Texas Hold 'Em, Hollingshead could give Wilkes a run for his money.

"Most important," he continued, "and why we're here now, is the fact that we know she's planning on having you executed at midnight. That is, in"—he checked his watch—"about ten minutes."

"We'll keep you safe, sir," Wilkes said. He pulled a pistol from his belt and laid it on a table.

"If that's even necessary," Chapel said. "I'm thinking that if Holman is here, her assassins won't attack. They'll abort, rather than risk harming her by mistake."

"Oh, you think so, do you?" Holman asked.

Chapel turned to face her. "Are you going to tell me I'm wrong?"

She gave him a nasty smile. "Yes," she said. "In a few minutes, Captain Chapel, you're going to be dead. So will Rupert. And there's nothing you can do about it."

IN TRANSIT: MARCH 25, 23:54

Up in the wind, high over Alexandria, the Reaper made one last, tight turn and began its final run, straight and true, straight for its target.

Normally it had to search for its prey for hours, sifting through signals in a variety of spectra, or homing in on a particular cellular phone or the IP address of a computer. This time its masters had made things easy. They'd given it a set of map coordinates. The Reaper consulted the GPS satellites one last time and began its descent.

Already the hunter was being hunted. Waves of active secondary radar washed over its hull, demanding its transponder codes. Fighter jets had been scrambled to bring it down if it didn't respond. None of that mattered—its masters had assumed this would happen, but they'd also known exactly how long it would take for the fighter jets to find and destroy the Reaper. Approximately three minutes too long, in point of fact. The Reaper's defection, the parameters of its final mission, had been designed around that timetable.

Nothing in the air could stop it before it could launch its deadly payload.

DAINGERFIELD ISLAND, VA: MARCH 25, 23:56

Wilkes lifted a hand as if he would strike Holman across the face.

Only Hollingshead stopped him. In this case by clearing his throat. "Is there something you'd like to tell us, Charlotte?"

"The assassination can't be aborted or stopped or even postponed," she said. "If we don't run away from here, right now and as fast as our legs will carry us, we'll all die. Even then, there's no guarantee we'll make it to safety in time."

Chapel stared at her. "Surely you don't want that."

"I don't have much choice. Unless you let me go. It's your only chance, Captain. It's the only chance any of us have. What time is it?"

He glanced at his watch. "Three 'til."

"And that's assuming your watch isn't slow," she told him.

Chapel turned to look at the director. "Sir, maybe you *should* get out of here."

Hollingshead sighed. "Unless that's what she wants. Perhaps there's a sniper out there waiting for me to step out onto the deck and make myself a target."

Chapel reached for the hands-free unit in his ear. "Angel, what about imaging? Do you see anyone out there? Anybody skulking around?"

"Negative."

"There's nobody out there," he told the rest of them. "Unless—" He slapped his forehead.

"You've figured it out, have you?" Holman asked. "We're the NSA, Captain. We don't have field agents. Much less human assassins. When we want to kill someone—"

"They send a drone," Chapel said.

Wilkes jumped up and ran to the stairs that led above deck.

"You can't send an abort signal?" Chapel asked. "Even if we gave you access to a computer, a phone, whatever?"

Holman laughed. "No. We knew we weren't going to change our minds. Hollingshead knows too much—he has to die. If I'm going to die as well, then so be it. The Initiative will go on without me. What time is it?"

"Thirty seconds," Chapel told her. "You could call them, call whoever it is you answer to, get them to—"

"There is no abort signal," Holman said. She closed her eyes. He could tell she was trying to play it cool, but she was shaking, her breath coming raggedly as fear overcame her. "Good-bye, Captain. Good-bye, Rupert—"

OFF DAINGERFIELD ISLAND, VA: MARCH 25, 23:59

An electronic signal from the Reaper's command module readied itself to trigger. It only needed to run down a length of wire, headed for a contact point where the aircraft met the AGM-114 Hellfire missile it bore. When the signal reached the missile, its thruster would fire and the missile would streak down toward its target, the yacht *Themis*. It was designed to blow apart armored vehicles. The yacht, which was mostly made of fiberglass, would provide little resistance.

Before the missile could launch, however, Julia Taggart stood up from where she'd been lying in a rowboat a few hundred meters south of the marina and lifted a FIM-92 Stinger missile launcher to her shoulder.

"Ten o'clock high," Angel said, in her ear.

The launcher weighed thirty-five pounds, but Julia had done a lot of Pilates and she managed it. She slammed the Battery Coolant Unit into the handguard, just as Wilkes had shown her. In the complicated eyepiece, the sky turned blue and yellow, with a big orange dot right where Angel had said it would be.

No need to aim. The Stinger was designed to be foolproof. Fire and forget.

Julia pulled the trigger. *Fwoosh*. The missile jumped out of its launch tube with a modest noise, followed a second later by a bone-shaking roar as its rocket motor kicked in.

"Drop the launcher and get out of there!" Angel said.

Julia tossed the launcher over the side of her boat and let it sink in the Potomac. She pulled the cord on the boat's little outboard motor and started downriver, away from the yacht, away from everything.

Behind and far above her, the Stinger tracked the Reaper by its heat signature. It adjusted its course to home in on the drone, and they met in a burst of light and heat and smoke that filled up half the sky. The noise followed a moment later, loud enough to make the boat rock back and forth.

Julia did not turn around to watch.

She did let a little smile cross her face.

"Badass," she said.

DAINGERFIELD ISLAND, VA: MARCH 26, 00:01

At the last second, Holman clamped her eyes shut and buried her face in her shoulder, as if that could protect her from a Hellfire strike. The noise and light of the explosion made her cry out in terror.

When she finally opened her eyes again and looked up, Hollingshead was standing over her, peering down at her through his thick glasses.

"Charlotte, my boys aren't fools. They knew you might send a drone."

Wilkes came thudding down the stairs from the deck. "It's awesome out there." He laughed. "Every car alarm from here to Foggy Bottom is going off."

Holman's eyes went wide. "You blew it up? You blew up a plane this close to Ronald Reagan airport?"

"To be fair, it was a drone, not a plane," Chapel pointed out.

Holman shook her head. "Every cop in D.C. is going to be after you now."

"Because of you they already were," Chapel told her.

He knew she was right, though. They had only a few minutes before the entire river would swarm with police boats. Still, heading out by water was the better option. Moving overland would be impossible. The capital police drilled constantly for something like this and they would act quickly to shut down every road in the city. Chapel didn't intend to go very far, but he wanted to be away from the epicenter of the search, and soon.

So he needed to get Holman talking now.

"Director, sir," he said, "forgive me, but we need to get you dressed, and we all need to get out of here." Hollingshead nodded and stepped out of the room. "But the big question," Chapel said, turning to Wilkes, "is whether we take her with us when we go, or just leave her here for the police to find her."

Holman snorted. "You think I'm worried about them finding me here? I can make up any story I want as to why I'm handcuffed in a traitor's yacht."

"I'm sure they'd believe you, too. A respected official of a government agency, held against her will. It would be hard to make anything stick to you, even your involvement in the Cyclops Initiative."

Holman narrowed her eyes. "There's a 'but' in there, isn't there?"

"Maybe an 'unless.' We can't make anything stick without evidence. The problem for you," Chapel told her, "is that we have some now. We have Wilkes."

"His involvement was highly compartmentalized."

Chapel nodded. This was where he had to start playing real poker. "As far as you know, yes. But he was there when you ordered us all killed. He was there when you said you planned on assassinating the director. And he kept his ears open the whole time. He met other people in the Initiative as well. Spoke with them. They're all dead now or out of the way. You're the only one left. The question you need to ask yourself is this: How much does he know? How much can he prove? And if the answer is anything more than 'nothing,' you know you're in serious shit."

She winced as if the obscenity stung her.

Chapel took a breath. "This 'Cyclops Initiative' thing? It's over. It failed. Now it looks to me like you have one chance to beat a treason charge," he said. "And that's to tell us everything, right now. Otherwise Wilkes is going to find the closest reporter and start giving interviews."

Holman turned to look at the marine. "You wouldn't dare. I know you well enough that—"

"You know me? I was a triple agent right under your nose for three years," Wilkes pointed out. "You know jack, lady."

Director Hollingshead stepped back into the cabin, dressed now in pants and a blazer over his pajama top. "Shall we head out, boys? I have a motor launch moored in the next slip over. It will allow us to make a, ah, more expeditious retreat than if we tried to move the yacht."

"On it," Wilkes said, and he stomped back up onto the deck.

"Sir," Chapel said, "did you hear my conversation with Subdirector Holman?"

"I did, son." Hollingshead took off his glasses and polished them with a handkerchief. "So what will it be?" he asked her.

She was breathing heavily by then, as if she were about to have a panic attack. "Rupert—I want your word as a gentleman. You'll protect me from any fallout."

"To the best of my ability," he said and gave her a little bow. "Of course, in exchange for my protection—"

"Everything," she said. "I'll tell you everything."

PART 5

"Okay," Angel said. She tapped the keypad of her laptop, and a green light came on next to the camera. "We're ready." She glanced over at Chapel, and he supposed she was asking him what to say next, but he had no idea. He'd never done this before. So he just nodded.

Angel swallowed and looked straight into the camera. "The following is an interview with Charlotte Holman, subdirector of the National Security Agency, recorded March twenty-sixth, 20—, starting at . . . 3:18 A.M." She nodded once at the camera, then turned the laptop around so that the camera faced Holman. "Please confirm your identity."

"I'm Charlotte Holman."

Chapel walked over to where Angel sat in a folding metal chair. It was one of two, and they comprised the only furniture in the tiny room. They were in the cellar of a DIA safe house just across the river from Washington. A place where foreign spies were taken to be debriefed. Hollingshead believed it was the safest place they had access to, a place the NSA didn't know about.

The perfect place to carry out an interrogation. "All the levels look good?" Chapel asked Angel. "You've got plenty of memory?"

"It's all fine, Chapel. Go ahead and start. You can—"

"Hold on," he said. His stomach had just flip-flopped. It had been doing that every so often. He'd assumed it was just nerves, or the fact that he wasn't eating properly. Normally it just twitched a couple of times and that was it. This time it lasted longer. It didn't hurt, it just felt weird.

Angel's expression changed to one of concern. "Are you okay?" she asked.

"Fine. A little exhausted. I'll try to get some sleep after this, if I can," he told her. Then he walked over to where Holman sat. He remained standing as he interviewed her.

"We want to ask you some questions," Chapel said. "About the Cyclops Initiative. First off, I'd like to know why."

Holman's brow furrowed. "Why?"

Chapel pinned her with his gaze. "Why you crashed a Predator drone into the Port of New Orleans. Why you took down the power grid in California. Do you admit that you did those things?"

"Yes, of course. We also manipulated the stock market. Oh, and we released a virus into the Internet that slowed down electronic transactions. That was one of Paul's favorite parts of this. He was really quite proud—you see, the people who run e-commerce sites are always looking for ways to speed up transactions, to make it easier to buy and sell online than it is in the real world. Just adding code to sabotage those transactions wouldn't have worked, because the software engineers would have noticed it right away and cut it out on their own. What Paul did was add an upstream checksum function at the level of the banks funding the . . ." She stopped herself. She blinked as if remembering where she was. "I . . . I'm guessing you didn't know about that. You look surprised."

"We'll get to that later. But you're not answering my question. Why did you do all this?"

"To soften the economy," Holman said, with a smile. "Do you have any cigarettes? I gave up smoking years ago, but this feels like a good time to start again."

"No. I don't have any cigarettes. Answer the question, please."

"The question?"

Chapel fought to control himself. "Why?"

"We attacked the economy because we wanted people to care."

"What people?"

"The American people, of course. That's where the name comes from. The Cyclops part. The American people are like a Cyclops, a giant of immense power but capable of seeing only one thing at a time. For years now, the leaders of the country have known this. They've used it to shape the discourse, to move national politics in the direction they want. Look at the Iraq war. After September eleventh, the people couldn't see anything, couldn't deal with any issue except terrorism. The Bush White House claimed that Saddam Hussein had weapons of mass destruction—well, who knows. Maybe they really thought that was true. Or maybe it was a convenient excuse. They got the war they wanted. Later on, after the economic collapse in 2008, the only thing the people could talk about was the economy. About money. Which provided the impetus to bail out the banks, the auto industry, later on the insurance companies and the hospitals. All of it on the dime of the people who were already hurting financially. Because we told them it would improve the economy."

Chapel gritted his teeth. "Maybe we can save the conspiracy theories for later."

Holman laughed. "Theories? This is all a matter of historical fact. For a generation now, the two political parties have exploited the public's single-mindedness to line the pockets of their friends and cronies. They've dismantled the American state piece by piece, sold it off to the highest bidder—"

"Enough," Chapel said. "This isn't a propaganda video. Get to the point. You don't like the way the country's being run, fine. So you started your own conspiracy to fight that?"

"The Initiative is made up of people who understand that the real problems of this country are being ignored," Holman told him. "Climate change running amok. Income inequality so profound the only logical outcome is class warfare. Globalism and automation leading to double-digit unemployment. These are the things that need to be addressed, and yet no politician will touch them. It was clear to us we needed to remove the politicians from the equation."

Chapel raised an eyebrow. "And how exactly do you plan on doing that?"

"By putting power in the hands of the one branch of government that doesn't take its orders from a fickle public: the military. The point of the Cyclops Initiative is to engineer a military coup in the United States."

ARLINGTON, VA: MARCH 26, 03:49

"The idea was quite simple. The people of this country care about only one thing right now: the economy. As long as the politicians keep making promises, though, the people remain complacent—unwilling to actually take any action on their own. They would rather let a few hundred people inside the Beltway make the decisions for them. We needed to wake the people up—wake the sleeping giant, as it were."

"By way of terror attacks on American assets," Chapel said.

Holman shrugged. "We would create a situation where the economy was in such a shambles that civil order would break down. We would incite riots and social disorder—which is exactly what we've accomplished in California. Soon that chaos will spread across the country. The governors of the states will call in the National Guard, but of course, they aren't prepared for something of this magnitude. They'll need to bring in the regular military for assistance in restoring order. The legislature and the executive will be forced to give the military more and more power to aid them in containing the panic, and in the end the Joint Chiefs of Staff will simply assume command. They will declare a state of emergency and dissolve Congress. At that point, the real work can begin."

Holman sat up very straight in her chair. She'd had a very long night, Chapel knew. She'd been kidnapped by a deranged marine. Dragged halfway across the city. Thought she was going to be blown up by a Hellfire missile, but instead she'd been brought to a windowless little room underground and forced to confess to all her sins.

But now she reached up and patted her hair. Brushed some lint from the front of her blazer. Suddenly she cared very much how she looked.

Chapel realized with a start that what he'd thought was an interrogation under duress was in fact a chance for her to say something she'd been holding in for a very long time. To express how proud she was of herself.

"We aren't terrorists, you see," she told him, and the camera. "We're patriots. We love this country. We love what it used to be. What it has the potential to become again. But if we continue down this same suicidal course, if we can't rise above ourselves to face the challenges of the twenty-first century, then—"

"Stop," Chapel said.

"You wanted to know why," she told him.

"Sure. I think we've got that. You think that to save America you need to cancel democracy. Depose all the elected leaders and put generals and admirals in their place."

"You're a soldier. You must know they would do a better job."

Chapel shook his head. He didn't want to get into an argument about this, but he could barely help himself. "I don't know that at all. The officers I've known have been mostly good people, sure."

"People with a firm grasp on reality," Holman said.

"Fine. Yeah, because they have to be. If every decision you make means life or death for somebody, yeah, you tend to drop the rhetoric and stop worrying about how popular you are. But there's another side to that. You get too focused. You have an objective to meet—say, you need to take a hill or secure a town. And everything you have goes into meeting that objective. But to do that, you sacrifice the bigger picture. You can't worry about why your superiors wanted that hill or that town. You can't waste mental energy thinking about why the war started. You can only think about how to finish it."

"And that's exactly the kind of focus we need," Holman insisted. "Get some people in place who can *fix* things. And then maybe in ten years, or maybe twenty, *then* the military can restore democracy and let us try again."

"Assuming that when that day comes, the generals and admirals just decide to hand power back to the people. Without a fight."

Holman shook her head. "Maybe it won't be that easy. But it's neces-sary. It has to happen."

"Except it isn't going to," Chapel told her.

"What?"

"It's not going to happen now. The Initiative is over, one way or an-other. Because you're going to tell me how to stop it."

All the air seemed to drain out of the room. Holman was beat, and she clearly knew it. But she was a proud woman. The kind of person who thought she knew better than everyone else, who was clear minded and certain about her right to be in charge. Chapel might as well have just slapped her across the face.

He might have felt bad about that, if she hadn't been responsible for dozens of people losing their lives and the West Coast descending into chaos.

"You're going to start by telling me the names of everyone you know who's part of the Initiative," Chapel told her. "Let's begin with the top level. You must have been pretty high up, since you were in charge of the operational end. But from what I've heard so far, none of this was your idea, originally."

"No," Holman said.

"So who's in charge? Who's number one in this thing?"

She blinked at him. "You don't know that? But—you must. I as-sumed . . . I . . . It's Patrick Norton."

Chapel's mouth went dry. He really wanted to sit down.

"Wait," he said. "Hold on. The secretary of defense—"

"Yes. The SecDef. He was the initiator for all this. He's overseen it every step of the way. Who else could engineer a military coup?"

Chapel had to go lean against a wall. He glanced at Angel. She looked just as shocked as he felt. He'd known this thing went pretty far up. But the cabinet—

"You didn't know," she said. All the color had drained out of her face.

She must have just realized that Chapel was bluffing. That he had far less information—and control over the situation—than he'd claimed.

He supposed it had to happen eventually.

Holman pursed her lips. She looked like she could barely sit still in her chair. "I think I may have made a mistake. You said everyone else was dead or under wraps. I assumed that meant you had Norton, too. That you had him in a room like this somewhere." She shook her head. "What a fool I've been. You didn't know anything, did you?"

"Let's get back on track," Chapel said. "Tell me about—"

"No," she said, her eyes wild. "I agreed to talk because I thought the Initiative was going to fail. My God, I gave Rupert far too much credit. You haven't stopped Norton. You haven't stopped anything."

"We can still—"

"No, Captain. No. You can't. It's already in motion. This is the day it happens. The day of the coup. And you aren't ready for it."

ARLINGTON, VA: MARCH 26, 04:09

Upstairs, they gathered around a kitchen table. Wilkes, Angel, Hollingshead. And Julia, who had a right to hear this if anybody did.

"Tomorrow morning—this morning, I guess," Chapel told them, "in about five hours, the president is going to make a speech before Congress. An emergency address to talk about the riots in California and how scared everyone is. From what we know, he's going to reveal that it's all been a series of terrorist attacks. We think he's going to blame the Chinese, although I doubt he'll come out and say so directly. As far as we can tell he has no idea about the Initiative or about Norton. It doesn't matter. He's not going to get to finish that speech."

Hollingshead blinked rapidly behind his thick glasses. "Son, are you saying—they're going to, ah, assassinate the *president*?"

"I believe that's the plan," Chapel said. "And not just him. The vice president will be there. So will the Speaker of the House and the president pro tempore of the Senate. If they all die, well . . . the head of the Initiative, Patrick Norton, has been chosen as the designated survivor for this speech. As secretary of defense, he's sixth in line to become acting president. If the secretaries of state and the Treasury are at this speech too, which is likely, then he could become commander in chief in one blow."

Julia gasped. Angel looked like she might be sick.

"Holman wouldn't give me any details of the attack. She shut down as soon as she realized Norton was still at large. She thinks he still has a chance to pull off a military coup. And if he does—"

"Then it won't matter what we know," Wilkes said. "He can throw us all in jail without a trial. Execute us without any fuss. Even if we tried to talk to reporters, he could just shut down the media. There'd be nothing stopping him."

Chapel nodded. "And between now and then—we can't show our-selves in public. The police were already looking for us, and after we fired a Stinger missile that close to the airport, they'll come at us with everything they have."

"I saw a news report," Julia said. "Somebody's covering up the fact we shot down a drone. There were lots of reports of the explosion, of course, but they're claiming it was a Cessna that crashed before it could land at Ronald Reagan."

Chapel nodded. "About what I expected. But believe me, there are still plenty of cops looking for us, cops who know the truth. We won't be allowed to just walk up to the president and give him a friendly warning."

"We can't drop him an e-mail, either," Angel said. "The NSA has every one of us flagged. If we try to go online or even call somebody on the phone, we'll just be telling them where we are."

"So what do we do?" Julia asked. "Just sit here and wait for them to find us and scoop us up?" She looked around at the rest of them.

Nobody seemed to have an answer for her.

"Come on," she said. "You can't just let him kill all those people. If he blows up the entire Capitol building, he's going to get a bunch of inno-cents, too." She grabbed Chapel's arm. "You're the good guys," she said. "*We* are the good guys. We need to stop this asshole. We can't let him win."

Hollingshead took off his glasses and set them on the table in front of him. "No, my dear. We can't." He looked around at the rest of them, his eyes as hard as wrought iron. "We won't," he said.

Chapel agreed with all his heart.

"Okay," he said. "Let's get to work."

ARLINGTON, VA: MARCH 26, 05:38

They set Angel up with a laptop, but she had no idea where to start. "I can go online if I set myself up behind an onion router," she told them, but then she shook her head. "But then I'll be anonymous. No way I can even access my old DIA files. I can send the White House all kinds of warnings, but they'll get logged and dismissed because they come from unconfirmed sources. I might as well phone in a bomb threat."

Julia looked confused. "Wouldn't that be enough? I mean, if there was a bomb threat to the Capitol, wouldn't that be enough to get them to cancel the speech? They have to take those seriously, don't they?"

Wilkes laughed. "You kidding? You know how many times a day the president gets a bomb threat? The Secret Service looks into 'em, but only as time allows, and only if there's some real chatter or analysis from their security advisers."

"Think about it," Chapel told her. "Let's say you're a political opponent of the president's. You want to keep him from getting anything done. Why not pay a bunch of people to call in a bomb threat once per day? If he had to change his schedule every single time, he'd be paralyzed. If we had time, maybe we could mail some talcum powder to the Capitol, that would probably shut things down for a few hours while they tested it for anthrax residue. But we can't do that now."

"What about the media?" Julia asked. "We could just call every television station in town, tell them what's going to happen. They would send enough camera trucks that the Secret Service would have to react."

"Right now I don't know—the country's ready to fall apart at the seams. Even just hinting at what's really going on might start a panic," Chapel pointed out.

"So what *do* you want me to do?" Angel asked.

"We're going to have to do this the old-fashioned way—in person. So we need to know where Patrick Norton will be during the speech," Chapel said. "That's going to be tough to find out. If he's the designated survivor, they'll have him somewhere secure, and part of that is not putting the location on his public agenda. But a guy like that can't stop working, even for an hour. He'll need to bring an entourage with him, have special communications arrangements made . . . there'll be a trail. Look for public buildings in D.C. that are scrambling to upgrade their phone lines, maybe. Look at his staffers' blogs and twitter feeds, see if they give anything away."

"I'll try," Angel said. She shook her head. "I've got limited access here, but—"

Hollingshead placed a hand on her shoulder and squeezed. "If anyone can do it," he said, "it's you, dear. You'll do fine."

Angel looked up at him with desperate hope in her eyes. Like she really wanted to believe him. Then she reached up and grasped his hand.

And then—incredibly—Hollingshead responded. Stroking her hair and cupping her cheek with one hand.

Chapel felt his jaw starting to drop, but instead of saying anything, he gestured for Julia and Wilkes to follow him out of the room. When the door was closed behind them, he said, "What exactly did I just see?"

Wilkes belched on cue. "Looks like maybe the director's got a girlfriend."

Julia shook her head. "No—no. She told us she isn't into that kind of thing. And anyway, he's nearly three times her age."

"Who was it said power was the ultimate aphrodisiac?" Wilkes asked. "Spiro Agnew or some dude like that?"

"It was Kissinger, but forget it—there's no way the two of them are— are—" Chapel found he couldn't even say the words. He kept remembering, though, how Angel had reacted every time Hollingshead was in danger. Like she would give anything to keep him safe. None of it added up. "Anyway. It doesn't matter. We don't have time to stand here gossiping. We need to make plans."

Wilkes nodded. "Yeah, okay. The big problem I see right now is what we do once we know where Norton's gonna be. If he's a designated survivor, he's gonna have T-men all over his butt, making sure nobody gets close to him. How do we get close?"

Chapel exhaled deeply. "It's not going to be easy. But maybe I have an idea there. I need to make a phone call."

WASHINGTON, D.C.: MARCH 26, 07:54

Traffic in Washington was more insane than usual that morning. It seemed a lot of people were heading into town to hear the president's speech.

"I don't get this," Angel said, keeping her head low as if to avoid the early sun coming through the car windows. "It's not like they're going to let all these people into the Capitol."

Julia had been keeping an eye on the news feeds all morning. "They're going to set up loudspeakers on the Mall. Everyone's supposed to gather there. People are really worried about what's going on—not just in California, but everywhere. They know something big is coming."

All of them were surprised, however, when they saw the sheer number of people who had made their way to Capitol Hill. The Mall was packed with them, standing shoulder to shoulder—huge knots of them carrying signs and chanting for public order, hundreds of them sitting on folding chairs and drinking coffee from thermoses—whole multitudes just milling around aimlessly, looks of desperate expectation on their faces.

"They really think one speech is going to turn things around?" Wilkes asked.

It was Hollingshead who answered. "People crave leadership in times of crisis. It's what Norton is counting on. If his attack succeeds, these people will accept anyone who claims to be in charge—no matter how brutal or dictatorial—because it means safety for their families. No, they don't expect a speech to save them. But they do expect a president to be there for them, to make things right."

Chapel nodded to himself, but he was busy scanning the streets around the Mall. "Angel," he said, "what do you need? A coffee shop with Wi-Fi? Or something more?"

"An Internet café might do," she said, frowning. "I'd say we should use one of the Smithsonian buildings; those have good libraries and that means solid Ethernet connections, but—"

"But they're also going to have a lot of security," Chapel agreed. "Especially today. Okay, Internet café it is." He worked the car's GPS unit. "Great. There's one pretty close—except it's on the far side of this crowd. It'll take another hour to get around them all, an hour we don't have."

"It's okay," Julia said. "We can walk across—on foot we can get through them."

"Speak for yourself," Angel said, her eyes bright with sudden panic.

There really wasn't any choice, though. Wilkes pulled over on a cross street and let the two women out. He held out his hand to Chapel, who shook it heartily, and then the marine got out as well. "I'll keep them safe," he said.

"You'd better," Chapel told him. Then he scooted over into the driver's seat. From the backseat Hollingshead watched him in the rearview mirror.

"You sure you want to go through with this, sir?" Chapel asked. "I can intercept Norton myself."

There'd been a great deal of discussion about how they would handle Norton if they could get to him. Wilkes had wanted to assassinate the man, of course. Chapel had wanted to exfiltrate him back to the safe house where they could hold him in the cellar room with Charlotte Holman until both could be brought to justice. Hollingshead had his own idea. He said he wanted to talk to Norton. Reason with him.

Chapel had no idea what the director hoped to achieve. But he was still the boss.

"I'm sure, son," Hollingshead replied.

Chapel put the car in gear and got moving again.

CAPITOL HILL, D.C.: MARCH 26, 08:01

The noise and the press of bodies got overwhelming as soon as they pushed their way onto the Mall—even for Julia, who was used to the crush of New York City, this was bad. She worried about Angel, but she knew they had to get across.

Somewhere close by someone was playing an acoustic guitar, belting out an old Bob Marley song about people loving each other. From the other side came the noise of chanters demanding the government reduce the cost of bread and milk immediately. A woman with no top on but with her breasts painted like butterflies came running past and nearly knocked Julia down. She was followed in quick succession by three young men with video cameras and iPads.

Inside the throng of people you couldn't see the roads, you couldn't see the Capitol building—you could barely tell which direction you were headed. You could see arms raised against the blue sky and you could see a lot of feet moving in every direction. Julia reached backward and grabbed Angel's hand while Wilkes moved ahead, steamrollering his way through the crowd.

Angel didn't look good. She was pale and she squinted as if the sun hurt her eyes. "Are we almost there?" she asked.

"Almost," Julia lied. She smelled cooking food and then nearly stepped in somebody's hibachi. Looked like they were making tofu burgers, she thought. Someone shouted right in her ear, but she just kept moving, pushing forward. Wilkes did a good job of making a hole for her—nobody wanted to get in his way—but still sometimes she had to squeeze between people who didn't want to move, who cursed at her and refused to move.

The throng looked like the New York peace demonstrations she re-membered from the start of the Iraq war—like hippies and college students and people just out for a pleasant afternoon on the grass. But once you were inside the crowd you felt their mood and it was toxic. These people were scared. They didn't know any way to express that fear except by gathering together and shouting slogans—but Julia was pretty sure that if something bad happened here, anything the crowd didn't like, they would remember how to riot pretty fast.

"This way," Wilkes said, bellowing back over his shoulder. He veered into the middle of a drum circle, pushing his way past a dancer who was clearly on so many drugs he didn't even see Wilkes, much less have a chance to step aside. The drummers looked up in horror as the big marine plowed through them. Julia smiled an apology down at them as she stepped over their ranks, but she was glad for Wilkes all the same.

There was a little moment inside the middle of the drum circle where they could breathe air that hadn't just come out of somebody else's lungs. Angel's hand nearly slipped out of Julia's. The younger woman was shaking. "I don't like this," she said.

"Tell me what you don't like," Julia said, pulling her close and getting an arm around Angel's shoulders. "Talk it out."

"I don't trust them," Angel said. "I keep expecting them to grab us, to throw us down on the ground. To trample us. I think they're going to just close ranks and smoosh us. Suffocate us."

"None of that is happening," Julia said. "They're people like you and me. Nobody wants to hurt anybody."

"It's not a question of what they want, it's just physics, it's differential equations," Angel protested.

"It's going to be okay," Julia told her, because what else was she going to say?

"Come on," Wilkes said. "Stay close."

Julia hurried to move forward a little faster and obey. The last thing she wanted was to get separated from him in the crowd.

GEORGETOWN, D.C.: MARCH 26, 08:09

Driving away from the Capitol was a lot easier than getting close had been. Chapel headed up Massachusetts Avenue and then across into Georgetown and soon had left the bulk of the traffic behind—meaning that while they still crawled along in typical D.C. gridlock, at least they were moving more often than not. As he drove, Chapel occasionally glanced in the rearview, looking at the director.

Hollingshead seemed perfectly calm. A little surprising, considering what he was about to do. Hollingshead was a spymaster, a spider in the middle of a web. He had never in his life, as far as Chapel knew, gone out on a field mission. But now he was going to be right in the front lines.

"You all right back there, sir?" Chapel asked.

"Fine, son. Fine."

"I'm not going to let you come to harm. I promise, sir."

"Captain," Hollingshead said, leaning forward a little and smiling in the mirror, "given the situation, it's perhaps best if we don't make promises we can't keep. I know the risks I'm taking with this plan, and how to minimize them. I also know what's at stake. I'm actually more concerned for you. The lovely Julia tells me you were wounded a little while ago. Shot by your own comrade."

Chapel grinned in the mirror. "I'm fine, sir." He shook his head. "You know, it's funny. This business, I mean. It wasn't long ago I thought that Wilkes—well—I thought you had brought him in to replace me."

"I beg your pardon?"

Chapel shook his head. Now wasn't the time, given what was about to happen. But then again, he was unlikely to be alone with Hollingshead much in the near future like this, with time to talk. "I'm sorry, sir, do I have your permission to speak candidly? I should have asked before."

"It's all right, son. After all you and I have been through, I think we can drop a little of the military discipline."

Chapel nodded. He had heard the way Wilkes spoke to the director, and Hollingshead never called him on it. All right, he would open up a little. "Back before all this began. Back when you had the two of us in that motel room down in Aberdeen running the stakeout. I was convinced you put me there to punish me. And that you brought Wilkes in to see if maybe he would make a better field agent than me. I thought you wanted to get rid of me."

"Is that right?"

Chapel could feel his cheeks getting hot, but he went on. "After what happened in Russia—"

"Which, I'll remind you, we agreed not to speak of again," Hollingshead pointed out.

"Yes, sir. But it didn't go as well as it could have. Not by a long shot. I thought maybe you had lost faith in me."

"I see," the director replied.

And then he didn't say anything else.

Chapel tried to focus on driving, on keeping pace with the cars ahead of him, but the silence growing inside the car made it feel like the air around him had been pressurized and was about to burst his eardrums.

"Well," Hollingshead said finally. "Well now, son. I suppose—from a certain perspective, ah, that is. Well."

"Sir?"

Hollingshead cleared his throat. "I suppose you could say most of that is true."

"I—sir, I—" Chapel's tongue froze in his mouth.

"You could say that. If you were feeling particularly uncharitable. You're not a fool, Chapel. I suppose I should have expected you to see what was going on. Though of course I couldn't tell you any of the facts of the case. As you know now, Wilkes actually had his own very specific mission—to infiltrate the Cyclops Initiative. That was why I gave him such light duty at the time. As for yourself, I put you in that motel because of what happened in Russia, yes."

"Sir," Chapel said. "If you found my behavior less than satisfactory—"

"Not," Hollingshead said as if Chapel hadn't interrupted, "as a punishment. As a sort of rest cure. For years I've sent you on mission after mission and you've performed flawlessly. But I knew how much I was asking and that eventually it would become too much. After your mission in Russia, I knew you were right on the edge of breaking and I could not afford to lose such an important asset. So I gave you light duty so that you could recuperate."

"Oh," Chapel said.

"As for replacing you, well, that was somewhat true as well."

"It . . . was?"

Hollingshead grunted in affirmation. "It isn't very easy for me to say this."

"Sir?"

"I'm getting old. Too old to do my job. Please don't suggest otherwise. I won't have any false flattery. I'll be eighty years old before the decade is out. It's only a matter of time before my faculties begin to decay. I'm going to have to retire—assuming, of course, I live through this day." Hollingshead gave a little laugh that didn't sound very merry. "Assuming we have jobs tomorrow. Or a country to serve. Anyway. I'll need to retire soon. Which means that I will need a replacement."

He leaned over the front seat. "Son," he said very softly, "I was hoping that would be you. I wanted to bring Wilkes into the fold as an agent whom you could direct. I want to make you the director of DX."

Chapel put his foot on the brake. He stopped the car in the middle of the street until he could catch his breath. The cars behind him started to lean on their horns, but he took another couple of seconds before he started moving forward again.

"I don't know what to say, sir," Chapel managed to get out.

"Then don't, since of course this is all, well, provisional. Contingent. Just tell me one thing. You've had a chance to work with Wilkes out in the field. Do you think he would be a good fit with any future directorate we build?"

It gave Chapel something else to think about, for which he was very grateful. He collected his thoughts and tried to think of the right way to answer. "He's good. Very good at fieldcraft, and he can definitely handle himself in a fight."

"That doesn't answer my question."

"No," Chapel said, "no, sir, it doesn't. Because I'm struggling with finding a nice way to say no." He took a breath. "Wilkes saved my life when Moulton would have killed me. He got us this far. I owe him a lot. But he's—he's a thug."

"Really?" Hollingshead asked. "You know I chose him personally."

Chapel swallowed uncomfortably. "I know that, sir. And you know I don't like to question your decisions. But he kills people."

"Part of the job," Hollingshead pointed out.

"No, sir. No. Sometimes it's necessary." But it wasn't what a field agent should do. Chapel had struggled with this the whole time he'd worked for the director. "Sometimes it's necessary, but it's always a mistake. When I have to, I will take a life. But I know it means I didn't do my job well enough, and every single time, I've regretted it. It's my absolute last option when I'm out in the field. But for Wilkes it's the first. It's what he's trained to do, and it's what he looks for."

"As they say," Hollingshead said, "when one has a hammer, every problem looks like a nail? Interesting."

"I hope I haven't offended you, sir."

"Chapel," Hollingshead said. He leaned back against his seat. "Jim," he went on. "I asked for your opinion. If you're going to replace me, you're going to need to learn to take a stand."

Chapel nodded. "If I were the director, my first act would be to transfer him somewhere else. I owe him, I even kind of like him. But I won't work with him again."

"That's what I needed to hear," Hollingshead said.

A few minutes later they arrived at their destination.

CAPITOL HILL, D.C.: MARCH 26, 08:14

"Get out of my goddamned way," Wilkes bellowed, and a group of pro-testers dressed like Revolutionary War–era soldiers blanched and quivered and finally moved. Wilkes reached back and grabbed Julia's arm and hauled her forward.

"Angel," she called out. She'd lost contact in the press. "Angel! Wilkes, where did she go?"

Wilkes didn't reply, except to pull her up onto a sidewalk. Then he dove back into the crowd, and when he returned, he hauled Angel behind him with a vise grip on her arm, tight enough to make her cry out in pain. Julia started to yell at him to stop hurting her, but the look on the marine's face stopped her cold. Then he raised an arm and pointed. Ahead of them was the glass front of a little shop—a bakery, by the look of it. He pulled the door open and got the women moving inside.

The shop was full of people but not quite so packed as the sidewalk had been. Every table had people clustered around it, a lucky few in chairs. A line of people was crushed up against the counter, all of them craning their necks around to try to see through the plateglass front of the store. Following their gaze Julia saw nothing but the constant crush out on the sidewalk and, off in the distance, the white obelisk of the Washington Monument framed by blue sky.

"This isn't the right place," Angel said. "This isn't right! We wanted the Internet café. I need real access. This isn't right!"

"Let's just catch our breath in here for a second, first, before we head back out there," Julia told her.

"Back? Out there? No no no no no no. No," Angel said. "No, I won't go back out there. Don't make me go back out there!"

"But you said it yourself," Julia told her. "You need Internet access."

Angel's face was wild, blotchy with fear. Her eyes were rolling like those of a panicked animal—something Julia had seen all too often in her veterinary practice.

Julia had to fight down the urge to slap her. The younger woman was sick. She was having a panic attack. Under any other circumstances she would have felt sympathy. She would have done everything in her power to calm Angel down. But now—

"Wilkes," Julia said. "We need to get her access."

The marine nodded. He reached in his pocket, and for a second Julia thought he would pull out a gun. Instead he took out a slim piece of leather like a big flat wallet. He flipped it open and held it over his head.

"FBI," he announced. All over the bakery people cried out, as if they expected to be arrested on the spot and dragged off to a police station. Despite the fact that even if that had been the case, even if Wilkes really had been arresting anyone, he would never have been able to get them half a block down the sidewalk in the crush out there. "I need the manager of this place, right now."

A middle-aged woman with streaks of gray in her long hair stood up from one of the tables. She looked terrified as she raised one hand.

Wilkes nodded at her. "Wi-Fi password. Right now."

"I—what?" the manager asked.

"Right goddamned now," Wilkes said again.

"It's—"

"Don't say it out loud," Angel interjected. Julia saw that she'd regained control of herself, a little. Angel looked around the bakery, at all the people craning forward to get a better view. "Otherwise everybody's going to use it and that'll slow the network down. Here. Type it on my phone."

The manager nodded and did as she was told, looking grateful that at least Wilkes wasn't shouting at her anymore.

IN TRANSIT: MARCH 26, 08:17

Over the Atlantic, the MQ-1C Gray Eagle banked and turned on its long mission guarding the sea lanes. It was flying on automatic pilot—a stick jockey back at Creech Air Force Base was watching the controls, of course, and after the Reaper had gone rogue the night before, every last thing the Gray Eagle did was closely monitored. But at the moment it was just keeping station, exactly as it had been programmed to do, running endless laps over the ocean waves.

This time, the base commander had assured the SecDef, there would be no deviation from standing orders. If the Gray Eagle were to fail to make a turn at the proper time, or if any of its systems came online when they should have been dormant, the drone would not be given a chance to do harm. An F-16 with a human pilot at its yoke was already in the air, ready to strike. All it would take would be one terse order from Creech and the Gray Eagle would be shot down.

The base commander had wanted to do more, of course. He had urged the SecDef to ground the entire drone fleet. The explosion over the Potomac had been covered up in an efficient manner, but the commander still had no idea exactly what had gone wrong or why his people couldn't seem to replicate the problem in simulation. A drone had just exploded without warning—and miles from where it should have been.

Given recent events, the only logical thing to do was to ground the fleet. But then the SecDef had responded in no uncertain terms. The drones were vital to national security. They would stay in the air. And you just didn't question orders that came from that high up.

So the base commander stayed on post all that morning, watching over the shoulders of stick jockeys and sensors as his robot planes carried out their given tasks. He was ready at the slightest provocation to send the kill signal, but he never had to.

The Gray Eagle, after all, never deviated from its mission. Or at least . . . it didn't appear to.

The base commander had to be reassured that the Gray Eagle was where it said it was. He could look at the telemetry data that gave GPS coordinates, altitude and the like, but all that could be easily faked. More reliably, he could watch the live video feed from the drone's camera eye and see the furrowed blue of the Atlantic roll by underneath the Gray Eagle's nose.

He had no reason whatsoever to suspect that that view, that video feed, wasn't live. That it was in fact a recording of what the ocean had looked like weeks earlier, the last time this particular Gray Eagle had been sent out on patrol.

Paul Moulton had been a very, very good programmer, and an even better judge of human paranoia. He had known perfectly well that at some point the drones would be monitored, that they would be under threat of being shot down. He'd gone to great pains to make sure they kept flying, right until the very last attack.

The Gray Eagle kept feeding false telemetry and video back to Creech as it turned on the wind, breaking away from its previous course. It headed straight for Washington, and Paul Moulton's final, glorious, posthumous strike.

GEORGETOWN, D.C.: MARCH 26, 08:21

Chapel's stomach was tied up in knots. Well, he supposed he was allowed to be a little nervous. What they had planned was one of the most reckless, dangerous stunts he'd ever pulled in the field.

It made him nauseated. Or maybe it was just the quick breakfast he'd wolfed down before they set out. Either way, he put his good hand on his stomach and held it there, as if he'd been cut open and needed to hold his guts from spilling out. There was some pain.

"Son?" the director asked.

"Hrm," Chapel said. Then he shook himself out of it and turned to face his boss. "Fine, sir. Just anxious. This is the place Angel told us about."

Hollingshead looked out his window and nodded.

The quaint brick three-story building across the street looked like every other quaint brick three-story building in Georgetown with one exception—there wasn't a coffee shop or a bank branch inhabiting its ground floor. Instead it just had an unmarked door and a couple of windows covered over by thick curtains. It looked, in fact, so much like a safe house that it couldn't be one. Any spy wandering past would immediately think they knew what it was, which invalidated its use as a safe house in any way.

Angel was absolutely certain that Patrick Norton was inside. Two of his low-level aides had complained on Twitter about being moved to a new location this morning, and while neither of them had given an exact address, one had said they were headed to Georgetown. Apparently they considered that to be vague enough to count as discretion. Meanwhile the Army Corps of Engineers had sent a team to this building in the middle of the night, and a local webcam had seen them. Angel had noted that they brought in some very high-tech communications equipment, including an entire crate of satellite cell phones. The kind of phones Norton would use if he needed to communicate with his generals during, say, a military coup.

To add to all that, the registered owner of the building was the Department of Defense. It was, she told Chapel, kind of obvious, once you saw the signs.

Chapel was just glad he had the twenty-first-century version of Sherlock Holmes on his team.

In the backseat, the director was growing antsy. "I trust him as much as you do, but if he's going to provide this diversion—"

"He'll be here on time. At eight thirty exactly," Chapel said.

Hollingshead nodded. "Very well. Then I suppose the next step is mine."

Chapel got out of the car and held the director's door for him. "Good luck, sir," he said.

"Hopefully I won't need it." Hollingshead looked both ways and then crossed the street, headed straight for the front door of the building. Chapel headed up the street, then crossed and jogged around to an alley that ran behind every building on the block. He made a point of not getting too close—the DoD safe house would have cameras watching its rear door, of course. But he wished he could get close enough to hear what happened when Rupert Hollingshead rang the place's front doorbell.

They were pretty sure the director would be taken inside. Hollingshead was still the biggest thorn in Norton's side, the one man the SecDef considered a genuine threat to his grand plan. If he just walked up and turned himself over to Norton, he wouldn't just be turned away.

They were mostly sure that he wouldn't just be taken inside and quietly shot. They figured that Norton would want to talk to Hollingshead first. For a little while.

Meanwhile it was Chapel's job to get inside the building and make sure Hollingshead had a way to get back out again. This was where the plan left a lot of room for improvisation. Chapel had to figure it out on his own, once he was in place.

At least he could count on a little help. His diversion should be showing up at any minute.

CAPITOL HILL, D.C.: MARCH 26, 08:24

"Angel," Julia said. "Angel—talk to me."

But Angel was hunched over her laptop, two fingers on the trackpad as she scrolled through endless pages of what looked to Julia like random numbers and letters. She didn't even glance up.

"Leave her alone," Wilkes said.

"She hasn't made a sound in a long time," Julia pointed out. "That's not—"

"Healthy?" Wilkes guessed. "Maybe. But it's the closest she's going to get. She's working. She's working 'cause it's all she can do right now. The only thing that keeps her from freaking out. So leave her alone."

Julia knew he was right. Fussing over people was what *she* did, though, to keep herself from freaking out. She turned her attention to the other people in the bakery. Most of the customers were still packed into the tables and up against the glass display counter. The street outside was just too crowded for them to flee the place when Wilkes commandeered its Internet connection, though a lot of them looked terrified of the big marine.

Julia didn't blame them. She might be a badass sometimes, and she might have seen plenty of this kind of action since she'd met Chapel, but still, the big dangerous soldier types like Wilkes bugged her. It wasn't so much that you thought he was going to hurt somebody. It was that he looked like he could, and that he wouldn't lose any sleep if it happened. It was something about the way he stared at everybody, she thought. Clearly sizing them up, assessing them as potential threats. He just made everyone uneasy.

Maybe she could help with that a little. She lifted her hands in the air until all the customers and the clerks and pastry chefs and the store manager were all looking at her. "No need to worry, folks. We're actually here to keep everybody safer," she told them. "To do that, we're going to need your help for a little while. We need you to stay calm, that's all." Her brain reeled as she tried to think of some innocuous reason the FBI would burst into a bakery like this. Then she realized that a real FBI agent wouldn't give one. "We'll be done in a few minutes," she said and lowered her hands. "Thank you very much for your patience."

It sounded lame when she said it out loud, but it seemed the civilians in the bakery were just glad for any sign that somebody was in control. What was it Hollingshead had said, about people craving leadership? She could see them start to breathe again, saw some of them even smile and roll their eyes at each other—which meant that what had seemed like a terrifying breach of the peace was now, to them, just a mild inconvenience.

At least that was something.

She turned back to look at Angel. The younger woman hadn't so much as shifted in her chair.

Julia knew what Angel was working on. There were radar dishes and optical sensors all over Washington, thousands of them, all tasked with different things. Some watched to make sure nobody landed a helicopter in the White House's Rose Garden. Others monitored planes headed into and out of Ronald Reagan International. Some, which hadn't been reassigned in a long while, were still watching for Russian bombers. Angel was checking all of them, all at once. She was looking for any sign of a drone approaching the Capitol.

Of course, she had no idea what kind of drone it might be, or what direction it was coming from, or whether it was flying low enough to evade radar. But if she found it, she could try to hack it in midflight. Gain access to its controls and send it back where it came from.

That was the plan, anyway. Angel had said there was maybe a one-in-three chance she could even find the drone, and the odds were even slimmer that she could gain control of it. But it wasn't like they had much choice.

If she couldn't get the drone to reverse course, a lot of people in the Capitol were going to die.

GEORGETOWN, D.C.: MARCH 26, 08:28

A white van pulled up right in front of the DoD safe house. Even before it came to a stop, a security guard in a dark suit came out the front door and started waving his arms at the driver, trying to get his attention. It didn't work. The driver parked the van and switched off the engine. The security guard tapped at the driver's window while simultaneously reaching for his phone.

The side door of the van swung open and a man in an army jacket jumped out, crowding the security guard back toward the safe house's door. The man smiled and his eyes twinkled, and he reached out to shake the security guard's hand.

"Name's Rudy," he said. "Pleased to meet you."

"You can't—" The security guard managed to say.

He didn't get any further because somebody else jumped out of the van then, somebody who was very difficult to ignore. This guy was missing an arm, a leg, and an eye, all three replaced by obvious prostheses.

"Morning, son," the man said. "We're here to meet with Patrick Norton."

"You can't—there's nobody here by—"

The amputee frowned. "He's the secretary of defense," he pointed out.

"Yeah," the security guard said, "I know who he is, but—"

"Good, then you go fetch him, we'll just set up here. And before you go telling me I can't use this particular stretch of sidewalk that my taxes happened to have paid for, I'll have to point out that you can't tell me why not."

"I don't need to—"

"So I think we'll just wait here until the cops arrive," Top pointed out. Behind him, more and more people came piling out of the van, some of them missing arms or legs, all of them carrying cardboard signs decorated with handwritten slogans:

RESPECT OUR VETS
VA CLAIMS TAKE
TOO LONG!
I SERVED MY COUNTRY,
WHY CAN'T IT SERVE ME?

"We've got a grievance, see, and we're not leaving," Top told the poor security guard, "until Mr. Norton comes down here and addresses it."

"But what makes you think he's even here?" the guard asked.

"Well now, friend, I wasn't entirely sure until I saw the look on your face just now. Why don't you go tell them we're here? We'll wait."

The security guard took one last desperate look at the wounded veterans marching in a circle in front of the safe house. Then he shook his head in disbelief and ducked back inside.

At the back of the building, Chapel could hear Top and his boys chanting out front, and he knew it was time to make his move.

GEORGETOWN, D.C.: MARCH 26, 08:32

They frisked him quite thoroughly and then bound his hands with a loop of plastic. Rupert Hollingshead had expected as much. But then they bundled him into a rather pleasant office on the third floor of the safe house, and perhaps out of respect for his age or perhaps for his former rank, they gave him a comfortable chair to sit in.

He sat there as straight-backed as he could and waited patiently. Outside, through the thick, bulletproof windows, he could just hear Top and his boys down in the street. That made Hollingshead smile. One thing had gone right, anyway, and the protesters had shown up on time.

The door opened. A guard with a very serious expression on his face came in and checked the corners of the room, as if he might find heavily armed gremlins had spontaneously appeared there. He looked Hollingshead up and down, then he nodded at someone outside the doorway, someone Hollingshead couldn't see.

It turned out, thankfully, to be Patrick Norton.

Of all the uncertainties and doubts that flitted around Hollingshead like a cloud of unwelcome gnats, there was at least one thing he was absolutely sure of. No one was going to put a bullet in the back of his head until Norton had left the room. It just wouldn't do to have the SecDef be a witness to murder.

It behooved him, then, to keep Norton in the room as long as possible. So he put on his merriest face, made his eyes twinkle, and said, "Sir. Forgive me for, ah, not saluting."

Norton grinned. "Rupert. I'm so sorry to have put you through all of this. I assure you, if I'd known you were coming, we could have met under more cordial circumstances."

"No doubt. My own fault, but it seems, well, it seems my personal assistant has been, ah, misplaced. Never was very good at making my own appointments."

"I see," Norton replied. "Well, under ordinary circumstances, of course, I'd be thrilled to meet with you on anything you like, but I'm afraid today I'm a bit busy. Perhaps if you could tell me what this was about?"

"I thought we might have a chat, sir, about the Cyclops Initiative."

The transformation that came over Norton's face was incredible to behold. The man was a politician, through and through. He had spent years bolting armor plate onto the smiling countenance he wore in public, hammering out any quirks of personality, polishing his mannerisms and gestures until any sign of ambition or lust for power were smoothed away. He had worked that face until it showed nothing at all except a love for civil service and the American people.

Now that armor came off, plate by plate, bolt by bolt, in the time it took for a smile to turn into a frown. The eyes hardened. The chin lifted in the air. The brow furrowed.

"You're a fucking idiot, Rupert," Norton said when the transformation was done.

"Ah, I wondered when we would get to the, well—"

Norton wouldn't let him finish. "What is this? You have a microphone hidden in your lapel, you think you're going to tape me saying something stupid? No, my men would have found anything like that when they searched you. So you came here to try to stop things somehow on your own. Not a chance. You're an idiot and a distraction. That's all. A distraction at a time when I really don't need one. Was that your whole plan? Is that why you brought this gang of cripples out to make noise in the street? You thought you could beat me through sheer inconvenience?" Norton studied him for a moment. "I find it hard to believe. But it's not like you have much else to play with. Your directorate is gone. Burned to the ground. Chapel's missing, presumed dead. Your Angel system is dismantled. By now you'll have realized Wilkes was one of us all along."

Hollingshead closed his mouth. He couldn't help but smile a bit.

"I think you got Moulton and Holman. They're dead, right?" Norton said. "It's what I would have done in your place. I take your knights away, so you took my queen and my rook? But you've already lost this game. I have more people I can bring into play. A lot more. And anyway, in half an hour, it'll be over."

Hollingshead nodded. "Yes, that's what I wanted to talk about."

Norton grabbed a chair and dragged it over to where it would face Hollingshead. He didn't sit down, though. Instead, he stood behind the chair, as if he was using it as a shield. As if he expected Hollingshead to lunge at him and wanted some cover to hide behind. Hollingshead tried not to read too much into it.

"You think you still have a chance," Norton said. His eyes narrowed as he watched Hollingshead very closely. "You think you have some play that will still bring me down. You had some kind of plan. But then you did the dumb thing and came here. What's to stop me from having you shot right now?"

"Nothing," Hollingshead said.

The SecDef raised an eyebrow.

Good, Hollingshead thought. He'd gotten the man to be quiet for a moment. Maybe now they could have a real conversation. "I know perfectly well that you aren't going to let me leave this building alive. But I had hoped we could talk for a few minutes, first."

CAPITOL HILL, D.C.: MARCH 26, 08:34

"Got it," Angel said. Julia came racing over to look over her shoulder, though of course she couldn't make any sense of the strings of numbers and letters on Angel's screen. "There," Angel said, pointing at a log entry that looked like all the others.

"You can just . . . look at all this, and see a drone coming at us?" Julia asked.

"No, of course not. But I can read a weather radar report. This radar is looking for clouds, right? So it has to screen out anything it sees that isn't made of water vapor. It's reporting here that it found something that it should ignore. There's a metallic object the size of a Predator or a Reaper or whatever reported here, at such and such an altitude, and that altitude fits with the flight profile we're expecting. It could be something else, of course. A small helicopter would match those numbers, and there are plenty of helicopters over D.C. But look at this." Angel tapped a key. Only a few of the characters on her screen changed.

"I have no idea what you just did," Julia pointed out.

Angel sighed. "Look, it's gone. This is one second after the first screen. The metallic object doesn't show up on the weather report this time. Which means it was moving so fast it passed right through the area that radar was sweeping in less than a second. A helicopter wouldn't move that fast."

Julia squinted at the screen. "That's not a lot to go on. It could be some other kind of airplane—"

"It could just be a glitch. It could just be a coincidence. Except for one thing."

"What's that?" Julia asked.

"There's no such thing as a coincidence. That's our drone. And it's going to be here very soon." Angel ran her hands through her hair. "I need to concentrate," she said. She looked at all the people in the bakery. Half of them looked back at her.

There wasn't much Julia could do about that. She knew Angel was struggling under the weight of all those stares, but the sidewalk out front was so crowded it looked like the mass of people out there was about to burst in through the plateglass windows. Julia couldn't clear the bakery.

"How about I get you something to drink?" she asked instead. "Do you want some coffee?"

Angel glanced over at the counter. "I only drink soda. Not coffee. This place doesn't have any soda."

"No," Julia agreed.

Angel leaned over her computer again, as if she could climb through the screen and escape that way. "A scone, then. Blueberry." she said.

GEORGETOWN, D.C.: MARCH 26, 08:35

The security guards flooded out into the street where Top and his boys were protesting. There was a lot of shouting about the First Amendment and a lot more shouting about how the protesters needed to clear the street right now.

Chapel didn't stick around to listen to all of it. He took a deep breath, then walked right up the alley to the back door of the safe house, right in view of its cameras. The alley was deserted when he started.

It didn't stay that way. The back door swung open and a man in a black suit stepped out. He had a pistol in his hand and a big hands-free unit in his ear. "Sir," he said. "You need to not be here."

Chapel kept coming, his head down, his hands shoved in his pockets. No point in subtlety here. The guard's job was to keep this alley clear. He wasn't going to listen to anything Chapel had to say.

So Chapel just waited until the guard started to raise his pistol. The man still didn't intend to shoot, just intimidate.

Which gave Chapel the advantage, since he had no such qualms.

Among the piles of handguns and assault rifles and carbines and grenade launchers in Contorni's arsenal, Chapel had found an entire crate full of military-grade Tasers. He had one in his pocket now. He shot the guard right in the chest and watched him shake and gag and then fall to the ground in a heap. Once the Taser had stopped clacking away and the current had stopped flowing, Chapel reached down and grabbed the hands-free unit out of the guard's ear. He dropped it on the pavement and crunched it under his heel.

Then he dug his fingers into the incapacitated guard's neck and slowed the blood flow to his brain. Not enough to do any permanent damage. Just enough to knock him out for a while.

When it was done, Chapel stepped inside the back door of the safe house. Beyond was a spacious kitchen full of stainless steel sinks and copper-bottomed pots hanging in neat rows on the brick wall. There was nobody else in sight.

Chapel closed the door behind him and locked it up tight. For good measure he grabbed a chair and shoved it under the doorknob at an angle. When the guard woke up, he would have a hard time getting back inside.

There was another security camera in the kitchen, watching the door from the other side. Chapel had expected as much. Hopefully nobody was watching those cameras—the bulk of the security detail being busy elsewhere.

GEORGETOWN, D.C.: MARCH 26, 08:36

There was a great deal of pushing and shoving and brandishing of signs, but it was clear the guards were about done with fooling around. "Now listen here, friend—and I do want us to be friends, ever so much," Top said as one guard tried to grab him by the shirt. "I want you to consider just exactly how this is going to look for the news media. Now, you and I both know that I'm some cussed fool who has refused to listen to any kind of reason, while you're just a workingman trying to do an honest job. And that's exactly the kind of moral equation that might lead you to start thinking you can lay hands on me. But I've got four different media outlets sending camera trucks in our direction right now. And when the two of us—cussed fool and workingman—are under the television lights, I wonder if things won't get a little less clear? If maybe it'll look like you're assaulting a multiple amputee who was intent on just a little harmless exercise of his First Amendment rights."

The guard pulled a gun and pointed it in Top's face. "Move now," he said.

"Point taken," Top said. "And I salute your initiative. But I'm afraid we have a new problem to contend with. I hope we can work together to find an amicable solution to this one, but I fear—"

"What the fuck are you talking about?" the guard demanded.

"It would appear," Top said, blinking his eyes in mock contrition, "that I've accidentally handcuffed my arm to the door handle of this van. And I've completely forgotten what I did with the key."

CAPITOL HILL, D.C.: MARCH 26, 08:38

"Come on," Angel said. She pouted at her screen. Took a bite of scone.

For a long, heavy second nothing happened.

"Come on!" she shouted as she lifted her hands away from the keyboard.

"Everything okay?" Julia asked.

"Arrgh!" Angel groaned. She tapped her fingernails on the table. "A couple of years ago somebody put a virus on the servers that run these stupid drones. Back then the command signal channel wasn't even encrypted. The virus didn't even affect that channel, just the back-end stuff, but still, they had to go and add serious military-level encryption to the command channel and make my life really, really difficult."

Julia frowned. "You're complaining because the military actually went to the trouble of making their drones *hard* to hack?"

"It's really adding to my workload," Angel said. "Okay, okay. Let me try something different. Every system has a weakness, right?"

"Um, sure," Julia said.

Angel nodded. "There has to be a channel I can exploit. Maybe something on the optical bus. The drone just has the one camera pod. If I can shut down that camera, it won't be able to find its target, and it won't ever launch its weapons."

Julia leaned back. "That's kind of brilliant."

Angel shrugged. "It's what I do. Now, could you just leave me to it? Maybe you should go talk to Wilkes. Make sure he doesn't accidentally kill somebody."

"Good idea," Julia said.

GEORGETOWN, D.C.: MARCH 26, 08:41

"I know," Hollingshead said, "what you're planning. What you're in the middle of achieving and it is, well, quite ambitious." He smiled at the SecDef. "I'd very much like to try to convince you not to go ahead with it, however."

"Oh? And why is that?" Norton asked.

"Because I think it's bad for America," Hollingshead replied. "I understand, really, why you would do this. You think the country is out of control. And I suppose it is. The legislature is frozen in constant gridlock.

The executive is stymied by special interests and a splinter party that viciously attacks its every move. Meanwhile the people refuse to even listen to the issues, much less debate them. The country can't move forward like that, can it? Not when our economic interests are threatened by global market shifts. Not when the very climate has turned against us. Not when we need to be unified now more than ever."

"You're making my case pretty eloquently, Rupert," Norton said. "This country needs a strong leader now. It can't wait until the next presidential election—not that that would change anything. We need a hand on the rudder if we're going to weather the coming storm."

"Indeed. And I believe that leader will step forward. But I don't think it's you, sir. With all due respect—"

"History shows us that the man who has the audacity to take power for himself is the only kind of man fit to hold it."

Hollingshead pursed his lips.

"Julius Caesar started an empire that would rule all the known world. Alexander the Great applied logic to warfare and won everything. Qin Shi Huang saw the petty warlords squabbling over pieces of China and knew they had to be brought together by force."

"Hitler," Hollingshead said. "Stalin. Mao."

"That's weak, Rupert. That's just special pleading. You really think I'm that sort? You think I'd use power for that kind of monstrosity?"

"No. But I'd like to point out one simple thing. If you seize America by military force, if you take away the basic freedoms of its people, then you will have gained nothing. Because without freedom, there is no America."

Norton laughed. "Over the last fifteen years we've been arguing this point endlessly. And the result? Americans are perfectly willing to give up freedom in exchange for security. If you want proof, look at what I've done in the last week. I've shown them what insecurity really looks like. By the end of the day today they will be begging me to take charge. To tell them what to do."

Hollingshead looked down at his shoes. "You took an oath to protect

the president. Now you're going to murder him so you can take his place."
He shook his head. "This goes against everything that you and . . . you
and . . . I— Patrick?" he said. "Patrick, are you all right?"

The man's face had turned bright red. His eyes bulged from their
sockets as if he was having a stroke.

Instead, though, his mouth opened, his head tilted back—and he
laughed. He positively guffawed.

"Kill the president?" he said. "*Kill* him?"

Hollingshead blinked in confusion.

"Rupert, why would I do that? The man and I play squash together,
for God's sake."

GEORGETOWN, D.C.: MARCH 26, 08:42

Chapel moved quickly out of the kitchen and through the first floor of the
safe house, keeping his back to each wall, flanking each doorway as he
moved but not wasting any time. He saw no one so he moved into a tasteful if somewhat cluttered parlor in the front. Peeking through the blinds
that covered the windows, he could see the guards still arguing with Top
and his boys. Chapel had to grin at that—he'd known his old physical
therapist would help, had known it even before he'd made the call. But
he'd had no idea that every single one of the boys would come with him,
or that they would commit to their ruse so intently. Chapel had mostly
expected them to show up, ask for Norton, and then politely leave when
security showed up.

Instead it looked like they'd installed themselves on the sidewalk for
as much time as it took for the guards to drag them away. Of course,
eventually Norton's people would just call the police. But maybe enough
of the cops were busy out on Capitol Hill, and it would take them a long
time to arrive . . .

Chapel was playing for time. If he could stay alive and free in the
house until Angel reported in, if he could confront Norton with the news

that his drone wasn't going to be killing anyone today, they might have a chance. Charlotte Holman had been as devoted to the Initiative as anyone, but she was also a practical woman. When she thought the cause was hopeless, she had folded in a hurry. Chapel thought Norton would do the same, especially if Hollingshead allowed the SecDef a graceful exit.

Of course, all that depended on Angel and Chapel pulling off a couple of miracles in the next fifteen minutes.

The first floor was empty. The security detail had been smart enough to leave one man on the back door, but otherwise all of them had flooded out into the street to deal with Top. Chapel moved into the front hall and up to the main door. He locked it and threw the dead bolt. That wouldn't stop the guards forever—once they realized they'd been locked out of the house, they would batter the door down if they had to—but it might buy him a minute or two.

He moved to the bottom of the stairs that led to the second floor. He drew a fresh Taser and started climbing the risers, one by one, careful to test each step with his weight, making sure it didn't creak. He thought he could hear people moving in the floors above him and he stopped perfectly still to listen for a second, but the sound didn't repeat.

He took another step. Another.

He couldn't see any shadows moving at the top of the stairs. No sign that anyone was aware of his presence. He didn't even hear anyone cough or clear their throat. He took another step.

He lifted his foot, got ready to take the next step, just three from the top of the flight. Put his foot down very gently.

That was when an armed guard leaned out into the stairs and started firing.

CAPITOL HILL, D.C.: MARCH 26, 08:46

Angel tapped at a key. Her screen filled with new data. She tapped another key and shook her head. "Okay," she said.

Julia nodded in excitement. She rubbed at her mouth because her lips were very, very dry. "Running out of time here," she said.

"How far away is the drone?" Wilkes asked.

"About ten kilometers. It looks like it'll be here right when the president starts his speech."

"How are we looking?" Julia asked.

"Bad," Angel told her. "I've got access to the onboard sensors, which is the first step toward switching off the camera. But I need more time, and—"

"And we're not getting any," Wilkes growled.

Angel shook her head. "I know, I know—Jesus. There are four bombs on this thing." She rubbed at her face. "Viper Strikes."

Julia had no idea what that meant, but clearly Wilkes thought it was bad. He actually went pale when he heard it. "Not Hellfires. You're sure."

Angel grunted. "I can tell the difference! And that's very bad, very, very bad. Because. Because I think I know how to stop this thing."

"So do it already," Julia insisted.

"I can release them," Angel said as if Julia hadn't spoken. "I can send the rails hot signal, and the bombs will just . . . fall off the bottom of the drone. Before they were supposed to. That means they won't hit the Capitol."

Wilkes nodded. "And they're Viper Strikes. Glide bombs, with GPS targeting. But they won't have targets."

"Yeah," Angel said. She took a deep breath.

"What's the big problem?" Julia asked. "Just do it already."

Angel looked up at her. "Julia, the drone is already inside the Beltway. If I release those bombs, there is absolutely no way of saying where they'll go. They're glide bombs, which means they can fly a little on their own, they don't just fall straight down. Normally they're guided to their targets, but because they won't have any target information, they'll just glide on the wind until they hit something. Maybe they hit an IRS building and blow up everybody's tax returns. Or maybe they hit schools and hospitals. If I do this, we can't predict how many people will die. But we'll be dropping four bombs on a crowded population center, and I guarantee you they'll hit somebody."

"It means saving the president, and everyone else in the Capitol," Wilkes pointed out.

"You think he's got more of a right to live than anyone else?" Angel asked. Julia was surprised at the younger woman's tone—she made it sound like an honest question, like something that could be debated.

"Yeah, I do. I think right now this country needs the president," Wilkes replied. "I think without him we're utterly screwed. So if you don't want to push the button—I will. And make up your mind right now, because we're out of time."

Angel stared at him for long, desperate seconds during which Julia felt like she couldn't breathe. Like her heart was just going to stop beating.

Then Angel nodded and broke the spell.

"I'll do it," she said.

She tilted the screen of her laptop back up and reached for the keyboard. Her finger hovered over the enter key. Then she tapped it, just once and closed her eyes. A shudder went through her small body. "Forgive me," she whispered.

Julia put her hand over her mouth. She couldn't bear to think what they might just have done.

She didn't get a chance to think about it. Someone on the other side of the bakery shouted "Hey!" and everything stopped.

All three of them turned to look at the middle-aged woman who had called out. She was holding her cell phone up as if she wanted to show it to everybody. "I had four bars," she said. "Four bars!"

A guy in a business suit took his own phone out of his pocket and stared at it as if it had turned into an avocado while he wasn't looking. "No signal," he said.

Angel stared at the man in horror. Then she looked down at her laptop. "No," she said. "No, no, no—not now!"

Julia looked out the plateglass windows at the front of the shop and saw something incredible. All over the sidewalk, as far as she could see in any direction, people were taking out their phones and staring at them, tapping wildly at the screen as if that would help, holding them high up in the air in an effort to catch even the slightest cellular signal, all to no avail. Her attention was drawn back when Angel tapped at the laptop screen, specifically at the icon in the status bar that indicated what kind of Wi-Fi signal the computer was receiving.

The icon had turned a useless gray, indicating the laptop had no signal at all.

"Not now!" Angel said again, grabbing her hair in both hands.

GEORGETOWN, D.C.: MARCH 26, 08:48

Chapel fell backward, half intentionally, trying to get away from the bullets that smashed into the wooden stairs all around him. He went down hard on his left arm—his artificial arm, which was good because if he'd landed on his right arm like that, it would have broken. The prosthetic twisted under him as he shoved himself downstairs, almost sledding over the risers until he reached the bottom. Then he twisted around to get the banister between himself and the shooter.

He was pretty sure he'd been hit, at least once. Looking up he saw blood on the risers and knew it was his. He also saw his Taser up there, sitting three steps down from the top of the staircase.

From above he heard the sound of a walkie-talkie, the voice of someone desperately trying to connect to his superior. There was no reply. Maybe the superior was busy out front with the protesters. Maybe he was the guy Chapel had Tased out back. What a lucky break that would be.

Chapel just hoped he would live to make use of it.

He didn't dare look—he had to keep his eyes on the top of the stairs, in case the shooter came back. But with his good, living hand, he reached down and tried to figure out where he'd been hit.

Two places, it turned out. Once in his right hip, though that just looked like a flesh wound. Once in his back, where he found a neat little hole that was leaking blood in a steady stream. That was a lot scarier. He couldn't reach the wound well enough to even put pressure on it.

Upstairs he heard a footstep creak on a loose floorboard.

He'd lost his Taser. But of course he'd come armed with more than one weapon. He drew a 9 mm handgun from one of his pockets and worked a round into the chamber. He hadn't wanted to kill anybody today. The guards in the safe house all worked for the Department of Defense. They were his colleagues. But if he had no choice, then—

Another footstep.

The shooter swung out into open space at the top of the stairs and fired three shots down in quick succession, none of them coming close to hitting Chapel, but it was enough to make him dive behind his cover. When he dared to look again, the shooter was gone.

Damn. The shooter had the high ground. To get a clear shot Chapel would have to run all the way up those stairs, leaving himself exposed the whole time. The shooter could just pick Chapel off at his leisure.

But if he stayed down at the bottom, Chapel knew he would bleed to death before he could get to Hollingshead.

He tried to think of what to do. He tried to—

More gunshots fell around him, still wide of the mark. Close enough to make Chapel throw his artificial arm over his head for protection.

The shooter pulled back and Chapel heard the floorboard squeak again.

Maybe. Just maybe, he thought.

The stairs ended at an abrupt landing and turned to the right up there. Where the staircase met the ceiling was exactly where the shooter's floor began. That creaky floorboard had to be about a foot and a half from the top riser, about . . . there . . .

Chapel heard the creak again, and this time he was ready. He aimed his pistol at the ceiling and fired six shots, one after the other.

Somewhere in the roar of the shots he heard a scream. He thought.

For nearly a minute he just sat there, bleeding. Waiting for the creak of the floorboard or the sound of gunshots coming from above. In the end, though, neither of those things gave him his signal. Instead, he looked up and saw the circular holes he'd punched through the ceiling with his own shots. A nice, tight grouping right where he thought the shooter had been.

As he watched, a drop of blood dangled from the edge of one of those holes. It grew larger and larger and then it fell to splash on the floor right next to where Chapel lay.

He didn't waste any more time. He got to his feet—which made his new wounds burn like fire, and his old, Wilkes-inflicted gunshot wound flare up like a smoldering ember—and staggered up the stairs, as fast as he possibly could.

At the top he found the shooter staring up at him, one hand reaching toward the stairs. One of Chapel's shots had gone through the bottom of the shooter's chin and out again through the top of his head.

The man was dead.

Chapel kicked his pistol away, back down the stairs, just to be safe. Then he started down the hall, toward the room where they were keeping Hollingshead.

Judging by the trail of blood he left behind him, he knew he'd better make this quick.

GEORGETOWN, D.C.: MARCH 26, 08:51

When they hadn't heard any gunshots in a while, Norton smiled. "That was your man, I think. The one we heard scream."

Hollingshead hoped not. For everyone's sake, he sincerely hoped not. "Then I suppose all is lost. I came here on a fool's errand and threw away the life of my last asset. And, ah, well, of course—my own."

"Looks that way," Norton told him.

"Then—since it no longer matters—maybe you can fill me in on a few details. Assuming, of course, that you aren't needed elsewhere."

Norton shook his head. "No, I'm fine right here. I'm expecting a phone call a little after nine o'clock. From the president. Until then my schedule is clear."

Hollingshead nodded. "Very good. A call from the president. And here I assumed your coup required that the man was dead. You set things up so you would be the designated survivor, then put most of the executive branch in one room—"

Norton waved a hand dismissively. "I had no idea I was going to be the survivor. I never planned to hurt anyone at that level."

"Then why—I'm sorry, I find myself baffled. Not that I wish to give you any ideas, but—why not? Why not assassinate the president, now that he's basically given you the perfect opportunity?"

"Because what you accused me of—of fomenting a military coup— that's impossible in America."

"Indeed?"

"Yeah. Aaron Burr tried it all the way back in 1807, and he failed. Douglas MacArthur and Alex Haig both considered it, I think—though neither of them went far enough for there to be any proof. I like to think they figured out the same thing I did. You can't pull off a military coup in America because we're a nation of loudmouths." He laughed. "You know how many people would have to be in on such a thing? How many generals and colonels and majors I'd have to swing over to my side? And if even one of them decided they didn't like my scheme, all they would have to do would be to make one phone call and I'd be in the stockades by dinnertime. Forget it. And even if I could get all those officers on my side, what about the actual soldiers? American soldiers are the best trained and best equipped in history. They're also the best educated. You really think there's a single private anywhere in the army who would shoot the president because I asked him to? No, they know their rights too well. They would just refuse."

"I can't say it's something I'd considered before," Hollingshead said.

Norton got up and paced around the room, waving his arms in the air as he spoke. "No, a coup was out of the question. Anyway, why would I want to be chief executive? The second I declared myself president for life, the UN would be on my ass. China and Russia would send their navies to blockade our ports. There would be no shortage of Americans calling for me to step down, and no shortage of self-styled patriots willing to martyr themselves if it meant they got a good shot at me."

"So you don't want to be in charge," Hollingshead said. "You don't want power. Despite everything you said about great men taking control of history."

"Oh, I'm going to have the power. But I'm going to stay anonymous at the same time. I'll be the man behind the throne."

Hollingshead squinted at the SecDef. "And how, exactly?"

"By making myself so vital to the president that he won't dare make a move without consulting me. When this country is reduced to utter chaos—when people are running wild in the street—"

"Ah!" Hollingshead said. "Of course. It will become necessary to declare martial law. And you will, of course, most modestly and in the service of your country, agree to take charge of the military clampdown that will follow."

"Now you're getting it, Rupert," Norton said, his eyes shining.

"And lo and behold, the drone attacks will stop. Your efforts to protect the nation will bear fruit and you'll be proclaimed a hero. Except, no—they won't quite stop, will they? Any time there's a threat to your power, there'll be another attack."

"Well," Norton pointed out, "it's not like anyone expects you to *win* the war on terror."

"Oh, of course not. And if the president begins to suspect that you engineered the entire thing?"

"Presidents only get eight years, and that's only if they can keep the American people safe. Cabinet positions like mine can last a lifetime."

"Ingenious," Hollingshead said. "Perhaps so brilliant that I feel like I'm still missing one piece of the puzzle."

"Oh?"

"I was under the impression that you were going to use a drone to attack the Capitol and kill the president. I can see how silly that idea was, now. But there was—I mean, that is to say, Charlotte told me there was one more attack coming, and—well—"

"Oh, there's going to be a drone attack today, definitely," Norton said. "It's just not aimed at the Capitol building."

"Ah."

"No. So far we've managed to cause panic and fear without too much loss of life. That poor bastard at the Port of New Orleans, of course, and some people in California when the lights went out. But I'm afraid you can't really get the American people to panic without a good old-fashioned massacre."

Hollingshead's eyes went very wide.

"You saw how many people are out there on the Mall, today, Rupert. Maybe a quarter million. The people who came to hear the president's grand ideas for how to fix the present crisis. I'm not proud of this. I ordered it with a heavy heart. But I need to utterly destroy confidence in the president's ability to control the nation. So quite a few of those people out on the Mall . . . well, they're going to have to make a sacrifice for the greater good."

CAPITOL HILL, D.C.: MARCH 26, 08:53

While the customers inside the bakery kept checking their cell phones, Julia leaned over Angel's shoulder and said, "What's going on? What just happened? What about the drone?"

Angel shook her head in irritation. She looked right into Julia's eyes, not four inches from her own, and stared until the other woman backed off. Then she grabbed up her laptop and jumped off her stool. She ducked under the counter and squeezed in between the manager and the employees back there, who protested volubly but ineffectively.

"I tried," Angel said. "I tried! I sent the rails hot signal. I told it to drop the bombs, but . . . hold on."

"Angel, report," Wilkes demanded.

"I was locked out," Angel said from under the counter. "I got in, I had a clear signal to the drone. The second I sent a command, though, the system knew I was there. Moulton must have expected we would try something like this."

"He knew what?" Julia asked. She shook her head. There was no time. "You were locked out of the controls? So you didn't drop the bombs?"

"No," Angel said.

"So just . . . just hack the drone again," Julia suggested. "Try from a different direction or something."

"It didn't just lock me out. When it detected me, it locked out *every-body*. The drone has an ECM pod," Angel said. When no one reacted, she added, "Electronic countermeasures. There was this . . . there was . . ." She ducked back down below the counter and rummaged around down there for a second. The store manager stared daggers at Wilkes, but he just flashed his fake FBI card at her again.

Finally Angel popped back up, yanking a credit card scanner after her. She pulled the cord out of the back of the scanner. She threw the scanner away, then jammed the cord into a port on the side of her laptop.

"In Iraq and Afghanistan, they had this problem," she said, even as she typed furiously on her keyboard. "Insurgents were burying IEDs all over the place, bombs they could detonate with their cell phones. Bombs like that are super cheap to make, you can hide them easily—it was a nightmare for our guys. So the Pentagon started putting ECM pods on their drones. You know what jamming is?"

Julia frowned. "It's like—you block somebody else's, I don't know. Radios."

Angel didn't even look up. "Good enough. The principle is basic, and it's been around for more than a century. Your enemies are using some radio frequency to communicate, so you just broadcast a ton of noise— just static—on that same frequency and they can't talk to each other. The jamming hardware on the drone is a lot more sophisticated, but it basi-cally does the same thing. It's knocked out every cellular connection, every Wi-Fi network, every television, radio, and satellite broadcast for a hundred miles. Just in case anybody tries to interfere with its programming." She shook her head. "This sucks! I was in. I was *in*, Julia. I had this thing. I had the drone . . ."

"So if it blocks out all communications, what are you doing now?" Julia asked.

Angel tapped the cord she'd plugged into her computer. "You can't jam wired connections. At least, not as easily. I'm still getting a signal through this thing, though ninety percent of the Internet around D.C. is down. Way too many vital connections being shared over Wi-Fi in this town. Damn it! I can't even contact the drone now."

"Why not?"

"Signal fratricide," Angel said. She must have seen the look on Julia's face, because she visibly calmed herself down and explained. "The big problem with jamming like this is that you jam your own connections, too. The frequency I was using to communicate with the drone is one of the frequencies it's blocking. I just lost everything."

"What does that mean?" Wilkes demanded.

"It means we're screwed," Angel said, putting her hands on her cheeks as if to warm them up. "It means I can't stop the attack."

Something happened to Julia then. Maybe it was just fear, maybe she'd had enough. She wanted to shake her head, she wanted to shake her whole body. Her stomach did somersaults as Badass Julia rose up inside her and took over.

She stood up very tall and stared down at Angel, forcing the younger woman to meet her gaze. "No, it doesn't."

Angel clearly wanted to look away. Julia grabbed her face and made Angel look into her eyes.

"I'm telling you," Angel said, "even if I could get a good broadcast signal, which no, I can't—even then—*I can't contact the drone*. I can't hack it if I can't even talk to it."

"Angel," Julia said, "the attack isn't going to happen for another . . . six minutes. Until then, I don't want to hear the word 'can't' out of your mouth. You think of something. You think of something right now."

Angel turned and stared at Wilkes, as if for sympathy, but the marine had nothing to offer her.

GEORGETOWN, D.C.: MARCH 26, 08:54

Chapel heard something, the scuff of a shoe on the floorboards, maybe just the rustle of a cheap wool jacket. Somebody was up there in the hallway ahead of him. Doors lined either side of the hall and he had no idea where the attack was going to come from, but he knew—he positively knew—that someone was about to try to kill him.

It wasn't like he'd never felt that sensation before.

Two guards stepped out of a room at the end of the hall, then, their pistols already up in the air. They fired without a moment's hesitation.

But Chapel was already moving. He swung around, bringing his left arm up high, over his face and the upper portion of his chest. The first bullet missed him entirely, digging a long trench through the hardwood floor. The second bullet sank deep into the silicone covering his prosthetic. The energy of the shot pushed Chapel sideways, not enough to knock him off his feet but enough to knock him off course as he threw himself at the nearest doorway.

His right shoulder hit the wooden door hard, hard enough he worried he might have dislocated the joint. The door resisted for a second, then wood cracked and the door latch gave way, sending Chapel tumbling into the room beyond.

It proved to be a disused storeroom, full of old furniture covered in dusty sheets. He collided with something soft—it felt like a sofa—and he let himself flop down, his feet going wide as he sank to the floor.

There was blood everywhere, all over the room, the sheets, the door. It took him a while to realize it was his own.

Yep. He was definitely getting light-headed.

He craned his head around to look at the hole in his back and saw that his shirt and pants were both soaked in blood. The flow of blood seemed to have decreased to just a trickle, but he'd already lost so much.

The pain was manageable—adrenaline was helping with that—but he knew that shock was going to catch up with him soon. If he didn't get a proper bandage on the wound, he could just bleed out as well.

A weird whining noise came from his left arm. He tried to make a fist with his artificial fingers, but they wouldn't close properly. The prosthesis had taken a shot for him, probably saving his life, but it was done for now. Useless.

Out in the hall, he could hear two sets of footsteps coming closer. They were coming slow, giving him plenty of time to show himself, but they weren't even trying to be quiet.

Chapel was pinned down by multiple enemies, stuck behind cover waiting for someone to just walk up and shoot him. He knew how to handle this situation.

But he also knew the odds.

A lot depended on how well trained these guys were. The MPs at the marina had been easy. Nobody had ever bothered to teach them more than basic hand-to-hand combat and simple overwatch tactics. Chapel had a feeling these two would be a little more advanced.

If they knew how to do their jobs, and if he just let them walk up to the doorway and start shooting at him, he was going to be killed. There was no question about that. He was going to have to take the fight to them. Jump out of that doorway, guns blazing, and hope he caught them by surprise.

It was just about the worst plan he'd ever heard. If there had been anything else, any other way . . .

Well, he told himself, there wasn't.

Slowly, aching and bleeding and gritting his teeth, Chapel levered himself back up onto his feet.

Outside in the hall the two guards were only seconds away.

CAPITOL HILL, D.C.: MARCH 26, 08:55

"Okay, okay! Just let me think," Angel said. She rubbed at her temples. She stared at the screen of her laptop as if the answer was there, as if a riddle was written there that she could potentially solve.

"There's gotta be something you can do," Wilkes pointed out. "Take over a cruise missile from an air base around here, send it after the drone. Or, hell, send another drone."

"No time, and even if I could launch a missile, I wouldn't know where to shoot it. Right now I don't know where the drone is."

Julia just leaned against the counter and folded her arms.

"Jesus, that is not helping," Angel said. She couldn't even look at Julia.

"What about—I don't know," Wilkes said. "When they taught us to infiltrate buildings, they said, if the doors are locked, make 'em open the doors. Set off a fire alarm so they all come rushing out. Or just set the place on fire."

"What does that have to do with anything?" Angel demanded.

"I'm just trying to think a different way. You know, outside the box. Or inside the box in this case. Listen, the drone is jamming us, right? What if we jammed it? Like, its radar or something."

"Possible," Angel said, "but then it still has its cameras and the best pattern recognition software money can buy. If its radar went down, it would just ignore the radar. Unless—unless we spoofed it."

"What's spoofing?" Julia asked.

"That's when, instead of jamming a signal with white noise, you actually send a false signal. Make the radar think there's something in front of the drone, that it's about to collide with another plane or something. It would veer off course." She shook her head. "But that's no good. Again, it's got that camera. It would check the camera, see there was nothing there, and ignore the radar. And there's no way to spoof the camera—at least, no way we're going to make happen in five minutes."

"Okay," Wilkes said. "But if we had more time, how would we—"

"Wait," Angel said.

A look of utter concentration came over her face. She put her hands out at her sides as if warding off distractions.

"Wait," she said again.

"Okay," Julia said. "We're waiting."

Angel looked her right in the eyes. "The drone has that fancy camera. But the bombs don't."

"How does that help?" Wilkes asked.

"We wait until it drops its bombs. These aren't Hellfire missiles, they're Viper Strikes. They're guided after they drop. Guided straight to their targets, by GPS."

"Okay," Julia said.

"So we don't spoof the drone's radar. We spoof the entire GPS."

GEORGETOWN, D.C.: MARCH 26, 08:56

"You're going to kill thousands of people," Hollingshead sputtered. "Just to make the president look like a fool."

"No," Norton said. "I'm going to kill thousands of people so that the president looks *weak*. So that it's clear to everyone he can't control his people through ordinary channels. Even if he doesn't declare martial law on his own, Congress will insist on it. I have a few senators I can count on. And once martial law is declared—"

"—the military will be in de facto control of the entire country," Hollingshead said, nodding. "And you control the military. You'll be given the justification to do whatever it takes to restore order. You'll have power over every aspect of American life. You'll tell people where they're allowed to move, what time they have to be inside at night. You'll have the power to nationalize whole industries and commandeer any goods or services you claim to need. And of course, suspend all elections as you see fit, until the time of crisis has passed."

"And I'll be the one who decides when that is," Norton pointed out.

"The people will be very angry," Hollingshead said. "They'll hate this. But they won't blame you—after all, you'll just be doing what the president asked you to do. They'll blame him." Hollingshead very much wished his hands were free. He would have liked to polish his glasses. It was what he did when he needed time to think. "Simplicity itself. A flawless plan. I suppose one doesn't rise to a vital cabinet position if one isn't a little brilliant."

"Thank you, Rupert. That actually means a lot," Norton said, with a genuine smile.

Hollingshead grinned back. "Of course, it won't last. Tyranny never does. The people will revolt."

Norton opened his mouth to say something more, but he was interrupted by the sound of more gunshots out in the hall.

"Do you suppose," he said when silence fell again, "that was mine or yours?"

"I imagine," Hollingshead said, "we're about to find out."

GEORGETOWN, D.C.: MARCH 26, 08:57

Chapel had lost so much blood he could barely stand upright, but he was still strong enough to shoot. He leaned against the wall of the storeroom, right next to the door. He closed his eyes—the better to hear the approaching guards, he told himself. It had nothing to do with the fact that he was about to pass out.

He could hear them getting closer. Since his only plan relied on getting off two perfectly placed point-blank shots the second he stepped into the hallway, he wanted them as close as possible. He forced himself to wait, to concentrate.

He kept thinking about the fact he hadn't said good-bye to Julia. Not properly, anyway. Nor had he told Angel what she'd meant to him over the years.

He hoped that she knew.

He forced open his eyes.

He stepped out into the hall and started shooting.

CAPITOL HILL, D.C.: MARCH 26, 08:58

"More," Angel said. "One more. Come on!"

At least now Julia could understand what showed on the laptop's screen. It showed a simplified map of Washington, covered in tiny red dots. Each of those was a cell-phone tower. As Angel seized control of them, one by one, they turned green.

"I don't understand," Julia said. "I thought the drone was jamming all the radio frequencies."

"It is," Angel said. "Those towers aren't getting any phone signals through. But GPS is different. It was designed by the military, originally, and it includes a technology called DSSS to get around jamming. Anything I send through those towers, if it uses DSSS, is going to look like GPS coordinates. If I can send the bombs fake coordinates, I can fool them into hitting the wrong targets."

"Doesn't GPS come from satellites, not cell towers?" Wilkes asked.

"Yeah. The drone would know it was being fooled, but the bombs aren't smart enough to tell the difference. Any radio signal with DSSS looks the same to them. The trick," she said, tapping at her trackpad until another tower turned green, "is to get enough towers up and running. The bombs are still getting *real* GPS data from the satellites. That signal is still stronger than what I'm putting out. But if I can take over enough cell towers, I can overwhelm the satellite signal and fool the bombs."

Wilkes started to ask another question, but Julia put a hand on his arm and shook her head. Angel needed to concentrate.

On the screen another tower turned green. And another. Angel nodded encouragingly. Then she spat out an obscenity as one of her green towers turned back to red.

Wilkes bent his head down to whisper to Julia. "Is this going to work?"

"No idea," Julia told him. "Normally I'd say it was impossible. But it's Angel. So—maybe?"

On the laptop, three more towers turned green.

A fourth.

Two more.

"Please," Angel said. "Please just work."

Julia glanced out the plateglass windows of the bakery, as if she could see the drone out there. As if she could see the bombs falling from the sky.

"Please," Angel said.

"Please."

OVER CAPITOL HILL, D.C.: MARCH 26, 09:00

A logic gate in the electronic guts of the Gray Eagle clicked open, and a signal moved forward through the maze of its processors. A circuit was completed and a command issued.

Under its belly, four clamps opened simultaneously. The clamps were all that held the Viper Strike bombs to the drone, and now they dropped away.

At first the bombs fell like ungainly bowling pins, tumbling through the air. But after a second of free fall, spring-loaded wings and tail fins popped out of their fuselages and they caught the air, pulling out of their spins like diving birds. They settled into long, shallow trajectories as if they wanted to take their time and enjoy the breeze.

The bombs lacked jet engines or propellers, but by adjusting their fins they could change their course radically after they were deployed. One by one they turned away from the path they'd been on, the same path the Gray Eagle had flown. They sniffed the air for the signals they were de- signed to follow, the GPS coordinates programmed into their tiny brains.

But something was wrong. There seemed to be two signals, with very different values. The two targeting solutions were nearly a kilometer away from each other.

Which signal was correct? There was no way of knowing. For the first few seconds of their descent, the bombs' fins twisted back and forth helplessly and their warheads swayed like dogs choosing between two perfectly identical bones.

An insoluble problem for computers as simple as those inside the bombs. They might have just kept twisting back and forth until they simply fell out of the sky. But then the problem solved itself, as things always do—for better or worse.

Little by little, one of the GPS signals grew stronger. Little by little the computers grew sure and certain of where they should go.

Down on the Mall a quarter million people waited to hear what the president had to say. One of the GPS signals indicated that the bombs' target was right in the center of that crowd. Right where their explosions would do the most damage.

Kill the most people.

The protesters might hear a whistling sound, in the last moment. The bombs would be moving too fast for them to see their deaths streaking toward them.

At least . . . that might have happened. But the second GPS signal was stronger. At the critical moment, the bombs twisted away from the crowd and headed west. They stretched their wings as wide as they could to gain distance as they slid toward the ground, their noses coming up as they tried, desperately, to reach their new target, nearly a kilometer away. They flicked over the roof of the Bureau of Engraving and Printing, just barely avoiding a collision, then nosed down to strike their target with pinpoint accuracy.

Their computer brains were not smart enough to wonder why. Why they had been told to attack a target fifty feet below the surface of the Tidal Basin, the nearest body of deep water. They were deeply submerged when they detonated. The high-explosive warheads sent a shock wave through the water, a concussive blast of incredible magnitude. The whole surface of the basin lifted and then a plume of water shot fifty feet up into the air.

Those few people who had gathered outside the Jefferson Memorial, perhaps to see the famous cherry trees, were soaked to the skin. Some of them screamed in panic—some ran for shelter. Most stared at each other with wide eyes, wondering what had just happened.

Antiterrorist units and uniformed police were mobilized and they raced to the scene, but there was nothing for them to see when they arrived except for some very wet, very confused tourists.

The attack was already over.

Meanwhile, over in the Capitol building, the president took the podium to enthusiastic applause and began to deliver the most important speech of his career.

GEORGETOWN, D.C.: MARCH 26, 09:01

Patrick Norton's cell phone rang inside of his jacket.

Hollingshead did not know at the time about the ECM pod mounted on the Gray Eagle. He did not know that for the last ten minutes or so not a single cell phone in Washington had been able to receive a call. He did not know that the drone had now switched off its jammer, specifically so that this phone call could get through.

Nor could he know who was calling or what they had to say. He could only hear Norton's side of the conversation, which was limited to a scant few words. "What? What do you mean— I see. All right, just stand by for now. Soon."

That was all the information Hollingshead had. Those few words. But it was enough to let him inhale deeply for the first time all morning.

He waited for Norton to put the phone back in his pocket.

Then Hollingshead asked, "Things not going exactly to plan?"

Norton was too good a politician to let his face show any real emotion. Still, he couldn't quite control the tic that made his left eyelid jump. "You didn't come here to talk me out of the attack, did you?"

"No, I knew from Charlotte that it couldn't be aborted," Hollingshead agreed.

Norton lowered his head a fraction of an inch. He appeared resolute and determined, though, when he looked up again. He went to the window and looked down into the street. "Those protesters of yours are still down there. I'll have to go out the back way. I'm sorry, Rupert, but you've pushed me too far. I don't have any more time to talk." He shook his head. "I'm afraid this is it for you. I still have a chance, I have plenty of people in sensitive positions who can arrange another attack, but—"

He stopped because there was a knock at the door.

Norton stared at the door for a moment, breathing heavily. Then he called out, "Come in," in a clear voice.

The door swung open.

Jim Chapel stood there, covered in blood, holding a pistol tight in his right hand.

He took a staggering step inside the room, lurching like an incarnation of red vengeance.

"I didn't come here to dissuade you from the attack," Hollingshead said. "I came here today to make sure, when the attack was foiled, that you didn't get away. This has to end, Patrick. It has to end this instant."

Norton watched Chapel carefully. He licked his lips, as if they were suddenly very dry. Hollingshead wondered if the man would try to run. Force Chapel to shoot him. Suicide by field agent might seem better, perhaps, than facing what was to come.

Norton surprised him, however. The SecDef set his face very carefully. Then he lifted both hands in the air in surrender.

For a moment no one moved.

It was like they couldn't believe it was over.

Eventually, though, Hollingshead decided the time had come to speak. "Mister Secretary, you're under arrest for the crime of treason. Captain Chapel, would you please secure the prisoner?"

Chapel took out a pair of plastic handcuffs and locked Norton's hands together. He frisked the man and took away his phone. Then he told the SecDef to sit down while he went over and cut Hollingshead free.

"Are you hurt?" Chapel asked.

"Son, you're not the one who should be asking that question,"

Hollingshead whispered back, while rubbing at his chafed wrists. "Are you going to—"

"I'll be fine, for now," Chapel told him.

He handed the SecDef's phone to Hollingshead, then went back to watching Norton. Hollingshead made a few quick phone calls. Within minutes a squad of military police arrived at the safe house. They stood down Norton's security guards—the ones out front, still arguing with Top—then came up the stairs to the room where Hollingshead waited for them. Their commander, a second lieutenant, blanched when he saw who he'd come to arrest.

"It's all right," Hollingshead said. "He's been removed from office. You can take him into custody."

Hollingshead didn't technically have the authority—or the rank—to do that, but Norton didn't protest. The MPs took him away without another word.

Only when they were gone did Hollingshead see Chapel sway on his feet.

"Is it hot in here?" Chapel asked. "It feels really hot."

Hollingshead went over to his agent and placed a hand on his forehead. Chapel was burning with fever. "Son—maybe you should sit down," he said.

"Not until," Chapel said. But he didn't finish the sentence.

"Not until what?" Hollingshead asked.

Chapel looked at him with the strangest expression. Then he collapsed, tumbling headfirst toward the floor.

GEORGETOWN, D.C.: MARCH 26, 09:33

It took forever to get over to Georgetown, creeping along through every traffic light, fighting weird traffic patterns as people kept trying to cram themselves into the Mall. Wilkes drove because Julia kept thinking she was going to throw up.

In the backseat, Angel was all but catatonic. Whether that was because of the news they'd gotten from Hollingshead or if she was just burned out after having to work so hard in the middle of so many people, well, who knew? Julia had stopped worrying about Angel.

She had somebody else to occupy all of her worrying faculties, now.

When they reached the DoD safe house Julia pushed open her door and jumped out onto the pavement even while Wilkes tried to park the car. Ralph, the one-armed vet, was standing by the door and he tried to say something to her as she pushed him away. He tried to grab her hands. She bulled past him and inside, then realized she didn't know where to go next.

"Where is he?" she demanded.

Ralph tried to calm her down. "Just—"

"Where the fuck is Chapel?" she said, and then there was somebody else there. The house was full of Top's boys. They tried to talk to her, maybe they even tried to answer her question, but she couldn't hear them. Her heart was pounding in her ears and she wouldn't have heard anybody. She couldn't think, could barely see. Dolores appeared, briefly, but didn't even try to get in Julia's way. Somebody pointed up a flight of stairs stained with blood. She should have known. Blood in the hallway upstairs. You want to find Jim Chapel, follow the trail of blood. Inside Julia's head a whole symphony of worry and fear was just tuning up.

Top himself opened a door for her. She stepped through into a little room.

The floor was littered with torn paper and foil wrappers and pieces of plastic tubing, a bright blue latex glove. The debris left by a team of paramedics. Blood everywhere. Stained towels and sanitary wipes. A syringe with no needle, lying on a carved wooden end table.

But no Chapel.

"Where is he?" she asked again, softly this time, because one of the possible answers was going to destroy her.

"Walter Reed," Hollingshead said. He was there. She hadn't noticed that before, but Rupert Hollingshead was there and he was alive and even unhurt. "He held on just long enough, you see. He waited until Norton was taken away, until he was sure we were done and then. Then he. Well. I, ah—he had sustained, that is—"

"Gunshot wounds, I'm guessing," Julia said. Not because of what the paramedics had left behind. Because that was what happened to Jim. He got shot. All the fucking time. She put a hand to her forehead, then dropped it because she didn't know why she'd done that. She thought maybe she should sit down. She thought she should run back downstairs and tell Wilkes to take her to the hospital, so she could see Jim again.

"What's the prognosis?" she asked. "Is he going to live?"

"Ah," the old man said.

Then Angel came running into the room. She ignored Julia and the very obvious absence where Jim Chapel should have been. Instead she ran over to Hollingshead and threw her arms around his neck and held on to him for dear life. Hollingshead closed his eyes and hugged Angel back and kept saying, "Oh, my dear, you're safe."

Julia wheeled around and stared daggers at them. Jim might be dying, right then, and all Angel wanted was to hug her sugar daddy. "You two are awfully glad to see each other," she spat out, as if the words tasted nasty in her mouth.

"I imagine that's, well," Hollingshead said, "natural enough. Given that Angel—Edith—is my granddaughter."

EPILOGUE

THE WHITE HOUSE: MARCH 27, 09:06

The attorney general carried out Patrick Norton's debriefing the next day. The two of them sat in a small room in one of the White House subbasements, a room that was fully wired to record sound and video. The session went on for many hours. Norton was provided with food and water as requested.

Rupert Hollingshead observed the proceedings through a one-way mirror from a rather underheated adjoining room. Present with him were three of the Joint Chiefs of Staff, including the vice chairman. It was one of the very few times in his adult life when Hollingshead had found himself in a room full of people who outranked him.

No one in the observation room spoke during the debriefing. They were too busy listening to what Norton had to say. The former secretary of defense made a full and detailed confession of everything he had attempted. He described every one of the drone attacks and how it was carried out. He named all his confederates, starting with Charlotte Holman and Paul Moulton.

There was a certain . . . excitement in the observation room when Norton named one of the Joint Chiefs as a coconspirator. The man resisted briefly, but he was eventually convinced to leave the room in the company of a pair of armed MPs. After he was gone, the chilly room seemed positively arctic.

Norton did not spare himself in his confession, nor did he offer any apology for what he'd done. Not even an explanation of his motives. He simply laid out the facts of the case and answered the AG's questions as they were asked.

When the AG had finished with his questions, he thanked Norton for his candor. Then he packed up his briefcase and left the room. Norton remained where he was, shackled to the table. He did not seem particularly worried or afraid, as far as Hollingshead could tell.

Then again, Norton had proven already that he would make a very good poker player, based on his ability to bluff.

The door of the observation room opened and the AG stepped through. He addressed the Joint Chiefs with deference and nodded at Hollingshead. "It's clear that he's indictable under any number of statutes," the man told them. "I'm going to advise we go ahead and just charge him with treason. If we had to try him for every attempted murder and violation of national security protocols, he'd be in court for a hundred years."

"What's your recommendation on sentencing?" the chairman of the Joint Chiefs asked.

"I think we have to seek the death penalty," the AG said. "I respect the man's office and his military service, but . . . this isn't something we as a nation should ever forgive."

There was no dissent among the Joint Chiefs. Hollingshead had been invited to the room as a courtesy—his opinion was not of interest to anyone there.

The AG and the Joint Chiefs filed out of the room then. Hollingshead waited at the back of the line out of respect, but before he could reach the door, he saw motion inside the debriefing room and he stopped to look.

The door had opened and Walter Minchell, the president's chief of staff, entered with a single piece of paper in his hand.

Hollingshead stayed behind to see what would happen next. When the last of the Joint Chiefs had left the room, he closed the door behind them.

In the debriefing room, Norton looked up at Minchell with a warm smile. Ever the politician.

"This is how it's going to be," Minchell said. "You're not going to trial. You're not going to jail or the gas chamber, either. If you sign this piece of paper, the president will give you a conditional pardon and send you on your way."

Norton had the good grace to at least look confused. "A . . . a pardon?"

"The conditions are these," Minchell told him. "You will go immediately to Guam, and you will never come back. You'll be put on the no-fly list without possibility of appeal. We'll do what we can to make you comfortable there. Do you agree to these conditions?"

Without even waiting to hear an answer, Minchell slapped his piece of paper on the table and handed Norton a pen.

Norton signed.

Hollingshead was on his feet in the next instant, headed out the door. He caught Minchell in the hallway and grabbed the young man's arm.

Hollingshead summoned up every shred of authority and command he'd ever possessed and put them in his voice. "Explain this," he said.

Minchell looked at him with tired eyes. He didn't pretend he didn't know what Hollingshead meant. "The country is too close to falling apart right now. Revealing that the terrorist attacks came from so high up would be—deleterious to public order."

"So he goes free? He gets the deluxe retirement package like a deposed dictator? Nobody is going to be punished for any of this?"

"Not exactly. Somebody has to be blamed. The prevailing wisdom," Minchell said, "is that Moulton was the main bad actor here. He programmed the drones and orchestrated the attacks."

"He happens to be dead," Hollingshead pointed out.

"That is a problem," Minchell replied. "We need to show that we're tough on this kind of thing. So Charlotte Holman is going to take the fall."

Hollingshead felt rage building inside his chest. "I promised her she would be spared if she helped me bring down Norton. I gave her my word."

"The president didn't," Minchell pointed out. He slapped Hollingshead on the arm. "Rupert, he's sensitive to your role in all this. He knows what you did for him."

"For the nation, you mean," Hollingshead pointed out.

"Yes, of course. And he's very grateful. He mentioned to me that he's thinking he might need a new director of national intelligence."

"I gave her my word," Hollingshead repeated.

But he already knew he'd lost.

BETHESDA, MD: MARCH 30, 11:39

The food at the new Walter Reed's cafeteria wasn't anything special, but Julia was getting used to it. It also had the advantage of being in the basement of one of the main buildings, so it didn't have any windows. Angel looked almost comfortable as she sat down at Julia's table.

"I went and saw him, but he was asleep. I sat with him for a while," Angel said. "How's he doing?"

It was the main thing Julia thought about these days, so she was always happy to answer that question. "Better," she said. "His pulse ox is up, which is really good. He's conscious sometimes. He sleeps a lot but . . . that's a good thing. He was in really bad shape. Crazily enough, if he hadn't gotten shot that day, he'd probably be dead right now. It turned out he had an infection from the time Wilkes shot him. If they hadn't caught it when they brought him here, it would have killed him." She ran one hand through her hair. "Funny how things work, huh? When I closed up that wound, I thought I was healing him, but in fact I might have killed him."

Angel reached out one tentative hand. Julia grabbed it up like a lifeline and held on while her chest surged with all the tears she wasn't going to let herself cry. Not yet.

"How are *you* doing?" she asked.

"We don't have to talk about—"

"Goddamnit," Julia said, "yes, we do." She stamped her foot under the table. "Give me this, Angel. Give me some small talk. I've been in this hospital for nearly a week with nobody to talk to except doctors. And do you have any idea how doctors talk to veterinarians? They assume we wanted to be like them but we weren't smart enough. It's about all I can do not to stab one of them. And then show him how good I am at field-treating lacerations."

Angel laughed, which was good. It helped Julia get things back under control.

"So how are you doing?" Julia asked again.

Angel nodded. Shrugged one shoulder, looked around. She tried to pull her hand back, but Julia held on to it. "I'm good. They have me back to work, which is really good. I'm not supposed to tell you any of this, of course, but Wilkes is doing field agent stuff now and I'm his operator."

Julia nodded in understanding. She kind of wanted to yell at Angel for cheating on Jim, but that was absurd. "They've got you in another trailer, then."

"Yeah," Angel said.

"That bastard. Hollingshead, I mean. I can't believe he'd do that to his own granddaughter. I'm never going to see him the same way again."

Angel yanked her hand back. She leaned back in her chair and just listened, though Julia could see by her face that she was offended.

"Angel—he owes you better than this. He uses you. He knows you have this, this problem with open spaces—"

"There's nothing wrong with me," Angel insisted.

Julia was on a tear, though. "He knows you're terrified of being outdoors, so he shoves you in these little boxes and makes you work for him. That's like—that's the opposite of what a grandfather should do."

"There's nothing wrong with me," Angel said again.

Julia tried to smile at her. "I know he's convinced you that what he did was okay. But you have to know he's using you, that he just wants to hold on to his best operative so—"

Angel nodded. "Are you finished? Maybe you want to judge him some more?"

Julia sighed. *You can't help somebody,* she thought, *if they won't acknowledge they have a problem.*

"Maybe you'll let me talk now. When I was fifteen years old," Angel said, her voice only a little too loud, "I had already graduated from high school, and I was incredibly good with computers, and I was very bored. And within a month I was all set to go to prison for the rest of my life on an espionage charge."

"I know this story. You were just a kid and you accidentally hacked into a Pentagon database. You didn't even know what you were—"

"I knew exactly what I was doing," Angel said. "There was a boy. A very nice boy, who I met online, and who I had a huge crush on. Do you remember what it was like to have a crush on somebody when you were that young?"

Julia nodded.

"This boy meant everything to me. He taught me so many different techniques—hacks, exploits, stuff I didn't even know was possible. And he never asked me for anything. Until the day he did. He asked me to break into a certain database and get some files for him. I didn't know at the time that he was actually a persona shared by a group of Chinese spies. That he was a complete illusion made to appeal just to me. I had no idea why he wanted the contents of that database. But I knew how to get in. My grandpa, after all, had access. So I broke into his study and stole his password and that was how I got in. Because I was young and stupid, I got caught. Luckily for all of us, I was caught before I found what I was looking for."

Julia just stared.

"They took me right out of my bedroom, with no shoes on my feet. They put a sack over my head and drove me to an interrogation center. They told me they were going to send me away forever. I was going to be subjected to extraordinary rendition and taken away to a CIA black prison overseas. They kept telling me I was a terrorist. And then my grandfather stepped in and pulled me out of there."

"I didn't know—"

"He took me out of there and sent me home. I didn't know at the time how much that cost him. He was already in trouble, since it was his password I used. It very nearly ended his career, but he didn't give up on me. He made sure I didn't have to go to jail. He wanted to send me home to my parents. Set me up with a nice therapist and lots of nice pills and let me have what they call a normal life. There were conditions, though. One was I was never going to be allowed to touch a computer again."

Angel rubbed at her face. Was she crying? Julia didn't see any tears. But she could tell how much it hurt Angel to talk about this.

"The one thing I had. The one thing that made any sense of my life. Imagine it, Julia. Imagine if someone told you that you could never touch a dog again. Never work with animals, and if they caught you within a hundred yards of so much as a gerbil, you would go straight to prison. Forever."

"It's not the same thing—"

"It's exactly the same," Angel told her. "I know I'm not like you. I know I'm different. But I am what I am. So I went to my grandpa. I got a hearing with a special group in the Justice Department, and then another meeting at the Pentagon. I laid out my argument as carefully, as logically as I could. When they didn't listen to logic—people so rarely do—I played on their emotions. I cried and told them how sorry I was, how I was duped, how I felt so bad about the whole thing. Then I asked them for a job. I asked them for a way to redeem myself."

"This—this life," Julia said, scarcely believing it. "This was your idea?"

"I had to beg them to let me actually work. I had to beg them to give me those trailers. Do you understand? I had to fight for what I have."

"You couldn't have known what it would mean."

"I wrote my own job description," Angel said. "When he heard it, my grandpa tried to stop me. He tried to convince me that a life of pills and no computers and maybe a job somewhere flipping burgers was worth it. I pointed out that I wouldn't be allowed to run a cash register. You need to run a cash register if you want to work at a fast-food place. There was nothing else for me. So he relented. He said yes. And now every year on my birthday, he comes and has lunch with me in my trailer. And he asks me if I still want this life. If I still want to be me. He says he can pull some more strings, call in some more favors. And every year I smile and kiss him on the cheek and say no. I'm not a prisoner, Julia. I make my own choices."

Angel stopped talking then. She'd said all she had to say on the matter, clearly. Julia wasn't sure how to respond.

"I didn't know," she said finally.

"No, you didn't. And you weren't supposed to. All that is classified."

Julia nodded.

Angel got up from the table. She started to turn away, but then she stopped herself. She took a piece of paper from her purse and wrote a phone number on it. "The next time Chapel wakes up, just call that number. It won't pick up no matter how many times you let it ring, but that doesn't matter. I'll see the call came in."

Julia took the scrap of paper. "When he wakes up—"

"Sugar," Angel said, "I'll come running."

SOUTH HILLS, PA: MARCH 31, 07:42

"I know you need to get to work, and it wasn't my, ah, intention to detain you. Mostly I just came to thank you, of course. After all that you"— Hollingshead waved his hands in the air—"after all you did. Quite frankly, you saved my life. But that's not the only reason I came. I did wish to speak with you quickly about, well. About this house."

Top's hand lay on the table, the fingers flexing as he gripped it hard enough to damage the veneer. He said nothing. He didn't even blink. He just nodded.

"It's a fascinating arrangement here. All the veterans, all your—your boys—living under one roof. Struggling through their PTSD and their physical rehabilitation together. A brilliant stroke, that. I remember how terribly alone I felt after I came back from my first tour overseas. How a situation like this might have helped! And you manage on such a shoe-string budget. I know that in the past you've managed to get by with do-nations from certain of your boys. Myself, of course, included."

Top nodded again. Hollingshead had needed physical rehabilitation after a hip replacement a few years back. Top had been his therapist. The fact that Hollingshead outranked Top by several orders of magnitude hadn't mattered in the slightest—from that day forward, Rupert Holling-shead had been one of Top's boys. He was rather proud of the affiliation.

"You may have heard—that is, I don't know if you've heard but my, well, my job title has recently changed. To be blunt I've moved up in the world a bit."

Top finally spoke. "Are you saying you want to give us more money?" he asked. "Admiral, sir?"

Hollingshead smiled and took off his glasses. He began to polish them with a silk handkerchief as if he needed time to think of how to frame his reply. "About that, well, certainly. I mean, if you think you could use more of, ah, a stipend. But what I was really thinking was, we could set you up as a pilot study. Get some data, crunch some numbers, as it were."

"A pilot study?"

"Well, yes," Hollingshead said. "The government does prefer hard data when it can come by it, you see. I think we can prove that a house like this does our veterans more good than—well, than the programs we have in place now. Ah, I know that look on your face. I remember it from our days together when you taught me how to walk again. You're wishing that I would get to the point."

"With all due respect, sir."

Hollingshead nodded. "What I'm suggesting is simple: that we start up houses like this all over the country. Hundreds of them—as many as necessary. Places for our returning veterans to stay, to get back on their feet. To make sure that every one of your, well, metaphorically let's call them your boys, has a chance like this. Now, of course, you and Dolores would be the directors of this program, which would mean a substantial yearly salary and—"

"You know I would do it for free," Top interjected.

Hollingshead smiled.

"Damn," Top said. "Maybe I shouldn't have said that."

Hollingshead tilted his head to one side. "Said what?" he asked. "At my age, of course, one's hearing is the first thing to go."

BETHESDA, MD: APRIL 2, 21:13

It was very quiet and very dark in the hospital room. They'd turned the lights out so that Chapel's roommate could get some sleep.

Julia didn't mind. She climbed into the bed with Jim and curled up against his side, careful not to disturb any of the tubes or sensors attached to him. It wasn't the first night she'd done this, and she knew how to get comfortable.

It helped that they'd removed his artificial arm. That made some room for her on the bed. They'd stored it in a cupboard nearby, out of sight— apparently it creeped out some of the nurses.

Julia kissed Jim's cold cheek. Laid her hand on his chest.

He stirred. He did that sometimes, in his sleep. But this time his eyes opened, just a crack, and he whispered her name.

"I'm here," she said.

He nodded. Licked his chapped lips.

"Angel came by earlier," she said. "She wants me to call her when you can actually talk to her—"

"Not . . . now," he told her. The effort of talking visibly drained him. But he shifted a little in the bed, turned so he could face her better. "Now." He took a long, deep breath. "Want to talk . . . to you."

"Sure," she said.

The words came out slowly, each one costing him a little strength. It was all right, though. This was the most he'd said since he first regained consciousness. Weak as he seemed, he was getting stronger. All the time.

He was going to make it.

"When you . . . broke up with me," he said. "I had a little box. I put it on the . . . on the table by the door."

"I remember," she said. There'd been a diamond ring in that box. She'd already broken things off, and she was walking out the door for what she thought was the last time. She'd seen it sitting there and it had destroyed her. She'd spent that whole night crying and drinking and trying to not think about what the box meant.

"I want . . ." he said.

Then he stopped. His eyes closed, and she thought maybe he'd fallen asleep again. She knew she shouldn't wake him up, that he needed his rest. She desperately wanted to know what he had been trying to say, though.

Fortunately for her sense of medical ethics, he opened his eyes again on his own. "Director. The director said . . . he said he wanted to give me a new job."

"You're not exactly ready to go on another mission," Julia pointed out.

He smiled. "A desk job."

"You know you couldn't work at a desk again if—"

"*His* job. His old job," Jim said.

"Oh," Julia said, so surprised she had no idea how to react.

"You'd know where I was. All the time. And not as many people would . . . try to shoot me. Virtually none."

She laughed.

"You should . . . go home," he told her. "Get some sleep. You look tired."

"You're not one to judge," she told him.

"I have an excuse. Go home." He grasped her arm, ran his fingers up her biceps. It sent shivers down her spine, like it always had. "Go home. Get that box and bring it back here," he told her. "I have a question I want to ask you."